Dedication

To Mikey Brooks: author, artist, and formatter extraordinaire!
You have my grateful thanks.

Acknowledgements

Once again I find myself indebted to many people for help in bringing this novel, *The Circle*, fifth in the Artesans series and second in the *Circle of Conspiracy* trilogy, to publication.

As ever, thanks and love must go to my husband, Dave, and my parents, Barbara and Dennis. Also to my two gorgeous pooches, Milly and Milo. All of the above are ever ready with encouragement, interest and support, and also cuddles and love whenever required.

Thanks are due to my brother, David Snell, for writing, playing on, recording and mixing "Larksong," the music associated with this book. Also to David Shepherd for the same, and his wife Catriona for making sure Milly and Milo didn't get bored. Special thanks go to Sue Mallett for agreeing to play violin and viola, and playing them so beautifully.

For the fabulous cover of *The Circle* I must once again thank Mikey Brooks, artist extraordinaire. You just get better and better!

Also to Diane Dalton for the cover copy, for editing, and for her brilliant suggestions.

One person I keep forgetting to thank is Bob Watson, who manages my website. I would really struggle without his knowledge and expertise.

I must also thank Amy Del Rosso, owner of Lady Reader's Book Tours, for organizing the promo for my books. Also to Kriss Morton for help with the same.

Many grateful thanks to Janet Morris, both for her effusive and enthusiastic endorsement and support, and also for allowing me to use and quote from it.

And of course I must say a huge "thank you" to all my readers, and especially those who have left me such wonderful reviews and comments. I hope you all enjoy *The Circle* as much as the novels that went before.

Praise for the Artesans of Albia series:

"Cas Peace's *Artesans of Albia* trilogy immediately sweeps you away: the drama starts with *King's Envoy*, continues unabated in *King's Champion*, and climaxes in *King's Artesan*, yet each volume is complete, satisfying. The Artesan series propels you into a world so deftly written that you see, feel, touch, and even smell each twist and turn. These nesting novels are evocative, hauntingly real. Smart. Powerful. Compelling. The trilogy teems with finely drawn characters, heroes and villains and societies worth knowing; with stories so organic and yet iconic you know you've found another home—in Albia. Now there's ... Peace's forthcoming sub-series, the *Circle of Conspiracy* trilogy, proof of more Albian tales on the way. So start reading now. I, for one, can't wait to find out what will happen next."

~Janet E. Morris: author of *The Sacred Band of Stepsons* series; the *Dream Dancer* series; *I, the Sun; Outpassage*.

✣ ✣ ✣ ✣ ✣

"The overall storyline is driven forward very well, with a huge amount of tension and build up early on, and then later on the reader is left with the feeling events will not proceed at all predictably. The Challenge moves the series up a gear in terms of scope, plot and character development. It was very satisfying and sets the series up for further greatness as the overall arc progresses."

~Dan G, Amazon reviewer.

✣ ✣ ✣ ✣ ✣

"Having read the last trilogy I was thrilled and not disappointed with this book. Lots of twists and turns but keeping with the essential characters. Can't wait for the next book."

~Gary Harvey, Amazon reviewer.

Published by Albia Publishing 2014

First American Paperback Edition

This is a work of fiction. Names, characters, places, and incidents either are the product of the author's imagination or are used fictitiously. Any resemblance to actual events, locales, or persons, living or dead, is entirely coincidental. The publisher does not have any control and does not assume responsibility for author or third party websites or their content.

Visit Cas Peace at her author website: www.caspeace.com

ISBN-10: 1939993512
ISBN-13: 978-1-939993-51-9

The Circle

Circle of Conspiracy

Book Two

Cas Peace

Albia Publishing

The Kingdom of Albia in the Realm of Albia. (not to scale)

Realm of Andaryon. (not to scale.)

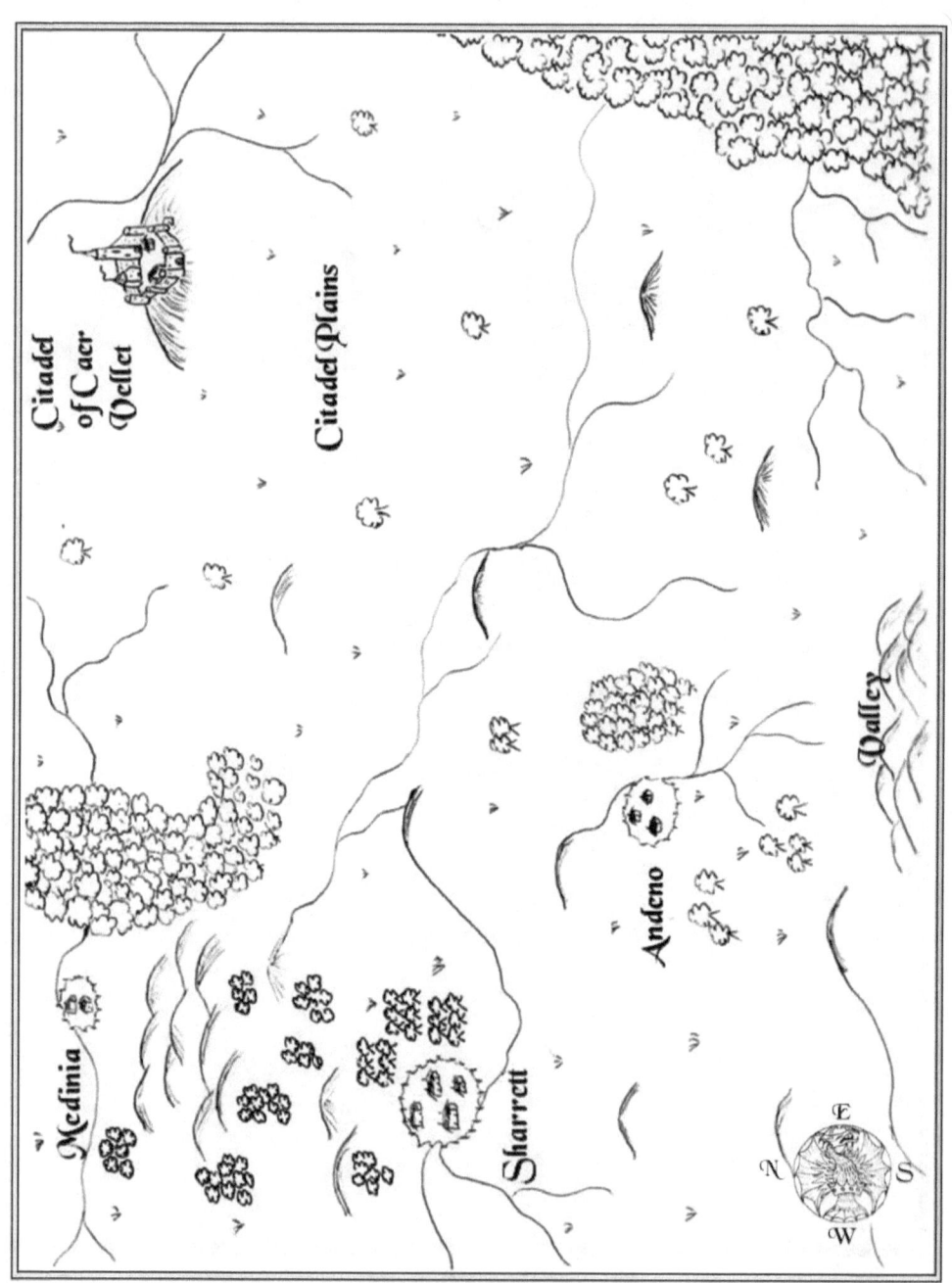

Citadel of Caer Vellet

Citadel Plains

Medinia

Sharrett

Andeno

Valley

N E S W

Andaryan Battle Site, (not to scale)

Chapter One

The summons came just as Rienne was preparing to go off shift. It was clearly urgent and she dropped the pile of clean bandages to answer it, yet now she had to lean against the wall a minute to catch her breath. Her pregnancy didn't allow her to rush around these days. Panting, she tried to calm herself.

Tad, the cadet who had brought Chief Healer Hanan's summons, didn't tell Rienne the reasons behind the urgency. He simply gave his message and ran off, but his tone and serious expression sent shivers of fear down her spine. Something dreadful must have happened.

Her fear was confirmed by the anxious bustle along the infirmary's corridors. It seemed every available healer was hurrying to Hanan's office. Had there been another invasion? Had the demons who had been raiding recently committed an atrocity? Oh, she hoped not; the infirmary was already as full as she'd seen it. They'd be hard put to cope with a large influx of wounded.

Rienne's heart was pounding by the time she reached the office, and not just from her physical condition.

There was quite a crowd of blue-clad healers around Hanan—the entire day shift, as far as Rienne could see. The Chief Healer wore a somber expression. The woman was tall and strongly-built, with a severe face that transformed when she smiled, which was often. Now, however, there was something else in her eyes.

"Healers," she began, "I have some grave news for you. A

couple of hours ago our King received a message telling him that his son, the young Prince Eadan, has been abducted by demons."

There were cries and exclamations of shock.

"It seems he has been taken by minions of the Hierarch of Andaryon in revenge for the abduction of his own son."

Rienne gasped. She knew this couldn't be true.

Hanan continued. "The King is understandably distraught, and I have to tell you all that he has just declared war on Andaryon."

"No!" Rienne was unable to stop the outburst. Eyes turned her way, but hers hadn't been the only protest. They all knew how highly the King had valued his alliance with the Hierarch, but Rienne thought she was probably the only one whose protest was as much for Pharikian's sake as it was for Elias's. She shared Sullyan's fondness for the demon ruler of Andaryon.

Chief Healer Hanan wasn't finished. "King Elias has summoned us all to attend him at midmorning tomorrow on the parade ground. You will arrange your duties accordingly, and we will also take all patients who are capable of being moved. That is all. You may return to your duties."

Rienne turned away, her hand to her mouth. She had been too young to remember much about the civil war in Albia, and had not experienced first-hand Rykan's war on Pharikian. She had no clear idea how this dreadful news would affect her on a personal level. More work, more patients, more wounded; she could be certain of that. Some of the wounds would be severe, and some fatal.

With a sudden cold shock, she realized that Cal would be involved and in the thick of the fighting. Her heart sank as it dawned on her that, as an Artesan, it was far more likely that he would be fighting in Andaryon rather than staying to defend Albia. What if she lost him over there? What if he became too injured to return home? What if he developed some virulent alien infection and was trapped there forever until he died? Her trembling hands protectively clasped her belly as tears started in her eyes.

Only then did she register that someone was standing before her. It was Emos, Sullyan's valet, and she thought he'd probably spoken her name at least twice. "Oh, Emos, it's you. I'm sorry, I was preoccupied. We've only just heard the news."

The small man regarded her with a worried expression. "Healer Arlen, I'm sorry to intrude when you've your own troubles, but I'm concerned about Colonel Sullyan. Could you come and take a look at her?"

"Why, what's wrong with her?"

Emos took Rienne's elbow and guided her out of the infirmary. "I'm not quite sure. I came across her in the hallway halfway between the General's office and her own. She was leaning against the wall, staring into nothing as if she didn't know where she was. She looked dreadful—she was pale and trembling and her brow was damp. I called her name, but she didn't seem to hear me. I touched her arm, and that's when she finally realized I was there. She didn't answer me when I asked if she was all right. I couldn't just leave her there, but I could see she needed some help. I managed to get her back to her rooms so I could come and find you. I just hope she's still there."

Rienne frowned. She didn't like the sound of this. Sullyan was bound to be distressed, even angry, over the King's announcement, but Rienne wouldn't expect her to react as badly as this. She glanced at the valet. "Was Robin there?"

He kept his eyes straight ahead. "No, Healer."

Rienne's anxiety grew as they hastened to the Colonel's chambers. Sullyan hadn't been herself for some time now, and Rienne was developing her own suspicions as to why that was. This time, she wouldn't be sidetracked or fobbed off; she would do a thorough examination whether Sullyan liked it or not. At least it gave her a temporary distraction from her fears for Cal.

The valet received no response to his tap at Sullyan's door. They entered to find Sullyan sitting just as Emos had described leaving her; staring blankly ahead, a slight frown on her brow. The valet stood aside as Rienne approached her, softly calling Sullyan's name.

She eventually got a response, but only when she knelt down in front of her and put both her hands on Sullyan's arms.

"Brynne!" she said urgently, giving her friend a gentle shake. Some semblance of life came back to the clouded golden eyes, and Sullyan blinked.

"Rienne?"

The healer turned to the valet, who was hovering at her shoulder, his face a picture of worry.

"It's all right, Emos. I'll look after her now."

"What's wrong with her, Healer? I've never seen her like this before."

"She's in shock. I've seen its like before. Just leave us now; peace and quiet are what she needs most."

The small man left, muttering that they'd be lucky to have much in the way of peace or quiet from now on. Rienne waited until he had closed the door and then she stood, still looking intently into Sullyan's unseeing eyes.

"Brynne!" she said sharply, but there was no response, not even the flicker she had seen just before. Rienne sighed deeply; she wasn't going to enjoy this. Steeling her resolve and making very sure there were no sharp weapons nearby, she drew back her hand and slapped her friend resoundingly across the face.

Sullyan's head snapped back and she hissed in a breath, but otherwise didn't react. Rienne was afraid she'd have to do it again, though her palm already stung and there was a bright red mark on Sullyan's otherwise pallid cheek. But when the younger woman slowly turned her head back to face Rienne, her eyes were normal, albeit tear-filled.

"Oh, Rienne," she whispered, "I am so sorry."

"You're sorry?" Rienne smiled in relief. "I'm the one who slapped *you*!"

"I am sorry you had to do it. I cannot think why I reacted that way. I seemed to have no control over my body."

"It's just shock, my dear, that's all. It's quite a natural reaction." Rienne sat down beside her friend. Seeing the tears begin to slide down Sullyan's face, she gathered her into her arms.

"Rienne, what am I going to do?" Sullyan's voice was hoarse with emotion. "Elias has declared war on Andaryon. I couldn't stop him—he wouldn't listen. As if that wasn't bad enough, he has commanded me to tell him everything I know about the Citadel's defenses and Anjer's battle strategies. How can I possibly obey him?"

Rienne gasped. "He asked you to do that? Doesn't he realize what he's doing? There's no way on earth Timar's involved in Prince Eadan's abduction."

"I know, Rienne, I know. I have told Elias so, but he does not wish to hear me. He is full of fury and avid for revenge and the need to do something to regain his son. I cannot blame him for that. But war! It will achieve nothing but death and the destruction of the alliance. This could put us back decades and resurrect all the old grievances still simmering beneath the surface. Which is exactly what our enemy wants, of course."

Rienne stared at Sullyan, totally overwhelmed. Events were moving too fast for her. "What will you do? What *can* you do?"

"I have no idea. I need time to think. But I simply cannot use my knowledge to help Elias attack Timar."

They were silent a moment, deep in their own depressing thoughts. Then Sullyan told Rienne everything that had happened that morning, how Pharikian had collapsed after finding his son's severed finger in a box, and how upset she was by Pharikian's condition, as well as Aeyron's maiming and probable death. Rienne felt herself turn pale and fresh tears welled in her eyes. She could understand Pharikian's belief that his son was dead.

"And what do you think?" she asked.

Sullyan shrugged. "He may well be right. I have searched and searched for Aeyron's signature in the substrate and can find no trace, not even one dulled by spellsilver. I very much fear that he is indeed dead."

Full of grief, Rienne shook her head. "This could kill Timar."

Sullyan nodded. "Let us hope that Idrimar's pregnancy will sustain him. The promise of grandchildren may serve to give him some hope." Her words clearly reminded her of Rienne's own condition, and she eyed the healer. "How are you faring, Rienne? All this must be a great shock to you, and you are still in the early stages of your own pregnancy. You must try not to let all this distress you too much."

Rienne found a smile for her friend. This was much more normal. Sullyan always was far more concerned for the welfare of others than she was for herself. Feeling easier about Sullyan's state of mind, Rienne said briskly, "I didn't come here to talk about me, Brynne. Emos came for me because he was worried about *you*, and so am I. You have experienced far too many of these little 'indispositions' lately, and today we're going to get to the bottom of them."

Sullyan shrugged. "We have tried before and each time you have found that I am healthy."

"Yes, I know. So today I want you to start from the beginning. Go back to the very first time you remember feeling unwell, however slight, and tell me everything. Leave nothing out. Even those things you felt were connected with Rykan's ... abuse. I want it all and I'm not leaving until I get it."

Sullyan gazed at her and then capitulated, telling the healer everything she could remember, going back five or six months.

Rienne was startled when she heard this. "Five or six *months?* I thought we were talking weeks!"

Sullyan gave a small smile. "Well, you said to include everything."

"Why didn't you say something sooner?" demanded Rienne. She waved a hand, knowing how heedless Sullyan could be of her own health. "Oh, just go on."

The catalog of minor irritations continued. The intermittent nausea, the lack of appetite, the metallic taste in the mouth that had put Sullyan off her fellan, the strange numb and tingling sensations in her wrist and forearm, her uncertain temper, her inexplicable weight gain; all were listed for Rienne's benefit. The healer heard it all with growing conviction and heightening exasperation. She couldn't blame Sullyan though, not really. After all, she'd had very good reasons for not seeing the obvious.

When Sullyan had finished, Rienne bade her sit quietly and open herself to Rienne's examination. She wasn't as competent at this part as Sullyan, but her experience in healer matters stood her in good stead now that she knew what she was looking for. Sullyan complied in mystified silence. When Rienne finally let go of her hand and sat back with a sigh, Sullyan watched her.

"Well? Are you any the wiser? Do you have any answers for me this time?"

Rienne looked her in the eye. "Oh, yes. That I have."

The tone of her voice, somewhere between excitement and sorrow, alerted Sullyan's senses. Rienne noted the sharpening of her gaze.

"Come on, then. You cannot keep it to yourself. What is wrong with me?"

Rienne smiled gently. "There's nothing wrong with you,

Brynne. You're in a very healthy condition."

"Do not play games, Rienne, please! I am in no mood—" She stopped short, something about Rienne's phrasing having got through to her. "Healthy condition?"

"Yes, my dear." Rienne smiled through a sheen of tears. "If you hadn't been so sure it was impossible, you'd have seen it for yourself. Brynne, you're six months pregnant."

Chapter Two

Rienne thought the silence might stretch on forever. Eventually, Sullyan found her voice.

"That cannot be!" She spread her hands helplessly. "Rykan—"

Rienne shook her head. "I think you've underestimated your body's capacity to recover from what Rykan did to you. Your part-demon blood allowed you to live in Andaryon all that time without ill effects, didn't it? So perhaps it helped you overcome your barrenness, too. You can tell me this is impossible until we both grow old, but it won't change the fact that you are pregnant."

Sullyan just stared at her, and Rienne's heart sank. She could see her friend was having trouble taking this in. Sullyan was already fearful and worried about the current political situation. Now she had another life to consider, and this one was dependent solely upon her. How was she going to cope? Rienne wanted her friend to experience the same joy she had upon learning of her condition. She spoke softly, putting as much encouragement into her voice as she could.

"My baby is more than four months younger than yours, but I can still link with her in the womb if I concentrate. Why don't you try with yours?"

Instead of doing as Rienne suggested, Sullyan looked critically at herself. "At six months, shouldn't I be showing more than this? And what about feeling the baby kicking? I have experienced nothing like that."

Rienne gave a small laugh, grateful for a lightening of mood, at least. "You're so small and slender, Brynne. If your baby is built anything like you, you may not show much at all until the final few weeks. And your muscles are so strong and developed that your baby will be held very firmly and may not kick at all. It's not unknown, you know, for some women to go through a whole nine months of pregnancy completely unaware, right up to the moment of birth. So you're not that unusual." She gave a broad smile. "But what do you think Robin will say? He's going to be so delighted."

The look of horror that came over her friend's face dismayed Rienne. The harsh tone of Sullyan's voice distressed her even more.

"Rienne, you must promise me that you will say nothing about this to anyone. Do you understand me? Not to *anyone*!"

"But—"

"Promise me!"

The strange look was back in Sullyan's eyes, and Rienne realized that this revelation had only added to her problems, not relieved them. Discovering that she wasn't barren after all was one thing; knowing she would be giving birth to a new life in the midst of a war was quite another. Not to mention being estranged from the baby's father. Reluctantly, Rienne had to give in.

"All right, all right," she soothed, "I'll leave it up to you to tell Robin. But as a Manor Healer, I'm duty-bound to inform the General. I can't keep quiet about something that will affect the physical capabilities of one of his senior officers."

Rienne started as Sullyan jumped to her feet. "*No*, Rienne! He will not know, and neither will the King."

Rienne's eyes stretched wide. "Whyever not? Brynne, you *must* tell them!"

"I can tell no one," the younger woman burst out. "Rienne, I want your solemn promise that you will keep this strictly between us. This is my responsibility and I will deal with it in my own way. Do I have your word?"

Tears pricked Rienne's eyes. This should be such a happy time. She remembered Cal's reaction to their own success, and Rienne couldn't bear for her friend to be denied the same. But Sullyan was still standing over her, implacable. What could she do?

"I promise, Brynne," she said softly. "I wish I didn't have to. I also wish you wouldn't put me in this difficult situation. I don't like lying, especially not to the General, who has been very good to me. But if you say I have to, I will."

✤ ✤ ✤ ✤ ✤

Sullyan needed time to think. There were priorities to be observed, and the fact that she was carrying a child would have to take second place to more immediate concerns. Besides, she knew it was likely that Cal would be ordered to fight in Andaryon, and she wouldn't keep Rienne from his side any longer than necessary. So she convinced Rienne that she needed time to rest, and the healer left her with admonitions to eat properly and take better care of herself from now on.

Once she was alone, Sullyan sat on the couch, her head in her hands. She was appalled by how quickly the alliance had unraveled and very fearful for the safety of both Prince Eadan and Prince Aeyron. Despite her searches and what she had told Rienne, she was far from convinced that Aeyron was dead. If it was indeed the Baron who was behind all this, she didn't think he'd throw away such a valuable bargaining piece until the final move was played out. And this war was only the next stage in his game, not the end itself. Of that she was certain.

If only she could figure out what his real goal was. What was the significance of the thirty pounds of reverse-polarity spellsilver, stolen before it could be delivered as ransom? And were the two princes part of the larger plan, or had they simply been taken to foment this war? She didn't know, and now she had no one to turn to for help and advice. Pharikian was the only one to whom she could have gone, and she herself had seen to it that he was unavailable.

She sat puzzling over the problem until her head began to pound, then turned her attention to exploring her options in the light of the King's declaration of war.

They were few. To be precise, there were two.

She could follow orders and allow Elias to use her knowledge to attack her foster father. Or she could disobey him and risk her whole life and career. Both were stark choices with no hope of peace whichever way she turned. If she obeyed Elias, she'd be betraying the love and care Pharikian had shown her, not to mention his invaluable help in ridding her soul of Rykan's poison. She also felt she'd be betraying her own sire, who had been such a true friend and ally to the Andaryan ruler.

Her whole being cried out against the King's demands, yet she was sworn to serve him. If her oath was not binding upon her, then what had her whole life been about? What was her worth? She had always upheld his interests and served him most faithfully. How could she turn from that now? It would be tantamount to denying her very reason for existence, and she knew she could not do that.

And yet....

She raised her head, her eyes unfocused. Might there be another way? A third option? An option that would allow her to serve her King without betraying her love for Pharikian? She thought there just might be. The roiling sensation in the pit of her belly calmed as she explored this new idea. It was still fraught with dangers, still carried the taint and appearance of treason, but it was the only course that might salvage something from this dreadful mess. And if she failed, well then their enemy would win and it would hardly matter anymore. For she'd likely be dead, and every Artesan with her, sooner or later.

She was under no delusions about their adversary's intentions—even less so if it was the Baron. Merely discrediting those he reviled would not be sufficient for him. He would never rest until all his enemies were dead, and she very much feared that he counted King Elias among the worst of them.

She was still hopeful of persuading the King to reason before he made his announcement on the morrow, especially if Blaine would back her up. She was convinced that the General felt as she did, but even he could push Elias only so far. Much would depend on whether the flash of insanity that Eadan's plight had raised in Elias would die down in the cold light of a new day. If it did not, then this risky third option might prove to be her only viable choice.

She would soon know.

She made up her mind in an instant and, having done so, could be still no longer. She caught up her cloak from its peg and left her rooms. She had little time. It was already dark outside and she needed to reach the inn before it closed its doors for the night. She sprinted for the horse lines. Elias's mad decision had brought one blessing at least; the steeds of the mounted companies would be kept in constant readiness now that things had escalated so far.

Sure enough, Drum was ready for her and she only had to slip on his saddle before cantering him out of the yard, watched by Stablemaster Solet's night lads. They were left wondering what would take her out at this hour, and what was behind her odd request to them for the next day.

The rhythmic movements of the stallion beneath her helped soothe and calm Sullyan's thumping heart as she rode. She had had very little to eat that day and not much more the day before, and she was beginning to feel lightheaded. She really ought to have drunk some fellan before she left, but this was more important. She could always persuade Milo to provide some if necessary once she reached the inn.

The night was dry but starless. Drum moved easily beneath her and she kept her senses alert in case of raiders. It was unlikely there'd be any this close to the Manor—the surrounding villages were too well protected to be easy targets—but she was still cautious.

She arrived at the inn just as they were closing up. The commons was emptying of the last few patrons and she had to call for a stable lad to take Drum from her.

"Leave him harnessed," she said. "I will need him again soon."

She strode into the inn, discarding her cloak at the door. The interior was only dimly lit now that the evening business was drawing to a close. She found Milo clearing up, and he was astonished to see her.

"Colonel Sullyan! Twice in three days. This is a rare occurrence."

"I am here to see Taran, Milo. Is he in his room?"

"Yes, Colonel, he went up about an hour ago. I imagine he'll be abed by now. You're a little late for visiting."

"Never mind that, this is urgent. Send us up some fellan, will you? And make it strong. I have ridden hard."

She brushed past the startled landlord and strode toward the darkened back stairs which led to the guest rooms. At the bottom step, however, she faltered. The reason Taran was here at all was because of rumors involving the two of them alone in a single bedroom—the last thing she needed was to give those rumors more fuel. Sighing in vexation, she returned to the bar.

"Milo, will you please go up and ask Taran Elijah to join me?

14

We will have our fellan over there by the fire."

She didn't need to see the landlord's expression to sense his confusion, but he said nothing as he climbed the stairs. The sound of his footsteps faded as she took a seat by the dying fire. A door opened and closed somewhere above, and then came the sound of footsteps clattering down the stairs. A disheveled-looking Taran came into the commons, concern apparent in his eyes.

"What's happened?"

She waved him to a chair. She had intended to maintain an air of calm while she told him what she wanted, but his presence was so comforting and she'd badly missed the love and support of her life mate over the past few days. Until now, she'd not realized how much. Tears came unbidden to her eyes, and she silently cursed her weakness.

Taran stepped toward her and laid a hand on her shoulder.

"Tell me what's happened. Is it Robin?"

That he could still care about Robin after the Major had believed such horrible rumors about him and driven him away almost overcame Sullyan's resolve. She had to swallow down the rising sob that threatened to break free. If she gave way to it now she'd break down, and she couldn't risk that. It wasn't fair to Taran.

He dropped his hand. "Shall I send for some fellan?"

She found a small smile. "I already have. Perdition knows I need it."

He sat in the chair she had indicated and watched her, concern plain in his honest, hazel eyes. She clasped and unclasped her hands, and then stopped herself when she saw this uncharacteristically nervous gesture only heightened his fears.

"Earlier today the King received a message telling him that his son, the young Prince Eadan, has been abducted."

Taran went deathly pale in the amber lamplight, but he made

no comment.

"This news, as you can imagine, sorely distressed him. He was so distraught, in fact, that he was pushed beyond reason. Taran, he has declared war on Andaryon."

Taran gasped. "Declared war? But he can't!"

Sullyan allowed herself a humorless smile. "So I told him, my friend, and he was none too pleased to hear it. Given how angry he was with me, I am fortunate to be sitting here now."

She could see Taran struggling to take it all in. Just then, Milo arrived with the fellan. Sullyan nodded her thanks and the landlord departed, curious yet silent.

Taran poured her a mug of fellan and Sullyan inhaled its bitter aroma gratefully as she wrapped her hands around it. While she waited for the liquid to be cool enough to sip, she told Taran of the distressing events of the day, both in the Citadel and at the Manor. He sat aghast while he listened and his eyes were troubled when she was done.

Pouring more fellan for them both, he said, "What do you intend to do? And what do you want me to do? I imagine you didn't come here just to tell me the news."

Grateful for his compliance and trust, she smiled in genuine warmth. "Ah, thank you, Taran. I knew I could rely on you."

Her praise brought the color to his face and he looked away.

She sobered. "I am going to ask something of you, my friend, but I want you to know that you are in no way obliged to agree. Indeed, I sincerely hope that what I am about to propose will not, in fact, be necessary. I will try my hardest to persuade Elias to reason tomorrow, and to withdraw his declaration, but I need a contingency plan in case he will not be swayed. If I am forced to that course, then I shall have need of you."

She sat for a while telling Taran her plan and ensuring he understood what she was asking of him. He was unsettled by it, she could see, and far from happy. But then she wasn't happy about it either, so she could hardly blame him.

"Do you really think it will come to that?" he asked.

"I hope not, but I fear Elias is too far gone in desperation to listen to reason. And Mathias can only do so much. When it comes to it, he will obey the King, even though he knows it is not a sane course of action. He has more to lose than I."

Even as she said it, she knew Taran doubted her. What she was proposing was a very final act, and even she could hardly see how she would find the strength to carry it out. He watched her as she sat cradling her cup, now nearly empty again. When she met his eyes in query, he drew and held a breath.

"You know you can count on me," he said as he let it out. "I don't see what help I can be to you, but I'll do what I can. You only have to call. I'll be ready."

Her eyes filled again. She didn't want him to see how much she feared this proposed course of action, but the uncomplicated support he was offering her had strengthened her resolve.

She stood, as did he. Then, much to his shock, she laid aside her cup and deliberately stepped into his arms. He only hesitated a moment before closing them about her as if he had every right. She laid her head upon his breast, feeling the pounding of his heart and knowing her own matched it. She had only intended to convey the depth of her gratitude, but this was dangerous ground. She wasn't emotionally stable, and once again she was being unfair to him. She moved, and he released her instantly.

"I had better go."

Why did her voice sound so hoarse? But the tall Adept said nothing and watched her move toward the door with an unfathomable look in his eyes.

"If I need to call on you, meet me outside the back entrance to the Manor grounds," she said, only flicking him a cursory glance to catch his nod of agreement.

She slipped out of the inn, closing the door behind her.

Sullyan arrived back at the Manor just before midnight. She would be able to snatch a few hours of sleep before daybreak, and she only had two other tasks to accomplish before attending the King. The first she would see to when she got back to her rooms and had access to parchment. The second involved the Paymaster, but it was far too late to rouse him now. She'd have to wait until daylight. Once those matters were settled, she'd be as ready as she could be for what might come. Whatever came, it was likely to change all of their lives, and not for the good.

Chapter Three

First light found Duke Marik in the lesser audience chamber meeting with Anjer, Ephan, and Barrin. He told them about the discovery of Lord Corbyn's name in Rykan's records, and the sizeable payments the former Duke had been making to him. They had all believed that the mysterious Albian responsible for providing Rykan with the Staff had other allies in their realm, and now that Corbyn had been implicated as the probable traitor they felt vindicated. Relieved too, as now, at last, they had something to work with. His disappearance was inconvenient, but not surprising.

Anjer almost smacked his lips as he said, "We'll soon track him down, your Grace, never fear. And then we'll see what information he carries. Once I've finished persuading him to tell us where Prince Aeyron is being held, I'll have his head on a pole for his treachery. I can hardly believe he used his own son in the abduction." He grimaced. "Can you imagine putting your own flesh and blood at risk like that? What if the Albians had killed Kethro and Rand instead of trussing them up?"

"Oh, I'm sure they were paid not to harm them," commented Marik dryly, "although you can never fully trust mercenaries. I suppose they removed the boys from the scene of the attack in case either of them had managed to call for help through the substrate. It would have made us waste time searching for them instead of tracking the raiders."

The lean Duke steepled his fingers and sat forward in his chair. He was beginning to enjoy the experience of rulership, even though—or maybe because—it was only temporary.

"We need to lay our hands on Corbyn as soon as possible, but if he's bolted like a rat for his hole in the north, we'll be hard pressed to force him out. Don't forget, he does have the support of his nobles. How will you go about it, Anjer?"

Anjer ran a hand over his black mustache, his dark eyes thoughtful. "Before we go haring off after him, it might be an idea to follow Brynne Sullyan's suggestion and question young Rand. He and Kethro are friends, and he might be able to give us a clue as to what Corbyn's been up to. I would bet Kethro didn't keep entirely quiet about his father's plans on that hunting trip. What young rake could?"

"All right, but we'll have to be careful," warned Marik. "We can't afford to antagonize Tikhal. He's the only one standing between us and Corbyn in the north should the traitor decide to call his nobles out against us."

Anjer bristled. "He wouldn't dare!"

"I wouldn't be so sure, my friend," Marik murmured. "Corbyn's been very vocal lately. Would he have been so confrontational if he didn't think he had sufficient strength behind him? He never did appreciate having to back down in front of you, and he's been pushing you hard recently. You've only just been able to keep him in line, and that was only because he wasn't in the bosom of his supporters. Don't underestimate him. If he is our traitor, he may have other resources that we know nothing about, supplied by his Albian ally, perhaps."

The Lord General's mouth thinned with displeasure at Marik's referral to Corbyn's arrogant defiance.

"It's a pity he was allowed to leave so abruptly," commented

Ephan.

Marik shrugged. "He wasn't a prisoner, General, he was an invited guest. He wasn't even a suspect until yesterday, so he was free to leave whenever he wished." He shook his head. "But he held his nerve, I'll give him that. It was quite a risk he took, waiting for that final message to arrive before making his escape. It was fortunate for him that we didn't know about those records of Rykan's earlier, or we'd have had a reason to call him to account. We could legitimately have detained him then. The timing was very convenient."

"Barrin, have a word with the sentries, will you?" said Ephan, turning to the commander. "Find out exactly when Lord Corbyn and his son left the Citadel. It might prove interesting."

Barrin inclined his head.

There was a short silence, then Anjer finally voiced the question they all wanted to ask. "Has there been any change in the Hierarch overnight, your Grace?"

Marik's long face fell. "He's much the same, I'm afraid. Idrimar's with him constantly, as is Deshan. They're both wearing themselves out over this, and Idri's still distraught over her brother. I wish there was something I could do to give her some ease, but she won't leave her father's side."

"I'll get Torien to take Brianne along to sit with the Princess," offered Anjer. "Brianne's enough to make anyone smile at the moment. I'm sure Idrimar will be cheered by her. She needs to be mindful of her twins. You don't want any upset caused to them."

"I don't know which I'm more worried for," admitted Marik, "Timar, Aeyron, Idri, or the twins. But thank you, Anjer, I'm sure the presence of your daughter will ease Idri's heart." He smiled gratefully at the huge man.

Forcing himself away from these dismal thoughts, he said,

"Right, let's get about it. Barrin, bring me the information on Corbyn as soon as you have it, please. Anjer, you'd better send someone to summon Lord Rand, but do it discreetly. We'll interview him together, and let's be subtle about it. If he knows nothing, I don't want Tikhal complaining to the Hierarch that we were unduly heavy-handed with his son."

"Of course, your Grace." Anjer bowed himself out behind the others, his expression grim.

✤ ✤ ✤ ✤ ✤

Sullyan woke with a sinking heart and an all-too-familiar sensation in the pit of her stomach. Groaning, she barely made it to the little privy before her intermittent sickness reasserted itself. Was it her pregnancy, she wondered, apprehension over what the day might bring, or lack of decent food? She didn't know and was presently too ill to care. The sickness left her shivering and weak and feeling truly wretched.

Splashing water from the nightstand onto her sweating face, she straightened and went to put water over the cook fire to heat. At least she had no aversion this morning to the smell of fellan. That would be all she'd need.

After taking some of the warming water for washing, she dressed. This in itself posed a dilemma. Should she dress to indicate her loyalty to the King, or should she dress for the eventuality she was dreading? Either way was a gamble. In the end, she dressed simply in her normal combat leathers and cream linen shirt. She put out her jacket, ready for when she went to see the King, the parchments she had written before retiring tucked safely inside.

She consumed two cups of fellan before feeling ready to leave the room. She had no wish to break her fast in the senior officers'

22

hall; there was too great a chance she'd meet Robin and she didn't think she could cope with him right now, despite Blaine's order to settle things between them. If the King could be persuaded to drop his plans for war, she'd address her problem with Robin. If he couldn't, it would keep. It would have to.

But she really did need some food. Rienne was right. She couldn't afford to neglect her body, especially now when she needed all her strength. So she made her way to the kitchens without going near the commons, which was doubtless more crowded than usual due to the tense situation.

One of the cook-boys saw her by the main kitchen door and scurried to do her bidding, bringing her warm new bread with butter and a slab of ham. She thanked him and sat quietly in a corner of the busy kitchen, ignoring the looks of surprise she was thrown. She knew that if she left this haven, someone would see her and demand answers she couldn't give.

When she was replete, she made for the Paymaster's office. Sullyan received a colonel's pay every month, and it was a tidy sum. As she wasn't one to spend much of her pay, she had amassed a considerable amount over the years. This was lodged with the Paymaster, who generally kept any gold owing to the men as it was safer in his strongroom.

Aside from new strings for her harp and guitar, and the occasional garment for personal use, Sullyan's only regular expense was Bull. Since his retirement from active service she had retained him as an aide, not only because she valued his love and friendship, but also because he was useful to her. And apart from drinking himself into a stupor every night, she knew that Bull could imagine doing little else with his life. So Sullyan had come to an agreement with General Blaine that Bull could continue in his quarters and that the King would supply his clothing and food,

as Bull's duties often included the King's business, but that
Sullyan would see to his pay. She found this a suitable
arrangement, and Blaine was well satisfied. As for Bull, well, it
had hardly changed his way of life. He drew his pay from the
Paymaster as usual; it just came out of Sullyan's private account
rather than the King's.

Sullyan found Serrell, the King's Paymaster, in his office as
usual. He was surprised to see her, as she was a rare visitor.

"Colonel Sullyan. What can I do for you? You know, I'm
thinking of asking for larger premises to house what you've
accumulated. My strongroom can hardly hold it all."

Sullyan grinned at the man, grateful to him for briefly
lightening her mood. She liked Serrell; he was a plain-speaking
man who engendered trust, and Sullyan considered that a useful
trait in a Paymaster. His eyes widened in astonishment when she
told him what she wanted him to do.

"What, *all* of it? Colonel, are you sure?"

"I will take a small pouch for myself, but all the rest, yes. It
may not be for long, but until I come to you to rescind the
arrangement, that is how I want it to be. And, Serrell, would you
tell him for me? Later this afternoon will do."

Serrell agreed with a mystified look, but made no other
comment. He disappeared into his strongroom and came back with
a bulging leather pouch.

"Thank you, Serrell. You have always been scrupulous in your
dealings, and I thank you for your care of my affairs."

Serrell stared after her as she left, and she knew that had
sounded too much like a farewell.

✠ ✠ ✠ ✠ ✠

Marik and Anjer awaited the young Lord Rand in Pharikian's lesser audience chamber. They had chosen to sit in chairs against the wall, with a low table between them, rather than at the more formal oval table. Marik had asked a page to bring them some refreshment. A relaxed atmosphere, he felt, would be more encouraging and less intimidating to the young lord.

When Rand arrived, bowed into the room by the same page who had brought them the wine, Marik and Anjer both rose to greet him. The young man was looking decidedly uncomfortable and wore a puzzled air.

"Rand," greeted Marik affably, "good of you to come so promptly. Come and have a seat. Have you had any of this Cheosian red before? It's a very old vintage and really rather good."

He poured the ruby wine for Rand and passed him the glass.

"Thank you, your Grace," said Rand.

"Oh, I think we can dispense with the formalities," said Marik. "We only want to have a little chat to see if you can shed any light on a rather perplexing problem we have."

"I'll do my best, sir," said Rand, accepting a seat and sipping his wine.

Marik leaned back in his chair. "Now, Anjer and I have been talking, and we believe that you may well be the only one who can help us with a particular problem."

"Would it have anything to do with Lord Corbyn, sir?"

Marik's eyes narrowed. Rand's demeanor so far had been quiet and self-effacing, and Marik hadn't expected him to put himself forward. But he was growing up fast, and the Duke knew that Tikhal had begun including his son in council meetings as well as consulting him on decisions concerning the governing of his lands. Rand was obviously no longer a callow schoolboy, and Marik revised his opinions swiftly.

"Possibly, Rand, possibly," he replied, watching the young man carefully. "Why? Is there something you'd like to tell us?"

Rand shifted uneasily, plainly unwilling to say too much. Marik suddenly realized that he had been anticipating this interview ever since Corbyn's absence had come to light. The Duke would have given much to know exactly when Rand had learned of Corbyn's departure, if indeed he'd needed to be told. Maybe that would become evident as the interview went on.

"Why don't you ask me what you want to know, sir, and I'll see if I can help you?" Rand suggested cautiously.

Tikhal was teaching the boy too well. Marik hoped he had hidden his annoyance.

"I'll be open with you, Rand. For some time now we've been trying to find out who might have been in league with Lord Rykan, and who could have backed him in his challenge to the Hierarch."

"But that would have been Lord Sonten, sir, surely," Rand said quickly.

His attitude was too much for Anjer. "Yes, boy, we know that!" he growled. "Just listen to his Grace and stop interrupting."

Rand flinched. "Sorry, sir."

Marik continued after a cautionary glance at Anjer. "We know that Sonten was involved up to his neck, but we have reason to believe he wasn't Rykan's only ally in Andaryon. We also strongly suspect that Rykan was working with someone of standing in Albia, someone who was able to provide him both with significant funding and also Artesan support. Now, Rykan and Sonten are dead, but the Albians' activities have continued, as the raids and now the abduction of Prince Aeyron have proved. And the ease with which that abduction was carried out strongly suggests that the Albians had another ally or informant, one we knew nothing about."

Rand had gone rather pale, convincing Marik that he knew something of relevance. He watched the young man closely as he continued.

"We asked Lord Nazir to gather up all of Sonten's records and bring them here to Gaslek. My people brought Rykan's records, and the Baron has been sifting through them all very carefully. Would you have any idea what he found?"

"No, sir," murmured Rand, his eyes resting anywhere but on the faces of the two men before him.

"He found that Lord Corbyn's name appears regularly in Rykan's accounts, going back quite some time. Can you think why that should be?"

Marik studied Rand's face and knew Anjer did, too. The pallor was still there, but Marik could swear Rand seemed relieved.

"I really wouldn't know, sir, but I imagine that because of it, you suspect Lord Corbyn of being Rykan's ally and the Albians' informant."

"Exactly right, young Rand!" said Anjer loudly, his black eyes snapping at Rand's faintly patronizing tone. Marik unobtrusively nudged Anjer's foot with his own and the huge man subsided.

"Yes, that's correct. Now, what we wanted to ask you is whether your friend Kethro ever mentioned anything in your hearing that might have made you suspicious of his father's loyalties?" Marik tried his best to keep his tone light. He was worried that if they intimidated or antagonized the young man, he might clam up.

The boy appeared to be considering Marik's words. Then he looked up. "My Lords, I can honestly say that Kethro never said anything to me about his father's affairs that would make me suspect his loyalty to the Crown."

Marik frowned and leaned forward in his chair. "Lord Rand, I want you to think very carefully about this next question. Remember what has happened, and how it has affected the Hierarch. Remember also that Lord Corbyn's lands border your father's, and if Corbyn is planning some kind of rebellion, you and your father will be the first to feel its effects. Do you understand me?"

Rand nodded, although his face had turned even paler and his eyes shifted nervously.

Marik phrased his question with care. "Have you ever, during all the time you spent with either Kethro or Lord Corbyn, suspected that either of them were involved with outlanders who might have supported Lord Rykan?"

Rand sat twisting his hands together, thinking. Marik could feel Anjer's growing impatience and hoped the Lord General would control it long enough. He thought that Rand just might open up if left to himself. But Marik was destined to be disappointed.

The young lord raised his head. "Sirs, I can honestly say that I have never heard either Lord Corbyn or his son say anything against the Hierarch, or anything that hinted at rebellion against the Crown."

Anjer shot forward in his chair. "You do know the pair of them vanished sometime in the night, don't you?" Rand recoiled from his irritation. "They crept out like criminals, and in the light of that terrible message concerning the Prince's fate, their actions appear suspicious in the extreme. Did you know they were planning to leave, boy?"

"Anjer," murmured Marik.

"No, sir, I didn't," said Rand quietly.

"And you expect us to believe that? Like you expect us to believe that Kethro never let slip anything about his father's plans or allegiances at all?"

"Yes, sir!" replied Rand, looking scared. "I mean, no, sir. That is...." He was flustered; an aggravated Anjer was a disturbing sight.

"All right, Rand," soothed Marik, kicking Anjer's foot hard under the table. The man was as subtle as a rock!

The Lord General shot Marik a sour glance but fell silent, glowering at Rand, his mouth a disapproving line beneath his mustache.

"We believe you," continued Marik smoothly. "But if you think of anything that might help us, anything that might shed some light on whoever is holding Prince Aeyron, you will come and tell us, won't you? I'm sure I don't have to remind you that his Majesty is grieving deeply over the loss of his son. We who are loyal to him must do everything in our power to recover the Heir. Do you understand me?"

Rand nodded unhappily. Every time Marik mentioned Aeyron's name, the pallor came back to his face. Marik had no doubt that Rand was deeply affected by his unwitting involvement in the Prince's abduction.

"If you do think of anything, Rand, come to me with it, all right? Just send a page. I will always be available to see you."

Marik watched Rand closely. He hoped he had conveyed to the young lord that any information he might have would be treated confidentially. Rand nodded, seeming to understand Marik's tacit reassurance.

"Will that be all, your Grace?"

"Yes. You may go."

When the young lord had left the room, Anjer turned on

Marik. “Why did you stop me? That young whelp knows something.”

“Yes, thank you, Anjer, I’d worked that out for myself. But trying to intimidate him wasn’t the way to get him to trust us and tell us what he knows. You saw how troubled he is. Something is worrying him and he needs to sort it out in his mind. Perhaps he thinks he’ll be betraying a confidence if he talks to us. He’s friendly with Kethro, and he’s obviously worried about getting Corbyn—or even Kethro himself—into trouble.”

Anjer exploded. “I’ll give him trouble! The Heir’s been abducted, maimed, and possibly killed because of Corbyn. How much trouble does he want?”

“All right, that’s enough!” snapped Marik, testing his temporary authority for the first time. Anjer’s eyes widened at Marik’s unexpectedly sharp tone. The Duke held him with a pale gray stare.

“Yes, your Grace,” muttered the huge man after an evaluating pause.

Marik continued more calmly. “Believe me, Anjer, I want to find the Prince and punish his abductors as much as you do. But until we know the facts, we’re shooting in the dark. We don’t know for sure that Corbyn’s involved, although I agree it looks that way. But I don’t want us to become blinded by our suspicions. I don’t want to rush into anything or miss any information, however insignificant. Do you understand? For what it’s worth, I agree with you about Rand. He knows more than he’s saying at present. Let’s give him some time to search his conscience, and maybe he’ll come to us of his own volition. And until his Majesty recovers and commands otherwise, my Lord General, we’ll do this *my* way!”

✣ ✣ ✣ ✣ ✣

The High King's summons came at midmorning as expected. The entire Manor was abustle with people moving toward the parade ground, and it was astonishing to see how many there were. Apart from the men of the fighting forces, there was also a veritable army of support staff. Solet's stable lads and cadet riders were probably the most numerous, closely followed by the kitchen staff and Manor servants. The healers made a tidy crowd, and the craft workers, smiths, and groundsmen swelled the throng until the vast parade ground was heaving.

Sullyan made her way to Blaine's office, experiencing the strongest feeling of reluctance she'd ever known. When she collected her jacket from her rooms there had still been no sign of Robin, but she knew he would be in attendance on the King. She had to put all thoughts of their personal problems out of her mind for now, but it wasn't easy. Her spirit missed him as much as her body did, and seeing him—and anticipating his probable reaction to what she intended to do—made her want to turn and run.

Making two stops on the way, she walked slowly and deliberately to Blaine's office door, feeling the tremble begin in her bones. She tried to control it; she had to stay strong.

She could hear the hum of voices and knew she was the last to arrive. She had been accused before of making entrances, but now she wished she could slide in unobserved. She pushed open the door and was confronted with a room full of people.

Mathias Blaine and the King were by the window, holding a muted discussion. Colonel Vassa stood nearby with Lieutenant-Major Baily, who was his second-in-command. Captain Parren and the rest of Vassa's captains were also there. Captain Dexter and Robin stood together on the other side of the room, both watching Parren with closed faces. The scarred captain ignored them.

The talk died down as Sullyan entered, and both Blaine and Elias looked over at her. She was dismayed by the demeanor of the King. He was haggard and strained, dark circles shadowed his eyes, and he appeared far older than his years. She couldn't judge his mood for his face remained impassive, almost as if he didn't see her, although his eyes were locked on her face.

Blaine was watching her intently and she had the impression he was trying to convey something to her. He wouldn't dare try for contact with her under the circumstances, and so she had no idea what he was trying to tell her. There was a warning of some kind in his expression, and she could well imagine what had put it there.

Ignoring the other people in the room, she walked slowly toward the King. He watched her approach, still with that cold, detached look in his eyes. No one hindered her or spoke. Everything was suspended as if the slight, tawny-haired woman and the tall, sandy-haired monarch were the only people there.

She halted before him and accorded him her most respectful obeisance. Now she saw a flicker of something in his eyes and hope flared within her. Maybe the situation hadn't gone completely beyond redemption.

"My King," she said softly, no hint of challenge or censorship in her tone.

"Colonel," he replied, his own voice lacking inflexion. She held his dull blue eyes steadily, willing him to see her devotion, her trust, and her sworn and unwavering loyalty.

She gathered her courage and took a breath. "May I ask, your Majesty, whether you have reconsidered your decision to wage war on Andaryon?"

She had spoken as quietly as she could, but the others in the room still heard her, and there were one or two sharply indrawn breaths. She was aware of the thudding of her own heart.

The King had stilled, his breath suspended. Watching his eyes, her hope slowly died. She could see that the strange taint of instability still lurked below the surface, just waiting for a goad, a reason to strike. She was very much afraid she was going to give him that reason.

His chin came up as he stared at her, and a challenge lit his altered eyes.

"Have they returned my son unharmed?" he demanded, his voice flat and cold. "No, Colonel! My decision stands. The messenger carrying my declaration to the Hierarch has already been dispatched. The decision you must make is whether to obey your King or be forsworn and accused of treason."

An icy chill settled over all assembled as they waited for her response. Her gaze never wavered.

"I am loyal to my Oath and to my King," she said clearly. "I exist to serve and I will do all that I can to preserve the Crown and the security of my country."

Plainly, this wasn't what Elias had been expecting. He blinked. Against her open declaration of duty, he could say nothing. But Blaine was watching her through narrowed eyes. Damn him, she thought, he knew her too well. He said nothing, however, and the King eventually turned from her to address the room.

"Gentlemen, Lord Blaine and I have discussed our battle strategies and come to a decision. It is my intention to send Albian forces into the realm of Andaryon in order to show these demons that they cannot take my son with impunity. They cannot be permitted to threaten Albia's ruling House. I have ordered the men to assemble and I will speak to them now and assign you all your duties. Lord Blaine." Elias beckoned and the General followed the King as he strode out of the door. The others did likewise. No one spoke to Sullyan as they passed her, and Robin didn't even cast her a glance.

Fighting back tears and trembling in every part of her body, she sent out the call to Taran. The King had just forced her feet onto a perilous path, a path that might very well lead to her death and would certainly change her life forever.

Chapter Four

"**E**ast? What's in the east that would interest Corbyn?"
His Grace the Duke of Kymer was still in the lesser
audience chamber, from which he had hardly moved
all day. He and Anjer had just been given the news that Lord
Corbyn and his son left the Citadel at around midnight the previous
night, and that they had been seen riding east instead of north.

Anjer considered a moment before slowly replying, "Sonten's
old demesne of Durkos is to the east."

Marik froze, his thoughts a jumble. He had granted Sonten's
estate and mansion to Nazir, his highest ranking noble. The man
had stood by him during Rykan's ungentle overlordship of Cardon,
and Marik had been pleased to reward him. Nazir was true, Marik
knew, but what had become of the rest of Sonten's people? As a
region, Durkos was large and underpopulated. Had a body of
Sonten's men remained loyal to their lord's ally in Albia and
pledged their support to Corbyn, just biding their time to strike? It
would answer the riddle of where the unmarked raiders who had
troubled Albia had come from. And Corbyn's son Kethro was an
Artesan. He was only a Journeyman, but well able to pass
information across the Veils, or to receive instructions.

Marik thumped his hand on the table in frustration. Could he
spare the men to seek out Corbyn? Should he?

The dilemma was abruptly and unexpectedly answered for
him. A young page entered quietly and requested permission to

admit an Albian messenger who bore a parchment sealed with the sun-circled crown emblem of Elias Rovannon.

Glancing at Anjer, Marik gave his permission. He watched as the messenger approached him, knelt, and offered the parchment. Frowning, Marik took it, noting the yellow bandolier across the man's breast—the token of free passage for messengers and a good indication that this message truly came from the High King of Albia.

A little reluctantly, he broke the seal. His face drained of color as he read the declaration, and Anjer moved around the table, taking the message from Marik's suddenly nerveless fingers. The huge man's face turned thunderous as he scanned the note.

"How *dare* he do this!" Anjer's deep and resonant voice boomed about the room, causing the messenger to jump. "How can he believe we would take his son? It is Albians who are holding the Hierarch's Heir. It is *we* who should be declaring war on *them*!"

Anjer viciously crumpled the parchment and threw it across the room. He swung round on the messenger, who stepped back a pace. Anjer was a truly imposing sight when he was angry.

Marik roused himself just in time. "Lord General!" he barked, slapping a hand on Anjer's arm. The huge man subsided, but only marginally.

"You may go," Marik told the nervous messenger. "I advise you to leave the Citadel swiftly. There will be no reply."

The man afforded the Duke a cursory salute and fled. Marik ignored him. He slumped to a seat at the oval table. How was he to deal with this? With Aeyron lost or dead and Pharikian insensible, all decisions came down to him. Idrimar was too bowed with grief to help him much, and Anjer looked intent on murdering someone. Was he the only one who could keep a clear head?

He briefly thought of asking Anjer to link with him so that he could bespeak Sullyan, but then thought better of it. Had she wished to, she could have warned him of this; she must have known of it. The fact that she hadn't meant that she was as swept up by this course of events as he.

A cold hand of dread clenched around his heart, and his spine froze.

"Anjer!" he said in a strangled voice. The huge man turned his head slowly, still fuming over the King's message. He quirked his black brows at the Duke.

"You do realize that Elias has access to detailed information about our forces and battle strategies, don't you?" Marik's voice sounded strange even to him. Anjer frowned. "Think, man!" urged the Duke. "Who knows us best? Who knows our numbers, the terrain, our weaknesses? Who has seen you command before?"

Anjer's face paled. "Sullyan wouldn't betray us!"

Marik held his gaze. "She won't have any choice. How would you react in her shoes? Would you risk being branded a traitor to your country? Would you refuse a direct order from Timar?"

Anjer stared at him, real pain in his eyes.

Marik looked away. "You're going to have to plan our defenses very carefully, my friend."

✤ ✤ ✤ ✤ ✤

From where she stood with the other healers, Rienne watched as King Elias strode across the covered walkway that led to the raised platform overlooking the parade ground. The serried ranks of fighting men were marred and blurred by the masses of support staff milling amongst them. Only the healers in their light blue garb formed an orderly group.

An expectant hush fell over the crowd when the King reached

the platform. Rienne studied those who stood with him.

General Blaine was beside him, with Colonel Vassa to his right. Robin, Baily, Dexter, Parren, and the other captains stood at the back. Bull stood below the platform, next to the King's swordmaster, Ardoch. The big man was frowning, not bothering to hide his anxiety and apprehension. Rienne knew just how he felt.

She turned her attention to Robin. Like Bull, he looked anxious, but there was no hint he'd been told his life mate's incredible news. Rienne supposed Sullyan was waiting until the announcement was over, but even then it wouldn't be easy. It ought to heal the rift between them, but it didn't change the fact that this new life might soon be brought into the world in the middle of the most ridiculous war of all time.

Her lips thinned. Would she have told Cal her own news if she had known how things would turn out? How would knowing she was pregnant affect Cal's commitment? Would it interfere with his concentration? She was suddenly more frightened for him than ever and came closer to understanding Sullyan's motives.

She was jerked out of her thoughts as Elias started speaking.

"My people, I have asked you to assemble here today to hear and witness an important announcement. You are probably all aware by now that the demons of Andaryon have abducted my son, Prince Eadan, in revenge for the taking of the Hierarch's Heir.

"As you well know, we had nothing to do with that, and so I have no option but to view the abduction of my son as a hostile act. It is with great regret that I have to tell you that, as of now, we are officially at war with the realm of Andaryon."

There was an uneasy stirring among the masses on the parade ground, although there couldn't have been many who hadn't already heard. Elias's formal declaration just made it irrevocable.

The King raised his right hand and silence returned.

"All patrols are canceled with immediate effect. Although we must wait for the militia, and for reinforcements to arrive from the surrounding garrisons, you are to hold yourselves in readiness for attack, and to ensure that you can obey the orders to move out as soon as they are given by your commanders. This is how I intend to deploy our resources."

The King was interrupted by sudden movement behind him. Rienne saw him turn, frowning with displeasure. She expected to see Sullyan step onto the platform and was puzzled when instead a young cadet handed a parchment to Lieutenant-Major Baily. Baily glanced at it and immediately handed the message to General Blaine. The General unfolded the parchment and briefly scanned the message. Rienne saw the look he gave the King, and both monarch and general moved to the side of the platform. Heads together, they read the message.

"This is outrageous!"

The King's outburst shocked many, judging by the expressions Rienne could see. Her heart lurched—what atrocity had occurred now?

Elias was visibly trembling with fury as he strode back to the end of the platform. Blaine followed, his face pale and serious. Rienne shivered as she waited to hear what had happened.

The King's voice shook with anger. "It seems we've been harboring a traitor in our midst! Brynne Sullyan has decided she no longer serves her King and country and has resigned her commission. In the light of her misplaced affections for our demon enemies, we have no alternative but to declare her guilty of high treason."

Gasps and murmurs of disbelief ran through the crowd. Bile rose in Rienne's throat and she fought to push it down. She hadn't foreseen this. Neither had Bull, judging by the pallor of his face and the shock in his eyes. Her gaze then skated across the odd quirk on Parren's lips and settled on Robin's frozen expression.

The King brandished the parchment, his fury plain. "I refuse to accept this letter of resignation! I hereby cast the former Colonel Sullyan out of my forces. I strip her of her rank, her battle honors, and King's Envoy title. Furthermore, I issue a warrant for her immediate arrest. She must not be permitted to use her knowledge of our strategies to aid the demons. I will deal with her under a martial court once we have shown the demons how true Albians defend their own. General Blaine, send a detail to arrest Sullyan."

A smothering hush descended over the crowd. Rienne saw many of the men of Sullyan's company glancing at each other, puzzlement and anger in their eyes. She watched with a hand to her mouth as Blaine stared at his King. For one brief moment she thought the General might try to support Sullyan, but the strange light in Elias's eyes brooked no argument. Blaine turned to Vassa, who spoke to Baily. The small man left the platform, calling for some of his men. Rienne saw Robin slip from the platform, too. Everyone else stood in stunned silence, their eyes fixed upon the King.

"Is there anyone else who doubts my decision?" snapped Elias. "Anyone else who doubts my right to wage war on those who have taken my son? I tell you now—I will tolerate nothing but total obedience. Those Andaryon devils have raided us for the very last time. Now I intend to give them a taste of our courage and steel. We will carry war into the heart of their strongholds and we will force them to return my son. Are you with me? For if you are not, you are with my enemies, and I will show you no mercy!"

There were cheers from some of the men, but not all. Sullyan's company in particular seemed unsure how to respond. Rienne hoped their reticence wouldn't be noticed by the King.

Fortunately, the cheers grew in strength until most of the crowd were shouting for Elias. Rienne turned away, tears pricking her eyes. Her world had just fallen apart and she had no idea whether it would ever mend.

✤ ✤ ✤ ✤ ✤

The King, still fuming, dismissed the men, and the huge throng in the parade ground began to disperse. Parren came down from the platform and walked among the jostling throng. He heard murmurs of astonishment over what had just happened, and now that the King and the General had left, he even heard some of the men—those of Sullyan's company in particular—criticizing the King. He briefly considered informing on them, but thought better of it. He had more important matters on his mind. He intended to send a runner immediately to Port Loxton; how the Baron would enjoy this news!

Parren shook his head as he walked, as astonished as anyone else. But he had always suspected that Sullyan was more than part outlander, and her refusal to use her knowledge to help the King regain his son merely confirmed where her true allegiances lay. He chuckled. It was a shame Vassa hadn't tasked *him* with leading the detail to arrest Sullyan, but never mind. He could still enjoy rubbing Robin Tamsen's nose in it. He felt totally vindicated in every insult he had ever flung Sullyan's way. How triumphant the Baron would be to hear of her disgrace! She was effectively nullified as a threat to them, and she was out of Parren's hair for good. He whistled tunelessly as he went to write his message.

✤ ✤ ✤ ✤ ✤

Sullyan collected the pack of clothing she'd left ready. She tried not to look at Robin's things in the room, or her own. Her sight was blurred with unshed tears, her soul felt like lead within her, and her heart was full of sorrow. For the first time since she'd saved Mathias Blaine's life all those years ago, she was homeless and adrift. Yes, she had a purpose, and yes, she still considered that what she was doing was serving her King and country to the best of her ability; but at what price? And what would become of her even if she was successful? She had as good as cast herself out of the only life she'd ever wanted, and she didn't know how to survive without it.

She knew her earlier attempt to make Elias see reason was risky. He could easily have turned on her then, ordering her confined to the cells. It would have been safer to have left the Manor before the King made his announcement, long before the cadet delivered her letter of resignation. But her sense of duty wouldn't let her. She had never backed down from what she felt was right, no matter the personal cost. So she had gambled on Elias not noticing she wasn't present on the platform, and that his having gathered everyone on the parade ground would give her time to slip away from the Manor before the contents of her letter brought a detention detail down on her. She knew how to hide from her own.

Throwing an encapsulating shell around the hurt and the shame, she walled it off. Time to dwell on it later. Now, she had to leave.

She made it to the horse lines unobserved, and collected the sturdy chestnut gelding one of the stable lads had readied for her. It was the mount Taran had bought from the Livery at Hyecombe for Rienne to ride on the journey to the Manor and, as such, didn't belong to the King like the other Manor horses. Taran had taken his own bay gelding with him, of course, and the third Hyecombe horse, a piebald cob, was still out with the general herd. The chestnut wasn't exactly what she was used to, but as she wasn't planning to take it into combat, it would do.

She fastened her pack to the saddle rings and mounted.

She rode down the track which led to the manned barrier in the Manor's encircling wall. She reached out quietly with her mind and touched Taran's waiting presence. He was already in place, and a measure of relief went through her. At least she didn't have to face this completely alone.

The sentry on the gate couldn't have heard of her resignation yet. He glanced at her in surprise and was about to ask where she was bound on the day the King had declared war. But hoof beats from farther up the lane diverted him.

Sullyan shot a glance over her shoulder, fearful that a detention detail had sighted her already. A voice rang out from the lone rider.

"Sentry! Open the gate for the King's messenger."

As the sentry ran to obey, Sullyan's pounding heart slowed. No one hindered Elias's runners, and the sentry had the barrier up before the messenger's athletic horse dashed through, scattering dust from its steel-shod hooves. Sullyan watched the woman, finding it incredibly hard to come to terms with the idea that she was no longer a part of life at the Manor.

She shuddered. She was suddenly, pathologically, terribly afraid to cross the boundary of the Manor's protective wall. Within the wall was familiarity, duty, responsibility. Without was... well, just that. Without everything that had ever made her life worthwhile. She trembled in the saddle. But the sentry wouldn't wait forever and was already fidgeting at her hesitation. She had sealed her own fate and had no choice. Gathering her remaining courage in both hands, she prepared to cross that line.

"Sullyan."

The instantly recognizable and much-loved voice behind her caused her heart to race again. He'd found her! Had he come to take her to the King? Or maybe he'd come to his senses. Maybe he wasn't going to let her go without healing the breach between them.

"Robin."

She turned the chestnut so she could face him. He was unable to look her in the eye, even after visibly steeling himself to do so. Their last meeting had been so painful. She watched him, fearful of saying the wrong thing, unable to read his shielded thoughts but seeing the wash of conflicting emotions chase across his much-loved face. She was innocent of what he had accused her so bitterly. But she had used her powers on him and that was unforgivable, no matter what had caused her lapse of control. She wavered. Should she apologize first or leave it to him? He had come to her, after all.

He had. But now that he was faced with her, Robin didn't seem to know what to say.

"I don't know what's got into you, Sullyan," he said finally. "Betraying me is one thing and bad enough, but I never thought you'd turn against the King."

Her heart lurched with pain. "I would have thought that you, at least, would understand." Her voice was flat with the effort of reining in her chaotic emotions. "What would you have me do, Robin? Could you betray them after everything we went through? Have you forgotten their care of us during that terrible time? Can you lay aside their friendship so easily? It was only two weeks ago that you were training alongside them."

Robin's temper flashed and she frowned; his anger flared so readily these days.

"Yes," he snapped, "and Barrin was very quick to accuse us of breaking the treaty and sending raiders into their lands. *That's* how deep their friendship runs."

She stared in dismay. He hadn't come to put things right after all; he'd come to berate her.

Infinite sadness settled in her soul. "Is that all there is between us now? Accusations and mistrust? Once it was very different. I thought we were bound together for life. I thought you felt the same."

He looked her in the eye for the first time. "I did!" he cried. "I wasn't the one who ruined all that."

His hands were gripped tightly together at his breast and she had to look away from the betrayed hurt in his pain-darkened eyes. He truly believed what he had accused her of; that she had deceived him and been false to the vows she had made. How could she convince him otherwise? How could she take away the hurt that had been done them by the vicious rumors? There was a way, only one sure way, but it was a way she could not use. She could not unleash her powers on him again, not even to convince him of her innocence. She had already abused his trust that way and she would never allow herself to make that mistake again.

She was about to plead with him once more when movement on the other side of the wall attracted Robin's attention. Taran's horse stamped its hoof and shifted its position, and Robin caught sight of the tall Adept where he sat silently waiting.

The Major's face tightened, paling dangerously. He turned burning, furious eyes on Sullyan.

"Oh, *now* I see! You're going off with *him*. I've been an idiot again, haven't I? I really should have guessed. Well, I wish you much joy of each other."

He glared at Taran, who was watching nervously, doubtless remembering Robin's furious assault on him the other day. "I was right about you, you back-stabbing bastard!" Robin yelled. "Well I hope she betrays *you* one day and then you'll know how it feels!"

He swung back on Sullyan. "The King refused to accept your resignation. He's stripped you of your rank and titles and cast you out of his forces. There's a royal warrant out for your arrest. I should do my duty and drag you back to face the consequences of your betrayal."

She stared at him, her soul crumbling. Would she be forced to fight him? She couldn't afford to let him stop her.

Robin held her gaze, his eyes hot with rage and shame. "Oh, just go, the pair of you. I'm going to pretend I never saw you, because I never want to see either of you ever again for as long as I live. Not even to see the King make you pay for what you've done."

He turned his back. Sullyan, her heart ready to burst for grief, stretched out one hand as if to reach for him. But he beckoned abruptly to the bewildered gate sentry and shoved the man into the gatehouse, disappearing inside behind him. He didn't see her gesture.

Sullyan gave a violent sob and wrenched the startled gelding's reins, sending it out onto the road. She kicked the chestnut into a flat-out gallop, Taran hastening to follow. They left the Manor in a cloud of scattered dust.

Chapter Five

The sentry was a member of Sullyan's company. Robin trusted his assertion that he wouldn't mention seeing him that morning. His soul in turmoil, Robin walked slowly back up to the Manor. He was numb, shocked, and angry. Discovering that she was going off with Taran—and the fact that he hadn't even suspected this might happen—had shaken him to his soul. The angry words he had flung at her, at the pair of them, had been born of jealousy and hurt. If he thought about it rationally—if he could be rational just now—he could accept that she wouldn't go off alone if she could help it, and apart from Bull she had no one else. He knew she wouldn't risk Bull's heart again, and so he shouldn't have been so surprised to see Taran there.

Yet this realization only confused Robin's tangled emotions further. Had Taran agreed to accompany her out of friendship, or because they really were involved with each other? Robin didn't know, and the more he worried at it, the more confused he became. One minute he believed every word Denny had said, and yet the next minute, he found himself doubting everything. He felt hurt and betrayed, yes, but there was something else. Could it be guilt? Was he feeling shamed because he'd been so quick to judge her? Because he'd swallowed the lieutenant's story without speaking to her first?

If he had spoken with her before flinging accusations, he knew that the first thing she would have done would have been to open her mind to him so he could read the truth of her words. He was well aware that this was what she meant when they had argued in their rooms, when she had told him there was a way in which she could convince him of her innocence. She had said and meant the same just now. The fact that she hadn't used that way was beside the point. Why say it if she hadn't known it would prove her fidelity?

He shook his head; he was talking himself round in circles. Why hadn't he spoken with her first? It was because he had been so sure that Denny was speaking the truth. Even when dealing with non-gifted people, an Artesan could usually detect a lie. Robin knew Denny hadn't been lying. But as he suddenly realized, that didn't necessarily mean that what Denny had said was fact. He might have put his own interpretation on what he had seen and heard.

So where did this leave Robin? He was coldly aware that he'd left it a little late to be having doubts about the rumors. The damage was done and she was gone. But Robin knew that damage would also have been done to his own credibility in Elias's eyes; his own loyalty would now be in question. With Sullyan gone, the only other person who held similar detailed knowledge of Andaryon and its forces was Robin himself. The very least the Major could expect was that Elias would demand the same of him as he'd demanded of Sullyan: that he use his knowledge to help his King. The worst would be incarceration and possible dismissal if Elias could not be convinced of Robin's loyalty. The Major knew he faced a very difficult interview.

He reached the Manor and made immediately for Blaine's office. Time was of the essence here. He must prove himself to Elias before the King even had leisure to suspect him. Angry voices reached him before Hyram, Blaine's valet, opened the door for him. King Elias turned on him the minute he entered.

"Well? Have you arrested Sullyan?"

Robin held Elias's gaze as best he could. "I believe she has left the Manor, your Majesty. I doubt the detention detail will find her."

He could see the General watching him and suspected Blaine knew he was dissembling. Robin was fairly confident the General wouldn't challenge him, though.

Blaine turned his attention to his King. "If she has already left the Manor, Baily's men won't find her. Leave her, your Majesty. We have more pressing concerns right now."

The fuming Elias seemed about to press the matter. To forestall him, Robin stepped forward, drew his sword, and knelt before the monarch's feet. He held his blade out to Elias.

"Your Majesty, I wish to reaffirm my Oath in the light of Sullyan's actions. I realize my association with her and with the Andaryans might lead you to suspect my loyalties, but I want to assure you that I remain true to my sworn word. I will serve you in any way I can. Command me."

Elias considered him in silence. Blaine looked on, his face expressionless. Light quivered off the sword in Robin's hands. Eventually, Elias reached out to touch its hilt.

"Rise, Major. We accept your pledge. Sullyan's treachery shall not taint your service provided you obey my commands. My Lord Blaine, is it your opinion that Major Tamsen would best serve our cause by remaining here to guard the Manor?"

Blaine considered Robin before replying. "Your Majesty, I understand your reluctance to trust the Major's ability to lead his men into Andaryon against those he considers his friends. Yet I believe that commanding him to remain here would deprive you of a valuable resource. Major Tamsen's familiarity with the terrain would be a great asset in the field. We could, of course, access his knowledge through the Veils if necessary, but that can be tiring and time-consuming, and in battle we would not be afforded the leisure. If you remain unsure of him, he could accompany us in an advisory capacity rather than as a commander. Would that be acceptable to you?"

Robin fixed his gaze upon the King. If Elias accepted the General's compromise, Robin's career should be safe. If Sullyan was no longer to be his life mate, then the Manor meant more to him than ever. His breath caught in his throat.

The King held Blaine's gaze before turning to regard Robin. "Very well, Major. You will accompany us to Andaryon in an advisory capacity. But be aware—I will be watching you. One misstep, even the slightest misdemeanor, will see you sent back to the Manor under guard. Your future is at stake here. I trust you understand that?"

Robin's heart still pounded. He bowed his head. "I will not fail you, your Majesty."

The King waved a hand and Robin left the room. He sensed Hyram's following gaze like an itch between his shoulder blades as he walked away. He needed to find somewhere quiet, needed time to deal with hurt and the conflicting emotions pulling his soul apart.

✣ ✣ ✣ ✣ ✣

Rienne looked down at the parchment in her hands, the words blurred by her tears. She had found it when she returned to her rooms after the distressing events of the morning. Wiping her eyes, she read it once more.

Rienne, my dearest friend,

I ask you to forgive me for leaving you this letter, but I fear I will be unable to see you in person. The King's actions have forced me to resign my commission and I must leave as soon as possible. We will meet again, never fear. I am going to try to find and rescue Eadan and Aeyron, if Aeyron still lives. Elias will send no one to do it. He firmly believes Eadan is in Andaryon. I have just staked my life and career on my own conviction that he is not, and I am now free to follow my own way. If I can find them, perhaps I can avert this war. If I cannot ... we must face what will come. But I must try. My love for Pharikian and for my King will let me do no less. I hope you can understand.

Look after yourself, Rienne. I will try to reach out to you now and then, so you will know I am thinking of you. Take care of Cal and ask him to look after Robin. I am still hopeful of healing the breach between us, and he will need much love and support in the difficult times to come.

Do not fear for me. I have Taran to help me.

Your loving friend,

—Sullyan

Tucking the folded parchment into a pocket, Rienne left the room. She had to know if Sullyan had told Robin her news. She searched the Manor and grounds for the Major, asking among the scurrying cadets and swordsmen. No one had seen him. She eventually found him up near the horse lines, sitting disconsolately on a mounting block in the deserted yard, his shoulders bowed as if under a great weight. She could see he'd been weeping.

He heard her approach and looked up at her with dull, dark

eyes. She drew in a breath at the state of him. She simply couldn't believe that the deep love he and Sullyan had shared had been reduced so easily to this. She stopped in front of him, something inside her wanting to take him in her arms for comfort. Instead, she said, "Has she gone?"

Robin nodded.

Rienne twisted her hands. "Did you see her? Did she…say…anything?"

Robin frowned. "Nothing I hadn't heard before."

His raw voice made Rienne look away, her sorrow deepening. "Oh, dear gods … And you just let her go?"

His head came up sharply. "Would you rather I'd arrested her? Fulfilled my duty to the King? I'm as bad as she is now … forsworn of my Oath. I just … I couldn't … I just tried to contact her, but she's shut me out."

Rienne shook her head in despair. "Robin, you've no idea what you've done—no idea what you've just lost. I only hope you can live with yourself."

Unable to speak further round the lump rising in her throat, Rienne walked away. She would spend some time with Cal, try to recover her joy in their future family. There wasn't much joy left anywhere else.

✤ ✤ ✤ ✤ ✤

Parren had watched the runner leave with his letter to the Baron. He could just imagine the swarthy man's pleasure when he read it. If this was what he had meant when he had told Parren he could "influence" Tamsen and Sullyan, then Parren was impressed. The Baron must have access to some pretty powerful "influence" if it could destroy such a strong bond so thoroughly. A warm glow of satisfaction filled his heart. He was looking forward to distinguishing himself in the forthcoming war. This time, Blaine would be unable to block his promotion. And even if he tried, Parren had faith that the Queen would override him. His future was secured. He couldn't possibly fail.

He turned a corner in the track and stopped, seeing the hunched figure sitting forlorn in the stable yard. When he registered who it was, a malicious smile stole across his scarred features. Now here was a fortuitous meeting! With any luck, the Major would be feeling more than wretched. Parren was going to enjoy this.

But then he stopped. This was a rare opportunity and one he should not let slip away. The thought of goading Robin was a pleasurable one for sure, but might there not be more to be gained here than a moment's gratification?

Parren pondered, his mind awhirl. If he threw his dice right, he might just be able to maneuver Robin into a very vulnerable position. It might take some time, but the wait would be worth it. And even if it didn't work, Parren would still have the satisfaction of causing his enemy more confusion and pain.

An even nastier smile quirked his lips. He'd have to be very careful, but he was beginning see a very gratifying outcome from what would be a difficult but worthwhile charade.

Schooling his features and calming his mounting excitement, he moved toward Robin. He tried for a sympathetic expression, but it was so alien to his nature that he settled for neutrality. Sympathy would be too much anyway; he didn't want to arouse Robin's suspicions.

As he walked closer, Robin raised his head and saw him. Parren noted the look of disgust in those pain-darkened eyes and clamped down on his temper.

When he realized Parren was intent on approaching, Robin

glared at him. "I came here for some peace and quiet, Parren. Piss off."

Parren ignored the profanity, although his lips tightened. Swearing was not encouraged among the senior officers, and it was considered a serious insult incurring disciplinary action when directed against one of junior rank. Parren ignored this opportunity for petty revenge, reined in his ire, and turned to lean on the paddock railing. He had a much larger goal in mind.

Robin continued to stare. "I'm not having a good day. If you've come to gloat, you'll get more than you bargained for."

Parren replied as levelly as he could. "Actually, I haven't, although I don't suppose you'll believe that."

There was a brief silence. Parren knew this wasn't what Robin had expected. They rarely exchanged civil words.

"What do you want, then? I'm in no mood for company."

Robin didn't bother to disguise the contempt in his voice. Parren knew that his company would be the last Robin would seek, even in a good mood.

Parren stirred, then stilled again. "If you really want to know, I came to see if you were all right."

Robin's jaw dropped. "You *what*? Don't make me laugh! What's it to you, anyway? Don't try to tell me you're not glad about what's happened. I know how you feel about me."

Parren was warming to his role. "I wonder if you really do? Yes, I know we've not exactly seen eye to eye in the past"—he ignored Robin's strangled choke—"but all along my problem was really with Sullyan, not you. Now that she's gone and you've found out what she's really like, well, I thought it might be time to set the record straight. There are hard times ahead of us, and we're both on the same side, after all."

Robin stood abruptly. "What the Void are you talking about?"

He stared hard at Parren, doubtless looking for the habitual cruel smile. "And what do you mean, 'found out what she's really like'?"

Parren faced Robin as openly as he could. Dissembling was not something he was used to. He thought very fast.

"She did something similar to me once." Catching Robin's scornfully dismissive look, he added, "Yes, I know what you were told, that I'd tried to force myself on her. But it wasn't true. It was a story concocted by her and Blaine to make me out as the villain. You ask Denny if you don't believe me. He was there at the time. It was jealousy, if I'm honest, that set me against you when you first came here." He watched Robin's reactions carefully. "It goes back a long way, and I daresay you're not interested. I can't say I blame you. I just wanted you to know that my grievance was never really with you personally. You just got caught in the volley."

Robin narrowed his eyes. Parren had said his piece, and he could see it would be enough. He'd sown the seeds of doubt and now they must be left to grow. There was a grain of truth in what he'd said, after all, and Denny would back him up if Robin bothered to check. Parren was sure of that.

With a flash of uncharacteristic intuition, Parren did the best thing he could have done; he left it alone. With a last glance at Robin's face—it would have been a bad mistake to smile, and Parren didn't make the error—he left Robin standing dumbfounded and confused for the third time that day.

✣ ✣ ✣ ✣ ✣

They were some miles down the road before Taran caught up with Sullyan. She had finally come back to herself enough to recognize what she was doing to her horse. It was a good enough beast for a hack, but it was no match for the powerful Manor horses, and certainly not for Sullyan's own treasured Drum. She had eased it to a walk and was stroking its lathered neck. Taran could see the heave of its flanks and sense Sullyan's chagrin at her ill-treatment. She had allowed her inner turmoil to affect her behavior, and he knew she was shamed. She retreated further into her own thoughts and sat with her head bowed, ignoring Taran.

They rode on into the afternoon, seemingly with no direction. Taran could think of nothing that would ease her pain. She stayed tightly shielded, a rarity in itself, and this alone told Taran how desperately she was hurt. If he had been able to reach out to her tortured spirit perhaps he could have helped her, but she remained walled off from him. He let her be. He rode close behind her in silence, hoping and trusting she would eventually come back to her senses.

The afternoon wore on toward evening. He couldn't tell if she knew where she was going, or if she even cared. She was hardly taking notice of her surroundings, and he didn't think she'd brought any supplies with her. He carried enough to make them both a light supper, but didn't know whether she planned to stop at an inn or whether she had made any plans at all. He had attempted to speak to her once or twice but got no response, and he couldn't tell if she had even heard him.

She rode with her eyes downcast, her hand loose on the reins. The chestnut, recovered now from the wild flight from the Manor, ambled along at a sedate pace, pulling at leaves and grass along the way. Sullyan never checked him.

The light was beginning to fade and Taran was becoming concerned. He had just made up his mind to rouse her from her lassitude and insist they stop for the night when she abruptly reined the gelding to a halt. Her head had come up, but her eyes were still unfocused. Taran could see the tremble of the hand that held the reins.

She slid slowly down the chestnut's shoulder and stood unsteadily upon the grass. They had been following the road westward and had just come upon a wide grass verge. Trees had given way to grasslands, and they were nearing the easternmost edge of the Downs. The Adept dismounted also and loosened his horse's girth. He glanced over at the silent Sullyan. She had dropped the chestnut's reins and was ignoring the grazing horse. Alarmed at her lack of movement, Taran came up behind her.

Only now could he see that she was shuddering, and she suddenly wrapped her arms about her chest as if it was the only way she could hold herself together.

"What have I done?" he heard her desperate whisper. "Oh gods, *what have I done?*"

He couldn't bear the desolation in her voice, and before he could stop himself he had taken her in his arms. She didn't pull away as he had feared. Instead, she turned to him and sobbed against his chest in a surging release of emotion, crying out her hurt as if her heart was breaking. He held her more securely, trying to convey love and comfort without complications. This was what he had dreamed of for so long; having her to himself, depending on him, leaning on him for strength and support.

It might only be a fleeting moment born of desperation, but still he savored it.

His unconditional and bolstering presence revived her after a while. Her shuddering body calmed; the sobbing quieted as the storm blew itself out. But she still didn't push away, and her willingness to remain within the shelter of his embrace told him how badly she needed his help. Very gently, he bowed his head and kissed her hair.

Now she did move. She slowly raised her eyes to his and they glittered with the moisture of her deep unhappiness. He saw their brightness cloud when she looked into his face.

"Ah, Taran!"

Gently but firmly she pushed herself away. He let her go reluctantly. The moment had indeed been fleeting, but very sweet. She had not released his gaze and held it still as she spoke.

"I cannot tell you how much pain it gives me to see the depth of love in your eyes and know that I can never return it as you would wish."

He could not prevent the expression of loss that crossed his face. She saw it, and the ache in her eyes intensified.

"It was not my intention to give you more pain," he said sadly.

"I should not have presumed so on your friendship," she murmured. "I am sorry."

"You've nothing to be sorry for. You know I'll always help you if I can, always be there if you call. You know how much I love you. Oh, it's all right," he said as he saw the leap of alarm in her eyes. "I know how you feel. I'm not asking for anything you can't give. But you're alone right now and you need a good friend. That's what I am. That's why I'm here. Anything else, well, that's down to fate."

He was dismayed by the reaction his words caused. He had intended to reassure her, but her strength suddenly gave out and he had to hold her fast or she would have fallen. The day's events had obviously been too much for her.

"Come on," he said, "we've been riding for ages. We can camp here, unless you were making for somewhere else?"

He felt her shake her head. "Taran," she murmured, "there is something I have to tell you."

"Let it wait," he replied, "you need to rest."

But she was adamant and he couldn't refuse her.

"I had not intended to tell you this." Her voice was so low he had to strain to hear her. It made him fearful. What else had happened that day? She moved slightly away from him, as if to distance herself from what she would say.

"You have been so good to me. You are the best of friends. You have risked your life for me on more than one occasion, and so I have no right to keep this from you, especially as you have been so willing to put everything aside for me yet again."

He placed a hand on each of her shoulders and looked down into her face. "What is it, Sullyan?"

He could feel her gathering the tatters of her strength as she said, still unable to look him in the eye, "I am pregnant. I am carrying Robin's child."

✤ ✤ ✤ ✤ ✤

There was shocked silence. Sullyan closed her eyes, unable to bear the expression on Taran's handsome features. How could she lay this burden on him as well? Yet she knew with certainty that he deserved her trust and honesty. He could make no considered decisions without knowing all the facts.

At last she opened her eyes and managed to look at him. His face was frozen; she couldn't tell his thoughts.

"But you said ... I thought you couldn't...."

"As did I. Believe me, it was as much of a shock to me as it is to you."

He was aghast. "Yet Robin let you go without him? How could he do that?"

Now came the hard part. "Robin does not know."

"He *doesn't know*? Sullyan, are you out of your mind? You *have* to tell him! You can't keep this from him. It changes everything."

She snapped out of her lethargy, finding nervous energy. "No!

It changes nothing." She pleaded for his understanding, clasping his forearms in her small hands. "How could I tell him? How could I tell him that the impossible has happened? With all this mistrust and betrayal hanging over us, not to mention a declaration of war, how could I tell him he will be a father in three months' time?"

Taran gaped at her. "You're *six months* pregnant?"

His eyes traveled her slender form, clearly unable to credit it. She found his expression almost funny and struggled for control. If she was not very careful, her knife-edge emotions could very easily spill over into hysteria. She forced them down.

"I know this is hard for you to understand. It was hard for me, too."

He swallowed. "How long have you known?"

That nearly made her smile too. What was wrong with her? "Since yesterday."

He closed his eyes, his breathing uneven and harsh. "Gods, I need to sit down."

He walked a few paces away and sat heavily on one of the chalky boulders marking the edge of the road. She stood where she was, watching him in silence, until he turned to look at her over his shoulder.

"I can't believe you found the courage to do what you did today after finding out something like that."

She folded her arms and moved closer to him. "I could do nothing else. It was not courage that drove me."

"Presumably you didn't tell Blaine or the King either?"

Sullyan sat upon the ground beside him. She plucked a blade of grass and turned it in her fingers. "No. The King would have ordered me confined to the Manor, even without my resignation. And until Prince Eadan is found, this war will not end. The Andaryans do not have the King's son and cannot return him, and so Elias will have no reason to cease his attacks. He is driven by his desperate heart at the moment, not reason or logic.

"Whoever has taken the princes—and you know my suspicions about that—has made the most meticulous plans. An all-out war culminating in the death of Elias and as many of our kind as possible is exactly what he wants, but unfortunately I could not convince Elias of that. I cannot allow it to happen, and so I had no choice but to do what I did. But if it comforts you any, Rienne also thinks I should have told the King."

"Rienne knows?"

She nodded. "It was Rienne who finally found out. She was right; had I not been so convinced pregnancy was impossible for me, I surely would have guessed months ago. I just thought I was unwell."

He stared at her, and she managed a small smile.

"I am a hybrid of sorts, and, as far as I know, the only one of my kind. It is hardly surprising that this is not turning out to be a normal pregnancy so far."

Taran shook his head and just stared down at her. She fell silent too, concentrating on the grass she was shredding in her fingers, her gaze turning inward. Then she tossed aside the ruined blade of grass, unfolded from her cross-legged pose, and rose to her feet.

"I really must care for that poor horse. I rode him far too hard today."

Taran also stood to care for his own gelding, but she laid her hand on his arm before he moved away.

"I must ask you not to mention what I have just told you to anyone else. I have sworn Rienne to secrecy and I must ask the same of you. This is my problem and I will deal with it as best I can. So please, if you are in contact with Cal at any time, do not let slip what you know."

He held her gaze. "Whatever you say."

"Thank you."

They spent some time tending to their mounts, Sullyan taking great care to brush out all the dried sweat from the chestnut's coat. The physical work helped calm her. Taran, who finished first, laid a small fire and brought out his few supplies. He stopped and jumped to his feet in alarm when he heard Sullyan cursing under her breath.

"What is it?"

Her tone was urgent. "Do you have any fellan in your pack?"

He frowned. "No, only some bread, cheese, and cold meat."

She spat a blistering profanity. Used as all her friends were to her occasional foul language, Taran still looked shocked. Sullyan slapped the chestnut on the rump rather harder than necessary, sending it ambling away in search of grass. She had not thought to bring any fellan either, which said more about her state of mind when she left the Manor than anything else.

A morose atmosphere descended around the small, bright fire. Sullyan's earlier listlessness returned, her depression deepening without her much-needed anodyne. Taran sat in silence, picking at the food. Sullyan had taken some bread and meat, but had hardly touched it.

The shadows were lengthening and the sun was slipping behind the Downs when Sullyan's head came up sharply. Taran looked around but heard nothing, and relaxed when she made no move toward her sword. It was not a threat she had perceived in the dusky landscape.

Taran had lost interest and was reaching for more meat when Sullyan leaped to her feet. This time he heard it too: the far-off whinny of a horse.

Sullyan moved nearer the road, whispering, "Drum?" Taran's bay and the chestnut gelding had also raised their heads. Their ears were pricked and their line of sight followed Sullyan's.

The sound came again, now the unmistakably imperious clarion call of a stallion. Sullyan cupped her hands around her mouth and gave her characteristic whistle, pitched to carry. There was an immediate answering whinny, and then they could hear the hoof beats.

Moments later, an inky shadow could be seen careering down the road, snorting as it came. The coal-black stud thundered toward them; feathers on his legs and his full mane flying, tail streaming behind him. There were tears in Sullyan's eyes as she stepped out into the stallion's path.

The hurtling half-ton of horse skidded to a dirt-showering stop right in front of her. His nostrils were red-rimmed from his furious pace, and his eyes were edged with white. She put her hand to his nose and he pushed his head into her, nearly knocking her from her feet.

"Oh, Drum," she crooned, "you beautiful, big fool."

She ought to have guessed he would follow her. She had raised the black stud from a tiny foal, when the vicious mare that had been his dam rejected him. She and he were joined by an unbreakable bond, and he would have sensed her distress. Drum was much more intelligent than many horses; he'd had no trouble tracking her down.

Clever though he undoubtedly was, he was not capable of harnessing himself. Someone at the Manor must have sent him, for the huge stud wore his plaited bridle, its reins knotted over his neck. He also bore a pack tied to the rings of his saddle.

Sullyan led him toward Taran and unharnessed him, watching as Drum sidled over to the two geldings. The stallion snaked his head at them, his small ears laid flat and his teeth bared to emphasize his dominance. They turned their heads and licked their lips to indicate their lowly position. Satisfied, Drum moved alongside them and began to pull at the grass.

Sullyan rummaged through the saddle-pack.

"Someone had their wits about them," commented Taran.

"Undoubtedly Bulldog." With a deep sigh of contentment, Sullyan held up a leather pouch for him to see the plentiful supply of fellan grounds. "Ah, my friend, I could not begin to tell you how much I love that man."

The Adept smiled. Bull was her oldest and staunchest friend, and it wasn't surprising he had sent Drum to her. He knew how she relied on the black's battle skills. She wondered how the big man had gotten around Solet's vigilance. Taran stooped to put water over the fire, making sure there was plenty of it. It would likely take a deal of strong fellan to get her through the coming night.

She was on her second cup—the first had disappeared even before it was really cool enough to drink—when they again heard the sound of hooves on the road. Sullyan sprang for her sword and Taran drew his. They moved away from the fire so as not to cast a silhouette, but Drum's whicker of recognition had already reassured Sullyan. She turned to Taran.

"Remember," she hissed as she sheathed her sword, "not a word!"

Chapter Six

There was not one horse, but two. Neither Sullyan nor Taran was surprised to see Bull, but they were surprised to see he was accompanied by Master Ardoch. Taran saw the speculation in Sullyan's eyes as the old swordmaster slid down from his gray stallion.

"That's a quarter-pound in gold you owe me, old friend!" crowed Bull as he too dismounted. "I told you Drum would find her."

The old swordmaster gave him a sour look.

"Bulldog," said Sullyan as she embraced the big man, "that fellan saved my life."

The two men were drawn into the comforting circle of the fire, and more fellan was distributed. Bull and Ardoch had brought more food as well, both for themselves and for Sullyan.

"I found the letter you left me and then I checked with Goran," the big man said. "He told me you'd not sent for supplies. I take it you've heard what Elias did, that he refused your resignation and cast you out? Sully, why didn't you come and see me before planning all this?"

His tone was neutral, but his heart was in his eyes, and Taran could see she felt shamed. She probably hadn't wanted to risk bringing Elias's anger down on Bull if he suspected they'd planned this together, but he thought it more likely that her heart had been too full of pain. Maybe she hadn't been able to endure any more.

"I am sorry, Bull," was all she said, but her oldest friend could read under her words. He merely placed a huge hand over hers and smiled.

"So, what do you intend to do now?" he asked as he settled himself comfortably by her side, one arm thrown companionably across her small shoulders. She nestled into the safety of his embrace, and Taran suddenly wished that he shared such an easy relationship with her. But then, he reflected, Bull was that much older and had probably never seen himself as a potential mate. He had no idea how wrong he was.

Sullyan wasn't prepared to speak of the future just yet. "What was the situation when you left?"

The big man narrowed his eyes. "Elias was still in a foul mood, from what I could gather, but I don't think he's the biggest problem right now. It's the men of your company. They're so angry at what Elias did that many of them are on the verge of deserting. Dexter in particular is furious with the King—and with Robin too—and I think the men would follow his lead were he to refuse Robin's authority."

Sullyan's face paled and she sucked in a breath. "They must not rebel, Bull. They must not! Elias will need them. Mathias will need them. And I could not bear to have Elias punish them on my account. I will have to get word to them somehow, tell them to remain true to their Oaths."

She shook her head at this unforeseen complication. Loyalty to one's commander and comrades was one thing, and Taran knew that Sullyan's company was loyal to a man, but to put themselves at risk of their lives like this would do none of them any good.

"What was Elias doing when you left?" she asked.

"He'd called all the senior officers and captains into the hall for a council of war. It all seemed a bit frenetic to me. If he's not careful, he'll go too fast and commit himself too deeply. I didn't like the look of him, Sully. I don't think his mind's working right."

The old swordmaster stirred. "Careful what you say, big man. That's treason you're talking."

Bull was unmoved. "Not among friends. And can you think of another reason why he would cast aside the most skilled and experienced officer in his entire fighting force?"

Sullyan sighed deeply. "A pity Elias does not share your sentiments, my friend."

"But he does," asserted Bull, "underneath it all. The little Prince's disappearance must have shocked and unhinged him; otherwise he wouldn't have done it. Blaine did try to convince him to retract, I think, but even he can't gainsay the King."

"No," she murmured. "Not without the direst of consequences."

Bull's face fell and he hugged her. "Don't worry, dear heart. Blaine knows you're no traitor. He trusts you. He'd have supported you today if he could. I know because he saw us letting Drum out, and he stopped Solet protesting. We wouldn't have got past the little weasel if he hadn't. He'll keep working on the King, you can be sure of that."

"Oh, Mathias," she breathed. "I just hope I can avert this war before things get seriously out of hand."

"That's why we've come," said Bull, indicating himself and Ardoch. "We're going with you."

"No!"

The vehemence in her tone startled them all. Taran saw fear come into her eyes as she turned to face Bull.

"I cannot let you do that," she insisted. "I will not risk your heart again. I will not risk losing you. Whatever would I do without you?"

"Is that why you turned all your pay over to me?" he demanded suddenly. Taran's eyes widened. "Serrell told me this afternoon that you'd arranged for me to draw on your account. He said you'd withdrawn all claim to it. Why on earth would you do that?"

Sullyan cast down her eyes. "I have no way of knowing what will happen. I have to do this. I have to try to find Aeyron and Eadan. It is the only way of averting the war. With any luck, I can prove the Baron's involvement. I hope at least to discover his plans for all that spellsilver. I will wreck those, too, if I can. But it will be dangerous. If I fail, I will have no more need of that gold. But you will, and I am not prepared to see you suffer because I am out of favor with the King. If I succeed, Serrell knows that I may return to claim what is mine. But if I cannot, if Elias proves firm in his resolve and refuses to rescind his warrant, then at least you will be provided for."

"But what about you?" Bull protested. "Even if Elias won't take you back—and I can't see that happening if you can rescue the Prince—you'll need that gold to live on."

Taran noted the pallor that came over Sullyan's face, and the way she wouldn't look at any of them. She spoke in a very soft voice.

"Even if I am successful, I may not return to the Manor."

Bull's voice shattered the evening stillness. "What? But where else would you go?"

Sullyan was in no mood to discuss painful possibilities, and she shrugged her shoulders listlessly. "It is futile to speculate. Who knows what will happen?"

The big man frowned. "You still need help, though." Taran could sense he was desperate to be allowed to go with her. "You can't do this alone."

"Taran has agreed to help me," she said, still not meeting his eyes.

Bull glanced over at Taran, who held his gaze.

Ardoch stirred again. "One's not enough," he said firmly. "I'm not bound to the King, lassie, nor am I under your command. But I happen to agree with what you're doing, so, if you'll have me, I'll ride with you."

Her smile was warmer and Taran saw Bull relax. If she wouldn't accept him, at least he trusted the two she would.

Bull stayed a little longer, drinking fellan and holding Sullyan in his arms. Taran could see she was lapsing once more into her lethargy, and he wondered whether he should try for contact with Bull to explain about her mood. But he wasn't confident of achieving this without her knowledge, and he daren't take the risk she might sense him. She had had enough upset for one day, and so wisely he left it alone.

Eventually she stirred and let Bull know she thought it was time for him to leave. He was clearly reluctant, but she was adamant. So he collected the reins of his stallion and also those of the chestnut she had used. He would return it to the Manor now that she had Drum. Sullyan walked with him to the road, still within earshot of Taran and Ardoch.

"Speak to Dexter and the men on my behalf," Taran heard her ask. "Tell them I ask them to stay true to their Oaths. They will be doing me no favors by angering Elias. Tell them I am relying on them to keep the King safe. Tell them all to take care."

"You take care, too, Sully," Bull said softly, turning to face her before mounting his horse. "It seems to me like we've been here before."

An expression of pain crossed her features, and Taran remembering their leave-taking at Marik's mansion before she had ridden to her first meeting with the Hierarch.

"But this is nothing like that time, my friend," she said, taking his large hand in hers. "This time I intend to stay in touch with you. You will be my lifeline. I need you to keep me informed about events at the Manor and how the war goes. And I especially want you to look out for Robin. He is hurting too, no matter the rights or wrongs between us, and he will need someone to look out for him. Can you do that for me?"

Bull growled. "I'll try, but I can't guarantee not to knock his teeth out if he won't see sense."

"Then try to knock out ones that will not show."

Her attempt at levity didn't ring true, and Bull hugged her, making her gasp with emotion.

"If anyone can find Eadan and Aeyron, it's you," he said fiercely. "But if you run into trouble, if you need help of any kind, promise me you'll call."

"I promise, Bull." She smiled. "Now go. The hour is late, and I need to know you are safe."

"You sound like my mother," grumbled Bull, but he mounted his stallion and moved off down the road, the chestnut gelding jogging alongside. He turned to wave just before the darkness swallowed him in inky shadows.

Sullyan returned to the fire and her own chaotic thoughts. Bull's departure seemed to plunge her ever deeper into her morbid depression, and neither Taran nor Ardoch could snap her out of it. After a few desultory attempts, they gave up.

The two men decided on watches for the night, as no one knew whether there might still be raiders in the area. Even if there weren't, there would be Kingsmen and militiamen passing through over the next few days, answering the King's call to war. Taran offered to take the early watch and Ardoch took the middle, leaving Sullyan her preferred dawn watch. She made no response when Taran told her. She simply sat staring into the fire as if she were reading her whole life's history in the leaping flames.

It was deep into Taran's watch when she finally laid herself down, but Taran could tell by the glitter of reflected starlight in her eyes that she did not sleep.

✤ ✤ ✤ ✤ ✤

Arousing in the early light of a cloudless summer day, Taran stirred and sat up, stretching cramped muscles. He looked around, noting the light dew on the grass. Ardoch lay curled in his cloak beside the dying fire, his head pillowed on his saddle. When Taran had woken the old swordmaster for his turn on watch an hour past midnight, he had thought that Sullyan had finally closed her eyes to the night. But whether she had slept or lain wrapped in her sorrow, he didn't know.

He looked about for her now and spotted her sitting on one of the larger boulders by the road, her sword across her knees. She was motionless, just staring ahead at the gently rolling Downs in the distance, where the rising sun was only now kissing the grassy hills with gold. Drum stood half-asleep at her back, one hind hoof resting, his nose inches above her hair, his lower lip hanging loose.

Taran rose stiffly and went about coaxing the cook fire back to life. Now would be a useful time to have mastery over Fire, he reflected sourly. He had to make do with dry moss, flint, and steel, and he soon had water on the boil. Ardoch stirred at the sounds and rolled over. He, too, looked about for Sullyan.

"How's our lassie this morning?"

Taran couldn't disguise his worry. "I don't know. I've not been over to speak with her yet. Let the water boil and I'll take her some fellan. That usually revives her."

The swordmaster grunted and rose to help Taran prepare food for the morning meal.

"Has she given you any hint of what her plans might be?"

Taran shook his head. "I don't think she has any. Events moved so fast yesterday. She left without any supplies, not even fellan, and that's not like her. I know she has … things on her

71

mind"—Taran had to be careful not to reveal too much—"but I think the King's reaction yesterday affected her more deeply than even she knows. It must be a terrifying shock to have everything that made your life worthwhile suddenly ripped away from you."

"You care very deeply for her, don't you?"

Taran turned his head slowly. The older man's dark gray eyes were clear and shrewd, and Taran remembered that he probably knew more about Sullyan's character than Taran did himself. He felt a tremor of fear.

"Don't tell me you've been listening to those rumors, too? They're not true, you know."

"Ach, I didn't believe them, laddie. I saw the two of you together, remember? And I know how much she loves that fool life mate of hers. You'll get no accusations from me. No, you just keep on loving her. It's what she needs right now."

He filled a mug with fellan and held it out toward Sullyan.

"Come and break your fast, lass," he called. "This is no time to be sitting on your ass. Tell me your plan. You do have one, don't you?"

Sullyan shook herself out of her reverie and rose to join them at the fire. Sheathing her sword, she accepted the fellan. "My plans are not yet fully formed. I need a little information from you first, Ghyl." She told him her suspicions concerning the abductions of both princes, and then asked the Torlander what he could tell her of Baron Reen.

"Denny told me that he retains his own guard," she said. "Do you know how many men he has?"

"Not exactly. They're not stationed at the castle garrison. At a guess I'd say he has around thirty."

She was surprised. "Thirty men of his own? Why would he need so many? Did they all come with him from Bordenn?"

"I couldn't say. Yon Baron is a secretive man. Certainly their commander did. Izack, his name is, and a nastier piece of work you'll not find. The others, I don't know. He may have recruited more since he's been here."

"Where does he quarter them?"

The Torlander stared at her. "On his estate, of course. Where else?"

A light kindled in Sullyan's eyes and she glanced briefly at Taran. "Baron Reen has his own estate? Gifted to him by the Queen, I presume."

Ardoch nodded. Sullyan began to smile—a predatory and not very nice smile.

"And just where is this gifted estate, Ghyl?"

"Right outside the city, on the north side. It runs up to those cliffs overlooking Loxton Bay."

Her eyes widened. "Just how large is it?"

Ardoch shrugged. "Must be a few thousand acres. There's a mansion-house and a small village, too. Has its own kirk an' all. Reen keeps a huge staff to run it for him."

"Does he, indeed? And I suppose that any of the estate workers would answer his call for fighting men should he need them." She sat a moment in thought before saying, "Ghyl, do you know if there are any stone circles or ancient places of worship around Port Loxton?"

The unexpected tack of her question clearly startled the Torlander. "Why on earth do you want to know that?"

She merely raised her brows.

"Can't say I do," he replied.

"Well, then, that must be my first task. Taran, I will need your assistance. We will make for the stone circle on the way to Loxton Forest."

She stood fluidly, her strength of purpose clear. "Come, gentlemen, we have no time to sit around on our asses." She grinned slyly at Ardoch. "We have work to do."

The old swordmaster rolled his eyes as he rose to saddle his horse.

Chapter Seven

"Ah, Izack, there you are."

Baron Reen looked up from the two parchments in his hand as his commander entered the room. "Read this, will you?"

The stocky man took the parchment Reen held out to him and quickly scanned its contents. He glanced up at the Baron with a sneer on his lips.

"'No longer a threat'?" he said scornfully. "My Lord, who is this idiot?"

Reen smiled. He had known Izack would react like this. "One of the captains at the Manor, a very embittered young man. He's been useful to me in a small way, although that's over now. I had intended to tell him so, but this piece of foolishness has dissuaded me. He obviously needs to learn some of life's harsher lessons, so I shall keep him dangling a little longer before I burst the bubble of his expectations. You never know, he might just get himself killed in the coming war and save me the bother."

Izack grinned. "I must say that your latest ploy has worked very well, my Lord. The King is emptying Loxton's garrison and leaving only a token force to guard the Queen. You were right. The disappearance of his son and heir was the key factor."

"Of course it was. Her Majesty took a little persuading, but she eventually saw sense. Now, I have told her that the majority of my personal bodyguard will be at her disposal during this time, for her added protection. See to it, will you? And I trust the little Prince is safe and well?"

"Oh yes, my Lord. No harm will come to him, you can trust me on that. His nursemaid is very attentive, if a little dim, and he's not had so much as a single crying fit. This custom of the higher nobility of not raising their own children certainly has its benefits. The young Prince hasn't missed his mother once."

"Which is more than can be said for the mother," replied Reen. "Concealing her son's whereabouts from her was a masterly stroke of yours, Izack. Her grief at the separation is real and no one could suspect her of complicity in his disappearance."

Izack made an ironic bow.

"So this means," continued Reen, "that we are very close to our final goal. I have to send another message to our contact in Andaryon. I must instruct him to organize the assault which will ensure the Hierarch's forces engage those of the King when he sends them. I can't afford to have any of these Artesans unoccupied when we activate the spellsilver. It's a pity Colonel Sullyan won't be out of the way in Andaryon, but at least the King won't have her advice and experience to rely on. Let us hope that our disaffected young captain is correct after all, and that she is no longer a threat.

"Where's that young idiot, Izack? Why is he never around when I want him? Perhaps I should have taken your advice and locked him up somewhere, but I didn't want to take the chance he'd turn nasty on me. We have him pretty well terrified, I think, but he's unpredictable and very strong, and I can't afford to lose control of him until we're ready to use the spellsilver. After that, we'll have no more use for him and you can follow your instincts. I do wish he wasn't quite so stupid, though. I've still not been able to make sense of what he said about containing the spellsilver the last time I tried to get it out of him, but the more I threaten him, the more incoherent he gets."

"Might I make a suggestion, my Lord?"

"Of course. What is it?"

"Well, you do have another of these Artesans in your power. Why not make use of him? He's a good deal more intelligent, for all he's an outlander. I'm sure he could tell you what you want to know."

A smile broke across Reen's features. "Izack, you're a genius! Why didn't I think of that?" Then the smile faded. "But will he cooperate? And is he in any fit state to answer questions?"

Izack's expression was predatory. "I'm sure I could persuade him, my Lord, given a little time."

"How much time?"

"An hour should do it. I'll have him ready to dance for you by then."

Reen was quite taken with the image of the Crown Prince of Andaryon being forced to dance for his pleasure. He chuckled. "That won't be necessary. Just see that he's able and willing to talk. I have to go attend the Queen, but I'll be back to see the results of your handiwork."

Izack bowed himself out of the room.

Reen approached his Queen across the lushly carpeted floor of her solar. "Madam, calm yourself, I beg you," he soothed, although in truth her weeping was playing admirably into his hands. Sofira raised her tear-streaked face to the Baron's. No one who saw her pallid, blotched countenance would suspect her of any involvement in this deception. Personally, he was amazed at her display. She'd never shown this much interest in the boy before. Yet she was obviously suffering and he genuinely regretted putting her through this.

Reen thought that the depth of her reactions had probably surprised even her, and she was only now realizing how deeply her feelings ran for Eadan. Now that her husband was no longer here, Reen imagined she was seeing the boy as *her* son, and not simply Elias's heir. He knew she didn't love Elias, but she knew she owed him at least a semblance of loyalty. It was Elias who had made her Queen, after all. But even if Elias was killed, she wouldn't lose her position. As there were no other Rovannons to lay claim to the throne, she would remain in power as Queen Regent until Eadan was old enough to rule. And with Reen to advise and guide her, sole governance should not be too great a burden.

That thought had revived her in the early days of Reen's plan, and had banished all thoughts of loyalty to her husband. Reen had told her to think about how proud her father would be of her. To think that the only daughter of the ruler of such a small province as Bordenn should rise to govern all Albia!

"My Queen, let me assure you, Prince Eadan is quite safe. I'm told he has suffered no ill effects from the move. He is well cared for and happy. And I have today received news that may mean your separation will not last much longer."

Sofira brightened. "What do you mean, Hezra? What news?"

Reen handed her the parchment he held.

"So," she said once she had read it, "he has finally declared war. Will he strip the city garrison, do you think?"

"I am told so, Madam. He has also called on every able-bodied man in the city to join the militia. They will leave under the command of the garrison forces. But he will not leave you unprotected, and you shall have my own hand-picked guards to ward you and the Princess, never fear. A small contingent of Kingsmen are returning from the Manor as we speak, led by Lieutenant-Major Denny. He has not yet fully recovered from the injuries he received during the demon attack on the King and is not fit enough for battle. He will command here while the war lasts.

"So it would appear, Madam, that all is proceeding as we would wish. Once our troops have crossed into Andaryon and engaged the demon forces, I will be free to put my final plan into action and the fate of all these outlanders and unnatural Artesans will be sealed. Let's see how well they fare once they have no powers to work with!"

He bowed himself from Sofira's presence, leaving her with the parchment of the King's Declaration. The other message, the personal one from Captain Parren, he kept to himself. He had decided not tell the Queen that Colonel Sullyan—*ha! Colonel no more!*—had been cast out in disgrace. She had finally shown Elias her true colors. If Elias ever did return to Port Loxton—and Reen was seriously considering taking positive steps to prevent that— the Baron would enjoy taunting him for his misplaced faith in her.

Well pleased with his plans so far, the Baron went in search of his messenger.

✠ ✠ ✠ ✠ ✠

The squalid dungeon cell smelled worse than ever. Apart from its original damp mustiness, which had lately been augmented by the stench of ordure, blood, sweat, and fear, it now also exuded the rank miasma of infection. Neither of the captive's wounds had been tended, and the slashed arm had started suppurating days ago. The wound on the right hand where the little finger had been hacked away had never been staunched or cleaned, and the whole hand was now black and swollen, its condition aggravated by the cruelly tight spellsilver cords binding the captive's wrists. It was excruciatingly painful.

Mercifully, Prince Aeyron was rarely in a condition to feel it. Lack of adequate water and food, coupled with abuse and sickness, had brought him so low that he now longed for death. In his rare moments of lucidity, he fantasized about it. He yearned toward the velvet Void of oblivion with a strength that tore at his heart. Had he but for one moment been able to breach the spellsilver, he would have leaped for the yawning abyss like a drowning man after air.

It seemed he was to be denied his desire for a little longer yet. His tormentor had ordered that he be given water, and even a small amount of thin meat broth, and although Aeyron had done his level best to refuse both, he had no physical strength left with which to fight. In the end, his desperate body had betrayed him by taking sustenance from his enemies' hands, and a highly unwelcome semblance of life had returned.

And with life came the pain.

He lacked even the strength to scream; a constant, low keening was all his raw throat could produce. Izack found it irritating and had slapped Aeyron's face in an effort to quiet him. But the sound continued and Izack, skilled though he was in inflicting pain and torment without permanent damage, clearly feared to push his alien captive too far. At least not until the Baron was done with him.

Vaguely, Aeyron heard footsteps on the slick dungeon stairs. He gasped in shock as Izack dashed icy water full in his face. The water's extreme cold against his abraded, naked skin made Aeyron shudder. A measure of awareness returned.

The Baron stepped into the cell around the half-open door, his usual scented cloth held delicately to his nose. He moved fastidiously around the mess of ordure in the cell and glanced over at the commander.

"Well, man? Is he fit to talk?"

"Oh, he'll talk, my Lord. Just ask your questions. I can persuade him if he's reluctant."

Aeyron barely registered this exchange. The world had long ceased to hold any meaning for him. He wasn't even sure who he was anymore. Reen casually kicked his leg, more to gain his wandering attention than with any intent to cause pain. Aeyron's sore eyes flicked to his.

"My dear Prince," said Reen through his cloth, "it is my pleasure to tell you that your ordeal is nearly over. Even now King Elias readies himself to march his forces against your father, and very soon now I will fulfill my dream. You know, I had intended that you should die down here in the dark, like the vermin you are, but now I think it would be more fitting if you were to witness this apocryphal event. I might even permit you to be a part of it, but first I have a few questions."

The Baron squatted on his haunches beside his captive. "You are what they call an Artesan, are you not?"

Aeyron blinked slowly. Izack moved to Aeyron's other side where his maimed and blackened right hand lay. He prodded the hand with the toe of his boot, and Aeyron discovered just how far a tiny morsel of sustenance could go toward reviving tortured nerves.

Once the harsh scream died away, the Baron repeated his question. Aeyron rasped out an affirmative reply.

"What rank do you consider yourself?" The Baron watched Aeyron's face to ensure he'd heard and understood the question.

"Master," he croaked.

"Ah!" Reen gave a satisfied smile. "Lord Rykan was also a Master, was he not?"

Aeyron nodded.

Reen smiled up at Izack. "Maybe this demon might be able to tell me what I want to know after all." He turned back to Aeyron. "Now, my fine Prince, I have another question, and it's really quite a simple one for such as you. Answer me well and you shall be given no more pain. Listen carefully.

"I have acquired thirty pounds of reverse-polarity spellsilver. I want to use it to create a metaphysical explosion, but I gather that if power is channeled into the silver, it will just pass straight through. How do I ensure the silver will collect the power, and build it up enough to trigger an explosion?"

"Contain it." Aeyron's mind had fixed on the question with no thought to the consequences. His powers of logic had virtually shut down and he was using surface memory only. What he was saying had no real meaning for him.

The Baron tutted impatiently. "Yes, yes, Rykan said as much when we discussed how the Staff could be made. But this is thirty pounds of silver, not two. What is strong enough to contain that much silver, considering we don't have any ceramic?"

Aeyron's eyes flickered closed and Izack lazily employed his boot again. This time Aeyron's agony produced only a strangled gasp. Whatever energy he had gained from the little food and water he'd received was fast evaporating.

"Earth," he rasped faintly. "Rock."

Reen waved a hand at the stone walls of the cell. "What, like in here?"

The Prince's mouth twisted in a grimace; it could have been a smile or the rictus of pain. One good explosion of Earth-power in here and his suffering would be over for ever. "Yes."

His voice was so hoarse and breathless that Reen must have known he'd get no more. Izack picked up the jug, but Reen stopped him, his eyes alight with unholy anticipation.

"No, Izack, that's enough. I know what the boy meant now. He was rambling earlier, but the few words he did manage now make perfect sense. Give this creature some of that water to drink. I've decided not to let him die just yet. He can witness my final triumph. And unless you feel like carrying him, it would be in your interests to get him strong enough to walk. Once Elias is fully committed and on the battlefield, we'll be moving our demonic friend."

Aeyron barely registered Reen leaving the cell. All he could hear was Izack cursing the vagaries of the Baron's whim. The commander stood, hands on hips, muttering about how he had spent the last six days ensuring that the demon was on the verge of death. Now he'd have to reverse some of that work, and if Aeyron died on him just when the Baron wanted him to live a little longer, it'd be Izack who got the blame.

Pouring vituperative curses on the instability of the minds of nobles, Izack went about using his skills to ensure Aeyron's immediate survival. The Prince, desperate to die but lacking the strength to goad Izack into killing him, let him do what he would.

✣ ✣ ✣ ✣ ✣

"He really is a fine-looking beast. Have you raced him often?"

The youthful voice behind him startled Ozella out of his preoccupation. He turned to face Tad, still leaning on the door of his horse's stall where he had come to ponder his situation. Spending time with Felika always soothed Ozella. He'd imagine himself leaping aboard that creamy back and sprinting out of the yard and far away—all the way to Beraxia, where he would find that his sisters were safe and well and that this whole episode of living under Captain Parren's thumb had been some vile and tortuous dream.

"Yes, he's won me lots of races. He's the fastest horse in my father's stable."

"Did you breed him yourself?"

It was the right question to ask. Ozella knew all the bloodlines of his father's horses going back generations. Once they had exhausted the subject of Felika's pedigree, Tad said, "Colonel Sullyan told me that the Manor horses were crossed with your desert racers in the past. Long time ago."

Ozella was surprised. "Really? I've never heard that."

"We could go and ask Solet if you want to hear more about it. He's a bit crusty and he's not as knowledgeable as the Colonel about the various bloodlines, but he does know horses. I wonder if your Felika could outrace the Colonel's Drum?"

"Easily," asserted Ozella.

Tad frowned and Ozella thought he might argue the point. Tad was always eager to defend any of his fellow Artesans, or anything to do with the Manor. Ozella hoped he wouldn't, though. In order to meet Parren's demands, he needed to win Tad's friendship, not start a rivalry.

After a moment, Tad's face cleared and he laughed. "I'm not so sure, but it'd be fun finding out. Not that we'd get the chance, mind. Drum's a warhorse, not a racer, although he's won races in his time."

Ozella saw his chance to prolong the conversation. "Not our sort, I'll bet. Our races can go on for days at a time. They're tests of the horse's endurance, not just a short burst of speed. Your horses are fine for what they do. They're bred heavier, with more bone to carry greater weights and also to use their bodies to help their riders in battle. Our horses don't fight. They're bred to withstand the heat and go long distances without tiring. Their paces are different, too. But they also have great short-distance speed due to their long legs and lighter mass."

He turned back to Felika as he spoke, Tad joining him to lean over the stall door as Ozella pointed out the finer details of his horse's confirmation.

"I'd love to ride him," said Tad. "It'd be good to ride just for fun for once, rather than for training."

Ozella glanced at him. "Don't you have a horse of your own?"

"No, not yet. I won't be assigned a permanent mount until I've passed my final tests and taken the King's Oath. And I'll only get one then if I decide to ask for secondment to a mounted company. Which I will."

Ozella shook his head at Tad's youthful assurance of his future. His heart lurched; he wished he felt so confident of his own.

"Did you always intend to join the military?" he asked, interested despite himself. He'd always considered Tad to be a mere boy, but the way he was talking belied his few years.

Tad's eyes shone. "Oh yes. I was born and brought up here, and although I spent my childhood in the kitchens, it's always been my dream to take the Oath."

"Why?"

Ozella could see that his question had surprised Tad, as if the boy couldn't conceive of anyone doing anything else.

"Why? Well, just look around you!" Tad threw an arm wide to encompass the whole of the Manor and its grounds. "Can you think of doing anything more worthwhile with your life than being a part of this? Serving your King and country, keeping order, defending the right of ordinary people to live out their lives as they choose? I tell you, Ozella, there's nothing like belonging to a band of comrades who trust and rely totally on each other, under the leadership of an experienced and courageous commander. Like

Major Tamsen."

"You really admire him, don't you?" Ozella recognized hero-worship when he saw it.

Tad ducked his head. "Is it that obvious? I try not to let it show too much, but apart from Colonel Sullyan"—his face fell as he said her name—"I think he's the best and the fairest commander here. I want to be just like him when I get command of my own company. Until then, I want to learn as much as I can from him, both about military matters and about being an Artesan."

Ozella felt gloom descend once more and turned back to watching his horse. "I wish I had your ambitions."

Tad frowned. "Is that why you don't try very hard at your training? Because you've got no ambitions?" His tone conveyed disbelief. "You must have some idea what you want to do with your life. You're old enough to be independent. Married, even. Your father must be very indulgent or very rich to let you drift along like this."

Ozella was stung by Tad's incredulity, although it was clear the boy didn't intend to be critical. It was all very well for Tad, he thought. He had a clear desire and the means by which to achieve it. Ozella had far more grievous problems right now than what to do as a career. And he doubted he'd have much of a life left once his betrayal was discovered. He had no illusions about coming out of this unscathed. Even if he managed to save his sisters by his treachery—and he doubted that very much—it was bound to come out. Parren would denounce him to the King if he tried to tell anyone what had been happening, he was sure of that. Either that or he'd be discovered as a spy and informant and, at the very least, be sent home in disgrace. His sisters would die or be injured, his father would disown him, and then he'd be nothing.

He became conscious of Tad's scrutiny and sensed a softening of the youth's attitude.

"Tell you what," the boy said quietly, "no one's going to bother with us now there's a war on. Sure, we'll have duties to attend to until the companies leave, but once they're gone we'll be left to our own devices until it's all over. Why don't we work together? Falkerk will give us some sword-practice, and we can fence against each other. After all, we both need the practice. And in the afternoons we can share our exercises in influencing Earth. I can help you, if you'd like, although I think you only need to learn to concentrate. You're easily as strong as I am. What do you say?"

Ozella turned to look at Tad. He was touched by the lad's offer. No one else had made friendly overtures to him since he'd been here. Not that anyone had been *un*friendly—with one notable exception, of course—but they all seemed so focused, and none of them understood his sense of separation at being so far away from his home and culture. Tad's innocent offer of friendship was like a balm to his soul.

Disarmed by Tad's empathy, Ozella felt an overwhelming need to pour the whole sordid tale of Parren's blackmail into the young lad's ears. He'd nearly forgotten that it was supposed to be *him* befriending the boy, not the other way round. He sharply curbed the dangerous impulse. The idea of a confidante was too seductive, and he had to turn away. He said, in a voice only slightly choked by emotion, "Thanks, Tad. I'd appreciate that."

"Come on, then," said the boy. "There'll be no one in the College right now. Let's go and see if there're any jewels left. I want you to show me how you shattered that topaz!"

The lad's enthusiasm was infectious. Grinning despite himself, Ozella followed him.

Chapter Eight

Marik found it hard that Idrimar was living almost exclusively in her father's suite. She took her meals there, sat by him, held his hands, talked to him, and tried feverishly to get him to respond to her.

Despite Deshan's assurances that he was improving slowly, Idrimar could see no sign of it. She found it hard to accept that his shrunken and seemingly lifeless shell was ever going to recover. His face was white, his lips bloodless. The skin was papery, transparent. His breast rose and fell with his breathing, but the breaths were shallow and slow. She felt the beat of his heart in his aged wrist, but it seemed to be weak. To comfort herself, she talked to him. She tried to pour all her love and care for him into her words and her hands, and sought to keep life within him.

Deshan had explained to her the futility of her actions. Out of necessity, Sullyan had cocooned him so deeply within the complexities of his own psyche that outside influences had no effect. If Pharikian was to recover, he must not be exposed to anything that might cause his frail and ravaged soul to despair, and that included the grief and sadness of his daughter.

Still, Idrimar insisted on keeping vigil. Marik hated to see her so bereft, so anxious and afraid. She was convinced she had lost her brother. Were she to lose her father also, he feared not only for her sanity but also for the lives of her babies. He sat with her whenever he could, giving her the comfort of his strength and love.

He persuaded her back to their rooms at night, to lie quiet and exhausted in his arms, but she only went because Deshan stayed with the Hierarch all night long. Otherwise, she'd have slept by her father's side, too. Marik was beginning to lose hope himself that these distressing times would ever end.

Heavy-hearted, he left her at her father's side that morning and walked toward the audience chamber, which he had taken as a temporary office. Things had taken a depressing turn, what with King Elias's declaration of war, and Marik feared his assumed command of the throne would be sorely tested. He would have to rely heavily on Anjer's military expertise, and he could have done with Idrimar's insight into her father's control of state affairs. But she was too distraught for him even to consider asking her. He found himself wishing for Sullyan's confident presence and wondered, not for the first time, how she felt about this and what her reactions had been.

Marik brooded on these melancholy thoughts until a deferential page snapped him out of them.

"Your Grace?"

"What is it?"

"The Lords Tikhal and Rand have requested a few moments of your time, your Grace. They await you in his lordship's suite."

Marik pursed his lips. Maybe something would result from his interview with Rand after all. Or maybe Tikhal wanted to task him with speaking to Rand without his father's knowledge. Either way, Marik would respond. He sent the page scampering on ahead and strode toward Tikhal's suite. The page was waiting by the door and bowed him in. Tikhal rose from his seat by the window. Rand stood apprehensively at his back.

"Your Grace," Tikhal greeted him. "Thank you for agreeing to see us at such short notice. I do know how busy you must be, but I felt this couldn't wait. Will you sit?"

Marik accepted Tikhal's offer, and also the glass of wine Rand poured for him. Marik thought Rand looked nervous; he wouldn't meet the Regent's eyes.

Tikhal seated himself opposite Marik and began without preamble.

"Your Grace, my son has told me of your…conversation with him yesterday. He begs your pardon most sincerely for not speaking out then, but he wanted to seek guidance first."

Marik's eyes narrowed, but he nodded silently. Rand visibly relaxed. Tikhal turned to his son, taking up his own goblet of wine.

"Go on, Rand. Tell his Grace what you told me."

Rand moved to stand before Marik and looked him deferentially in the eye.

"Your Grace, I beg your forgiveness for my reticence yesterday. I know you suspected I could tell you more than I did, and you were right."

Marik raised his brows at the lad's perception and indicated he should continue. Rand swallowed.

"Your Grace, I told you the truth when I said that neither Lord Corbyn nor his son ever said anything to cause me to suspect their loyalties. Corbyn was far too clever for that. But while Kethro and I were away hunting with the Prince"—Rand turned pale at the memory—"something happened to make me think things were not as they seemed. With hindsight, I now believe that the course we took over those few days was not random. I believe the quarry we followed was driven in the direction we were intended to go, but I didn't suspect it at the time. On that final night, it was Kethro who convinced Prince Aeyron to dispense with two of the dawn sentries, but I didn't remember that until I learned of your suspicions. It was also Kethro who broke out the brandy the night before the attack, and he tried very hard to get the Prince and me to drink more than we should. I was not, I'm ashamed to say, too hard to persuade." He hung his head, and Marik would have grinned under less serious circumstances. "At the time, I thought Kethro was as drunk as I was, but I doubt that now. When Prince Aeyron refused more brandy, I suspect Kethro poured the rest of his own drink on the ground."

Rand paused and looked up, catching Marik's eye. "Your Grace, are you aware that the attackers came out of the substrate right on top of us?"

Marik nodded. He'd heard the details of the abduction from Pharikian.

"Then that must surely mean the raiders knew exactly where we were, down to the nearest few feet. And the fact that they came immediately for me, Kethro, and the Prince must also mean they knew who we were, and that the three of us were the only Artesans present. That's why they had the spellcord ready before they reached us, to tie us with."

Again Marik nodded.

Rand took a breath. "I've already said that I heard one of the humans say they had to deliver the Prince to the 'King's man.' But what I never said"—he glanced apologetically at both Marik and his father—"was that when they pounced on Kethro and me, I'm sure I heard one of them whisper to Kethro, 'don't worry, my Lord, just lay still and pretend fear. You won't be harmed.'"

Marik sat bolt upright. "Gods! Are you sure?"

Rand's face flamed. "As sure as I can be, your Grace."

Marik exploded. "Why on earth didn't you say something before? Why didn't you tell this to his Majesty?"

Rand fell back before his anger and Tikhal raised a hand. "Gently, I beg you, your Grace. Rand knows he's done wrong, and he's showing great courage in telling you this now. He could just as easily have kept quiet, but his fear for Prince Aeyron will not let him."

"It's a shame his fear couldn't have given him the courage before, when Corbyn was still here!" Marik's tone was harsh, but he did calm down. What was done was done. "All right, Rand, go on. Tell me why you've kept this to yourself until now."

Rand's face was pale again and he seemed acutely uncomfortable. "In all truth, your Grace, I had forgotten it in the terror of the moment. When his Majesty questioned us after we woke from the effects of the spellsilver, I was disoriented and confused. I could only remember snippets of what had happened. It was a few days later when I remembered, and then I couldn't be sure I'd heard correctly. I couldn't believe it of either Corbyn or Kethro. We've been friends since childhood, you know. But when Father and I heard they'd fled the Citadel, and you told me what Baron Gaslek found in Lord Rykan's records, well, I grew frightened and I wanted to speak with my father. I wanted to be sure I was doing the right thing and not leading you on some wild boar chase."

Marik stared at Rand, unable to be too angry with him. For all his maturity he was still very young, only just beginning to learn about governing a province and eager to prove himself. But he also had the loyalty of the young to old friendships and hadn't yet been exposed to the sly, underhanded backstabbing of the Andaryan nobility.

Fortunately for him.

"Very well, Rand. Thank you for telling me. I commend you for your honesty, even if it came a little late. If there is anything else you remember or can tell us, however slight, my door is always open. At least now we know for sure who our traitor is."

Rand's eyes widened and Marik realized what the young man thought. He tried to give him some reassurance.

"Just because the raiders knew who Kethro was doesn't prove he was in on the treachery. Corbyn would have wanted to guarantee his son was unharmed, and so would have taken care that the raiders knew him. Kethro may still be innocent. If he was instructed to get the Prince drunk, he may not have known the reason for it. We'll have to question both him and his father before we learn the truth. Rest easy, Rand. I assure you, your friend will not be condemned unless he's proven guilty."

Marik turned from the worried young man to face his father. "Now, Tikhal, have you had any word concerning your mine workers and the theft of the ransom silver?"

Tikhal laid aside his empty goblet, and Rand moved to refill it. "I've had reports from those I sent to investigate, your Grace. It seems you were right. The mine foreman, who was an old and trusted employee of mine, gathered the silver together and loaded it on a cart ready for shipping. He intended to accompany it himself, but early in the morning, before it was light, the shipment was attacked. The foreman and his guards fought back, but they were driven off. The foreman was killed, and it was his horse that was used to bring the message to his Majesty. The other guards, once they recovered from their injuries, reported that their attackers were human, and that they wore clothing similar to that of King Elias's men."

Marik frowned. It was as he had feared. Whoever their adversary was, he was being very clever. Marik had no doubt whatsoever that Elias wasn't responsible for the theft of the silver or the raids on Andaryan soil. He was being duped and manipulated as much as the Andaryans were. All this talk of "the King's men," the ransom notes, the use of royal seals, and the clothing the raiders wore was purely circumstantial and meant absolutely nothing. But the raids suffered by both realms were real and damaging. Elias's reaction to the supposed abduction of his son by Andaryans, and his declaration of war, were real and damaging. Many of Pharikian's and Tikhal's nobles had heard the rumors and believed the fabrications. They would be all too eager to engage Elias's forces to exact revenge for Albian raids on their lands and people. It was a mess that would only get worse unless their adversary was found and stopped.

Marik sighed and stood, setting down his empty goblet.

"Tikhal, I thank you for your hospitality. May I ask what you intend to do about Lord Corbyn? The initial responsibility for his apprehension lies with you. He is one of your nobles, after all."

Tikhal also stood, his expression grim, his demeanor rueful. "I don't know, your Grace. I've heard he headed east when he left here, so I can only assume he has allies and supporters awaiting him. But whether they are here or in Albia, I couldn't say. I have already called for my nobles to send what men they can spare to swell his Majesty's forces in this coming war. It will leave Morvaigne vulnerable, and it may be that Corbyn will try to take control of it while I am occupied here. If that is so, I will be forced to request assistance from the Crown to crush his rebellion once the war is over."

Marik noted the apprehension in Tikhal's eyes. He was aware that Tikhal was attempting to wring a promise from him that he could use against the Hierarch later should Corbyn prove troublesome to shift. But Marik was learning fast and had no intention of letting himself be trapped into that kind of indiscretion. He didn't blame Tikhal for trying, though. Such maneuverings were the stuff of Andaryan politics.

"That possibility is too far into the future, my Lord. We have other, more immediate, concerns. I have a feeling Corbyn isn't finished with us yet. Let's wait and see what comes. We'll deal with his treachery in our own time, and you have my word on that."

Tikhal and his son bowed as Marik left the room.

✢ ✢ ✢ ✢ ✢

The Manor was becoming crowded. The surrounding villages were sending their men to join the militia in response to the King's summons. It was Elias's intention to use the commoners' militia to defend Albia against any retaliatory attacks by the demons, thus freeing his trained and deadly forces to penetrate Andaryan territory and carry out punitive strikes around Pharikian's Citadel. Elias had charged Vassa with the organization and deployment of the militia, using whichever captains he chose to train them and to lead the militia companies.

Vassa had already issued orders to the captains under his command. To Parren's utter disgust, he found himself placed in charge of two hundred or so farmers, laborers, smiths, and the like, and tasked with forming them into a creditable fighting force.

He raged inwardly against what he saw as an insult to his capabilities, considering himself to be far above nursemaiding a load of country bumpkins. His dearest ambition was to be sent into Andaryon, and his soul thirsted for the blood of demons on his sword. Besides, Tamsen would be there, and Parren's scheme was to get close enough to him to get in an unseen sword thrust.

Once he recovered from the shock of Vassa's orders, Parren went in search of Robin. When he found him, Parren didn't immediately speak, but stood considering his words. Robin watched him warily, and the thought that their previous conversation had left the young officer off-balance stoked Parren's self-esteem. Had he not been so furious about Vassa's orders he might have smiled.

He finally spoke, striving to sound neutral and keep the habitual sneer from his voice. "Have you heard Vassa's plans for the deployment of the militia, Major?"

Robin looked away, clearly finding the experience of standing here talking normally to Parren surreal. "I have, Captain."

Parren continued in a low voice. "He's put me in charge of one of the rural companies."

Robin frowned. "So I heard."

Now Parren could afford to give vent to some of his frustration. Equanimity was not, after all, in his nature. "But I'm worth so much more than that," he snapped, taking care not to make direct eye contact with Robin. He didn't want the Major to think his irritation was directed at him. "Vassa knows that. Why hasn't he seconded me to his Majesty's spearhead, to the invasion force? I'd be of far more use there. I'm a very experienced field officer. Surely he knows that?"

Despite Parren's natural lack of human empathy, he could see that Robin thought he knew where this was going. He'd always suspected Parren of hidden motives, after all.

"I'm sure Colonel Vassa knows what he's doing." Robin placed a slight emphasis on Vassa's rank.

Parren had to bite back a stinging reply. Treading carefully was not something he was used to, but he had to try. He changed tack. "How many men is the Manor sending to Andaryon, Major?"

Robin held his gaze. "In total, a thousand."

Parren was surprised. "A thousand? Under how many captains? Two?"

"Three."

Now it was Parren's turn to frown. "Three? Dexter and

Harker, I suppose, but who else?"

He was trying not to sound indignant, but he was only too afraid he knew who the third man was.

"Cal Tyler is Acting Captain and will have command of two hundred and fifty men."

It was as Parren feared, and he let his incredulity show. "Tyler? He has no experience of battlefield command! How can the King rely on him? Surely he needs all the field experience he can get with a force of a thousand men?" His outburst had angered Robin, but he continued regardless. "Major, why don't you speak to Colonel Vassa? Why not request the services of another, far more suitable captain to lead that third company? Or better yet," he rushed on in the face of Robin's stony expression, "I could lead a fourth company and free you to watch over Tyler. He really isn't up to this, you know, not on his own. It would be such a waste if he fell in this war, or lost his men due to some ill-considered decision. Especially as his wife is pregnant."

He fell silent and watched Robin considering what he'd said. Despite his self-interest, Parren thought he might actually have hit on the one aspect of this coming conflict that gave Robin the most concern, apart from the folly of fighting the Andaryans in the first place, of course. Parren knew Robin had faith in Cal's growing command abilities, but it was true that the man was completely untried in a serious combat situation. He'd heard rumors that Robin had intended to present Cal to the King so he could be formally promoted, but it hadn't happened yet. Even if it had, Cal would still be facing this trial with only a few sorties against raiders under his belt. Parren *was* vastly more experienced; even Robin couldn't deny that. But Parren was also under Vassa's command, so the Major had no say in how Parren's skills were used.

Parren watched the consideration in the other man's eyes, willing him to agree. Robin eventually glanced at him and gave a small shudder.

"You may be right," he said slowly. "But Colonel Vassa is your commanding officer and I have no sway with him. Besides, I'm only accompanying the King in an advisory capacity, I'm not commanding. We will also have Captain Valustin from Port Loxton with his three thousand five hundred, so we will not be without experienced leaders."

Seeing his chance slipping away, Parren had to stop himself from sounding too angry, too fervent. Neither would help him. "But you could still speak with the Colonel, Major. He's a reasonable man and will listen to a sound argument."

Robin abruptly caved in, probably to get rid of him. "Very well, Captain, I will speak to him. But it's his decision. If he wants to keep things as they are, you'll just have to accept it."

"Thank you, Major." Parren spoke stiffly, words of gratitude coming awkwardly to his lips. He hated that Robin would think he was doing Parren a favor. He comforted himself with imagining his sword passing through the Major's back and emerging out the other side. That would be his reward for prostrating his pride like this and humiliating himself in front of his arch enemy. He stared hungrily at Robin's retreating back as he walked away, already tasting success.

Cal returned to Rienne's side after waving off Lieutenant-Major Denny and his thirty or so walking wounded, who had just left for Port Loxton. In the seven days since receiving his injury, and despite being tossed out of the infirmary by a furious Rienne, Denny had recovered sufficient strength to be able to ride again.

He was returning to the capital with the others of the King's Guard who were unfit to fight in the war, and he would take command of Loxton's garrison until the King returned. He took his leave of Cal and rode out at the head of his small contingent. He left just as another group of militiamen arrived, striding in with their varied assortment of weapons.

Cal's feelings toward the coming war were ambivalent. He was proud and excited when told he would be keeping his temporary officer's status, and that he would hold a command. When he realized they would be sent across the Veils to fight in Andaryon, however, his heart misgave him. He simply couldn't imagine fighting against those he thought of as friends, and he also had Rienne to consider. He didn't need to ask her what her opinion was. Since the King's declaration and Sullyan's shocking dismissal, Cal had done some painful soul searching. The time had come to share the results with Rienne.

He found her in their rooms, where she had been sent to rest by Chief Healer Hanan. The older woman had wanted Rienne to stop working as soon as she learned of Rienne's pregnancy. Rienne wouldn't hear of it. She loved her work and knew that very soon now they'd need all available hands. She said she would monitor her own condition—being an empath, it would be simple—and Hanan reluctantly acquiesced. Still, she made sure Rienne rested a part of each day.

The healer looked up with a fond smile as Cal came into the room. His new responsibilities had brought a maturity to his bearing that he had formerly lacked, and he knew she liked it. Today his expression was grave, and he noted the beginnings of concern on his life mate's face.

"What is it, Cal?"

"Nothing bad," he reassured her. He crossed to the table and poured himself a shot of firewater brandy before sitting on the couch by her side. She had her feet propped comfortably on a cushion and was reclining against the arm of the couch. He kissed her before sipping his drink.

"I've just been seeing Denny and his men off on their way back to Port Loxton."

"Good." Rienne sniffed disdainfully, her tone reminding Cal that she hadn't forgiven Denny for spreading cruel and damaging gossip. Cal shook his head. He wasn't convinced that the damage was all Denny's fault, but had no proof to back it up. He wasn't about to start that argument, though. He had other things on his mind.

"I want to talk to you about the war," he said, not knowing how else to begin. She brought her gray gaze to bear on him and he found it hard to return the look. He studied the liquid in his glass instead. "You know I've been asked to lead a company against the Andaryans?"

Rienne nodded.

"I tried to talk to Robin about it, but he brushed me off," he continued. "I think what happened with Sullyan has shaken him badly."

Rienne pursed thin lips. "He should be more than shaken by what's happened here over the past week!"

Cal nodded. He knew she wouldn't trust herself not to fly screaming at Robin for his unreasoning jealousy. Any mention of his name was guaranteed to sour her mood. He was aware that her emotions, always near the surface anyway due to her empathy, were being affected by her pregnancy. He dearly wished none of this had happened—that they'd waited a little longer before removing the restrictions on her fertility—but they'd had no foresight of these distressing events. They'd have to make the best of it, which was why he was making this painful offer now. He drew a breath.

"Rienne, my love, you know I'm not happy about fighting the Andaryans. We have too many friends there, even if we believed they had something to do with Eadan's disappearance—which we don't."

Her face fell. "Some Andaryans were involved in it, though, that much is for sure."

"Granted, but they're likely to be old allies of Rykan's or Sonten's, and nothing to do with Pharikian."

She glanced at him where he sat beside her, nursing his glass. "What are you saying, Cal?"

"What I'm saying is this: If you think I'm doing the wrong thing by agreeing to go, if you'll be too upset and worried by what might happen, I'll do what Sullyan did. I'll ask the General to leave me behind, and if he won't, I'll rescind my Oath."

Rienne sucked in a breath. "You'd do that for me?"

He had to be honest. "Yes, but not just for you. *I* don't want to fight them. I agree with Sullyan. It's not right. Pharikian would never abduct Prince Eadan, nor would he charge anyone else to do it for him. He's as much a victim as Elias, maybe more so."

Cal laid aside his glass and took up Rienne's hands, looking intently into her pale and wide-eyed face. "We've been happier here than we've ever been. I've found something I didn't even know I was looking for, and it's made me complete. You love your work in the infirmary, and you'll be in charge there if and when Hanan goes. And now that we're to be a family, well, my heart could burst for pride. But this war could ruin everything. Even leaving aside the danger of injury or death in Andaryon"—he steeled himself against the sob that escaped Rienne's throat—"there's the moral question of being forced to take action against your friends when you know it's wrong. I just don't know if I can do it.

"And afterward, what then? What happens when Elias discovers they don't have Eadan? Or when this mysterious enemy succeeds in using that spellsilver for whatever purpose he has? What will life be like then? Even if we're still alive, if Artesans do survive, the Andaryans won't want to have anything more to do with us. They won't be impressed by the old excuse that we were just following orders. We all have a choice, and it's up to us to search our consciences and use it well.

"What I'm trying to say, my love, is that if you think we should, we can leave here, refuse to be involved, go somewhere else and be safe."

Rienne couldn't take her eyes from him. He was asking the impossible of her, he knew, asking her to make the right choice for them both. Was he being fair? Probably not. But it was something he'd had to say.

"Cal." She had to swallow and start again. "Cal, I'm so proud of you for thinking that way. So proud. But this war will happen whether we're here or not. We just can't run away 'somewhere else and be safe.' For all we know, there isn't anywhere safe for our kind. Sullyan believes our enemy's plans will affect all living Artesans, and that includes our daughter. She'll be an Artesan too, don't forget."

Cal's heart lurched. "Daughter?"

Rienne smiled. "I'm sorry. I didn't mean to tell you just yet. I've been able to touch our child's developing mind, and she's a girl. But I'm not going to be sidetracked. I admire Sullyan's courage in doing what she did. You have no idea what she's risked on the strength of her convictions. But I'm not so sure it would be right for us. If anywhere is protected from this enemy, then it's here. I feel safe here and I don't plan to leave unless there's no other option. There's still Taran and Sullyan to consider, and Bull too. I can't abandon them, and if Sullyan's successful, things will go back to how they were. At least, I hope so. And if she isn't successful, what will happen then is likely to affect us wherever we are.

"And there's something else. Robin needs our help. I don't understand why he reacted so badly over those rumors, but I still believe he and Sullyan can work this out, given a chance. There's a very strong reason why they should. No, don't ask me. I won't say any more. But they do need our help, and despite his attitude recently, you and Bull are Robin's closest friends. Bull won't be going to Andaryon because of his heart. He'll stay here as the General's contact and help guard the Manor. So it's up to you, my love. You must decide whether to go to Andaryon, if only to help keep Robin safe and stop him making decisions he'll regret later.

"I know it'll be hard, my dear, and I know you don't like it. Neither do I. The thought of you fighting our friends fills me with horror. And if I were to lose you…" she choked but then carried on, "I should never forgive myself. But I can't see any other way of fulfilling our obligations to our friends without compromising our consciences. Can you?"

Cal stared at her in amazement. That was quite some speech. He'd had no idea she felt like this. She'd obviously given the problem far more thought than he had. He became aware that his mouth was hanging open and closed it with a click of his teeth.

"Well, I see you've not been sitting here contemplating the paintwork. You've really thought this out, haven't you?"

Rienne gave that gentle smile he loved so much. "Someone had to. I knew you'd come and say something sooner or later, so I had to sort my feelings out. I won't pretend I'm happy about it, but

I think I'll be happier this way than if we turn our backs and run. Remember, Cal, you've taken the King's Oath. That has to mean something. Yes, I know what Sullyan's done, but she thinks she's fulfilling her vow by her actions. You'd just be dodging the issue, and so would I. We can't do that."

Cal nodded slowly. "No. I suppose you're right."

"I know I am. Now, put your arms around me and let's see if I can help you link with our daughter. It's quite an experience. Do you have any favorite names for girls?"

Chapter Nine

Sullyan, Taran, and Master Ardoch rode northward for the rest of the day, making for the stone circle she and Taran had stopped at previously on their way to Loxton Forest. Their pace was slow, limited by the stamina of the gelding Taran rode. It was a good beast, but it couldn't hope to match the pace of Drum or Ardoch's gray stallion, Morlech. They stopped for frequent short rests, followed by bursts of a steady hand-canter, and as time drew on Taran could tell Sullyan was growing impatient.

"Why don't you and Ardoch go on ahead?" he suggested during the next stop. "I know where you're headed. I'll follow on and catch up with you later."

Sullyan smiled. "I thank you for the offer, Taran, but that will not be necessary. We are nearly there now, and it will be too late to use the circle tonight anyway. Dusk is not far off, and I will need daylight to see what the circle may show me. So there is no hurry today, my friend, although tomorrow may be a different matter."

They mounted again and moved off at a steady pace. Taran drew his bay gelding alongside Drum, who ignored it; he was too busy trying to intimidate Morlech.

"How soon do you think the attacks on Andaryon will begin?" he asked.

An expression of pain crossed Sullyan's features and she stared resolutely through Drum's laid-back ears. "Soon, I would think." The musical lilt in her voice was suppressed by her unhappiness. "Elias will use the militia to defend Albia, and will send as many of his trained forces into Andaryon as he can spare. I really must let Marik know what he intends. I should already have forewarned him of Elias's declaration. I cannot leave him thinking I might lead the assault myself."

"He surely won't," protested Taran.

Sullyan glanced at him, a wry twist to her lips. "None of us are free, Taran. We all have a higher authority to obey. Were it not for my convictions about the whereabouts of Aeyron and Eadan, I would have no choice but to bow to the King's will."

Her focus turned inward, her eyes dark with pain. "I cannot imagine how it would feel to have my knowledge used against Anjer and Ephan on the battlefield. It would be a profoundly disturbing experience. The eyes of the Citadel would be upon our forces, passing judgment on what would be the most fundamental of betrayals. I have been offered a home there. How could I have lived with myself?"

She fell silent and Taran let her be. The dreadful images her words had conjured up went spiraling through his brain. The consequences were just too painful to contemplate. Ardoch glanced at them both, but he held his peace when he saw their expressions.

The sun was setting over the open countryside to the west by the time they reached the circle. They had spotted and avoided many small groups of militiamen, and even some trained swordsmen marching toward the Manor, but the only band Sullyan feared to meet—the garrison forces from Port Loxton under Captain Valustin—would most likely have passed them farther west. Taran knew she had no wish to encounter anyone who might recognize her as Elias's former colonel.

They drew rein at the foot of the little hill whose crest bore the ancient ring of standing stones. They avoided the nearby village, although it was probably as stripped of men as the others they'd passed. Nevertheless, Sullyan chose to make camp on the northwestern side of the hill so their small fire would be hidden from any villagers who were late abroad.

They dismounted and saw to the horses. Sullyan had to reprimand Drum twice, quite sharply, for his dislike of Ardoch's gray stallion, but Morlech was being stubborn about accepting Drum's dominance. Sullyan feared to let the black loose in case he attacked Morlech. This bother over the horses shortened her temper, already friable over recent events and her physical condition.

When she was done and Ardoch was busy preparing their evening meal, Sullyan stood and held out a hand to Taran. He rose to take it, a query in his eyes.

"Come with me, Adept," she requested formally. "We shall use the circle to contact Bulldog and Marik. It will be useful practice for you and will preserve our energies for the morrow."

Hand-in-hand, they ascended the small hill, watching the heads of the monoliths appear over the crest of the rise, dark forms rearing to the clear, turquiose sky. With the approach of dusk, the place took on an aura of ancient peace and mystic majesty.

They passed through the ring of monoliths and approached the central depression.

Sullyan's liquid gold eyes glowed as she faced him. "Raise the forces of Earth for me."

He did as she asked, seating himself on the flat stone to the edge of the depression and drawing the slow and ponderous might of the earth from the western cardinal stone. He felt the warm and amber complexities of Sullyan's psyche shift around him, interlocking with his, meshing and binding them together until they were one. He sat compliant, simply observing the fantastic new structure that was formed by this bonding. Once it was complete, he sensed her strength as she cast outward, questing toward the familiar and sturdy pattern that was Bull.

They made contact almost immediately, leading Taran to suspect that Bull had been waiting for them. The big man briefly gave them an update on the situation.

Elias is only waiting on the contingent from Port Loxton now, he reported. *All the companies here are ready. I imagine they'll leave around midmorning tomorrow. He's leaving me in nominal charge when Vassa's not here, as there are still pockets of militia expected over the next two days.*

Sullyan nodded. *How is Robin?*

Taran both heard and felt the pain in Sullyan's tone as she asked this. He wondered at the emotion darkening Bull's psyche at the mention of the Major's name, but understood when he heard Bull's reply.

He managed to persuade Elias of his loyalty. He's going to Andaryon as an advisor. Would you believe he's asked Jerrim Vassa if he'll lend Parren as a commander of one of the Andaryan companies?

Sullyan's startlement at this incredible news burst out as an expletive. *And what was Jerrim's reply?*

Bull chuckled. *He's got more sense than I ever gave him credit for. He refused, thank the gods. Apparently, Parren's spitting like a snake. Serves the bastard right.*

Be careful, Bull, said Sullyan. *Parren might give you trouble. And without Vassa there to back you up, you would have to go to the King.*

There was a brief silence. Both Sullyan and Taran felt Bull's acute discomfiture.

What? What is it? demanded Sullyan.

With uncharacteristic terseness, Bull said, *The King won't be here, Sully. It's his intention to go to Andaryon with Blaine.*

WHAT? No! He must not! Sullyan actually wrung her hands in anguish. *Oh, Bulldog, what madness is this? Surely Mathias will not permit it. What if all the Artesans are killed? Elias would be trapped. You* must *talk to the General. He has to prevent the King.*

Bull tried in vain to damp down her distress. Taran could tell that the strength of it was causing the big man pain. Finally, she realized what she was doing to Bull and subsided. She carefully soothed away the headache her outburst had caused him, berating herself for her lack of control.

She murmured privately to Taran, "Maybe I ought to have let you handle this. I am clearly not capable of mastering myself at present."

Bull had recovered and was speaking again. *Do you really want me to? Because if Blaine can't dissuade him—and you can bet he's tried—then nothing I say will sway him. I really think some kind of madness has overtaken Elias. He's totally out of control.*

Sullyan's pain and sorrow at this news nearly broke the link with Bull. Taran could clearly feel the big man's concern. *Sully, I'm sorry, I shouldn't have told you. I should have known better.*

No, Bull, she sighed, *you were right to tell me. I am going to speak with Marik now. I will inform him of this and try to make him understand Elias's state of mind. None of the Andaryans want this war—with the exception of our enemy's allies, of course—and perhaps Marik can organize a parley with Elias before things get completely out of hand. Maybe he can convince the King of their innocence in Eadan's disappearance.*

It's worth a try, I suppose. Bull sounded dubious.

Sullyan passed him messages for Rienne and Cal from her and Taran, and then broke the link. She slumped onto the stone beside Taran, tears in her eyes and her face pinched and white. There was so much more riding on her efforts now.

Taran longed to take her in his arms for comfort, but didn't dare. She sat for a few moments before rousing herself. Their meshed patterns still bound them together, and he felt her drawing strength from the circle to reach out for Marik.

Contact wasn't so easy to establish this time. Marik had very little in the way of Artesan power, and he was, not surprisingly, preoccupied. Sullyan almost had to force herself upon him to gain his attention, and Taran could tell that without the aid of the circle she wouldn't have found the strength. This disconcerted him, used as he was to the seemingly limitless supply of power she usually commanded. It was brought home to him with stark acuity just how badly the recent events in her life had affected her.

Once Marik realized who was reaching out to him, the bond became easier to maintain. He told them what he had discovered concerning Corbyn and what Rand had been able to tell them. When he was done, she strongly recommended he send some men to search Corbyn out, even if he could only spare a few scouts.

You need to know what his plans are, she told him. *He is not finished with you or us yet; not by a long way. If he is the contact of our enemy, he will have a part to play in the coming war. He will need watching. Be sure to tell the Lord General this.*

Anjer is very unhappy about the thought of meeting you on the field, Brynne, said Marik.

Taran felt her grim smile. *Then you may tell him he will not have to go through that ordeal.*

She briefly told Marik what she had done. The Duke's

astonishment and dismay were plain, but Sullyan hadn't the strength to deal with his sympathy.

Tell Anjer that my fear and respect for him were too great, she said in a futile attempt at levity. Taran sensed Marik's distress. *But he may still have to face Robin,* she warned, pain suffusing her tone. *Ty, I have to tell you that King Elias plans to direct his forces against you in person, on Andaryan soil.*

This news rattled the Duke badly. Sullyan continued. *He is not himself. The abduction of his son has changed him, just as the maiming of Prince Aeyron did Timar. He is not thinking straight and is not wholly responsible for his actions. Ask Anjer to remember that in his defense of the Citadel. I know this is a long shot, but a parley might get through to him. Approach General Blaine on the field. I am sure he will be able to get Elias to agree to meet you under truce. Try to convince the King that Eadan is not in Andaryon. But be careful, my friend. Do not forget he is driven by distress and fear. He is not altogether rational, so take no risks.*

Once the contact with Marik was broken, it was left to Taran to damp down the Earth power he had called up and begin the delicate task of disentangling their meshed patterns. It was intricate work, and the owner of the other psyche usually helped, but Sullyan was deep in thought, so Taran did all the work himself. He knew Sullyan's pattern thoroughly now, and his own pattern, although growing and evolving with his strengthening confidence, was as familiar to him as his own hands. He soon completed the task.

He sat there quietly once he was done, allowing the sense of loss he always felt after such intimate contact to slowly dissipate. Neither of them spoke for a while. Then Sullyan roused herself from her morbid thoughts and turned the full power of her startling eyes upon him. He read there her gratitude, her approval, and her love for him, and his soul sang with it. He returned her a smile that held all his feelings for her and took no account of their present circumstances. It was spontaneous, fresh and honest, and spoke only of his joy at his successes and his deep and grateful acknowledgment of her help and support.

The simple and unconditional nature of his gesture very nearly undid her. She had to turn away from his warmth, and the tacit promise of shelter and safety his presence exuded. She needed them so very badly yet couldn't allow herself to partake of them. It would be too expensive, and he knew she feared to pay that price. He sensed the effort she made to steel herself against imminent breakdown.

"I thank you, Taran," she said, her voice sounding strained. "I suggest you get a good night's rest. Tomorrow's exercise will be draining for us both."

She didn't look back as she left the circle.

Taran remained within the ring of stones, staring across the darkening landscape until it was time for his turn on watch.

✣ ✣ ✣ ✣ ✣

Marik gave Anjer the news early next morning. The relief on the massive man's face when he heard he wouldn't have to fight Brynne Sullyan was plain to see. But then it faded and was replaced by an almost equal amount of dismay.

Marik nodded in understanding. "The good news is good but the bad is no better. Robin Tamsen is no fool, and he knows your strengths and weaknesses almost as well as she does. And there's more."

The Lord General's black eyes snapped with consternation. "How much worse can it get?"

They sat together with General Ephan and Commander Barrin

in the lesser audience chamber, lit by the glow of lamps against the gloom of a depressingly rainy summer's day. Far in the distance the low grumble of thunder could be heard, and the momentary flash of pink summer lightning flickered at the corners of their eyes. Anjer folded his arms across his enormous chest as if to ward off Marik's bad news.

"King Elias intends to lead his forces against the Citadel in person," said Marik. "He will be accompanied by General Blaine, who is an Artesan of the same rank as you, Anjer."

Ephan leaned forward, his nearly-white eyes wide. "The human King's coming in person? But he's not gifted. He'd be taking a huge risk. What if all his Artesans should be killed? He'd have no way of returning home." He snorted. "I hope he's not planning on asking any of *us* for help!"

Marik returned Ephan's gaze. "Brynne thinks he's not in his right mind. She says he's been unstable ever since his son's abduction. We know what Aeyron's fate has done to Timar, so we shouldn't be so surprised."

Anjer stirred. "Unstable? He must have gone completely mad."

Marik could only agree. "She thinks it might be worth trying to parley with him before joining battle. Apparently, General Blaine is a reasonable man and may still have some sway with the King, although he's obviously been unable to prevent things going this far. What do you think, Anjer?"

Anjer considered carefully. "I'm willing to try anything to stop this nonsense. But who would we send as our envoy? If Elias is that unstable, it'll be dangerous."

Marik smiled almost pityingly, reflecting that now he understood how Sullyan must have felt when he was being obtuse about the regency. He spoke clearly. "I will go."

Anjer and Ephan both objected. As regent and head of state during Pharikian's indisposition, Marik was too valuable to risk. If he should be killed, or become incapacitated, Anjer would have no choice but to declare military regnancy and take over himself. That had not happened for hundreds of years.

Marik understood their concerns, but he was determined.

"Tell me, gentlemen, who else could we send? It has to be someone who will not be perceived as a threat, so that rules out either of you, or even Barrin. Yet it has to be someone in high authority." He closed his eyes and sighed. "So in the absence of anyone else, I'm afraid you're stuck with me."

They debated it hotly. In truth, he did not relish the task, especially if Elias was as unstable as Sullyan feared, but they could not gainsay him. Surely, he thought, under the stricture of parley he would be safe. He wouldn't go alone, of course, and with sudden inspiration he decided that Pharikian's young page, Norkis, would make a good second. Norkis was only thirteen; might his presence rein in any unstable tendencies Marik's message might arouse in Elias? It was worth a try, and the boy's presence might also speak to the paternal instincts that were currently overriding Elias's normal senses.

That decided, Marik moved on. He instructed Barrin to select four trusted scouts to track Corbyn's flight east, to see if they could discover where he had gone and what he might be up to. They all agreed with Sullyan that Corbyn wasn't done with his treachery. He was obviously deeply mired in the plot, whatever it was, as the accounts from Rykan's palace containing his name went back more than two years.

"Tell them to report as quickly as possible, Barrin," instructed Marik. "Brynne believes Elias will be sending his forces through sometime today, although she has no knowledge of where they'll emerge. He has two Master Artesans to afford them access, so they won't take too long in reaching our doorstep."

Barrin took his leave to make the arrangements, and Marik, Anjer, and Ephan fell to discussing where the Albian companies might form their bridgehead. They needed to decide where to position their own scouts in order to bring them the earliest possible warning.

Anjer already had his forces out of the Citadel and camped upon the Plain. He'd had no time to call up all the Hierarch's reserves, although messages had gone out to some of them. Some were too far away to be of help at such short notice. It was Marik's thought, and Anjer agreed, that the humans would most likely approach from the southwest, as this would avoid the dense Haligan forest to the east and southeast. Although the forest would have given them cover, it would also hamper the fighting men. There were woods and villages to the southwest, which would also afford some cover, and Marik feared for the villagers. Their protection was the reason Anjer had decided to confront Elias rather than allow him to attempt a siege.

Now, however, in the light of Corbyn's unquantified threat from the east, they had two directions to guard. If Corbyn was gathering a fighting force, the forest would conceal his numbers until he was ready to strike. The three men sat deep in tactical discussions while thunder rolled heedlessly overhead.

✳ ✳ ✳ ✳ ✳

It was raining in Albia too, a light and refreshing summer shower that would soon pass. Sullyan and Taran had ascended the hill once more as soon as the hidden sun was high enough to illuminate the land for many leagues around. They had left Ardoch to care for the horses and prepare breakfast. The Torlander was busy making what he called "patties," which appeared to be lumps of a doughy, cereal-based mixture which he slapped onto a flat stone set over the fire. They were apparently some kind of Torland tradition, and he was adamant they try them. Taran had to admit that the smell of their baking was making his stomach growl.

Sullyan ignored the tempting smell. This was more important, and Taran could sense her eagerness to see what the circle could show her, even though he had no idea what she hoped to find. As they made their way up the hill, she explained what she intended to do.

"This will be very draining for both of us," she warned as they strode shoulder to shoulder. "We may need some time to recover from the effects. I believe the results will be worth the expenditure. If I can find what I seek, it may save us days of searching. A morning spent in recuperation will be a small price to pay."

"What exactly are you looking for?" asked Taran, pleased to see a clear sense of purpose in her after days of debilitating sorrow.

She glanced up at him. They had reached the top of the hill, and the ancient, lichen-spotted monoliths sparkled in the morning damp. The shower cloud shifted slowly and shafts of yellow sunlight lit her face, turning the tawny of her hair to red-flashed gold. The fire opals at her throat and ears spat back the light like cats' eyes.

"I firmly believe that Rykan's Staff was crafted here in Albia." She turned from him to gaze across the land to the northwest. "I also believe Baron Reen somehow had a hand in its creation. If I am right, then the odds are it was made not far from Port Loxton. We know from what Timar has told us that the silicon-ceramic which encased the spellsilver required intense and highly-controlled temperatures for its manufacture, and that an ordinary furnace could not have contained the energies needed to produce that kind of heat. But a powerful barrier of Earth element could."

She turned back to him, and he could plainly see the desperate hope in her eyes that she would be proved right in her assumptions. There was so much riding on her decisions; so many lives would be affected by her choices, for good or for evil. He had no concept of how she contained the risk and uncertainty.

She continued. "The most logical place to construct such an Earth barrier is within a stone circle, where the energies flow naturally and would need minimal attention to maintain them. Leakage would be virtually nonexistent, and the heat required to mold and manipulate the ceramic would be unable to escape, and could be stoked almost infinitely."

"And you're hoping to discover such a circle near Port Loxton?"

He was rewarded with a flash of approval from her golden eyes. "Exactly. But I intend to go much further than that. The energies raised to create the Staff must have been colossal. They would have left a deep and abiding imprint in the substrate—even after all this time. *That* is what I intend to look for."

Taran was doubtful. "But the Staff was created at least two years ago—maybe even longer. How the Void are you going to find an imprint that old?"

She closed her eyes as if in pain. "This is why we must use the circle. The search will take all of our energy, and all the power Earth can lend us. I must go back through the layers of time within the substrate. It will be arduous and difficult work. It is not a thing I have attempted often. I will not deceive you, my friend. There will be pain involved. It may prove too much for you. It may prove too much for me! You must monitor yourself carefully, and if you become fearful of permanent damage, you must pull out. Immediately. Do you hear me? I want no heroics, Taran. We must not overtax our strength. If this trial surpasses us, all is not completely lost. The mere presence of a circle or other ancient site near Port Loxton will give me hope. But if I can also find evidence of the Staff's creation, I will know for sure that my instincts have not misled me."

She gazed at him. "What do you say, my friend? Are you willing to make the trial? I assure you, I will not blame you if you refuse."

The question made him raise his brows. How could she think he could possibly refuse? This would be another new experience and he was keen to participate. Yet he knew it was this very eagerness that gave Sullyan pause, as his enthusiasm sometimes got the better of him. She stared hard at him until he grinned at her.

"All right, Brynne, I have heard your warning. I take your point and I'll be careful. Now, how do we start?"

She shook her head and led the way into the center of the circle.

Chapter Ten

Sullyan explained the process in detail, and Taran indicated his readiness. With her standing behind him again, her hands resting lightly on his shoulders to facilitate the link, they wove their patterns together.

He had worked with her like this many times before, but never had he experienced such a close sharing of his most intimate self. He felt as if their very souls were one, and he was profoundly glad she knew him so well. Any secrets, personal traits, or embarrassing quirks of nature would have been instantly revealed, they were so closely bonded. He could see that she had never attempted to hide anything from him. Her feelings for him were laid bare and he was astounded at their depth. But he could also see the breadth of emotions that she harbored for her other friends, and they were as deep and profound as those she kept for him. He was humbled to be so loved, and he felt her warm and generous smile as she noticed the focus of his attention.

"Concentrate, Adept," she admonished, but her tone was mild.

With an effort, he turned his will toward the western cardinal stone. Once more, the ponderous forces of Earth came flowing forth at his merest touch, running sunwise about the monoliths and linking each one in a chain of impenetrable force. The ancient stones seemed to glow, the spots of lichen to fluoresce, and the glints of mica within the granite flared with coruscations of power.

When the circle was complete, he drew the weighty forces toward him.

"Form the Powersink," Sullyan instructed.

He did so, the vast, abyssal structure snapping into existence just as the flow of energy reached him. As he watched, sluggish Earth power bled down into the maw of the Powersink, disappearing into the depths like a slow motion avalanche. He could feel it mingling and interlocking with their joined metaforce. It felt strange, almost like being violated, taken over. He wasn't at all sure he could stand it. Sullyan's calming presence soothed him and he heard her voice, strangely altered by the wealth of power surrounding them.

"Concentrate on the portion of our merged patterns that masters Earth. Then you will not feel so helpless."

He did as she bid, and found it true. Even she was doing the same. Now the alien forces felt more natural, and he could assimilate the strength they gave him without conflict.

When it was done and he was stable, she spoke again.

"I am going to cast the power outward. Its direction and flow will flood through your psyche. Try to remain calm and open. It will make things easier for me."

Trusting her implicitly, he relaxed. He felt her take hold of the Powersink and use its energies to cast her awareness over the land. Through their link, he could see what she saw, feel what she felt.

Across the wide green lands he perceived a glittering web of earth power punctuated by pockets and columns, indicating sites of raw and natural Earth element where those forces were strongest. They flowed upward and outward like shimmering pillars or pools of light, shot through with all the hues of life. It was an awe inspiring and fundamentally thrilling display.

Sullyan ignored it. Her focus lay to the northwest, toward the sea and Port Loxton. Taran could see there were no obvious areas of Earth power in that region, but this didn't seem to disappoint Sullyan. She merely took a firmer hold of the power and pulled strongly on the structure of the Powersink. Taran tried to focus his mind on holding the power flow constant, but he was fascinated by her casual use of this tremendously potent energy. Earth might be the least complicated element for an Artesan to master, but it could also be the strongest, and its possible uses obviously far surpassed Taran's meager experience. He wondered anew how she had learned all this so young.

Their joint awareness approached the environs of Port Loxton. To the perception of their empowered minds, the city appeared nothing like its physical presence. Taran could detect life force in abundance, but he saw no dwellings. Manmade structures made little impression on the substrate, and natural things like trees and animals left only vaguely recognizable imprints. Swirls and patterns impinged upon his mind, and he had no idea what they were.

Finally, just when Taran was beginning to feel the first effects of fatigue, Sullyan gave a start. With an effort, he split his concentration, still calling forth the power of Earth, but leaving part of him free to see what she had discovered.

Within the milky mire of the ever-changing substrate he saw an impression: a static and circular discoloration which exuded a faint miasma of power. Sullyan pounced on it like a starving cat.

Swiftly, without releasing her hold on it, she sent a warning to Taran.

Be strong for me, Adept. This is where the real work begins. Concentrate on the forces of Earth and not on me. I need you to call the power as you never have before. Try to drain the circle. Think of the power as lifeblood—keep it pulsing into the Powersink for as long as you can. If it becomes too much for you, if the pain becomes too strong, then you must step back. Give me fair warning, but then pull out. Do you hear me?

He agreed, determined not to fail her. He took a deep and steadying breath and then brought the full focus of his will to bear upon the western cardinal stone. The immediate and powerful response his will commanded startled even him. The power almost burst out of the stones, called from the very bedrock and foundations of the land, and it gyred around the circle until the stones thrummed with power. It poured toward him in torrents and, caught by surprise, he only just remembered to channel it into the Powersink. He was just in time.

Sullyan took command of the increased forces. Strongly empowered, she refined the natural element down until she could use it to delve and burrow her way through the complex layers of substrate which covered the circular depression they had found. They could both already feel the slow headache that was the inevitable result of long and intense concentration. Working as fast as she could, she delved deeper and deeper through the layers of time.

Taran sat motionless upon the stone, uncaring of the hands that gripped his shoulders like talons. Sullyan's mind had relinquished all control over her body, and the clasp of her hands was the only thing keeping her upright. Taran would have bruises, but neither of them took any notice. He was desperately trying to ignore the shooting pain in his head which the channeling of so much power was causing him.

Taran was beginning to fail. He knew it—knew it with a cold, dispassionate certainty that nevertheless tore at his heart. Why could he not be stronger? Why did his physical stamina always fail him? He couldn't possibly pull out now. There was far too much at stake. She had risked all on this one chance and he didn't intend to let her down.

Biting back moans and ignoring the warning red flashes before his eyes, he grimly hung on, using what Sullyan was thinking to distract him from the pain.

✢ ✢ ✢ ✢ ✢

Sullyan was beginning to feel she had risked everything on a non-starter. She had been so blindly sure she was right. She knew with instinctive certainty that Reen was involved in the plot and that he had been Rykan's backer, with or without the Queen's knowledge. Yet Sofira *must* have known, what with the amounts of gold that must have changed hands.

Rykan would have demanded much more than just a tool to enhance his metaforce before he'd ever have been willing to attack Pharikian. He would have had to outfit his forces and bribe the nobles whose lands he had usurped in order to stop them from rebelling once he started his campaign. She suddenly realized this must be the reason for Corbyn's name appearing in Rykan's records, although he might well have been retained as an ally, as his payments went much farther back. She also knew that Reen would never have had access to that much gold, despite having his own estate. No. Elias's protestations to the contrary, Albia's Treasury *must* have provided the funds.

Sullyan was equally certain the Staff had been made in Albia. Rykan hadn't possessed the power to create it, and Reen would never have crossed the Veils, notwithstanding the fact he had obviously suppressed his revulsion and compromised his conscience in order to deal with the rebel Andaryan lord. And as this was the closest site of available Earth power to Port Loxton, the Staff *must* have been made here.

And yet, she couldn't find it. She was expending every ounce of her own power, all of Taran's, and most of what was available through the Powersink, heedless of the cost. Still it eluded her. She was so determined to find what she sought that her guard over Taran's condition was forgotten.

✛ ✛ ✛ ✛ ✛

Taran already knew he'd gone too far. The pain in his head was excruciating, and it disabled him completely. The intensity of it transfixed and overcame him, and he was helpless. He couldn't even moan anymore. The power still flowed; he was locked on to it, his mind gripping the Earth forces with such desperation that he could not release them. He knew that were he to lose control now, the power would overwhelm him and absorb him into its depths.

The red flashes in his vision were coming more frequently, and he knew he would soon black out. Mentally screaming with frustration, he made one last superhuman effort to warn Sullyan.

✛ ✛ ✛ ✛ ✛

She jumped. Was there something here after all? Was that the glimmer of a deeply buried trace? Was it the suggestion of old forces, a flash like the remembrance of vast energies, of scorching heat? Grasping the power ever more tightly, heedless of the pain, she probed as deeply as she could, desperate not to lose this fleeting chance of success.

Taran's desperate scream shattered her concentration. With a vicious curse she wrenched her attention back to the present. She saw with cold dread that Taran had passed out. Berating herself soundly for not paying him closer attention, she withdrew from her goal and took full control of the Powersink, halting its immense drain on their life forces.

She carefully reversed the march of power from the stones,

marveling as she did so that the Adept had been able to sustain such a pace for as long as he had. Her anger at his reckless determination not to fail was mitigated by her recognition that his determination had mirrored her own. How could she blame him for sharing her desire?

Once the circle was dormant, she dismantled the Powersink and examined the complexities of Taran's damaged psyche with anxious eyes. There was scarring, of course; she knew there would be. He would have a fearsome headache for hours after this. Well, maybe it would serve to remind him to heed her warnings in the future. Her own head was pounding and sore. She had pushed them both too hard and very nearly reached her limits. Small wonder, then, he had passed his own.

Coming back to herself once their patterns were separate, she had to hold him upright or he would have fallen. He was out cold, which was a mercy as far as it went, for he couldn't feel his own pain. If he would remain so for long enough, maybe she could dampen it for him. She took a trembling breath against her own weakness and called as loudly as she could for Ardoch.

The old Torlander must have heard the fear in her voice, for he reacted swiftly. He rushed up the hill to her side, the consternation on his face increasing when he saw Taran's limp form.

"What happened, lass? Is he hurt?"

"Yes, but not too badly. He overtaxed himself, that is all. We both did. Can you carry him down?"

Taran was tall but slim, and the tough Torlander easily bore him down to the camp. He laid the Adept on the ground beside the fire and covered him with his cloak to keep him warm.

Sullyan sat by Taran while Ardoch brewed fellan. She rested one hand lightly on the Adept's brow, gently reaching into him to soothe away some of the burn scars of his overexertion. She was still weak herself, and when the pounding in her head grew too strong, she desisted. Taran would probably remain unconscious for at least a couple of hours; long enough for his psyche to begin to mend.

Ardoch handed her a steaming mug of fellan, the contents of which disappeared before his back was turned. She held out the mug for more and he obliged with a wry smile.

"Still addicted, eh, lass?"

She grinned back, but it turned into a yawn.

"You should sleep," he growled. She agreed, but suddenly found she was ravenously hungry, not a sensation she was used to. The smell of the baked patties still hung in the air, and the Torlander brought one to her. Its brown, crusty surface was liberally spread with honey warm from the hot stone. The golden sweetness had soaked down to the patty's soft inner core, and it crumbled deliciously in her mouth.

The sustenance revived some of her strength, but the fellan was making her drowsy. Seeing this, Ardoch fetched her cloak and bade her lie down next to Taran to sleep.

"I'll keep an eye on him, lass, never fear. Did you find what you were looking for up on yon hill?"

She rolled herself in her heavy woolen cloak after taking one last look at Taran, satisfied he'd taken no lasting harm. She smiled across at the old swordmaster as she pillowed her head upon Drum's light saddle.

"I did. My instincts were true; my sacrifice has not been in vain. We found the site of the Staff's manufacture. Now all we have to do is find the Princes, stop this senseless war, and make sure the Baron cannot carry out his plan."

Ardoch watched her as she settled to sleep.

"Oh, aye," she heard him mutter, "is that all?"

✣ ✣ ✣ ✣ ✣

Rienne came out of the infirmary to watch the departure of the companies which would form Elias's fighting forces in Andaryon. The men from Port Loxton, led by Denny's second-in-command, Captain Valustin, had arrived late the night before and were now drawn up alongside the Manor companies. Elias himself sat astride his roan charger as he addressed the assembled men. Rienne thought the King's aspect was strained, his face gray and gaunt. Only his eyes seemed alive, and even they held an unnatural glitter in their depths.

Elias wore tough combat leathers, as did all the men, his ornate but no less deadly longsword belted by his side. Over his combat jerkin he wore a scarlet cloak, which flowed down in supple folds to drape the hindquarters of the powerful roan stallion. His voice rang out clear and strident as he addressed the men, but it held an edge, a subtle tremor, and Rienne's eyes narrowed.

Hers wasn't the only concern.

According to Bull, General Blaine was a troubled man. He had argued long and hard with his monarch against this course of action. It was unnecessary and reckless to the extreme. And as a means of regaining his son, it was futile.

Bull had assured Rienne that Mathias Blaine had done everything within his power, short of following Sullyan's example, to dissuade Elias from it. But the King was adamant. The keen knife of his grief and outrage was twisting incessantly in his soul and goading him toward heedless action. He was in no mood to listen to reason, and had made very sure Blaine knew where his objections were likely to land him.

The General's suspicion that Elias would actually dismiss him as he'd done Sullyan had effectively silenced Blaine's protestations. At least Blaine would be with the King to protect him. Rienne could only hope the General would succeed.

The King finished his exhortation to the troops, and the men hailed him. Elias didn't notice—or chose to ignore—that the cheers were not entirely wholehearted. Rienne noticed. Her eyes were fixed on the face of her life mate where he sat his iron-gray warhorse at the head of his company. Although nominally intent on the King, Rienne knew that Cal's attention was focused solely on her. She could swear there were tears in his eyes.

They'd said an emotional farewell earlier that morning, before the sun was up. Lying warm in each other's arms, they'd taken what comfort they could. Words were useless. Anything could happen over the next few days and neither could guess how things would turn out.

At least Cal had the comfort of knowing Rienne would be safe. Hanan had brusquely refused her request to go with the small contingent of healers that had been assigned as field medics. Rienne, however, had no such comfort. Her fervent prayers that Sullyan would return with Elias's young heir had as yet gone unanswered, and anyway, she knew it was too soon. Even had Sullyan ridden nonstop like the wind and taken advantage of every runner staging post, it would take her two days to reach Port Loxton. And that was only the beginning of her task. No, there would be no last-hour reprieve for Cal, or for any of the men heading through the Veils. This course was set. All Rienne could do was wait and pray.

✤ ✤ ✤ ✤ ✤

Bull watched Robin from his place beside Rienne. On the surface, the young Major appeared as calm and assured as usual, but Bull thought he could detect a tremor in the hands which held Torka's reins, and Robin's face was paler than normal. Bull had considered but then thought twice about speaking to him before he left. They'd not parted on the best of terms the last time, and the barely believable news that Robin had requested Parren as one of Elias's captains had pushed Bull's tolerance to its limits.

If Elias was unhinged, he thought grimly, surely Robin was headed that way. His ridiculous behavior over those stupid rumors surely closed the case.

So Bull held his peace and kept his temper and said nothing. But he had seen Robin's eyes flick to his face at least once, and wondered what the young Major was thinking.

✶ ✶ ✶ ✶ ✶

Bull was correct in his suspicions. Robin *was* trembling. This whole situation seemed somehow unreal. The absence of Sullyan, the presence of the King, and the sheer folly of what they were about to do all combined to make this a completely surreal experience. Robin didn't like the feeling at all. It was too much like an omen of doom.

Yet he knew his orders, was confident in the captains, and was well-versed in the procedure to open a large trans-Veil tunnel for the men to travel into Andaryon. Robin had suggested the site of their emergence, as he knew the terrain around Caer Vellet well. There was a small, secluded valley just to the southwest of the woods around the southern borders of the Citadel Plain, and that whole area was largely uninhabited. It should provide them with a protected location in which to acclimatize the men who had never traveled the Veils before—which was most of them—and would be an ideal bridgehead from which to launch their assaults.

Robin's only concern was that Lord General Anjer would also have recognized its suitability, and would have men stationed there to hinder the humans' crossing.

He had put these concerns to Blaine and received the General's permission to accompany the small force tasked with scouting the valley. As soon as the King indicated he was ready, Robin and the scouts would cross the Veils.

Elias was speaking to Colonel Vassa, who had come up to wish his monarch good fortune and a swift and successful outcome to his venture. Vassa was happy to be left in charge of the militia and Albia's defense, especially as Bull would be remaining at the Manor to relay communications between Vassa, the King, and the General.

Watching them, Robin caught sight of Parren standing off to one side and registered the impotent fury in his dead eyes. He could not tell its direction. Was Parren more furious with Vassa for refusing Robin's request, or the Major for failing to persuade the Colonel? It mattered little and Robin dismissed the puzzle. At least Parren would be unable to take revenge on him while he was in Andaryon with the King.

Had he known exactly what was going through Parren's twisted mind at that moment, he might not have been so sure.

Finally, Elias seemed ready. He'd made his plans, instructed his officers, and deployed his men. All that remained was to cross the Veils and secure their bridgehead. He turned from Vassa, a strange excitement in his eyes. Robin knew the workings of Artesans had always fascinated the King, and now he was about to experience something of what they felt. Blaine had already explained to him what he would see and hear as they crossed the Veils, and Elias was clearly keen to get on with it. With a nod to Blaine and an abrupt command to the men, he urged his stallion forward, leading the massed fighting companies toward the ridge on the outskirts of the Manor's extensive grounds.

Captain Dexter had selected twenty men from among the mounted companies to be his scouting force. Robin fell in behind them. Once they were clear of the Manor and well away from any human habitation, Robin signaled to Blaine. The General spoke to the King, and Elias gave Robin his permission to cross the Veils. Blaine had been a little reluctant to allow Robin to join the scouts instead of merely affording them access to Andaryon, but as Robin had pointed out, he knew the terrain better than any of them, even Cal. He would be invaluable to the scouts.

Once Dexter and the scouts were in position, Robin closed his eyes and concentrated on his route. The shimmering opalescence of a trans-Veil corridor opened before him and he rode through it slowly. The men followed, and Cal came last to guard the structure.

It opened out as planned into the pleasant valley Robin had chosen. He cast about with his metasenses, questing for any signs of Artesans in the vicinity. There were none. Riding cautiously, sword drawn, he emerged onto the grass of the valley, the scouts spreading out around him. There was no sign of resistance, no shouts of challenge, no hint of movement. He looked about grimly. Had he chosen correctly? Had Anjer forgotten this little valley, or was he just biding his time? Robin handed control of the tunnel to Blaine and followed the scouting force farther into Andaryon.

✤ ✤ ✤ ✤ ✤

Lord General Anjer was far too seasoned a warrior to ignore or forget such a convenient location as the secluded valley to the southwest. Due to the unknown quantity of the threat posed by Corbyn and the necessity of initiating a parley, Anjer had instructed the scouts he had dispatched to the valley to do no more than watch and report numbers should Elias indeed chose it as his bridgehead.

Anjer had no intention of actually fighting Elias if he could avoid it. Sending forces against the Albian King was pointless, and would only serve to vindicate Elias's suspicions and give him a reason to press his attack. Containment and the defense of the people was Anjer's only motive in sending troops to meet Elias.

So, as planned, the Albians never saw Anjer's scouts who watched from concealment, and as Anjer had been careful to include no Artesans among them, Robin didn't sense them.

✤ ✤ ✤ ✤ ✤

Receiving Robin's all-clear, Blaine meshed with him, and the two Master Artesans widened and stabilized the tunnel so that up to five men could march through abreast. Elias wanted to be in the van as an example to the men, some of whom were plainly nervous of the experience. Blaine put his foot down at that.

"No, your Majesty," he said, holding the King's eye and speaking in low tones. "I cannot allow it. You are not an Artesan, and in this you will be guided by me. In all other respects I will obey you, but in Artesan matters, I will not. You will go through last, and you will be surrounded by a guard. Do you hear me?"

Although his mind was not functioning as rationally as usual, Elias was not so far gone as to be completely unreachable. He heard the logic in Blaine's words and decided to accept his General's recommendation. Now was not the time to argue; the men would hear.

He nodded curtly. "Very well, General, carry on."

Blaine gave a sigh of relief. This was the first sign he'd had that the old Elias resided somewhere within this wracked and driven shell. Perhaps there was still hope.

Blaine gave the order to march and the men began filing

through the tunnel, most looking about them with anxious eyes. Those with horses dismounted and led the beasts. There was no panic, and the transfer progressed steadily.

When the final fifty men were ready to walk the tunnel, Blaine sent the King into their midst, one of the guards leading his roan stallion. The General had also persuaded Elias to remove his scarlet cloak in case there were any concealed crossbowmen waiting to identify and shoot the King.

Once the transfer was over and the tunnel had been collapsed, Blaine ordered Valustin to deploy sentries around the access points to the valley. Then he gave orders for the setting up of the field camp. The rest of the day would be spent in camp duties and drill, while Elias and his officers discussed their next move. Much depended on the Andaryans' response to their presence, and should Anjer send a force against them, they would be ready. They would make no offensive moves until the morrow.

Well pleased with the discipline of his forces, Blaine left Valustin to instruct the captains and went to attend his King.

Chapter Eleven

Captain Parren watched the King's departure with rage in his heart and murder in his soul. He was convinced Robin had done no more than pay lip-service to his promise to speak with Colonel Vassa, and Parren didn't know which man to hate the most. Robin eventually came out on top, due to Parren's long-standing feud with him and Sullyan. He would pay Robin back for this snub, he promised himself.

Vassa passed him on his way back to the Manor and summarily sent him on his way. Parren was supposed to be assessing the newest arrivals, checking their weapons, and arranging billeting. He barely acknowledged the Colonel and glared at Vassa's retreating back. As he swung away to go about his demeaning duties, his eyes lit upon Bull and Rienne talking together.

Parren's eyes narrowed. The Manor now contained but few of its trained fighting men, and of those who were left, none outranked him except Lieutenant-Major Bailey and Colonel Vassa. Bailey had long since ceased to pay Parren any attention, and Vassa would be kept fully occupied. Parren suddenly realized he would never have a better opportunity to rid himself of those who had damaged and obstructed him over the years.

He had no real grievance with Rienne, save that she was friendly with Sullyan. Although, he reminded himself, she had been responsible for the discharge and imprisonment of the only two trusted supporters he'd ever had. She had informed on one of them after he reputedly attempted to rape her, and Parren was convinced it had only been a bit of horseplay that had spiraled out of hand. At the time, he'd heard Bull say Rienne had had little to do with it, as Morin, the sergeant in question, had confessed to the attack. Parren didn't believe it. As far as he was concerned, the whole thing was Rienne's fault. She shouldn't have paraded herself alone through the hallways of the Manor if she was so incapable of looking after herself. Maybe the place would be better without her.

Hal Bullen—ah, he was another matter entirely. He was already at the Manor when Parren arrived as a raw cadet. Part of Blaine's household before he was appointed General-in-Command of the King's forces, Bull had once been a sergeant-at-arms, and his military background had made him the obvious choice as sergeant-major once Elias bestowed royal status on the Manor garrison. Bull had immediately become responsible for training new recruits, along with Swordmaster Ardoch and Horsemaster Solet, and he had recognized very early the intrinsic cruelty of Parren's nature.

He had done his level best to work it out of Parren, without success. His efforts had only driven it deeper, where it was fueled by Parren's resentment and bitterness. Yet Parren's obvious grasp of the intricacies of leadership, his natural aptitude for military life, and his expertise with the sword had guaranteed his acceptance into the King's forces. Parren was aware that Bull would have prevented this if he could, and still resented him for it. Parren had nursed his grievances like festering boils, but due to Bull's position and power there was nothing he could do.

By the time Parren was promoted to captain, Bull was already semi-retired and had become Sullyan's personal aide. Her acceptance for training, her promotion to captain well ahead of Parren, and her rise to major on the death of Anton had infuriated Parren still further. His various attempts to discredit and harm her had all met with failure, but now—ah now!—he was finally going to reap the rewards of his long patience. She was gone, and his bitter heart was glad. Bull was nothing without her. With any luck, and perhaps a little help, he would drink himself to death. That only left Robin, and if Parren had been prevented from going with him and finding an opportunity for a sly knife in the back, well, he had other means of revenge at hand.

Still spitting with frustration, Parren went to take charge of his contingent of rustics. They would find him a harsh and unrelenting taskmaster.

✢ ✢ ✢ ✢ ✢

Once all the companies heading for Andaryon had received their supplies, Tad and Ozella kept out of the way by taking it in turns to exercise Felika. Tad, more used to the stocky, muscular Manor stallions, found the desert-bred animal's slim back and long limbs most ungainly. The horse's gait was different too, and he had been trained to pace: that is, to move both legs on the same side at the same time. This produced a smooth, swaying, energy-saving motion, but Tad found it most peculiar. He doubled over with laughter the first time Ozella demonstrated the action, and was convinced some dire cruelty had been employed to force the stallion to move in such a strange way. But Ozella convinced him that it was a natural gait in desert horses and only needed careful training to bring it out. No one who valued their horseflesh, he asserted stoutly, would descend to using cruelty to train a horse.

Then, of course, Tad had to experience it for himself. It took some patient explanation and much laughter from both boys before

Tad finally got the hang of the aids to give Felika. When the horse finally broke into the swaying gait, the boy nearly fell from the saddle in surprise, which immediately spoiled the dun's balance. Hooting with derisory laughter, Ozella made him try again.

Tired, hot, and sweaty, they called it a day around lunchtime. Tad helped Ozella rub down his horse and clean the harness, and then they parted to clean themselves up. Arranging to meet again in the afternoon at the College to practice their influence over Earth, Tad left Ozella and returned to the barracks.

Ozella gave his horse a final pat and the apple he'd saved, and then made his way back, whistling to himself. For the first time in weeks he'd been able to forget his unhappiness and the desperate plight of his sisters in the simple pleasures of friendship. He wished he'd realized sooner how much fun Tad could be, but he'd always considered the younger boy to be too much of a child to bother with. The young cadet's maturity had surprised him.

Once he was alone again, worry over his sisters' fate returned to sit on his shoulder like some malignant carrion bird, just waiting to stab his conscience with a beak of steel. How could he have laughed and joked with Tad while they languished gods knew where, in the power of that unfeeling thug's men? Ozella's face reddened and he cast down his eyes as he walked.

"Well? Do you have anything useful to tell me?"

The harsh, hated voice jolted Ozella's nerves. He'd not seen Parren come up behind him. The thin hand that descended on his shoulder in a cruel parody of friendship had the aspect of a claw, and its grip froze his skin. He looked up into Parren's pale, dead eyes.

Ozella's step faltered.

"I … I'm doing as you asked," he stammered, "but it takes time. You can't just befriend someone and get them to tell you their innermost secrets when you've steadfastly ignored them for the past nine months. You can't possibly expect—"

"Then you'll have to try harder, won't you?"

Parren thrust his face so close the younger man could smell his unsavory breath. It made him want to gag and he tried to back away, but Parren held his shoulder in a viselike grip.

"You're starting to annoy me, Ozella," he grated, bitterness and frustration boiling in his tone.

Ozella stared at him in despair. He recognized the crazed look in Parren's eyes. He was all too afraid he knew what was coming.

Parren mastered himself with an effort. He took a swift look around, checking they were alone and unobserved. He reached into his pocket and took out the slightly larger of the two rings he kept there. He held it up for Ozella to see.

"You know what this is, don't you?" It was a rhetorical question, but Ozella nodded. "Well?" Parren pressed.

"My sister Rozlin's ring," he choked out.

Parren grinned slyly. "Yes, Rozlin," he drawled. "The elder of the two."

Ozella paled.

Parren allowed his expression to darken ominously. "She, I'm sorry to say, has been proving troublesome."

Ozella's eyes widened. Parren pressed on, clearly enjoying the pleasure his power over Ozella gave him. "She's been trying to defend her younger sister," he said, observing Ozella's reactions from the corner of his eye.

Desperate and afraid, Ozella fell for it.

"Surine?" he whispered. "What's happened to her? Why did she need defending?"

Parren stared hard at him, a cruel smile tugging at the corners of his mouth. "I surely don't need to tell you what the presence of two such helpless young women is doing to my men, do I?"

This was too much even for Ozella. He lunged at Parren, but Parren was ready for such a move and had his sword out in a flash, arresting the younger man's blind rush. The Captain held his naked blade across Ozella's trembling chest.

"I have to tell you that it was necessary for them to, ah, 'discipline' Rozlin," he said.

Ozella gasped, the strength draining from his muscles. "If they've hurt her…" he whispered, stricken.

Parren casually sheathed his sword and placed his hands on his hips. "If they have, it's your fault! I've told you before. I need something concrete, something useful, from you before I'll exert the kind of control my men will need to stop them from going any further. She wasn't badly hurt … this time … but the next time might be another matter. Remember, Ozella, what's one girl to me, more or less? Maybe Surine will prove more tractable if we remove Rozlin. What do you think?"

Ozella gagged on Parren's threats. He could hardly open his throat to croak, "I think you're a vicious, sadistic bastard! You're really enjoying this, aren't you?"

Parren turned away languidly, smiling. "Not as much as my men will if you don't come up with what I want, my fine lord."

He sauntered back the way he had come.

Ozella stood there shaking, staring after him. His fists clenched and unclenched uselessly by his sides as tears poured down his face. He loved his sisters dearly and this torture was tearing out his heart. But what could he do? Who would believe him if he tried to denounce Parren? Who would be able to stop what was happening before Parren's men killed or maimed his sisters?

Ozella had no idea where they were being held, or how far

away they were. He couldn't take the chance that Parren could get orders to his men even if Ozella managed to convince someone of the blackmail.

And what proof did he have, anyway? No one else knew his sisters were missing. There was no way Ozella could even get a message to his father. Beraxia was too far away and Ozella didn't have the authority to use the King's runners. Parren could easily hide the rings if he needed to, and then it would be Ozella's word against the captain's. Parren had been here years and had status; Ozella was only a visitor and not a very useful one. Why would anyone believe him?

And besides, Ozella realized with a sinking heart, they were all gone now. He didn't know Colonel Vassa, had never spoken to the man. How would he react to Ozella's sudden denouncement of one of his officers? As for Bull, well, he clearly had a low opinion of Ozella. It would be no use going to him. No, Ozella was completely alone and defenseless. He had to do as Parren asked. His father would never forgive him if he allowed any lasting harm to come to Rozlin or Surine.

Friendless, comfortless, and bereft, Ozella gulped back more tears. He was doomed whatever he did and he didn't know how he would bear it. He staggered blindly away, his heart limping in his chest.

✠ ✠ ✠ ✠ ✠

"No, Barrin, we are *not* going to attack them while they're in the valley. We're not going to attack them at all if we can help it."

Commander Barrin stood before Duke Marik and Lord General Anjer, his face a picture of indignation. He had brought them word of the scouts' reports and was eager for action.

"But, your Grace, they have invaded Andaryan soil. They

have declared war on us."

Marik stirred. "Thank you, Commander, I am well aware of that. The Lord General and I have already discussed this and we have our strategy planned. General Ephan will no doubt explain it to you in due course."

Barrin's expression was sour. "What are we to do then, your Grace? Wait for them to raid our villages as they've done before? Allow them free access to our people and their homes? Why don't we open the Citadel to them while we're about it?"

Anjer was outraged. "*Commander!*"

Realizing he'd overstepped the mark, Barrin immediately backed down, his face flaming. "I'm truly sorry, your Grace, I didn't mean that. I just hate all this waiting around. It doesn't seem right. They did declare war on us, after all."

Marik spoke gently, darting a quelling glance at the rumbling Anjer. "Yes, I know. I understand your concern. But you must remember that they had no valid reason to declare war on us. Would you have me give them one? What do you think the Hierarch's reaction would be if I went in too hard? If I attacked Elias, who is, after all, still our trade partner despite his current misapprehension, and precipitated our realm into an all-out war? Is that good rulership, Barrin? Is it good leadership?"

"Did Vanyr teach you nothing, man?" Anjer was unable to keep a rein on his temper any longer. "I tell you, I wish he still commanded the Velletian Guard. He had a cooler head and a firmer grasp of politics than you."

Thoroughly cowed, Barrin turned away.

"Commander," Marik called, and Barrin turned slowly back. "I appreciate your thoughts. Ideas are always welcome, but for now our plans are going in a different direction. If we can avert this war without major bloodshed, we will do so. Now, I have decided to try to parley with Elias before he commits himself to attack, so I want you to pick fifteen trustworthy men to be my honor guard. And I want you to lead them. We leave before dawn tomorrow."

"Very good, your Grace." Barrin gave Marik his due salute and left the room.

Once the door had closed behind him, Marik eyed Anjer reproachfully.

"What?" demanded the huge man, folding his arms over his chest. "He shouldn't answer back like that. He's getting above his station."

Marik sighed. "Agreed, but I'd prefer it if he wasn't reprimanded quite so harshly for speaking his mind. That's what makes good commanders. You should know."

Anjer was silent, as if trying to work through the Duke's comment to see if it implied a compliment or an insult. Marik grinned at his expression, allowing himself to relax a little. He didn't mind admitting to a vast relief that Elias hadn't, as yet, led an attack on their people. Barrin's scouts had reported the setting up of the field camp and the activities therein, and Marik realized that the human King was allowing his men to become comfortable with their surroundings before he committed them. This gave Marik some breathing space, too; time to work out what he would say in his parley and how he would present it.

There was a discreet tap at the door, and Pharikian's young page, Norkis, came into the room. The boy was pale. He was very fond of his monarch and felt Pharikian's indisposition keenly. Throughout it, he had hardly moved from his station outside the door to the royal chambers, where he waited to run errands for the Princess or the Master Healer. He would be there even now if Marik hadn't summoned him.

He approached Anjer and Marik slowly, worry in his eyes. He was an intelligent and lively boy, his blond hair and pale blue eyes lending him an angelic air. The habitual cheeky grin that charmed everyone who met him was absent, as it had been since Pharikian's collapse.

Watching him, Marik hoped his request would bring some measure of purpose, some sense of pride, back to the young page. They all missed his usually irrepressible humor.

Norkis came to a halt before them. "You sent for me, your Grace?" He didn't return Marik's smile of greeting.

"I did, son. How is your master today?"

Marik usually spent a good few hours every morning with Idrimar at her father's side, but the arrival of Elias's troops had forced him to forego that ritual.

Norkis's face fell further. "There's still no change, your Grace. Her Highness is very worried."

Marik frowned. "Yes, I know. But we have to expect no great changes until Colonel Sullyan returns to awaken him."

The boy wrung his hands. "But what if she doesn't, your Grace? What if she can't? What if the war ... what if she...?"

He was voicing what no one else had dared, and Marik wished he had not.

"She'll come, Norkis." He spoke with more confidence than he possessed. "She'll find and bring back the Heir, and all will be well. We have to believe that. Do you hear me?"

"I hear you, your Grace."

The words were softly murmured, and Marik saw the glitter of tears under Norkis's lowered lashes. He took a deep breath. "Come, boy. I have a duty for you. Something that will serve his Majesty and all of Andaryon well if we can pull it off. I'm asking for your help, Norkis. Will you hear my request?"

The boy's eyes widened at Marik's deferential tone. People usually gave him orders rather than asking for his help, and even when they weren't being brusque they weren't usually so polite.

Marik's calculated use of this approach had the desired effect. Norkis momentarily forgot his sorrow. "Of course, your Grace. I am yours to command."

"This isn't a command, Norkis, it's a request." Once again, Marik subtly emphasized the word. "You are aware, of course, that King Elias has invaded Andaryan soil and that he intends either to assault the Citadel or attack our people, in the mistaken belief that this will force us to return his son to him."

Norkis nodded, eyes still wide.

"It is my intention to try to divert Elias from this useless war by initiating a parley with him. I want to meet him face to face, assure him that we do not have his son, that we were not responsible for Eadan's abduction, and that he will gain nothing but death and destruction if he attacks us. I have already asked Commander Barrin to lead the honor guard, and we will leave just before dawn tomorrow. I myself will be the envoy to Elias, but I need a standard bearer to carry the flag of truce. Norkis, will you be my bearer?"

Norkis's pale face flushed with pride and his mouth dropped open. He had clearly expected nothing like this.

Marik smiled at his flustered demeanor. "Am I to take it you're willing?" The page nodded emphatically, too overcome to speak. "Very well, then. Wear your ceremonial robes and meet us in the courtyard before dawn. We will ride out early and hopefully catch Elias before he orders his troops to attack."

He stared at Norkis intently and the boy sobered. "If we succeed tomorrow, we will save many lives. I won't deceive you— it could be dangerous. I don't think for one minute the High King of Albia would violate a flag of truce, but I've heard reports that the loss of his son has damaged his mind. Grief has made him unstable. This we can understand, given our own ruler's condition. But it also makes Elias unpredictable. Do you understand what I'm saying? I can't guarantee our safety, even though we will have Commander Barrin at our backs. Are you still willing to accompany me on those terms?"

Norkis didn't hesitate. "Of course, your Grace. I'll do anything I can."

Marik's grin widened. "Good lad. Go on, then, go and get some rest. You're excused from your duties for the rest of the day."

Norkis bowed and left the room, his head held higher than before. Marik sat back with a deep sigh.

Anjer steepled his fingers. "Do you think this has a realistic chance of working, your Grace?"

Marik closed his eyes. "It's in the lap of the gods, my friend. All we can do is try."

✤ ✤ ✤ ✤ ✤

Taran opened his eyes with a small groan of pain. Instantly, before he'd even had time to react, he felt a warm and soothing balm wash over his aching mind. It smoothed away the edges of his pain. Sighing in relief, he looked about for Sullyan and saw her sitting on the ground beside him, fellan in hand. He smiled his thanks even as he registered the strain on her pale features.

"I can manage now," he assured her, and took over his own healing. He felt her withdraw as he yawned and sat up.

Ardoch handed him a mug of fellan and he accepted it gratefully. Judging by the height of the sun, it was past midday, and he wondered that he'd been allowed to sleep so long. This thought gave rise to a sudden fear, and he turned back to Sullyan.

"Rest easy, Taran, we did not fail at the trial. Indeed, my friend, you surpassed my expectations, although you imperiled yourself to do so."

He heard the censure behind her mild tone and ducked his head. "How could I have let go?" he said softly, half to himself. "There was so much at stake."

"Your safety was at stake, man!"

Her tone was quite sharp and his eyes shot to hers. He lived in dread of the day she turned real anger upon him, having witnessed its devastating effects on others. But there was no anger in her golden eyes, only the memory and ache of her fear.

She sighed. "What did I tell you before we began? My warning was given for a good reason. Do not ignore it again." Then her expression softened. "I do not want to lose you, my friend, or see you maimed in my service. That, I could not bear."

She dropped her eyes, and he knew that the deep sorrow over the recent events of her life was still dangerously near the surface. He was shamed to think he had given her yet more pain, and resolved to heed her words in future.

"Did you find what you were looking for? I didn't think I'd been able to hang on long enough…."

The look of pride she gave him turned his bones to water. It shone through her limpid eyes and replaced the grief with hope.

"Oh, but you did, and I found the site of the Staff's creation. We were right, my friend. It was faint, for sure, and sunk far down in time, but I was just able to discern traces of the energy that was raised to fuse the silver and ceramic. You bought me the time to do that, Taran. I am very grateful to you. I owe you more than I can say."

Taran colored with embarrassment. Love and pride were still

shining in her sun-lightened eyes, and he had to look away.

Across the tiny fire, Ardoch smiled. "So, what now, lass? What's our next move?"

Sullyan transferred her attention to him, giving Taran time to compose himself. "We ride to Port Loxton, Ghyllan. For where we find the Baron, there, or somewhere close by, we will find Aeyron and Eadan. I did not have time to pinpoint the precise location of the circle Reen used to create the Staff, but I am sure that his acquisition of yet more silver means it will figure again in his plans. If that is so, then it cannot be far from the city. Perhaps he will lead us to it."

She eyed the Torlander thoughtfully and he cocked his head, waiting for the request that was clearly coming.

"What we really need is some idea of the Baron's movements since he returned alone to the Queen's side. I cannot enter the castle now, and even Taran would be viewed with suspicion. But you can move there freely. Would you be our eyes and ears in the castle and garrison? Could you make discreet inquiries and try to learn of the Baron's activities over the past few days? And, of course, there is another task, another question requiring an answer."

She had Ardoch's full attention. Taran wondered if he'd anticipated something like this. Was this why he'd ridden out with Bull?

"What question?" asked the Torlander.

Instead of answering, she asked a different question. "How well do you know the First Minister?"

He frowned at her apparent change of tack. "Levant? I know him reasonably well. I wouldn't go so far as to say we're friends, but I have spent some time with him. Where are you going with this?"

"Was he not Keeper of the Treasury before the Queen came to court?"

"Aye, that he was. Elias gave over control of the exchequer to Queen Sofira a year after their marriage. Said it would help her learn statecraft. Levant worked with her for a year or so, but since then she's run it herself. Why?"

Sullyan took another sip of fellan. "It is my belief that large amounts of gold changed hands when Reen acquired the original silver and ceramic that was used to form the Staff. Yet he could not possibly have supplied the gold himself. I believe that somewhere in the treasury records there will be a trace of that exchange— either in the accounts themselves, or in a lack of them."

Ardoch stirred as if he would protest, but Sullyan hurried on. "We need someone capable of searching the treasury records for these details, but it has to be without the Queen's or the clerks' knowledge. If I am to convince Elias of the Queen's involvement with Reen, I must have some proof of her treachery. Otherwise, the Baron alone will pay the price for their perfidy, and Queen Sofira will escape justice. I do not want to take the chance that she may work against her husband again."

Ardoch gaped at her. He clearly hadn't realized she meant to go this far. Taran was startled, too.

"You intend to impeach the *Queen*?" gasped Ardoch. "Don't you realize that's treason?"

"I already stand accused of treason, Ghyl."

Her voice was soft, and Taran, knowing how much this charge had hurt her, could only admire her stoicism.

She appealed to the Torlander, one hand spread toward him. "My suspicions are true, I know it. How can I leave Elias vulnerable, knowing what they have done? Will you do it? Will you speak to Levant for me? Or if you will not," she added, seeing his hesitation and taking it for reluctance, "will you at least bear a message to him and persuade him to see me? I will do my best to convince him myself. I would not put you in a position of peril."

Ardoch's lined face hardened. "I'm not frightened of Rendan Levant, lass," he growled. "And Elias has more sense than to cast away all his friends. Besides, I'm my own master these days." He shrugged. "Very well, I'll be your messenger and speak to Levant for you. But I'll not guarantee he'll do as you ask. He's a mind of his own, you ken."

"I thank you, Ghyllan," she murmured, a small smile on her lips.

He scowled at her, well aware she'd known all along he would not refuse her.

"Ach, lass." He spoke gruffly, climbing to his feet, preparing to extinguish the fire. "You could draw blood from a stone, you could."

She grinned, glancing sidelong out of merry eyes. "Do you know, Ardoch, I probably could."

The seriousness of her tone arrested Ardoch and he stared at her. Then he burst into peals of laughter.

In this lighter mood they broke camp, Taran feeling stronger by the minute as his own powers reduced the throbbing ache in his head. The more relaxed atmosphere of their success and purpose lent an air of anticipation to their venture.

All traces of their brief occupation erased, they mounted their horses and moved out toward the Loxton road in the afternoon sunshine, munching on the last of Ardoch's delicious Torland patties.

Chapter Twelve

Tad waited over an hour in the deserted College, amusing himself by calling Earth through the various rocks and gems in the Earth power study. Eventually he became bored, then cross, then worried by Ozella's failure to keep their appointment. Finally deciding the young lord didn't intend to show, Tad went in search of him.

He'd not seen Ozella around the barracks as he'd washed and changed out of his dirty riding clothes. Nor had there been any sign of him near the kitchens when Tad had gone to beg something to eat from his erstwhile colleagues. No one Tad knew around the Manor—and there were precious few left now—had seen anything of the young lord since earlier that morning.

Puzzled and more than a little concerned, Tad moved aside as Captain Parren, who gave him a stare that was even more morose and sullen than usual, led a group of militiamen past him on their way to relieve Colonel Vassa. Racking his brains, Tad tried to think where Ozella might have gone. Although they'd spent the morning with the horse, Tad knew that in times of stress Felika proved to be a source of comfort and a reminder of home to the young foreigner, so he decided to try the horse lines again.

His guess proved correct: Felika's stall was empty. Looking around the deserted yard, Tad went into one of the large barns that held supplies of hay and straw. A couple of the stable lads were there, turning the hay to keep it fresh. They told him Ozella had thrown saddle and bridle onto his horse and had ridden out like the very devil was on his heels more than an hour ago. Wondering what on earth could have possessed Ozella to do that when his dun had already been well exercised, Tad grew seriously worried.

Without seeking Solet's permission, he quickly saddled one of the messengers' mounts and rode out of the yard, tracking Ozella by the distinctive prints of Felika's small hooves. The trail led south, out into the extensive Manor grounds, and wasn't hard to follow. Tad was by no means an experienced tracker, but he could tell Ozella had been pushing his horse hard. He wouldn't keep that pace for long.

Alert for any signs, he trotted his bay along the track, watching his mount's reactions and straining his ears. He wished he were more skilled with his powers, but he'd not yet learned how to reach out with his consciousness toward another Artesan. He could hear a stronger person sending to him, but could not yet respond in kind. And Ozella was even less skilled, so Tad had to rely on his ordinary senses.

After around half an hour of searching, the bay suddenly flung up its head and gave a pealing whinny. To Tad's relief, that call was answered from somewhere up ahead. He let the bay's reins loosen and sent the horse onward. Giving a whicker, it cantered up the wooded track until the creamy yellow of Felika's hide could be seen against the trees. There was no sign of Ozella.

Tad rode up to the dun stallion and dismounted. Felika's reins had been hitched to a branch and his saddle removed. Tad could see where the sweaty patches on his back and neck had dried, testament to his earlier hard exercise. No attempt had been made to rub him down, although the saddle was resting on its pommel on the ground and the bit had been removed from the dun's mouth.

Looping his own horse's reins over the branch, Tad looked around.

He called Ozella's name, but there was no reply. Tad knew that a little stream ran through the woods nearby and, for want of a better direction, he headed toward it. He didn't call again. Ozella had come out here for a reason and might not want to be disturbed.

After ten minutes of quiet walking, Tad came upon the stream. It bisected his path and blocked his way. Upstream, it fell from a small waterfall into a deep, round pool before continuing on. Downstream, the way grew mossy and boggy. He turned upstream.

By the side of the gently gurgling waterfall, a few tumbled boulders brought down by some long ago flash flood formed ideal seats for watching the mesmeric flow of water and the bright kingfishers that flashed their jeweled plumage across the stream. It was here that Tad found Ozella sitting on a mossy boulder, his shoulders hunched with desolation, his head in his hands.

He didn't hear Tad's approach and the young lad faltered, unsure what to do. Was this grief or anger? Was it private? Would Ozella resent the intrusion, or would he welcome a friendly face? Their new-found friendship was too young and brittle to provide Tad with the insights he needed to answer these questions, but he'd come this far. He couldn't just leave.

Without speaking, Tad walked over to another of the mossy boulders and sat down, gazing across the stream. Ozella's reaction when he first heard Tad's footfalls was violent, but he subsided when he saw who it was.

Tad caught sight of Ozella's red-rimmed eyes and tear-streaked visage, and could sense the aura of a terrible dilemma emanating from him. It frightened the young lad and he found himself wondering whether he'd made a mistake in coming here alone. He didn't know very much about Ozella. The older youth made no move toward him and neither did he speak. The desperate hunger in his eyes, however, compelled Tad to break the silence.

"What is it, Ozella?" He kept his voice soft, still unwilling to look directly into the young lord's pain. "Do you want to tell me?"

"I can't."

The whisper was faint and full of agony. Tad wasn't sure at first that he'd heard it. He turned his head and looked at Ozella, reading the tearing indecision and desperate need within him.

"You've been unhappy for months," he said, still in an easy, conversational tone. "Can't you tell me why? Maybe I can help."

The strangled bark of mocking laughter was shockingly loud in the quiet woods. Tad's eyes widened in surprise. Ozella was weeping again, making no effort to conceal his grief.

"There's no help for me," he grated.

Tad frowned. "That can't be true. Nothing's that bad, surely?"

"Oh no?" Ozella's pain turned to anger, and his anger turned on the only target in view. "You have no idea!"

"Then tell me," ventured Tad. "Two minds are better than one. Perhaps you're too close to the problem to see the solution?"

Ozella's head came up, furious tears pouring down his face. "Too close?" He almost screamed the words. "You're damn right I'm too close! But there's nothing anyone can do about it. I'm trapped, boy, trapped! Don't you understand that?"

Tad didn't understand, of course. He could see Ozella's torment, but he couldn't believe it was as hopeless as Ozella thought.

"Who or what has trapped you?" he asked, trying to sound as non-confrontational as possible. At least Ozella was talking.

"I … can't say." Ozella dropped his eyes to his hands, the slim, dark fingers twisting feverishly.

Tad leaned forward. "There's no one here. We're well away from the Manor. No one will hear you. Not even the horses can hear you from here. And I won't say anything if you don't want me to. Maybe you're right. Maybe there's no cure for your trouble. But just talking can help, just sharing your pain and knowing someone else understands, that can be better than bottling it all up inside. Why not trust me? I'd have been your friend months ago if you had let me. I wanted to but you seemed so … self-contained, so cool, that I didn't like to approach you. But we get on fine, don't we? We could be really good friends. Why not give it a try?"

Tad watched the desperate need for companionship play across Ozella's features. He saw it chased away by doubt and fear, only to be replaced by a hopeless and despairing acceptance of his fate. But the young lad wasn't going to give up after coming so close.

"I'll swear, if you like," he said, holding Ozella's gaze. "I'll swear by anything you want. I'll swear by my powers as an Artesan; by my word as a cadet. I'll swear on my life. No one will ever hear of your troubles from me, unless you give me leave."

Tad's honesty and sincerity must have been obvious to Ozella. His embryonic Artesan senses could tell him Tad truly meant what he said. The last thread of Ozella's resistance dissolved and the tears came again.

"I'll hold you to your oath," he snapped, desperate hope flaring once again in his eyes. "If you betray me, Tad, I swear … I swear I'll kill you. This is more important than anything you've ever done, believe me. If you betray me, you'll be betraying something dearer to me than life itself."

Appalled by Ozella's fervor, Tad approached him and fell on his knees before the boulder on which he sat. He clasped one of the young lord's hands in his.

"I swear I will not betray your confidence."

Ozella snatched his hand away and stood, breathing heavily.

"Very well," he said in a low, harsh voice. "I'll tell you. I need to tell someone. I've needed to for a long while. But...." He fell silent and paced about the stream bank, still wrestling with his resolve. Tad merely re-seated himself and waited.

Ozella's pacing brought him closer to Tad again. Despite their isolation and the silence of the woods, he lowered his voice to a whisper and glanced about him before he said, in a voice racked by indecision and pain, "I'm being blackmailed."

Tad was shocked. "Blackmailed? By whom? With what? What for?"

Ozella slumped to the boulder as if the strings of his volition had suddenly been cut. Now that he had taken the first step, it all came out, his voice wooden with despair.

"It's Captain Parren. The bastard's kidnapped my sisters. He's holding them captive to enforce my silence and to make me gather information for him."

Tad's mouth dropped open. He'd never expected to hear anything like this. This was way out of his experience, and for a fleeting moment he heartily wished Ozella had refused to tell him. But Bull had charged him with finding out what was at the root of Ozella's unhappiness, and it looked like he'd succeeded. It wasn't his fault if the information was too much for him to handle. He would also have to somehow overcome the problem of his oath not to tell. However, Tad was nothing if not resourceful and had never yet balked at a challenge. He had offered Ozella his friendship; he wasn't going to back out now.

He whistled—a low sound of incredulity. "What information could Parren possibly want from you?"

Ozella's dull eyes met his. "Information concerning Artesans, and Major Tamsen in particular."

Tad paled. The first was incomprehensible—Parren had no

interest in Artesans—but the second made perfect sense. He was confused. "I think you'd better start at the beginning. Tell me all of it, don't leave anything out. Maybe I can help you after all."

Ozella shook his head in flat denial. "You can't." But the relief his actions had brought was too great. Tad knew he'd come too far to stop now. In a halting and emotional voice which sometimes filled with grief, he told Tad the whole sorry story.

The younger boy sat dumbfounded through it all. When Ozella finally lapsed into exhausted silence, his head cradled in his hands, Tad found that the tale stretched his credulity just that little bit too far.

"Hold on," he said. "This just doesn't ring true. It just can't be."

Ozella leaped to his feet, clearly fearing betrayal. "Are you calling me a liar?" he snarled, balling his fists.

Tad belatedly realized how his words had sounded. "No, no, of course not. That's not what I meant. Sit down, Ozella, let's talk this through."

Ozella subsided, hurt suspicion still haunting his eyes. Tad ignored it and carried on.

"I don't doubt for one minute that what you've told me is the truth. But I know how things work around here better than you do, and I know Captain Parren, and I can tell you that what he said just isn't possible. First, he doesn't have any men of his own. He only commands one of Colonel Vassa's companies, so he can't possibly be giving anyone orders concerning your sisters. Second, he only leaves the Manor on the King's business, so he can't possibly have kidnapped them."

Ozella goggled at him. "But he has their rings!" he cried, anguish rasping his throat. "Stop saying 'can't'. I've *seen* them."

"Oh, I've no doubt *someone* is holding them," asserted Tad

grimly, "it just isn't Parren. Hush, Ozella, let me think a minute."

The young lad was silent a while, musing over what he had heard. Ozella sat in his own despair, holding his head in his hands. Eventually, Tad's eyes refocused and he sat straighter with an air of decision.

"All right," he said, drawing the foreign lord's eyes, "this is what I think, for what it's worth. It seems to me that there're two separate issues here. When Captain Parren first told you to get Colonel Sullyan to take you on that diplomatic trip to Andaryon, he said to you '*we* want to hear every arrangement that is made.' Is that right? Were those his exact words?"

Ozella frowned. "As near as I can remember, yes."

Tad nodded. "Then that fits. And after that, after you'd told him what you'd heard during that trip, you had no more instructions from him for … how long?"

Ozella shrugged. "A couple of days. I was hoping by then he'd tell me I'd done what he wanted and that he was letting my sisters go."

"No, he wouldn't have done that."

Ozella's head came up, suspicion and indignation in his eyes. "What do you mean? What do you know about it?"

Tad regarded him with some pity. Ozella had obviously been in too much distress to work it out for himself.

"I think you probably had done what they initially wanted," he said, trying not to sound patronizing, "but if they'd released your sisters then, what would have stopped you from running to the General or the King with your story? Don't you see? They have to hold your sisters until whatever they're planning has happened. What were your next instructions?"

Ozella sighed. "He told me I had to befriend you. He said he wanted information about Major Tamsen and the other Artesans."

Tad's eyes widened at the coincidence, and he decided not to tell Ozella about Bull's identical instructions to him. Ozella was brittle enough already and their trust too new to withstand such a knock. Tad did genuinely like Ozella, but Ozella might not believe it if Tad told him of Bull's request. He wisely stuck to the problem at hand.

"He asked about Major Tamsen specifically? No one else?"

"He didn't mention anyone else by name. Just Artesans in general."

"That sounds much more like Parren." Noting the beginnings of interest in Ozella's despondent gaze, Tad elaborated. "Parren's hated both Major Tamsen and Colonel Sullyan for years. I don't know all the reasons behind it, but I do know he's insanely jealous of them. He'd do anything to harm them. He must have laughed himself sick when the King cast the Colonel out."

Tad fell silent, processing this new information. Tapping his chin thoughtfully, he continued. "All right, Ozella, this is what I think. Originally, when Parren first began to blackmail you, he was taking orders from someone else. Someone with the power and resources to kidnap your sisters and hold them to ransom. Trust me, there's no way Parren could have done that himself. But this latest plan, asking you to gather information from me about Major Tamsen, well, that's pure Parren. I think he's acting on his own now."

Ozella's brow furrowed. "So what does that mean for my sisters? Does he control their fate or not? Are they even still alive?"

Tad shook his head slowly. "We have no way of knowing. But I think we can assume they are. Parren has to have been passing messages to whoever took them, and he could still be doing that." A sudden thought struck him. "I wonder if he's been using the

King's runner service?"

An idea was taking shape in his mind, and he stared full and frankly at Ozella. "You know, you really do have to tell someone about this. It's very important stuff."

Ozella exploded. "No! You promised. I *can't* tell anyone else, it's too dangerous. I've taken a huge risk telling you. Who knows what will happen to Rozlin and Surine if Parren finds out? You'd better keep your promise, Tad, or it'll go hard with you."

Tad heard the desperation in the older youth's voice. He was in two minds about it himself. He understood Ozella's fear, but he also realized just how important this discovery could be.

"All right, all right," he soothed, "I won't tell. But do you realize what this means? It means we have a traitor in our midst—here, at the Manor. Someone who's been passing vital information to our enemy, information that could destroy all of us, even the King. Think about it! What if the person Parren's been reporting to is the one who made that terrible Staff? If it is and we keep silent, then we, personally and as Artesans, are helping him fulfill his plans against us."

Ozella's expression was frozen and Tad tried once more. "Please listen! Why don't you talk to Bull? He's discreet and very sensible. He won't go running to the King or the General unless he thinks it's serious, and he might be able to do something about Parren so he can't inform the people who are holding your sisters."

Tad could see it was no use. Ozella was badly frightened. The relief he'd shown at having a confidante had faded, replaced by the terrible fear he'd just signed his sisters' death warrants. Tad gasped as Ozella stood and drew his sword.

Tad stared at the naked blade with trepidation. Had he pushed Ozella too far?

Ozella's voice was harsh and unrecognizable as he said, "I

want you to swear."

Tad tried to remain calm. "I already have."

Ozella shook his head. "In blood." He hissed as he drew the flat of his palm across the tip of his sword, nicking the flesh. "Do it."

Tad saw the fanatical light in Ozella's almond eyes. He was trapped now and he knew it. "Oh, very well," he sighed, "but it's not necessary."

Ozella snarled as he flourished the blade under Tad's nose. "*Do it!*"

Tad reached out and drew his own palm across the sword's point. He gave a little gasp as the blood seeped forth. Ozella clasped his bleeding hand to Tad's.

"Now swear never to breathe a word of this to a living soul!" he growled, his face too close to Tad's.

Tad could feel the tremble of Ozella's tortured psyche. "I so swear."

Apparently satisfied, the foreign lord released Tad's hand, wiping the blood from his own on his breeches as he re-sheathed his sword. Then he collapsed back onto the boulder.

Tad let him be for a while and sat sucking at the small wound in his hand until the bleeding stopped. He couldn't yet control his life force well enough to stem bleeding. Instead, he used it to steady himself to make his next suggestion.

"Ozella." He spoke softly. He saw the flicker of the youth's eyes, but received no other sign of acknowledgement. He carried on regardless. "If we can't go to anyone else with this, then it's down to us. We can't let Parren get away with it. We can't sit back and let him, or whoever he's working for, destroy everything that Artesans and King Elias have achieved these past few years. And you can't just wait for him to kill your sisters."

Ozella's head snapped up again, fury in his eyes.

"You surely can't believe they'd be released alive?" Tad's expression was quietly sympathetic.

Ozella's face crumpled. Tad watched him sob. Words would have been useless, and physical contact no help. Ozella needed to find his own balance if they were going to make a difference.

After a while, Tad said, "I do have the beginnings of a plan, if you're interested."

Ozella's weeping eased and he raised a pale and red-eyed face. "What plan?" His voice held no hope.

Tad came closer and crouched down in front of him. "If we can find some evidence that Parren's mixed up in all this, something Parren can't refute, it'll give us something to work with. You said you didn't go to someone straight away when it started because it would have been your word against his. So let's find something to change that."

Ozella's gaze remained fixed on Tad's face. Tad took this as encouragement.

"If Parren's been sending messages, he's probably also been receiving them. And if he's been passing information, he may well have been paid for it. Parren never does anything unless there's a reward involved. Let's search his room. I'll bet there'll be something there to prove he's involved in this plot. And you never know; he might even know who's behind the kidnap of the Princes. Just think, Ozella, we might be able to find the Princes, avert the war, and save your sisters all at the same time! What do you say?"

Ozella stayed silent, but Tad could see the thoughts roiling through his mind. Was he assessing the risks? Surely he knew that at least some of what Tad said made sense? And Ozella only had two choices: to do Parren's bidding and let his sisters languish, or take action to rescue them himself. And if Parren—or whoever really had his sisters—wasn't intending to free them anyway, what did he have to lose?

Come on, Ozella, urged Tad silently, *let's* do *something!*

Ozella took a deep breath. "All right, but we'll have to be very careful." Tad hid an excited smile as Ozella carried on. "Parren's no fool. Sit down and tell me what you know about him, about his habits and his routine, and we'll see what kind of plan we can come up with."

✢ ✢ ✢ ✢ ✢

By the time Sullyan and her two companions reached the outskirts of Loxton Forest, it was getting dark. There was a half-moon, but it didn't give much light, and they entered beneath the trees cautiously, mindful of the ever-present footpads which haunted the forest depths. Now that the garrison had been emptied of King's Guard, the local thieves and cutthroats would be bolder. It was unlikely that three well-armed travelers would be attacked, but nevertheless they rode alert, ready for the slightest hint of danger.

Sullyan had retained her sense of purpose throughout the journey, and Taran was relieved to see she was much more her old self. The vindication she had found at the stone circle had clearly renewed her faith in herself, and it gladdened his heart.

They were still a couple of miles from the city walls when Ardoch turned to Sullyan.

"Have you anywhere in mind to spend the night, lass? I take it you don't intend to start any searches before the morrow."

Sullyan shook her head. "No, a night's rest and a hot meal will do us all good. Can you recommend an inn where we will not be too obvious? Preferably one near the city walls."

"I can do better than that, lass. I've a house you can use. It's small and I don't stay there often, but it's right up against the walls and not too far from the Forest Gate. It'll be aired and fresh for sure. I have a housekeeper who takes care of it for me. She'll not be there now. She only comes in twice a week to tidy and such like. We can pick up fresh food for supper on the way."

Sullyan reached out and laid a hand on his arm. "I thank you, Ghyl. The house sounds perfect. Are you sure we will not be remarked? I would not like to be the source of gossip about you."

Ardoch grinned, his teeth flashing in the dull gleam of the moon. "Ach, lass, a bit of gossip wouldn't worry me!"

Taran's heart fell at their jesting, remembering the gossip his last visit here had engendered. But the tawny-haired woman by his side showed no discomfiture at Ardoch's banter, and they rode on toward the city.

They entered the city by the Forest Gate, which was barred and guarded after dark. The sentry recognized and acknowledged Ardoch with no hint of suspicion, and took no undue notice of Sullyan's cloaked figure. The old Torlander's assurances concerning his companions were easily accepted. It seemed that the guards were not on high alert after all, and Taran could see that this concerned Sullyan. Surely the abduction of the King's son, purportedly by demons, would have produced more wariness than this? She remarked upon it to Ardoch, who looked grim.

"Yon guard was one of the Baron's men." The look he gave her was full of meaning.

She straightened stiffly and glanced behind her. No wonder he hadn't recognized her, thought Taran. Sullyan frowned, watching the guard as he returned to his hut after barring the gate behind them.

"I'll wager your man has offered some of his own guards to swell those left at the garrison," said the swordmaster. "I can find out from Denny or Levant tomorrow."

Sullyan nodded, her mouth a grim line as she assimilated the implications of such a generous offer.

They followed Ardoch through the mainly empty streets toward his house. It was just beyond the merchants' quarter to the east of the gate, set among many just like it against the outer wall. It was a two-story building, the lower half made of the local stone, the upper story of white plaster set between a wood beam framework. There was a livery stable close by, and here they left the horses in the capable hands of the stable lads.

Ardoch let them into the small house, lighting a taper from the street lamp outside and kindling oil lamps as he went. The dwelling had but two rooms on the ground floor: a small cooking room and a larger living room with comfortable seating. While Taran took their packs to the sleeping rooms upstairs, Sullyan used her skills to call Fire to the ready-laid hearth in the cooking area. Ardoch took himself off to see what food he could procure and soon came back with the makings of a stew. Sullyan had already boiled water, and she and Taran were on their second helping of fellan by the time the Torlander returned.

Once replete, they sat at their ease in Ardoch's comfortable chairs, drinking fellan and watching the progress of the half-moon across the dark summer sky. Ardoch produced a bottle of what he called "tarn-liquor," a grain spirit distilled through the characteristic brown waters of the Torland tarns. Taran was happy to try some, finding it very different in taste to Bull's heavier firewater brandy. Ardoch claimed his poison was far superior to Bull's, but Taran could appreciate the merits of both. Sullyan, as usual, eschewed the drink.

They discussed their plans for the next day. Ardoch was to try to get an appointment with Lord Levant, to see if he could persuade him to check the treasury records. Ardoch would have to tell Levant some of their suspicions, but Sullyan warned him against revealing she was in the city unless the minister refused to see him. After that, the Torlander would go to the garrison and see what gossip he could glean from the few men left to guard the city.

Taran had been wondering what his part was to be, and he soon found out. Sullyan asked him to wander about the city itself and listen to the populace. She was keen to know what Loxton's inhabitants were saying about the Baron, the war, the demon raids, and Eadan's abduction. She also advised the Adept to visit the dockside taverns, as trade-sailors were notorious for picking up and spreading gossip. She cautioned him against going anywhere near the castle or the taverns adjacent to its walls, as the garrison swordsmen often used these and she didn't want him recognized. Denny and his men would know Taran on sight. Sullyan bade him be wary.

Ardoch placed his empty glass on the table. "And what about you, lassie? What do you intend to do on the morrow?"

She stared into her half-empty fellan mug, her voice low as she said, "I intend to visit the Baron's estate to see if I can pinpoint the site of the Staff's creation. He has to have secreted that spellsilver somewhere close, especially if, as I believe, he intends to use the Earth power again. Maybe there will be signs of preparation at the site which will give me a clue to his ultimate purpose."

Ardoch and Taran shared a look.

"Is that wise, lass? Shouldn't you wait until one of us can go with you?"

She shook her head. "I will be better alone. It will be easier to remain hidden. Have no fear, I do not intend to reveal myself."

She glanced sharply at him. "It bothers me that there was no obvious sign of heightened awareness at the gate. I would be interested to know what extra protection, if any, is being provided for the Princess Seline in the aftermath of her brother's abduction. Can you find out at the castle for me tomorrow? Discreetly?"

Ardoch nodded. "I'll do what I can."

Their discussions over, they went to their rest. Taran unrolled his blankets on the floor of Ardoch's room, while Sullyan took the small bed in the guest room. Taran could only surmise what her thoughts were. Would she comfort herself with a brief contact with Bull before she slept? Knowing that Elias was likely to begin his assault on the denizens of Andaryon the next day lent even more urgency to her already belated rescue mission. And Taran couldn't begin to imagine what condition Prince Aeyron might be in by now, if indeed he was still alive. He more than half expected they would find his corpse if they found anything at all, but he knew Sullyan's love for and duty to Pharikian wouldn't let her lose hope completely.

His soul uneasy, he laid himself to sleep.

Chapter Thirteen

The moon had long since set over the Andaryan valley where Elias had his field camp, and dawn was only an hour away. Robin watched Valustin pace around the small tent, impatient for his scouts to report.

One of Robin's main concerns about using this valley as a bridgehead was that Anjer would also recognize its suitability and, once he knew where they were, would attempt to surround them and pin them within it, effectively nullifying their threat. Against this possibility, Valustin had posted sentries at all the valley's access points, and had also sent scouts out into the surrounding hills, from where they would see Anjer's forces approaching long before they could get into controlling positions.

He had also sent one such group toward the town Elias had designated as his first objective.

Although Robin had a good working knowledge of the Andaryan countryside, he had never been to the town Elias had chosen. They needed to know what defenses their forces were likely to meet as they approached. They all knew the King was anxious to leave the valley and begin the assault, and so Valustin awaited his scouts' return with barely-concealed frustration.

Soon, Robin heard the sentries challenging the returning scouts. He left the tent with Valustin and went to meet their leader, who came forward to report. General Blaine and the King also emerged from their tent to hear what the scouts had discovered.

The scout leaped from his horse and saluted Valustin, giving his news without preamble.

"The town isn't fortified, Captain, and there's no sign of organized resistance. It's quiet enough. None of the townspeople were about when we left. I would say they've been alerted to the possibility of action, and are keeping to their homes just in case."

Valustin frowned. "You saw no sign of enemy forces at all? You had the men search the entire area?"

"As well as we could, sir. There's a dense wood a mile to the east of the town. As far as we could tell, there's no threat there. If we approach from the south, we should have fair warning even if there is a force concealed within those woods. And the town itself would give us cover, provided we can secure it before we're attacked."

Valustin turned to Blaine. "What do you think, sir? It sounds as if our plan should work."

Blaine nodded, not waiting for the King's approval. "Rouse the camp, Captain. The sooner we get there, the more the darkness will aid us. It'll be light in an hour. I want this town subdued and under our control as soon as possible, and with as little bloodshed as we can manage. Get to it!"

Valustin had the junior officers rouse the camp. The men had been expecting it, and were ready to ride in short order. He still had other scouts that had not yet returned, but they knew where their fellows were headed and would follow on to the town if they hadn't arrived by the time the valley was vacated.

Leaving a small unit of swordsmen to guard the healers and other support workers who were staying behind with the tents of the field infirmary, the men formed their companies and began to move out. Robin saw Cal at the head of his two hundred and fifty men, and felt profoundly glad that Hanan had forbidden Rienne from coming. Cal couldn't have concentrated if she'd been left here. Once the town was secured, the healers and other workers would move up to join them. The healers would occupy some suitable building within the walls and set up their infirmary. Until then they would stay within the valley, hopefully unmolested. After all, they posed no threat to the Andaryans.

The vacating of the valley progressed smoothly. Elias and Blaine rode sandwiched between the Manor's and Valustin's forces. Gentle slopes led them up and over the rim of the valley as they rode north, giving way to broad grasslands dotted with trees and shrubs. Nearer their objective they encountered farmlands, streams, and cattle pasture, none of which impeded their progress.

As they advanced, Valustin and Blaine briefed the other captains and junior officers on the final approach and the method by which they intended to take the town. Even before the scouts' report they had not been expecting much in the way of fierce resistance, as this small town was basically a farming and trading center which produced food and shipped it to the Citadel. It would be populated mainly by farm workers and merchants, none of whom would have received more than rudimentary military training, if any. They would, of course, attempt to defend their homes, but it was Blaine's plan to surround the place and force their surrender, rather than sack it. He meant to send a statement of intent to the Citadel, not wantonly massacre the Hierarch's people.

Robin knew Elias didn't much care at this point. He wanted the town taken by the swiftest possible means, giving no quarter, but Valustin and the other captains heard Blaine's tacit warning and took heed. None of them had the stomach for needless violence, and were well aware that the townsfolk were innocent of any wrongdoing.

The light was increasing as they approached the town, and the scouts reported more in the way of movement among the houses. They had obviously been seen, and preparations were being made. The population was probably well under a thousand, many of whom would be women and children, and as Andaryan women didn't bear arms, they would be no threat. Valustin gave the captains their orders, and the forces split up to surround the town. Blaine held an impatient Elias well back from the action, although the King had his sword drawn in his hand.

At a prearranged horn signal, the companies charged the town. The scouts had been correct; there was little in the way of resistance. Robin realized Anjer couldn't possibly have sent men to defend each town, even if he had guessed which direction Elias's forces would take.

After a couple of hours, it was over. The townsfolk had immediately seen they stood no chance, and so no lives had been lost. There had been a few minor skirmishes with villagers furious at this cavalier and undeserved treatment, but mainly it was a bloodless coup. Elias and Blaine established themselves in one of the more comfortable council buildings and prepared to meet with the town's elders. Robin witnessed the meeting.

Four of them came, trepidation evident in their slit-pupilled eyes. Despite their fear they were angry, and neglected to speak respectfully to their new overlord. Indeed, they went so far as to demand he leave their town forthwith. Not prepared to deal sympathetically with these overbearing and disrespectful elders, Elias had them summarily thrown into the nearest strongroom and locked away, giving orders to the sentries to keep at bay all other petitioners.

Blaine just shook his head and sighed.

Once all was secure, Robin accompanied Valustin on his rounds of the town with some of the men, learning the street layout, looking for defensible places and vulnerable spots. Valustin congratulated his captains on an efficient and well-executed takeover. He would now have to send men to scout the area between this town and their next target.

Elias's plan, formulated with the aid of Robin's local knowledge, was to annex and hold three of the most important food-producing towns on this side of the Citadel. Once he had them under his control, the King intended to demand a response from the Citadel, namely the return of his son. If he didn't get what he wanted, he would fire the captured towns. Then, if the Citadel still refused to treat with him or return his son, he would fire the entire crop-producing countryside between those towns, thus destroying a sizeable section of the Citadel's vital food resources. It was a simple and effective plan.

When the tour was over, Robin was satisfied by what he saw. So far, the townspeople were being sensible. He didn't like to think of this simple, peaceful town being put to the torch, and knew he would have its demise on his conscience should Elias carry out his threat. He sighed deeply and climbed a bell tower to look out over the surrounding countryside. Joining the sentries already there, he was discussing the duty rota with them when one of the men spotted something and gave a shout. Shading his eyes against the sun, which was rising toward noon, Robin made out a small group of scouts making for the town at a gallop. Behind them, some way off yet through the woods to the west, he thought he could see the glint of sunlight on metal.

Descending the tower steps swiftly, he sprang for Torka's broad back and made his way to the town gates. Valustin was already there, and sent another group of men to support the scouts should they need it. Yet they were unpursued and soon gained the safety of the town, where he heard their news. He immediately sent them to Elias and Blaine.

One of the scouts, an old hand named Jona, told Elias what his group had seen. A large force of demons under the Hierarch's standard was approaching unhurriedly through the trees to the west. Elias and Blaine both looked to Robin at this news, although he could only make guesses.

"I imagine they'll be led by Lord General Anjer, your Majesty, as General Ephan usually commands the Citadel's defenses. Both men are able and experienced commanders."

Elias huffed, unimpressed. "And what do you suppose this Anjer's plans are?"

Robin didn't hesitate. "To prevent us from advancing farther and annexing more territory. I would say he'll attempt to surround us and pen us here, or drive us out and away from the towns."

Elias turned back to the scout. "Could you estimate his numbers?"

Jona shook his head. "No, your Majesty. The woods are very dense to the west and there were not enough of us. I took the decision to warn you as soon as possible rather than stay and count heads."

"Your Majesty," put in Robin, "if the Lord General has come directly from the Citadel, leaving behind an adequate defensive force, then I'd estimate he has four to five thousand men at his disposal. He would need to raise the Hierarch's reserves to field many more than that."

Blaine and Elias conferred briefly. Their numbers were fairly evenly matched if Robin was correct. Blaine turned to Valustin.

"Captain, leave an adequate force behind to ensure the town does not rise against our backs, and move the rest of the men out to the west so we are not trapped here. I would meet Anjer's forces with room to maneuver."

The Captain saluted and went to do the General's bidding.

✤ ✤ ✤ ✤ ✤

Riding with his honor guard ahead of Anjer's main body of troops, Marik advanced upon the town. He could see the masses of Elias's men drawn up outside the walls, and fervently hoped the townspeople had followed the advice Anjer had sent them some days ago. They were totally innocent in all of this, and it was now up to Marik to secure their release. At least, he thought, the Andaryans' show of force had drawn Elias's men from among the shops and houses of the town. If he should fail in this mission and the two sides fought, perhaps the town would escape the worst of the conflict. Then he realized how vain that hope was. Elias was bound to use the town both as cover for his men and as a threat to Anjer. The Albian King would know the Andaryans wouldn't want to see it destroyed.

He glanced across at Norkis, riding a showy, high-stepping black horse beside him. The boy was wearing his purple and gold ceremonial tabard and appeared very young and nervous. He was gripping the shaft of the standard he bore as if he feared he would drop it, even though the heel of the shaft was snugged within the leather sheath attached to his saddle for the purpose. The large, white-bordered green flag of truce snapped and streamed in the breeze over Norkis's shoulder.

Marik smiled to reassure the boy. "Don't worry so, Norkis. You're doing just fine. Look, there's a party coming to meet us. Keep your eyes ahead and don't react to anything they say. Just announce us and leave the rest to me." He turned to the scowling Commander riding at his other shoulder. "That goes for you too,

Barrin. I want you to keep your temper today. Don't forget that this is a parley, not a council of war. We're here to prevent bloodshed, if we can, not bandy insults with Elias."

Barrin looked stung by Marik's words, but the Duke knew they were justified. The Commander had already given his feelings away by failing to suppress a hiss of outrage at the sight of the well-armed party riding to confront them. Barrin positively bristled with indignation, and Marik could scarcely blame him. Why were the Albians carrying weapons? Couldn't they see the flag of truce? They were the aggressors here, not Marik's people. Their arrogance inflamed Barrin, and Marik knew he felt demeaned by his inclusion in this party of peace. Yet he subsided under Marik's unrelenting stare and muttered, "Yes, your Grace."

Sighing, Marik turned his attention to the commander of the approaching party, trying to control the trip-hammer of his heart.

The humans reined to a halt before him, and Marik saluted their leader in the Andaryan style. The commander returned his own style of salute, but in a rather more casual manner. Marik narrowed his eyes. The Albian commander sat in silence, waiting for Marik to announce his purpose, but this was a breach of etiquette as they were on Andaryan soil. Marik pursed his lips, determined not to be rattled.

"Norkis, if you please," he prompted gently. The young page swallowed, and Marik guessed he'd been expecting to answer the greeting of the human commander. He would have to improvise now.

He nudged his black two steps ahead of the Duke's horse, and cleared his throat.

"May I present his Grace the Lord Marik, Duke of Kymer and Cardon, Regent to the Throne of Andaryon, and Heir Elect to his Majesty the Hierarch, Timar Pharikian. We come under flag of truce to request a parley with King Elias of Albia."

Marik could not suppress a start of surprise at Norkis's inclusion of the title Heir Elect. He hadn't expected to hear it, but he knew Norkis was right. In Aeyron's absence, but lacking proof of his death, as second in line to the Throne, Marik *was* Heir Elect. Although saddened by the reminder of this fact, he silently applauded Norkis for doing his homework. Baron Gaslek had probably coached the boy in his speech.

The commander of the human troops inclined his head, barely enough to avoid insult. Marik's eyes tightened. He had hoped he might know the leader of this party, but he didn't recognize any of the men. If they had been familiar, it might have made matters easier between them. He suddenly wondered whether their unfamiliarity was a deliberate act.

"My Lord Duke," the commander said, "I am Captain Benett of the King's Guard. What message shall I bear King Elias?"

This also was only barely polite, and not the proper form at all. Marik could feel Barrin seething beside him and fervently hoped the man would hold down his temper.

"Captain," replied Marik, trying for the same casual tone the human had used, "I would speak with his Majesty, King Elias. As you see, we come under flag of truce. There are matters which should be discussed between us of mutual benefit to both our realms. We request audience."

A small smile creased the captain's lips as he acknowledged Marik's use of his own tactics. He inclined his head once again. "I will so inform his Majesty."

With no forewarning, he barked an order to his men to remain in position blocking Marik's path, then he wheeled his mount and galloped back to the King, who was waiting among the companies drawn up before the town.

Barrin very nearly lost control. Marik could see the man's fury in the white knuckles of the hands that held the reins. Had Barrin been wearing his sword, one hand would have been on the hilt. Marik tried to catch his eye to subdue him, but Barrin refused to look his way. Instead, Marik cast a quick smile at the increasingly nervous Norkis, and was pleased to see the boy respond. They mustn't allow these uncouth humans to unsettle them.

Presently, the captain returned. Marik could see Elias and a few other men dismounting, a space being cleared about them. The human forces only withdrew far enough to form a wide C around their King, and it was all too obvious that the arms of their formation could be drawn together swiftly at need, enclosing the parley party completely.

Marik didn't like this, but he had no choice. He'd made up his mind to speak with Elias and he wasn't going to back down now. He faced Benett squarely as the man said, "King Elias will speak with you. You may approach with your flag bearer and one other."

Marik gaped involuntarily and Barrin's indrawn breath was loud in the still air. "You can't possibly expect his Grace to go forward with no honor guard!"

Captain Benett stared unfeelingly at the demon commander and his voice was flat. "Those are the King's orders. They are the terms on which he will parley. Accede or ride away."

Marik placed a restraining hand on Barrin's trembling arm. He tried for a calm he didn't really feel. "Commander, I will be safe. We are under flag of truce. King Elias will not violate that. And besides, you will come with me. Ride ahead of us, Norkis. The rest of you, await me here."

He heard the men's disapproving mutters, but they stayed where they were as Marik rode forward behind Norkis, Barrin by his side. Captain Benett's men surrounded them. They covered the distance to the King in silence, and Marik halted them when they were just outside the pincer-like arms of the human formation. Benett tried to urge them closer, but Marik refused. He gestured to Norkis and Barrin, and they dismounted.

With a studied, casual motion, Marik flicked the reins of his warhorse at Benett, who caught them by reflex. The horse had been skittish enough before, sensing Marik's nervousness, and Marik had deliberately aggravated this as he rode toward Elias. The resulting head-tossing, snorting, and side-stepping of the nervous beast occupied Benett long enough for Marik to approach Elias unhindered by his unwanted escort.

Benett recovered swiftly and another of his men took charge of the three Andaryan mounts. The Captain strode past Marik just in time. He halted in front of King Elias and bowed low.

"Your Majesty, may I present the demon envoy, his Grace Lord Marik, Duke of Kymer and Cardon."

Elias watched Marik with hawk-like concentration. He stood easily upon the grass, his hands on his hips. He was flanked by General Blaine and Robin, and Marik was interested to note that Robin could meet neither his eyes nor Barrin's. The Duke was pleased that not everyone in this invading force shared Elias's resolve.

With a flourish, and ignoring Benett's insult in terming them "demons," Marik bowed respectfully to Elias, also turning to include Blaine, whom he knew only by sight, and Robin.

"Greetings, your Majesty, and to you, General Blaine. Major Tamsen, it is good to see you again."

Robin had the grace to color under Marik's friendly greeting. The Duke could only imagine what was going through the young man's mind. Images of their joint rescue of Sullyan from Rykan's dungeon were flashing through his own. He had thought the friendship that had grown between them since that day, cemented by a deep love of the same woman, was unshakable, and he suddenly felt incredibly sad.

"Your Majesty," he continued, "allow me to introduce my companions. On my right is Commander Barrin, leader of the Hierarch's Velletian Guard, and on my left is Senior Palace Page Norkis, who graciously consented to be my standard bearer today. As you see, we come under flag of truce with the earnest intention of resolving this unnecessary conflict between us. Will you hear us?"

Elias's piercing blue gaze flicked dismissively across Barrin and Norkis before fastening unblinkingly on the Duke. Marik thought the King's face appeared strained, and his eyes certainly held a hint of unnatural emotions. He wondered if he was catching a glimpse of the instability Sullyan had mentioned.

Elias stared hotly at Marik. "The only thing I want to hear, my Lord Duke, is that you intend to return my son. Immediately. Otherwise, your petition is purposeless."

Marik heard the unbending steel in the King's tone. He hardened his will but replied calmly. "And will you, your Majesty, return to us Prince Aeyron?"

Elias's face turned purple and his eyes bulged. "We are not holding Prince Aeyron! What would I possibly want with him? His abduction was none of our doing. How dare you accuse us of that?"

"Likewise," put in Marik before the furious Elias could continue, "we had no motive for abducting your son. He is not here, your Majesty. You have my sworn word on that. The Hierarch would not stoop so low. You and he are trade partners, and we do not treat our allies so falsely."

Elias's scowl deepened at Marik's implied criticism. "And yet you accuse us of holding Prince Aeyron."

Marik held up a calming hand. "I merely used that as an example. You do not hold Prince Aeyron. We know that. But neither do we hold your son. It is our common enemy who has set us at each other's throats like this and caused us to mistrust each other. We should be working together to find the Princes and their abductor, not turning on each other and threatening innocents."

"Oh, very convenient," snarled Elias. "You would have me slink away with my tail between my legs, and send me off on a wild boar chase over Albia when all along I know my son is here. He was taken by *demons*, my Lord Duke, not humans. Demons invaded my castle. Demons took my son from his nursemaids and rode off with him. Demons who left behind a parchment with your precious Hierarch's seal on the bottom. 'Fair trade' it said, fair trade for the abduction of Prince Aeyron. How do you explain *that*, my Lord? And if you're all so innocent, where is your precious Hierarch? Why does he send *you* here to do his horse-trading for him? I'll tell you why—it's because he can't face me, because he knows I'll see the truth. Send *him* out here with his apologies and then I might listen!"

Marik had retreated a step at the strength of Elias's spleen. The King was almost spitting with rage, and Marik instinctively knew his cause was lost. Nevertheless, he gave it one last try.

Softly, he said, "The Hierarch is still prostrate with grief, your Majesty. He knows his beloved son and only Heir has been severely maimed, and fears he has even been killed."

Marik let his own sorrow color his words, hoping to breach Elias's overwhelming and controlling anguish. Both Norkis and Barrin had turned pale, and there were tears in the young page's eyes.

Marik went on. "He received proof that Prince Aeyron had been taken in the form of a box containing the Prince's royal signet ring, unfortunately still around the finger that had borne it. And there was also a letter, your Majesty. A ransom note signed with your seal."

Elias was silent. Marik watched him carefully, berating himself for not having had the foresight to bring the parchment in question. Had the similarities between the two abductions dawned on the King? Was he even now reconsidering his position? Would he be prepared to listen further to Marik's reasoning?

He noted the expressions on Robin and General Blaine's faces. Both looked as though they were hoping the same thing. Had Sullyan argued a similar case? Would hearing the same argument from two sources trigger doubt in Elias's mind? There was nothing any of them could do to bring this about. They could only hope and wait.

For a moment, the King's resolve hung on a knife edge. Marik could see it. Elias was raging with grief inside, wanting desperately to strike out, to cause hurt to those who had taken his son. Had Marik's calm and non-confrontational manner struck a chord within Elias, worming through the fog of grief obscuring his reason? Marik was sure he could sense the rational part of Elias's mind telling him there was something to what the Duke was saying. He held his breath.

Elias raised his eyes to the Duke and Marik's heart lurched. He was going to stand his men down, move them back, and give the party more space so they could sit and discuss this in comfort! He could almost hear the words forming on Elias's lips. Then, on the King's other side, Robin stiffened and gasped, causing them all to turn their heads to see what had caught the Major's attention. At the same moment someone blew stridently on a horn, sounding the compelling call to horse, the alarm of attack.

Reacting instantly, Barrin grabbed Marik's and Norkis's arms and sent them forcefully stumbling toward their horses. Around the western edge of the town came galloping a small party of Albians, men who had probably been instructed to cover the rear of their forces in case of Andaryan attack from that direction.

And pursuing them—impossibly—crossbows and shortbows thumping, charged a large force of mounted Andaryans.

Marik heard Robin's shout even as he struggled to mount his curveting horse. "Form up, form up! Close and protect the King!"

The Duke saw Elias's murderous expression as he wrenched his stallion's head around to glare furiously after Marik.

"You lying, treacherous bastard!" the King roared as Barrin's men, taking full advantage of the ensuing confusion, wrestled their horses from Benett's men and galloped furiously for their escort which was thundering to meet them, swords drawn. "I knew we couldn't trust you, hiding behind children and speaking your smooth, deceiving lies! Well, you tell your skulking Hierarch that I hope his son rots in hell. I'll see you pay dearly for this."

Then the King was surrounded by his men as they wheeled to face their attackers. The crossbows and shortbows were silent now, but the noise of steel on steel was loud in the morning air. The fighting was joined in earnest.

Marik stared frantically at Barrin as they sped away among their escort, mercifully unpursued as the humans, aware of the presence of Anjer's forces somewhere behind Marik's party, concentrated on protecting their King.

"Who the Void were they, Barrin? Where did they come from?"

Barrin had no answer and didn't reply as they galloped madly back toward the security of Anjer's men. The Lord General had halted his forces well back among the trees and was sitting his warhorse restively. He could tell something was badly amiss, but hadn't seen what had happened.

"Prepare for battle, my Lord!" yelled Barrin once they were close enough. "Someone attacked Elias's forces and precipitated war, despite our best efforts. There'll be no holding Elias now."

Anjer returned a grim look as he ignored Barrin's shouts. He sent orders to his commanders that they should hold station unless they were attacked, and drew his horse alongside Marik's. "What in Perdition happened?" he demanded, following the Duke as he made his way through the massed companies.

"We nearly had him, Anjer." Marik slapped his hand hard on his saddle. "Against all the odds, Elias was going to listen. He was going to let me talk him out of this. And then he was attacked from behind. Don't ask me who they were, they were too far away to see. There were no obvious colors of allegiance and I wasn't going to hang around to look any closer. I'm afraid that's done it, my friend. Barrin is right. Elias is doubly convinced we're guilty now. I don't know who those bastards are, but they've made damn sure of that."

"*Corbyn*," snarled Anjer, his mustache bristling with fury, his black eyes snapping.

Marik's mouth dropped open. "You really think he'd go this far? If he has, he's a dead man."

Anjer threw him a vicious look. "You'll have to get in line. Now, back to the Citadel, if you please, your Grace. This will be a battlefield soon and no place for the Heir Elect."

Marik wanted to refuse. He wasn't used to skulking in safety while others risked their lives. But he wasn't lowly Count Marik anymore. He was Duke of Kymer and Heir Elect, and he couldn't be risked. He'd only distract and irritate Anjer if he insisted on staying. Calling for Norkis, he saluted Anjer and rode at speed for the safety of the Citadel, flanked by Barrin's honor guard. His heart was in ashes.

Chapter Fourteen

That first battle lasted barely an hour. Elias's forces were much larger than those that had taken them by surprise, and although the demons strove mightily to push the humans forward and into Anjer's massed ranks, they were too few to stop Elias's men from forcing a way through and taking cover in the town. Anjer, as enraged as the human King but for a different reason, had sent a couple of companies around to the west to try to trap the attacking force, hoping to catch Corbyn—if indeed it was he—before he was either killed or driven off. He didn't commit the main body of his men. He knew he couldn't stop Elias from gaining the town, and any escalation in the conflict would necessarily involve more damage and danger to the townspeople. Anjer wisely held back and awaited the return of his men.

⁜ ⁜ ⁜ ⁜ ⁜

The Albian forces drove their assailants off with no great losses. Some of the demons had been killed, and once it was over Valustin sent men to search the dead for any sign of who their masters were. Elias wasn't interested. As far as he was concerned they were simply dead demons, but Robin had registered the shock on Marik's face at the appearance of the attackers. The fact that Anjer had made no move against them as yet also gave him pause, for if the ambush had been of his devising, surely he'd have followed it up. Robin found that he still trusted Anjer, and also Marik; there was too much personal history between them.

The men found nothing incriminating on the bodies, but as they were piling them together outside the walls, Robin was approached by a diffident Cal.

Their relationship had never recovered from the incident at the farmstead. Cal had been deeply hurt by Robin's unfair treatment of him. Robin knew it, could see it every time he looked at Cal, and his actions that day still shamed him. Guilt made him unintentionally curt in his response when Cal said quietly, "Major? Could I have a word?"

"Later, Captain. I'm busy."

Cal flinched but held firm. "I don't think this can wait, sir."

Robin sighed. "Oh, very well, then."

"It's this man over here, sir." Cal showed Robin a body lying on its back on the ground, a grim and gaping wound in the belly. "I know him."

Robin's eyes widened. "You *know* him?"

Cal was quick to explain. "I mean I've seen him before. There was one other among the attackers that I've seen before, as well."

Robin stared at the Acting Captain. "Go on."

Cal looked away. "During that raid, you know, on the farmstead …." He glanced guiltily at Robin, who grimaced and waved a hand.

"Yes, Cal, I know the one you mean."

"Well, I thought I recognized one of the raiders that night. I wasn't completely sure in the dark, and he wasn't among the dead afterward, so I didn't say anything. Perhaps I should have, only…."

"Only I'd been a bastard that day and chewed you out for no reason? Yes, Cal, you're right, that was completely my fault." Robin gave a resigned sigh. "I never did apologize for that, and I should have. You didn't deserve it. I'm sorry, all right? Now tell me quickly—where've you seen these men before?"

"This man was definitely at the raid on the farmstead. And I'm pretty sure the one in command today was commanding that earlier raid—I think I remember seeing him in the ballroom at the Citadel. You know, after we were all married."

Robin froze for an instant, feeling a momentary flash of pain from that memory. Then he breathed, "Are you sure?"

Cal nodded. "Pretty sure. After that raid I kept trying to recall where I'd seen him. I think I remember him because he seemed angry or sour that day, and it was out of place when everyone else was so happy. But I never knew who he was. I don't think he was ever introduced."

Eyes narrowed, Robin crouched, studying the face of the dead demon on the ground. He straightened, slowly shaking his head. "I can't say I recall seeing this fellow before. What did the one in the ballroom look like? Can you give me his image?"

Cal accepted Robin's contact and did his best to hold an image of the man, but he could remember little except dark clothing and the man's sour expression and aura of displeasure.

Robin's mind was awhirl. "I don't recognize him, and it's not much to go on. He could be anything from a minor noble to someone with ambitions like Rykan's. But if we can find out who he is, you may well have solved the problem of who has been sending raids into Albia. I must report this to Blaine at once. He may want to hear it from you. This could be vitally important."

"Of course, Major, but what good will it do? We don't know who he is, and King Elias is going to be even less willing to listen to reason after today, isn't he?"

Robin's look was grim. "We'll let the General worry about that. Once we settle for the night, I'll get Blaine on his own and tell him. You just be ready in case you're summoned."

Robin swung away, then turned back. "By the way, Captain, good work." He laid a hand on Cal's shoulder. "You did well today, and I'm not just talking about recognizing those men. You kept your unit together and fought well. I'll be commending you to the General."

Cal ducked his head and grinned. "Thank you, Major." He turned away as Robin left, urging his men to finish up so they could return to the town before dusk fell.

Although he was supposedly here in an advisory capacity, Robin still went around the sentries, checking the billeting for the various companies within the town. As he worked, his mind was buzzing with what Cal had told him. If he felt like this, how would the news affect Elias? Would it make him more determined, or less? Surely if he came to believe that the commander of their assailants today was also responsible for the raids on Albia, it would only serve to harden his resolve to force a response from the Hierarch.

Robin didn't know whether their attackers were known to Marik and Anjer or not, but judging by Marik's reaction, he thought not. He couldn't imagine the Duke leaving himself vulnerable if he'd known a strike on Elias's forces was even likely, let alone imminent. And Robin knew that Sullyan had thought all along their enemies both in Albia and Andaryon were working independently of either ruler. Fortunately, the decision of what to tell Elias wasn't his. He would inform Blaine and let the General decide.

Once the town was quiet and the sentries reported no forward movement from Anjer's massed companies, Robin went in search of the General. He found him in the council building he and the King had selected as a command post.

When Robin explained what Cal had told him, Blaine frowned. "This is a complication I hadn't foreseen, Major. It puts a completely different perspective on things if we're going to be attacked on two fronts. Are you sure you didn't recognize the man?

If we could identify who is orchestrating these secondary attacks, we might be able to persuade Anjer to help us. It may be that Anjer's command will be attacked too, if this renegade's intention is to force us into all-out war."

Robin shook his head. "I don't remember seeing anyone matching Tyler's image, General. The Citadel was thronging with people. We could try asking Bull, though. He's been on more diplomatic missions here than I have. Shall I have Captain Tyler contact him and send him an image of the man, or do you want to talk to the Captain yourself?"

"You see to it, Major, and let me know if Bull can shed any light on the matter. We need every advantage we can get in this sorry situation. I don't know if Anjer intends to try to drive us out of here tomorrow or whether he's waiting for our next move, but I do know the King won't sit idle for long. He wants action— anything to force them into admitting they have Prince Eadan. He's quite simply beyond reason, and believe me, I've tried my best to dissuade him. I know he's frightened and grieving over the loss of Eadan, but I've never seen him lose all sense before. Not even when his father was killed and the throne in jeopardy. I'm at a loss to understand it. This campaign is tantamount to suicide, and I have no idea how it will end."

Robin agreed with the General's sentiments, but it wasn't his place to say so. He saluted the man and left him, going to seek out Cal again. He finally found him on the roof of one of the larger houses in the town, where he'd established a lookout post. Hearing Robin's request, Cal left the post to one of his men and swiftly made contact with Bull. The big man was on constant alert, having been left at the Manor to pass messages between the General and Vassa, and he immediately responded to Cal's questing touch.

He examined the image of the man Cal sent him, fuzzy as it was due to Cal's relative inexperience.

Well, I can't say I remember seeing him at any time during the weddings, he said, *but even so, I can tell you who he is. That's Lord Corbyn. I met him when I was at the Citadel with Sullyan the day Prince Aeyron was abducted. Corbyn's son was among Aeyron's hunting party, along with Tikhal's son, Rand. Both Corbyn and Tikhal were beside themselves with worry, but Corbyn was also furious and tried very hard to get the Hierarch to agree to punitive raids into Albia. He as good as threatened insurrection unless the Hierarch agreed.*

Robin, who had been listening in, cut impatiently across Cal's contact. *But Corbyn was present at the Citadel the whole time? He wasn't involved in the abduction of the Heir?*

Not in person, no, replied Bull, his mental tone colored by his disapproval of Robin's recent behavior and attitude. Meaningfully, he added, *But I know someone who could tell you far more about it than I could.*

Thank you, Bull, snapped Robin, and left the link.

He passed this on to Blaine, who was extremely interested and said he wished Sullyan, with her far superior knowledge of the Andaryan hierarchy and political system, was here to add her views. Robin didn't reply.

"Let's see how this unfolds over the next few days, Major. If this Lord Corbyn attacks Anjer, he may well get himself killed. And if Anjer's forces succeed in holding us here, Elias might lose interest or realize it's hopeless and return to Albia. I'll do my best to keep persuading him of that. Carry on, Major, and thank you. If you remember or hear anything else, let me know immediately."

Robin saluted woodenly and left, wishing to the depths of his heart he didn't feel so wretchedly maimed whenever someone mentioned Sullyan's name.

✤ ✤ ✤ ✤ ✤

Taran rose early after a restless night. The day was gloomy and overcast, warm and muggy. The louring clouds held a threat of rain and the air was oppressive. He made his way to the cooking room and started breakfast.

Hearing his preparations, Ardoch and Sullyan appeared. The Torlander accepted Taran's offering of fellan, and bread liberally spread with clear honey. Sullyan was too depressed to eat, although Taran tried hard to persuade her.

"I'll make some more patties later, lass," promised Ardoch, drawing a smile from her pale face.

Taran had hoped the promise of positive action and the thought of striking a blow against their enemy might have buoyed her flagging spirits, but it seemed to have had the opposite effect. He noted with sorrow that she wasn't even wearing her Artesan's rank badge, and the absence of the wealth of insignia over her left breast struck him an almost physical blow.

She was dressed in her usual combat leathers, topped by a dark green shirt in place of her usual cream or white, and she wore her leather jacket despite the day's warmth. Taran also noticed she wasn't wearing her sword belt but had only her long knife with her, snugged in its sheath as usual. She clearly intended to blend into the dark woods through which she would travel later.

Once they had eaten they split up. Ardoch made his way to the castle to speak with Levant if he could, and then to Denny. They wished the grizzled Torlander good fortune as he stepped out onto the street.

"Are you going to be all right?" Taran asked before leaving on his own mission.

She gave him a smile, although there was no emotion in it. "I will be well, Taran. My heart is heavy for the sake of our friends, both Albian and Andaryan. Every minute we delay brings greater danger to us all. But I must bide here a while this morning. I intend to use my metasenses to pinpoint that ancient signature we found in the substrate. It will be swifter than searching for it on foot. Once I know where it is, I can go directly there. I may be gone some time, and I may not return tonight, so do not fear for me. We have to bear in mind that somewhere nearby is a hostile Artesan of great power, and regardless of whether that hostility is inherent or coerced, we must keep contact to a minimum. I will be forced to shield myself while I am near the Baron's estate, so we will not be able to bespeak each other. But have no fear. If I need you, I will call. Otherwise, we will gather here again to discuss what we have found and then decide what to do. Off you go, Adept. Keep your ears open and be wary."

"You too," he said, strangely reluctant to leave her. This felt too final, and he disliked her going off alone, especially in view of her stricture against substrate communications. She had frequently kept herself shielded since they had left the Manor—he didn't know why and hadn't liked to ask—but then she'd not been alone. This was perilous territory they were entering, and he felt profoundly uneasy. Still, he had his part to play and didn't intend to shirk it. Feeling awkward, he embraced her, sensing the tightening of her muscles as she reacted to his unexpected emotion. She returned his clasp after a brief moment, and her eyes were damp when they parted.

"Go now," she whispered, turning from him. Unable to say more, he did as he was bidden, slipping unobserved out of the little house into the gray light of the heavy day.

✣ ✣ ✣ ✣ ✣

Once Sullyan was alone she found it even harder to master herself, as no one would see or know if she gave in to her deep unhappiness. But too many lives were dependent on her resolve. Thoughts of Aeyron's plight drove her on and stiffened her spine.

Wiping her eyes, she went back up to the small room she had slept in and laid herself on the bed. She closed her eyes and opened her senses, cautiously questing around the awakening city, feeling for anything unusual. She sensed Taran walking westward, toward the docks. Even shielded as he was, she could still catch the unease within him and the deep love he felt for her.

Pushing down her emotions, she turned from him and quested toward the castle. Here, she would have to be very careful. Somewhere close by was a mighty Artesan who could easily sense her and capture her mind if she wasn't constantly on her guard. Even if he was shielded, she ought to be able to sense something of him, but to her annoyance there was nothing. If Reen was somehow coercing this person and using ordinary spellsilver to control him, why didn't he break free and turn on Reen when it was removed to enable him to do Reen's bidding?

She shook her head, knowing she was missing something. Spellsilver made sense of her failure to locate the Artesan, but not of his compliance with the Baron. Irritated by her lack of success she cast her senses farther north, toward where Ardoch had told her the Baron's estate lay.

Here, she was more fortunate. Although she found no traces of the renegade Artesan or of the Hierarch's son, she did detect some kind of emanation from the ground, a hint of ancient power, and she homed in on it with the greatest caution.

Within the milky, opalescent substrate, she followed the unmistakable signature of Earth. As she neared it, she knew she was right: there was an incredibly ancient site of power here somewhere. It had not been used regularly for aeons, but she recognized the shape and texture of it from her exertions the day before. It was definitely the site she and Taran had discovered.

This close, she needed no strength but her own to probe its secrets. She found nothing odd about it; no taste of spellsilver and no hint of any psyche nearby but her own. Still, as she withdrew she spent time and energy covering the traces of her visit so that if anyone should chance to look, they wouldn't sense her.

Coming back to herself in Ardoch's house, she damped the slight headache her exertions had caused and went back to the small cooking area. Hot water still steamed over the fire and a quick mugful of fellan revived her. She now knew where she must go, and she intended to make her way there as soon as she could. She wanted to be in a place of concealment by evening when, hopefully, the gathering dusk would shield her from prying eyes as she explored the place fully.

Having decided against taking her sword or her pack for ease of movement, she slipped out of the house and made her way on foot.

The city gates were unbarred during the day and the Baron's guard was casual about his watch. She had no difficulty slipping out unobserved. Allowing the forest to swallow her, she began to work her way east and north around the city.

✢ ✢ ✢ ✢ ✢

Ardoch was surprised at the ease with which he secured an interview with Lord Levant. He had approached Elias's chamberlain, Lord Kinsey, and the thick-set man kept him waiting only a short time while he enquired whether the First Minister would see the swordmaster. Ardoch used Kinsey's absence to furtively glance at the papers on the secretary's desk, but saw nothing of interest.

When Kinsey returned with the news that Levant could spare Ardoch an hour or two later in the morning, his demeanor betrayed his curiosity. The swordmaster thanked him and left without enlightening him. He then headed for the garrison, where he knew he would find Lieutenant-Major Denny.

He eventually found Denny at the training ground, where he was watching his convalescing men train under Ardoch's assistant, Royen. The old swordmaster joined Denny by the rail and studied the young lieutenant.

"How're you mending, lad?"

Denny scowled. Ardoch knew Denny had never before been so severely injured. He was probably finding recovery a slow and boring process. Being back at Port Loxton and resuming his duties would help to a certain extent, but he was no doubt feeling inadequate, as well as stiff and sore.

"It's better to be back, Ardoch," Denny said, "but it's not right. I should be with the King, but I know I'm not really even fit enough to command here. What if we're attacked while he's away? What if the demons try to abduct someone else? The Queen, say, or the Princess? How can I and my men guard against marauders who can disappear into thin air? No one could have prevented Prince Eadan being taken, could they? What price my career if something similar happens while I'm too unfit to prevent it?"

Ardoch took his eyes from the exercising men and regarded Denny frankly. "No price at all, man. Do you know the full story behind the Prince's abduction? I've not heard how it happened yet."

Denny shrugged. "I wasn't here, of course, but I've heard about it. It seems the Prince was being taken for his usual walk in the castle grounds by one of his nursemaids when two demons ran out of the woods near the folly, grabbed both her and the Prince, and disappeared back into the trees. She managed to scream, but by the time the guards reached the spot, the Prince and his captors had vanished."

Ardoch raised his brows. "The babe was attended by only one nursemaid? That wouldn't have happened had Elias been here. Where was the other maid? Where were the guards?"

Denny leaned his elbows on the wooden rail of the exercise ground. "Guards went with them, of course, but there was only one nursemaid. It seems the other had fallen ill the day before. But the guards were called away, and the only other person near Eaden at the time was that poor backward boy, Huw. You know how much use he is."

Ardoch grimaced. He had as little to do with Huw as possible. A child in a man's body was outside of Ardoch's experience, and he always felt awkward around Huw. Had the lad been capable of learning some kind of weapons skill, however rudimentary, Ardoch would have felt more comfortable with him and could have looked beyond his mental inadequacies. As it was, there was no common ground, and Ardoch did what most people did—avoided the boy.

"Were the guards ours?" he asked. "What called them away?"

"There was some kind of disturbance at the castle gates. I don't know the full facts. Because the Prince and his nurse were well within the castle grounds, they felt it safe to go and investigate. And no, they weren't our lads, they were the Baron's. Apparently, once he heard of the King's plans for war, Reen offered his guards' services to the Queen to free the garrison swordsmen for other duties."

"How convenient."

Denny stared at Ardoch in surprise and the old swordmaster continued. "Someone was watching the wee Prince that day, just waiting for the opportunity to snatch him. Tell me, has the Queen ordered any special arrangements for the Princess?"

Denny opened his mouth to reply, frowned, then said, "Not from me, she hasn't. In fact, I've had no orders from her at all. She and Seline are guarded by the Baron's men, like Eadan, but the Princess doesn't seem to have any restrictions on her movements. Sofira doesn't seem worried about her. And now I come to think on it, she's not been quite so distraught about Eadan lately, either."

"As if she knows he's safe?" Ardoch's voice was low.

Arrested by his tone, Denny shot him a look. "What are you suggesting, old fox? You surely can't think the Queen had anything to do with this? There's no question Eadan was taken by demons. The nursemaid saw them clearly."

Ardoch gazed at him, unsure how much to tell him. If Sullyan was right, time was running out. In order to gain any answers or insights at all, a few risks had to be taken. He knew Denny well; knew his unwavering loyalty to Elias and also his dislike of the Baron. It was true that no one really liked the Baron, but would Denny go so far as to spy or inform on him? Ardoch didn't really have a choice and decided to trust him.

"I've no doubt of that, lad," he said softly. "We have no proof, but we do suspect the Baron. And he's very close to the Queen. If he's involved in this, he'd have told Sofira where Eadan is, you can be sure of that. Or at the very least, that he's safe. He wouldn't risk the Queen turning against him. He's also suspected of having dealt with demons in the past, despite his oft-aired opinions of them."

Denny took a while to consider this. "The Baron's been absent quite a bit lately, ever since Eadan's disappearance. He's reportedly been spending a lot of time on his own estate, which is unusual. When he's not there, he's with the Queen. He barely leaves her side. You'll see for yourself. Tomorrow's a holy day and they've both taken to attending the Minster practically all day. The Baron's even giving an address. He seems to be in very good odor with the Arch Patrio right now."

"Really? Now that's very interesting." Ardoch was thinking tomorrow would be a very good day to go looking round the Baron's estate. He would have to tell Sullyan later.

He spent a little more time with Denny without learning

anything else. Before he left, he let the young lieutenant know he'd be serving the King well if he kept his eyes and ears open.

Chapter Fifteen

At the appointed time, Ardoch presented himself outside Levant's chambers and sent the waiting page in to announce him. Levant met with him in his small but luxurious office, which was attached to his suite on the second floor of the castle.

"Master Ardoch, this is a rare occurrence. To what do I owe the pleasure?"

Levant gestured to the Torlander to take a seat and proceeded to pour him a goblet of wine. Ardoch folded himself into the encompassing leather chair and took the goblet from Levant's hand. As they both drank, Ardoch studied the slightly younger man, trying to decide how to begin.

Elias's First Minister was a tall man, dark-haired with silver at his temples and peppering his neatly-trimmed beard. His dark-blue eyes were shrewd and honest, never wavering in their regard. As usual, they showed a mild curiosity which belied his sharp and enquiring mind. He was in his early sixties, only a couple of years younger than Ardoch. They had known each other a long time. Both had been in service to Elias's father. Although neither disliked the other, their separate lifestyles had kept them apart.

Levant had spent his working life within the castle, immersed in politics and bureaucracy, whereas Ardoch had lived within the garrison, spending long weeks away from the city in training and maneuvers. He had also spent some years at the Manor, so the two men had never cemented a strong relationship. Nevertheless, mutual respect prevailed and there was no awkwardness or suspicion between them. Ardoch studied Levant over the rim of his goblet. He could only guess how the Queen's favoring of her sycophantic Baron had galled Levant. Enough to cause him to be sympathetic to Sullyan's request? Ardoch could only hope so.

"My Lord, I have only just returned from the Manor, from where his Majesty has launched his assault on the demon realm of Andaryon."

"Yes, Swordmaster, I heard about that," Levant replied dryly.

Ardoch thought he caught an undercurrent of censure and considered this a promising sign. "I'm telling you this in confidence, you understand. There are those of us who consider this war to be both unnecessary and wasteful. We're loyal to Elias, but we feel that the solution to his ... problem ... lies closer to home."

Levant sipped his wine. "How close?"

Ardoch was in a quandary. Levant was too sharp to give much of his own thoughts away, so the Torlander would have to lay himself open bit by bit as he tested the waters of Levant's tolerance. He decided to try an oblique approach.

"How much have you had to do with the treasury lately?"

Levant narrowed his eyes. "Not much, once the Queen showed herself capable of its control."

"So you wouldn't know the current state of it?"

Levant's frown deepened. "State? What do you mean, Master Ardoch? Speak plainly, man. Do you have cause to think there's something amiss with the treasury?"

The Torlander regarded Levant sidelong. "There's a possibility there might be less in it than there should be. Would there be a way to find out? Discreetly?"

Levant raised peppered brows. "Are you asking me to go

behind the Queen's back and check up on her accounting?"

Aye! That's it exactly.

Aloud, Ardoch said, "I believe the King hasn't taken any interest in the state of the exchequer since the Queen took it over. Is that true, my Lord?" Levant nodded cautiously. "Well, there's a possibility that a large sum of gold has been used for other purposes than the good of Albia, and that this ... transaction has been covered up. It would take someone who knew their way around the accounts to spot it."

"And you want me to be that one?"

The Torlander regarded Levant openly. "If there's no problem, if the accounts all tally, no one need know. But if there is a problem, whoever discovers it would be doing Elias a great service."

Levant pursed his lips. "I have no reason to doubt Queen Sofira. This conversation is getting perilously close to treason, Swordmaster."

Ardoch's heart sank. "Aye, it is." He held Levant's gaze, trying to show him how serious he was. "And you may not distrust the Queen, my Lord, but what about her Baron?"

At the mention of Reen, Levant's face hardened. "So that's who you suspect, is it? Well, I know for a fact that Elias has no love for the Queen's confidante, and I do think he's been unhealthily close to her of late. It's my opinion that had he not accompanied her from Bordenn, she and Elias would have stood a better chance of making a good marriage."

"Aye, my Lord, we agree there. And if it should turn out that his advice has caused the Queen to err, then it's our own duty to discover this before it goes too far. For the Queen's sake as much as the King's. He's a good ruler. You and I have known him longest of anyone here. When have you known him make such an error of judgment as he has over the little Prince's disappearance?

You know as well as I how pleased he was over his trade agreement with the Andaryans. Yet now he's making war on them. It's not right, my Lord. Someone is working against our King and the whole of Albia, and it's up to us to find out who's behind it. What do you say? Are you willing to help Elias and maybe put an end to this costly and unnecessary war?"

Levant stared at him in silence and Ardoch held his breath. Eventually, Levant sighed. "Very well, Swordmaster, I'll see what I can do. But it won't be easy. If the Queen discovers me, I'll have nothing plausible to tell her. She'll be very angry. And if it should come to pass that there're no irregularities in the exchequer accounts, then my career—if not my neck—will be forfeit."

"Is the Queen likely to have business with the exchequer today?"

Levant spoke slowly. "This morning, maybe. But in the afternoons she has taken to hearing petitioners and dealing with general city and trade matters. You want me to do it today?"

"The sooner it's done, my Lord, the sooner we'll know. I'll be in touch later, or send a page for me if you find aught. Good luck."

Levant muttered darkly about needing more than luck if he was discovered, but Ardoch was sure he caught a glimmer of what could have been eagerness in the First Minister's eyes. Smiling grimly, he bowed himself out of the office.

✢ ✢ ✢ ✢ ✢

Taran had left Ardoch's house with no clear idea of where he should start his search. Today was the last working day before the holy day, and so the city was bustling with merchants and traders, stallholders and farmers, all vying with one another to sell their perishable goods before the day was out.

Many of the city's womenfolk and servants were abroad too, hoping for bargains from those same vendors. Trade was brisk from what Taran could see. He wandered about the merchants' quarter, listening to the gossip of the women and the cries of the vendors, all against the backdrop of seabirds calling to one another as they swooped around the rooftops.

He heard nothing of immediate value among the shops and stalls, although many folk were discussing the possible whereabouts of the Prince. Unsurprisingly, most people believed the demons had spirited him away to Andaryon, and no one blamed the King for his punitive actions. Many sympathized with the Queen in her distress, and Taran heard no words said against her. Again this was unsurprising—most of the gossips were women and mothers.

The Baron's name was mentioned frequently, but most folk thought the Queen was fortunate to have such a loyal and staunch countryman on hand to comfort her while her husband was absent. There was a hint of lascivious suggestion in some of these comments, but again, no censure. The people of Port Loxton, it seemed, thought the Queen was entitled to whatever comfort she could get at such a harrowing time. Taran was disgusted both by the liberal attitudes of many of the women to a possible betrayal of marriage vows, and by their willingness to believe evil of the Andaryans.

The old prejudices against forcigners and outlanders were still firmly entrenched in the minds of the ordinary people. Indeed, most of them would have turned on him had they known he was an Artesan, and he was Albian through and through. Sighing for the ignorance and intolerance of Loxton's citizens, he made his way to the port.

He located it as much by smell as direction. Loxton Bay was a large and safe natural harbor on the western edge of the city. The strongest winds blew from the east, and the cliffs to the north sheltered the bay from the worst of the winter gales. Moles, baffles, and pontoons built out into the water provided safe mooring for ships when the infrequent western winds made anchoring in the roads unadvisable.

Loxton was a well-known and popular port, frequented by merchant ships from all over Albia. Goods of every kind could be had from the wharves, docks, and warehouses of the port. It was a bustling, cosmopolitan place.

Finding a busy tavern wasn't difficult. Taran was soon seated at an alcove table in the Leaky Clipper, ordering a foaming tankard of brown ale to keep him company while he eavesdropped. The ale was good, but not as good as the nutty brew he remembered with such pleasure from Jed's Hazel Tree.

The Clipper was full of sailors who had come in on the morning tide. Having unloaded their cargo, they were having a well-earned rest before the afternoon's toil of provisioning their ships before setting sail again. Taran downed two tankards of ale and learned much about the life of a trade sailor, but nothing pertinent to his search.

Downhearted, he left the Clipper and went in search of another tavern. In the Bearded Barnacle he had better luck, although only marginally. The men who were sitting at the table behind him were all local fishermen, and they were discussing the war. Almost to a man they were unanimous in their support of Elias's actions, and it was their opinion that it was about time he saw these unnatural outlanders for what they were and stopped trying to civilize them by making trade alliances. What could he possibly want from outlanders that Albia couldn't supply? It wasn't right, and the troubles that had beset him recently only went to show what you got for dealing with savages and barbarians.

It was all simplistic and depressing stuff, but what really made Taran prick up his ears was the tavern keeper's remark about the addresses at the Minster on the morrow. He'd brought replenishments to the fishermen's never-empty tankards and got drawn into their conversation.

"Oh, aye," the tavern keeper said magisterially, "all the nobility think the same, you know. Baron Reen is giving a sermon on the subject at the Minster tomorrow. There're notices all around the city inviting us to go and hear him. He's supporting the King by keeping the castle safe, and the Queen relies on him completely, so I hear. It was his idea that Elias should make an end of these outlanders once and for all, and once they'd abducted poor little Prince Eadan, well, Elias finally saw sense. Let's hope he kills the lot of them for abducting the Heir, poor little mite! Once this war's over and Elias has finally broken with the outlanders, I reckon the Baron's going to put himself forward for First Minister. You see if I'm not right."

The fishermen agreed heartily with the landlord, although after four or five tankards of his strong brown ale they'd have agreed with anything. Taran was only too afraid he was right. Feeling more depressed than ever, he placed coin on the table to pay for his largely untouched ale—he didn't have the stomach for it now—and went out once more.

Taran gradually left the port behind. It was coming on for noon and he was hungry. He decided to buy one of the pies Loxton's meat merchants were famous for and find one of the city's many parks to eat it in.

Purchasing the pie was easy, finding the park less so. Taran wasn't familiar with the city and wandered farther from the port than he intended before finding one. It was surrounded by small, well built houses, and was neatly kept. He realized he must be on the edges of one of the more fashionable areas, where the well-to-do middle classes lived. The park was quiet and peaceful, just what he wanted after the crowded merchant and dockside areas, and he found himself a comfortable wooden bench beside a stand of flowering shrubs. The scent of pale-pink blossoms chased the pipe smoke from his nose and the depression from his heart.

He ate his meal unmolested. Apart from the birds that hopped around him, hopeful of crumbs, he saw no one in the park, so when he heard the sound of soft sobbing coming from somewhere behind him, he was taken aback.

He sat quite still, feeling awkward and guilty, as if he'd been caught deliberately spying on someone's grief. The sobbing grew more pitiful by the minute. He was embarrassed to witness such unhappiness. This was a private trauma; the weeper had obviously come here for solitude and he was intruding. Deciding to leave as silently as possible, he stood.

He moved without a sound, intending to leave the way he had come. As he did so, he caught sight of the grieving figure, seated on another bench on the other side of the shrub. They'd been near enough to touch one another had they known. Only their silence had kept them ignorant of each other's presence.

The weeper was a young woman, and from the quality of her clothes Taran could tell she was nobility. He wondered why she was alone. Women of that class rarely went out without a maid or chaperone, but there was no one else in sight. And she was suffering so sadly. She was slumped over the bench, her blue satin gown draped becomingly about her legs and flowing down onto the grass. Her head was bowed over her hands, which bore numerous gold rings, and her shoulder-length blonde hair fell across her face as she sobbed into the delicate lace cloth she held to her eyes.

Something about her caught his attention. He looked closer, still undetected, and his unease at intruding upon her grief transmuted into amazement. He knew this woman. His presence would surely only increase her pain.

Then she saw him. That first storm of weeping over, she had

to come up for air. As she did so, she turned her tear-ravaged visage upon him. He saw the tears welling unchecked from the pale green eyes, the daylight gleaming in them as it did on the expensive diamond necklace she wore.

She looked him full in the eyes and gave a startled yelp. Discovered, he could only respond. To do anything else would have been craven, but he shied from it nonetheless.

He spoke softly, almost hoping she would flee from him.

"Lady Jinella. My apologies, I didn't know anyone else was here. I didn't mean to intrude. But you are distressed. Is there anything I can do? Are you hurt?"

Jinella gave a gulp and he thought he must be the last person she'd ever expected to see again. She sniffed and applied the lace cloth to her nose. When she didn't speak, he began to sidle away, but then she held out a small hand. Her voice was raw from crying.

"Captain Elijah, please don't go. Would you sit by me for a moment? I'm so very unhappy."

It wasn't the response Taran expected, but he couldn't refuse. His association with her had been the cause of much upset and grief, yet he couldn't find it in his heart to blame her. The fault was more his than hers. He approached her, took the small damp hand, and gallantly kissed it. He sat beside her.

"How can I help you, my Lady? Can you tell me the cause of your grief?"

She sniffed again, her eyes pleading. "Please call me Jinny. I know we didn't exactly part as friends, but I need a friend very badly just now. Could you bear to pretend to like me again, just for a few moments?"

Her unaccusing and pitiable state melted his heart. He smiled. "I can do better than that, Jinny. And my name is Taran, remember? I was never really a captain anyway, not in the true sense of the title."

She looked confused. "No? But aren't you from the King's forces at the Manor? Although if you were, I suppose you'd be fighting with him in Andaryon...."

"I've never taken the King's Oath," he explained gently. "I was only staying at the Manor because I'm an Artesan, and because of my friendship with Colonel Sullyan. I'm a member of the King's College, but not Elias's fighting forces."

He could tell she didn't really understand. "Oh," she said. "I'd heard Colonel Sullyan had fallen out of favor with the King. Is it true?"

Taran didn't want to discuss Sullyan's troubles with Jinny. "She still serves Elias."

Jinny's eyes welled with tears again. "I'm so sorry. I shouldn't have mentioned her name. It's none of my business."

She hung her head and Taran felt he ought to say something comforting. Before he could, she burst out, "Oh, Taran, I'm so very sorry about what I said to my uncle when you were here last. I just got so jealous! I know I shouldn't have, but when I saw you both together that night, I thought ... well, it doesn't matter what I thought. I've had time to think it over since then and I wanted so badly to apologize to you, but I didn't know how. Oh, I said some terribly dreadful things to my uncle about you. And then he told Lily—you know, my maid—and made her spread it all round the garrison. I was furious with her when I found out. I've dismissed the silly goose, but it's too late now. I've ruined everything. My uncle has thrown me out. I've no money, and no home. I'm staying with a friend at the moment because my mother's so disgusted with me. Oh, it's all such a horrible mess!"

She broke down again, burying her face in her hands. Taran stared at her, struggling between amazement and dismay. What on earth could have happened between Jinny and her uncle to make the Baron cast her off? Her confession about what she had said concerning him and Sullyan came as no surprise. He was, however, a little surprised to hear the Baron had deliberately capitalized on it by getting her maid to spread it around the garrison.

He studied Jinny speculatively. Maybe, just maybe, he could salvage something from this unexpected meeting.

He gently took the damp cloth from her and patted her reddened cheeks. "Come, Jinny, calm yourself. I'm not cross with you, and I'll stay with you until you feel better. All I ask is that you tell me the whole story. Tell me what happened after you saw me come out of Sullyan's room that night, what you told your uncle, and exactly what he did. And can you tell me why he cast you out? If you can, maybe we can put some things right that should never have gone wrong. At least three people's lives have been badly damaged, possibly forever, because of what happened the day of that fair. Can you bear to do that for me?"

Her pale green eyes were wide with sorrow and shame, and his words brought further tears. He held fast to her hand and smiled kindly at her, and she gradually calmed, nodding her head.

"I'll try," she whispered.

"Thank you, Jinny."

"But not here." She glanced about nervously. "It wouldn't be right for me to be seen alone with you like this. I'm in enough trouble as it is, and if the people who have taken me in should hear I was sitting alone in the park with a man, well, they'd probably throw me out too. I'm only here on sufferance. They hope I'll make it up with my uncle and that he'll recompense them for my keep."

Taran felt like telling her what he thought of such callous and venal people, but realized she inhabited a different world and lived by different rules to the ones he understood. She had to obey its dictates.

He stood, deliberately formal as he offered her his arm. "Very well, my Lady. Will you permit me to escort you through the city to a place where we can be private and unobserved?" Seeing the flash of alarm cross her features, he hastened to reassure her. "I mean you no harm. You were happy enough to accept me as escort on the day of the fair, remember? And I'm staying at the house of the King's swordmaster. He'll vouch for me if you're still troubled."

Jinny squared her chin and stood, showing Taran a hint of the backbone he'd feared she lacked. Having made up her mind to unburden her heart, she wasn't going to put obstacles in the path of her resolve. She took his offered arm with a fair approximation of grace.

"I thank you, my gallant escort. I'm sure I will be quite safe with you. And if we walk openly and swiftly through the town, no one will mark us. Shall we go?"

Taran used Jinny's superior knowledge of the city to find the most direct route back to Ardoch's house. They avoided the fashionable quarters and strolled purposefully along the streets as if they had every right to be together. They met no one Jinny knew, and only a very few people even gave them a second glance, no doubt wondering where the noble lady's maid was.

They soon gained Ardoch's small house and slipped thankfully through the door. The Adept showed her into the small living room and saw her seated comfortably. The day remained warm and muggy, but he didn't dare open a window. The oppressive air of the city would have given no respite from the heat, and he didn't want to take the chance they might be overheard. He brewed fellan and brought it in from the cooking room, serving Jinny as courteously as any manservant. She smiled gratefully at him, and he was reminded of how pretty she was. He seated himself across from her and once more asked for her story.

She sipped the fellan slowly, trying to order her thoughts. Taran let her be. She had to find her own strength and center if she was going to do this.

Her innate courage and determination finally won out. She cupped the mug in her delicate hands and brought her gaze up to meet Taran's, smiling hesitantly.

"I know you might find this hard to believe, Taran, but I really enjoyed our day at the fair. The only thing that stopped it from being perfect was the fact that you were forever talking about Colonel Sullyan."

Taran opened his mouth to protest, but she forestalled him.

"No, don't apologize. I knew you were in love with her, but now I can see she didn't return your feelings."

This oversimplified the truth by a very long way, but the Adept felt it better not to disabuse Jinny of her flawed understanding. He allowed her to carry on.

"There was something else that made me less than happy that day, something that made me more inclined to look for reasons to be upset."

She lifted her eyes in frank admission. "My uncle came to my rooms the day before the fair. He'd heard you'd agreed to be my escort, and he demanded I find out as much about you as I could."

Seeing the shock in his eyes, she hurried on. "I didn't want to do it, but you must understand—the Baron controls my inheritance. I'm only at court on his sufferance, and if I didn't do as he asked, all my hopes and ambitions would be ruined. He made that very clear to me.

"I decided I'd only tell him harmless and inconsequential things. And in the end, you didn't tell me anything important. But the fact that you left me so abruptly really annoyed me. I know it was silly and petty, but all I could see was that as soon as the Colonel snapped her fingers, you went running."

She held up a small hand as Taran tried once again to protest. "I know, I know. You'd come with her to help her, and I had no claim on you. I understand. You didn't really want to escort me to the fair anyway, did you? That was the Colonel's doing. It's just that I've never had it done to me before."

Seeing his puzzlement, Jinny almost smiled. "Remember when she told you you'd be free for the day? She was matchmaking, Taran. I've seen it a hundred times before. I've even done it myself. The Colonel's married, isn't she? You told me so yourself. She wanted you to direct your affections elsewhere. When you saved us that day in the Forest and I showed an interest in you, she saw an ideal opportunity."

Taran felt his face grow hot at Jinny's unexpected insight. She gave a small, girlish laugh at his chagrined expression, pleased to have been proved right.

"You don't have to be embarrassed," she said with a flash of her normal lightheartedness. "I was flattered. The Colonel is very beautiful and talented. I should be immensely proud she thought *I* might catch your attention."

Jinny sobered. "But you see, I've had time to think things through since then. I'm not as empty-headed as some people think. It's just that in the kind of society I move in, other things are valued more highly than intelligence. Once I got over your desertion, I felt ashamed of my jealousy. And when I heard you'd be leaving Port Loxton with his Majesty, I wanted to tell you how much I'd enjoyed our day and that I hoped we could see each other again."

Her frankness amazed Taran. He was surprised she'd even considered continuing their friendship after the cavalier way he'd treated her. She reddened as she added, "I also wanted to prove to myself that I could make you forget the Colonel, at least for a few hours. I feel so ashamed now, when I remember how shallow I was. I managed to give Lily the slip that night and came to your rooms in the hopes of … well, let's be honest. I intended to seduce you."

She dropped her eyes in embarrassment and Taran did the same. How would he have reacted had she turned up at his door with *that* on her mind? He didn't know and was very glad the opportunity to find out hadn't presented itself. After an awkward silence, she continued.

"That's why, when I saw you going into the Colonel's room half-naked, and coming out again a short time later with her standing there in nothing but a man's shirt, well, I felt incredibly angry and betrayed, and was quite prepared to believe she had got there first."

She raised her eyes in appeal. "It was stupid, I know. It was petty jealousy, but I was in no mood to be rational. I let my anger overcome my good sense. By the time I got back to my rooms, I was completely overwrought.

"Lily called my uncle, and because he was so supportive and caring—quite unlike him, really—I simply couldn't help myself. I denounced the pair of you and said some very stupid things. I told him you and Sullyan were having an affair, and he believed me. He told me how pleased he was with me, and that my position and inheritance were safe."

She spread her hands, her cheeks still red with shame. "That's what I'd wanted all along. It was all I cared about. I had to fight very hard to get my uncle to agree to sponsor me at court, so when he told me how pleased he was with me, it all seemed worthwhile. My uncle would release my inheritance to me and all would be well.

"The next day … well, that's when it all started going wrong."

Chapter Sixteen

Jinny looked guiltily at Taran, and he smiled in encouragement. He sensed that were he to show any negative emotion, she would retreat into herself and he would learn no more. He felt that if he kept very still and did nothing to disturb her she would eventually reveal something of vital importance. He had a sense of events shifting in this unexpected meeting, a movement in the machinations of Fate, and he couldn't afford to miss what might be uncovered. So he hid his annoyance at her immature intrigues, and tried to be uncritical.

"The morning after, I found my uncle had left this necklace for me, and I wanted to thank him before he left with the King's party. I ... also wanted to show you I didn't care about the way you'd treated me the day before."

Jinny couldn't look at Taran. She was reddening more by the minute, but she didn't stop.

"After you left and I got back to my rooms, I found Lily in a strange mood. She was counting a small quantity of gold. It was much more than she should have had, and she wouldn't tell me where it had come from. She was so furtive that I accused her of stealing it. She told me my uncle had given it to her as payment for spreading the gossip about you and the Colonel among the castle and garrison servants. She'd embellished my story and the whole castle was buzzing with it. It had even gone around the King's Guard, and they're a gullible lot sometimes. Even the smallest thing can be blown out of all proportion."

"Yes. I know." Taran's tone was bleak.

She winced. "Was that what you meant about people's lives being damaged?" He nodded and Jinny paled. "Is one of those people Colonel Sullyan? Is that why she fell out of favor with the King?"

Taran felt she deserved some honesty in return for her courage. "That's not why the King cast her out, but her life was damaged by the rumors. Her life mate, Robin, who is a Major at the Manor, heard the tale and believed it. I made matters worse by something I said, and he became … very angry."

He held her gaze. "Jinny, he and Sullyan are among my closest and most valued friends. They've both been hurt beyond measure by those rumors, so much so that they have become estranged. And Sullyan is—" He caught himself just in time. He'd never be forgiven if he let *that* secret out, especially to Jinny.

He carried on. "Robin refuses to talk about it, and he won't listen to any of his friends. And now I fear for his safety. He's in Andaryon with the King, and I know he won't be able to concentrate on the war with this awful situation hanging over him. It's affected us all, and I've no idea how it will end."

Fresh tears came to Jinny's eyes. She was so full of regret that Taran's anger melted. He came to sit beside her and put his arm around her.

"It might be that you can help put things right. Maybe it's not too late. When this war is over, perhaps you could tell the Major the truth. Perhaps he'll listen to you, and they can sort their problems out."

"If I can, I will. I promise you that."

"Thank you." He gave her shoulder a comforting pat and waited while she collected herself. "Do you want to tell me why your uncle cast you off?" She gulped and nodded. "Go on, then," he said, removing his arm so he could watch her.

She glanced down to her fingers twisting in her lap. "When I found out what Lily had done, and that my uncle had paid her to do it, I was furious. He'd already made me angry by asking me to spy on you at the fair, and this incident with Lily made me realize how much he must hate your kind. Then I wondered if he was planning something, and I thought about it more and more over the three days he was away.

"Then something really strange happened. On the morning he returned, he sent a page to my rooms with a message telling me to keep to my chambers all day. If anyone asked, I was to say I was very ill. I was puzzled, but mostly I was angry because I had to cancel the plans I'd made that day. But I did as I was told, hoping he'd come to explain. He never did.

"The next day, I left my chambers and went to find him. It took me ages to track him down. I finally found him with the commander of his personal guard, a horrible man called Izack."

Jinny shuddered. "I can't tell you how much I hate that man. He's cruel and brutal, and he doesn't care who knows it. Anyway, my uncle was furious with me for leaving my rooms and seemed very concerned that I might have overheard what he and Izack had been saying. I hadn't, though I got the impression they were talking about the abduction of the demon Heir. But it couldn't have been that because the message from the King telling us about it didn't arrive until the next day.

"I tried to tell my uncle I hadn't overheard them, but he wouldn't listen. He shouted at me and made me promise to tell anyone who asked that I'd eaten something disagreeable and that's why I stayed in my rooms the day before. He seemed really scared someone would find out I hadn't been ill.

"He made me leave then, and told me not to bother him again unless he sent for me. I was so hurt and angry that I decided to leave the castle. I went back to my rooms and began to pack."

"Leave?" asked Taran. "Go back to your mother, you mean?"

Jinny sighed. "What, give up my life at court and prospects of advancement?" With wry self-knowledge, she said, "It would have taken much more than harsh words to make me throw that away. What I meant was I'd decided to return to my suite at the Baron's mansion. It's where I usually live—lived."

Once again, Taran felt the cold echo of shifting events slither down his spine. He hadn't even considered Jinny might have apartments in the Baron's private mansion, but when he thought about it, it made perfect sense.

"So you left the castle and returned to your uncle's estate. What happened there to make him turn you out?"

Jinella paled and tears welled once more from her eyes. She wouldn't look at him and hugged herself tightly as if warding off pain.

"Would you like some more fellan?" he said, hoping the mundane offer would assuage her distress. "Or would you prefer wine? I'm sure I saw some."

Jinny shook her head. Sniffling, she murmured, "Fellan would be fine, thank you."

He left her alone while he made it, trying to control the quickening pulse in his chest. Her reference to hearing the Baron discussing Aeyron's abduction hadn't passed him by. The only reason the Baron could have known about it in advance of the message from the King was if he was involved. And if that was true, as Sullyan suspected, it was all the more likely he'd also had a hand in the abduction of Prince Eadan.

Taran could hardly suppress his impatience to hear what had occurred to cause the Baron to turn Jinny out. Returning with the fresh fellan, he found Jinella much more composed, although still pale. He passed her the fellan and reseated himself, schooling his impatience, determined not to press her.

"Are you able to carry on now?" he asked once she'd taken a few sips.

"You're being very kind to me considering the amount of trouble I've caused." She gazed at him and he flushed at the intensity of the emotions in her eyes.

"You're not completely to blame, Jinny. And I have a feeling what you're going to tell me may make up for any trouble."

Her eyes widened and he noticed the glints of gold among the green of her irises. They reminded him of Sullyan's eyes, and the smile he afforded her was warmer because of it. She returned it shyly as she resumed her tale.

"For two days I saw no sign of my uncle. That's not unusual. He's often at the castle dancing attendance on the Queen. On the third day, late in the afternoon, he reappeared. I thought he seemed inordinately pleased with himself. It was strange, as normally he's a very sober person, not much given to smiling. And there was something odd about his elation, something unwholesome...."

"Anyway, as soon as he saw me, his excitement vanished. He looked as if he'd forgotten I lived there and was none too pleased to be reminded. I wasn't sure what to do. After all, he'd told me not to approach him unless sent for. But the mansion was my home. Where else was I to go?

"I just bid him good day and made to walk past him, but he grabbed my arm. I was really shocked. He'd never laid hands on me before, and he was holding me so tightly he crushed the sleeve of one of my favorite gowns."

Taran had to suppress a smile. Jinny's priorities would always lie in a different direction to his.

"He demanded to know what I was doing there. I reminded him that I lived there, and his face actually went pale. I asked him if he was feeling quite well, and he snapped at me to mind my own business."

She frowned. "I wasn't going to take that. He was treating me most unfairly. I decided I'd had enough, and I told him what I thought of his hospitality and his rudeness."

She fell silent, tears sliding down her cheeks again.

"He was furious. He told me I was useless, a burden round his neck, and he refused to shelter me anymore. He said things were going to change, that he was going to be a very wealthy and influential figure at court, and that he couldn't afford to encumber himself with unnecessary baggage.

"*Baggage*, Taran! That's what he called me." She was crying openly now. "What did I do to deserve that? I was desperate to know, but he wouldn't tell me, although I begged him and begged him. The more I tried to placate him, the angrier he became.

"Eventually, he lost control completely. I've never seen anyone so furiously angry before. I thought he was going to have a seizure. He screamed at me, told me to pack my things and leave that very evening. He said he never wanted to see me or hear from me again. I was sobbing, but he just turned away. I had no choice but to go."

She was crying so hard Taran could hardly make out her words. Abandoning his fellan, he once again moved closer and enfolded her in his arms. She gave herself over to his comfort and sobbed out her misery on his shoulder. He sat in silence while the storm ran its course.

She finally calmed. Not troubling to dry her face, she drew in a deep and shuddering breath. "I still haven't told you the worst."

Taran gave a mental shiver. His senses felt sharp and honed, and he knew this was what events had been building to.

Her voice muffled by the circle of his arms, Jinny said, "I know he treated me badly, but I still can't believe I'm thinking this. He's my father's brother. Our family is loyal to the ruling house of Albia, and always has been. I *must* be mistaken, only...."

"Only what?" he prompted gently. When she didn't reply, he murmured, "Just tell me the facts, Jinny. Tell me as they happened. Let's see if I come to the same conclusions as you."

"Yes," she said. "Yes, that feels right. All right, then. After he told me to go, I sent a message to one of my friends asking if I could stay for a while. I began packing while I waited, but I needed to collect some gowns from the seamstress. I couldn't find a maid to send for them, so I went to the servants' quarters myself.

"I happened to glance out of a window that gave onto the stable yard. I noticed a horse and cart there. Two men were unloading small packages from it into one of the barns.

"I thought at first they were Kingsmen and I wondered why Kingsmen would be unloading my uncle's cart. But then one of them turned and I saw it was Izack, so they were my uncle's men dressed as Kingsmen.

"I put it out of my mind when I saw my uncle coming out of one of the maidservants' rooms farther down the corridor. He was facing away from me so he didn't see me, and I froze when I saw him because I was just so shocked...."

Seeing Taran's raised brows and guessing what he thought, Jinny pursed her lips. "I'm not as naïve as all that! I do know such things go on, and my uncle has never married. But it wasn't that. He doesn't seem to have that kind of interest in women. No, it was the shock of seeing him in the servants' wing at all. He's never set foot in the place as far as I'm aware. Anyway, he carried on down the corridor toward the stairs, and then I passed the room he'd just come out of...."

She faltered, but Taran had been drawn into the web of her telling. He'd seen what she'd seen, heard what she'd heard. Whether it was because she had some latent empathic talent, or whether it was the echoes of Fate shifting within the fabric of the world, he couldn't tell. Yet he knew, with a shock like ice water down his spine, what had rocked her so deeply that day and had led her to believe that which even now she strove to deny.

"You heard a baby cry."

He was unaware he'd actually spoken the words. Jinella gasped, her hand going to her mouth, her gaze locking on him with shocking intensity. He barely noticed. His inner eye was focused on the retreating back of the Baron, a man who never set foot in his own servants' wing. A man who'd been so pleased, so excited, so unwholesomely elated earlier that day.

Taran continued, affirming Jinny's worst fears, sealing the ruin of her hopes and dreams with the unavoidable conclusion.

"That was the day Prince Eadan disappeared."

Profound silence gripped the room. The oppressive heat of the afternoon weighed on their heads, draining their energy, stilling their tongues. Jinny's eyes were wide with a mixture of fright and awe.

"You really can read minds!" she breathed.

Taran frowned. The last thing he wanted was to scare her. They may be forced to ask for her help, and he couldn't afford to have her frightened of him. The charged atmosphere created by her tale, the ominous pressure of the approaching storm, and his intuitive grasp of her apprehensions had all combined to create a peculiar experience that she would never forget.

Giving himself a mental shake, he collected his thoughts.

"No, it was a lucky guess."

He smiled and she tentatively returned it. To bring her further out of her awe, he added, "Perhaps it was some servant's child you heard."

She shook her head. "My uncle doesn't permit his servants to keep children at the mansion. Those that have them must find their own homes."

Taran turned a sober look on Jinny, who still sat in the circle of his arms like she belonged there.

"It sounds as if you could be right."

She lowered her eyes, unwilling even now to accept her uncle could be a traitor. Taran released her and was about to go and brew more fellan—he certainly needed it after the revelations of the past few hours—when he heard the door latch. Ardoch had returned from his mission to the castle.

"I got back just in time. Looks like there's going to be a bad storm—"

The swordmaster stopped. He was surprised to see Jinella seated in his living room, but he greeted her cordially enough. "My Lady Jinella," he said, giving her a gracious bow.

"Master Ardoch," she replied, giving him the back of her hand to kiss.

Ardoch threw Taran a quizzical look over Jinny's hand. Taran explained Jinny's presence as he brewed fresh fellan, then asked Jinny to give her tale to the swordmaster. It would sound better coming from her, and besides, he felt a strong need to contact Sullyan and pass on this vital information. He'd not forgotten her stricture about substrate communications, but felt that what he had learned justified the risk. If he linked with her and she still felt it impolitic to talk through the substrate, at least he would have alerted her to the fact they had important news. She could then choose whether to return to hear it or continue with her own investigations. He left Jinny with Ardoch and went up to his room.

Lying on the bed and closing his eyes, he quested through the milky substrate for the familiar pattern of Sullyan's psyche. The soft murmur of voices from below was no distraction to his increasing control, but the ominous weight of the approaching storm Ardoch had mentioned, within which the signatures of both Fire and Water were strong, beat against his brain, threatening to swamp and distort his senses. Water he could master, and he brushed its threat aside, but Fire was another matter. He struggled to retain his sense of balance as he sought for Sullyan's pattern.

It was no good. He could sense her, but could make no contact. As she had warned him, she was tightly shielded. Taran was a mere Adept. No efforts of his could have breached or impinged upon that impenetrable wall, no matter how urgent or dire his need. Sighing in frustration, he struggled through the layers of substrate turbulence the storm had produced, and came back to himself in the darkening room.

When he rejoined Jinny and Ardoch he signaled his failure to the swordmaster with a shake of the head. They had no choice but to trust Jinny with their objectives and seek her help. After all, she knew the Baron's estate; she could direct them to the most likely hiding places for the baby Prince. Despite what Jinny had heard in the servants' wing, Taran didn't believe Reen would continue to conceal the boy within his own mansion. Surely it was far too risky. No matter how sternly he ruled his servants, some gossip or snippet of news was bound to leak.

He must have simply concealed the baby there that first day. He would have arranged a place of safety, somewhere secure and well hidden, from which he would undoubtedly "rescue" the boy when the time was right in order to be proclaimed a hero and savior of the Heir. This was the place they had to find.

Taran sat beside Jinny once more, casting a glance at Ardoch to caution him to silence. He took up both her hands, drawing her gaze.

"Jinny, painful and inconceivable though it is, let's agree to accept for the moment that your uncle was behind the abduction of Prince Eadan."

Moisture once again flooded Jinny's eyes. Seeking to comfort her, he said, "Neither of us believes he intends to harm the Prince.

He's doing this to increase his standing at court, to discredit the Andaryans, to gain favor with the people and the Queen."

Taran glossed over their suspicions as to the Queen's possible involvement, and Jinny made no connection.

"However, Prince Eadan is not the only Heir to go missing."

Jinny's mouth dropped and her eyes flicked to Ardoch's face. The Torlander didn't react and she turned her full attention back to Taran. Before she could speak, he continued.

"You already told me you thought you heard the Baron and Izack talking about Aeyron's disappearance. Let's assume for the moment this is exactly what you heard. They couldn't possibly have known about it at that time unless they were involved, could they?"

Jinny's cold fingers tightened convulsively in his. She shook her head.

"So, if they were responsible for taking Prince Aeyron, they'd have to have somewhere secure to hold him. Can you think of anywhere on the Baron's estate where he could possibly hold someone captive? A deserted building, perhaps, or an old strongroom? Maybe under the mansion itself? Does it have a cellar?"

Jinny's eyes were wide. He guessed she had originally hoped he would tell her what a silly goose she was, that her uncle couldn't possibly be involved or have any knowledge of these horrible events. Instead, here she was, sitting with two men who were taking her suspicions seriously. More than that, they were asking her to help them decipher and understand these momentous events.

He could see she didn't know how to react. She had never been intended to take part in history-shaping events. He noticed the pallor of her face and her unfocused eyes and thought she might faint. With intuitive sympathy, he realized they were going too fast for her. There was even a faint sheen of moisture on her brow, caused mainly by the increasing heat of the coming storm, but partly by her inner turmoil and distress.

He glanced at Ardoch.

"Ghyllan, do you have any wine to hand? I think the lady needs some fortification."

The Torlander rose. "If that's what she needs, I can do better than wine." He disappeared into the cooking room and came back with an exquisite little crystal bottle, delicately chased, holding a quantity of deep amber liquid. Taran recognized the ubiquitous tarn-liquor. Producing three small crystal glasses, Ardoch decanted a small amount of the liquor into each. He handed a glass to Jinny.

"Here, lassie, take a sip of this. Slowly, mind! It's powerful stuff."

Jinny eyed it dubiously and glanced at Taran, who nodded. As if she feared it would bite her, she took a tiny sip. The expression of delight that came across her face was soon replaced by shock as the fiery liquor burned down her throat. Taran was impressed by the ladylike cough that was all she permitted herself, refusing to give in to the breathlessness the first taste of such spirit usually produced.

"Oh," she exclaimed, holding her glass away from her to study its contents, "that *is* powerful stuff." She immediately took another sip, and Ardoch let out a gruff laugh. His approving bellow steadied her and she smiled shyly. "I've never had anything stronger than wine before."

"You took it like a true lady," said Ardoch, and Jinny stood and accorded the old swordmaster a dainty little curtsey. Courtly manners demanded he return a bow, and their easy jesting lightened the mood of the room considerably.

Once they had sobered, Taran asked Jinny, "Do you feel able to answer my questions now? I'm truly sorry to put you through all this, but I'm sure you can appreciate how important it could be. If it does turn out that your uncle is responsible for Eadan's abduction, then his fortune, his lands, even his very life, will be forfeit. You could get caught up in that by association."

Jinny gasped. "But I'm loyal to the King!"

Taran held up a hand. "I know you are, but Elias has been pushed to the limits of his endurance by Eadan's disappearance, as I'm sure you understand. He declared war on Andaryon because of his deep need to lash out at those he thinks responsible. He might not be capable of restraint once he discovers the true culprit. But if you help us recover the Heir, if you prove your loyalty by your actions, you'd be safe. Your inheritance would surely be restored to you, and who knows what else the King's gratitude might bring? What do you say, my Lady? Are you willing to help us find Prince Eadan?"

Taran had hit upon the one consideration guaranteed to strike a chord in Jinny. It wasn't that she was essentially shallow and materialistic, but she had been brought up with certain expectations, and the whole of her young life so far had been shaped to enable and motivate her to achieve them. Her eyes lit up at the prospect of finding such favor with the King.

"Of course I am."

Taran concealed a small sigh of relief.

He repeated his earlier questions, and Jinny gave thought to the problem of where the Baron might have hidden either of the Princes.

"As far as the demon Heir is concerned, I don't think I can help you. But if Prince Eadan is on the estate, there are a number of outlying cottages where a baby could be concealed amongst the families of the estate workers."

Taran considered this. He had never seen Eadan. The Prince would just be one blond baby among many. Even Jinny said she doubted she could pick him out from a group of similar babies.

"But," she added tentatively, "would he really leave the Prince so casually guarded? Believe me, he wouldn't trust his tenants to keep a secret like that, not if his own life were at stake. The only people he trusts are Izack and his personal household staff. So if he really is keeping Prince Eadan concealed on the estate, my money would be on him still being in the mansion. Far easier to keep control of who might see him than in a house belonging to a tenant."

Taran wasn't convinced, but left that problem for the moment.

"So," he mused, "if there's no strong place on the estate to hold Prince Aeyron, where else could he be? We know the Baron spends all his time either at the castle or the estate. And he can't have secreted Aeyron at the castle."

"Why not?"

Taran and Jinny turned to stare at Ardoch. He returned their gazes calmly. "There are dungeons under yon castle, you ken. They've not been used for countless years, since before the old King's time. I'd say they were perfect for yer man's purpose."

Taran frowned. "How would he get Aeyron down there? Wouldn't someone have seen them?"

Ardoch shook his head. "There are passageways in yon castle that are rarely used. Even I can't recall exactly where the entrance to the dungeons is, though I daresay Levant and I could squirrel it out if need be. Why don't I go back to the castle and see if I can talk to the First Minister again? If he's found anything of interest in the accounts, he might be willing to help us find the dungeons. What d'you think?"

"I think I wish our other colleague was here." Even now, Taran was hesitant to give Jinny too much information. But she was quicker than he gave her credit for.

"Are you referring to Colonel Sullyan?" At Taran's startled

look she said archly, "Well, you did say she was still serving Elias. It's not too hard to work it out."

Taran shook his head and smiled. "Yes, you're right. She's off on an investigation of her own at the moment and I'd feel much happier if we could tell her all this before we go any further. She really needs to know."

"Can't you just ...?" Jinny tapped the side of her head.

"I've tried. She's shielded." He and Ardoch studied each other. "Ghyl, check in with Levant and see if he's had enough time to look through the treasury accounts. If he's happy to help us further it would be advantageous. Jinny and I will wait here in case Sullyan returns. When you come back, we'll decide how to proceed."

The old swordmaster nodded. "Aye, that seems sensible. I'll be as quick as I can."

They watched him depart, and then Jinny and Taran sat together in the lamp-lit gloom of early evening, listening to the first heavy raindrops from the overburdened sky. The faint grumble of thunder rolled inexorably closer.

Chapter Seventeen

The weighty potential of the storm nagged at Sullyan like an aching tooth. She sent her metasenses toward it, but once she discovered it was perfectly natural—although she was surprised at the immensity of it—she ignored it. It was yet far away and wouldn't hinder her search. Indeed, a heavy downpour might work in her favor, keeping unwanted attention away from her activities.

Her dark leather clothing, although uncomfortably warm, allowed her to blend in with the undergrowth and dark tree trunks of Loxton Forest. She remained alert during the day and saw only one band of brigands within the Forest. They were laughably easy to avoid. Once the war was over, she really ought to offer to clear the Forest of these parasites for Elias.

A sudden pang under her heart reminded her she was no longer an officer in the King's forces. She gritted her teeth and tried to ignore the pricking behind her eyes. Inhaling deeply, she left the brigands to their sloppy habits and pushed on northward, toward the Baron's estate.

It took her until early afternoon to come upon the outer fringes of Loxton Forest, where she caught her first sight of the Baron's farmlands. A broad, thick hedge separated the straggling trees of the Forest's edge from the neat pastures of the Baron's lands. The hedge was fully twenty feet high in places; unkempt on the Forest side, managed and clipped on the other. She wondered how many foresters the Baron employed to keep it in shape.

Scouting carefully along the hedge, she soon found a deer trail through it. The hedge was only meant as a boundary to the Forest, not an impenetrable barrier, and she was able to squeeze through easily, emerging onto the Baron's estate.

There was no one in sight. The fields before her were arable pasturelands dotted with sheep and cattle in the distance. It was still too early for milking, so she wasn't likely to meet shepherds or cattle herders just yet. Once she was certain she was unobserved, she delicately reached out with tendrils of metaforce, seeking the direction of the Earth power site. Alert as ever for signs of the renegade Artesan, she ranged over the estate, finally locating what she sought farther to the northeast. Satisfied, she quenched her power and continued on her way.

She skirted farms and outlying houses, and passed fields of wheat, barley, and lavender slowly ripening in the summer warmth. Many a farmer would have cause to curse the heavy rain of the approaching storm when it unleashed its might over such tender crops.

After another hour of stealthy travel, during which she had to avoid several carters and laborers carrying out their duties, she saw in the distance a dark smudge which looked to be a remnant of woodland, left over from when the Forest had covered this entire region. The ground to the west had been steadily rising, and a few miles away it sloped sharply upward to merge with the chalk cliffs overhanging the sea. She could even hear seabirds crying, and guessed she was leaving the estate's small village behind and approaching the environs of the Baron's private mansion.

From Ardoch's description, she knew the mansion itself was situated in extensive fields and pasturelands adjoining the chalk cliffs, accompanied by a few workers' cottages, where the families of the household servants, gardeners, and cooks lived. She approached cautiously, wary of being seen. Away to the east of where the mansion must be, the dark smudge resolved itself into a large area of thick woodland. As she neared it, skirting the beginnings of what must be the mansion's private land, she realized her first impression was correct. This woodland was ancient indeed.

Brambles choked the edges and the trees were crowded, jostling together for space and light. She couldn't see far between them in the fading light of the approaching storm, for thin birches and whippy firs had fallen and intertwined to form a dense barrier. Her senses, however, told her that the area she sought was within this ancient wood, and so she moved around its perimeter to seek an entrance.

It was late afternoon and the iron-gray sky was turning ominously purple. She could hear the occasional rumble of thunder off to the east, and realized the storm would hit before nightfall. This didn't bother her; she had slept out in the rain many times before, and the very thickness of the wood should provide some cover. Besides, it was far too humid and a good downpour would freshen the air.

She came upon another deer path, this one more overgrown than the last. The brambles tried to snare her legs as she brushed through them, but her protective leathers shed the barbs easily. Then she was past the bramble barrier and slipping into the deeper gloom of the trees, where only occasional patches of undergrowth grew under gaps in the canopy.

It was eerily still. The approaching storm had dampened even the spirits of the woodland creatures. They had already taken cover, perhaps mistaking the heavy purple cloud-pall for true dusk. Slowly, questing delicately with her metaforce, Sullyan moved closer to her goal.

She knew she was nearly there. She could taste the raw Earth force in the air even through the heavy elemental signature of the fast-approaching storm. This must be a very ancient site indeed for the natural element to have saturated the area in this way. The stone circle she and Taran had used on their way here had not exuded its latent potential with such ponderous and archaic majesty, and she was eager to stand within the site and absorb its atmosphere. Her curiosity was piqued even as her caution and the recollection of the imperative nature of her search reasserted themselves.

In the end, and despite its awesome ambience, she still nearly missed it. The raw element was discharging in such a way as to percolate over an area far larger than the site itself. She had been expecting to find a stone circle such as the one she and Taran had used, or the one to the north of Pharikian's Citadel. This site was more ancient by far than either of those.

She ascertained the boundaries of the power leakage and traced it to its exact center. Only when she stood directly in the middle of the ferny area did she realize what she had found.

Once, aeons ago, it must have been a mighty monument of vast proportions. Megaliths such as she had never seen lay buried all around her, their weighty capstones tumbled and broken. All were overgrown by generations of vines, ferns, brambles, and creepers. Many of the huge stones had weathered over the ages until they were little more than humps under the moss and leaf litter. Trees had rooted within the circle, grown to maturity, fruited, and died, leaving their crumbling husks behind.

She saw that once there had been a double ring of stones; a rare configuration in her experience. The outer or "guard" ring was of the massive bluish stone which came from far to the north. These had once been crowned by equally impressive granite capstones. The inner or "sacred" ring, which interlocked with the guard ring, was of granite also, but these had been smaller, no taller than a man when they had stood erect.

Most of the stones had fallen over the centuries and moss cushioned everything. There was no clear patch of stone visible anywhere—except in two notable places.

Only three of the prehistoric megaliths still reared in place, although Sullyan thought they were probably less than half their original height. One was the western cardinal stone in the guard ring, and this monstrous megalith had been cleared of much of its lichen covering some time recently. The symbiotic little plants were beginning to recover much of their territory, but it was all too obvious that only a couple of years ago someone had scraped all the crustose growths away to leave the stone clean.

Also, someone had sunk two iron rings into the megalith, about six feet apart and approximately three feet from the ground.

The two other stones which still stood also bore such rings, and Sullyan spent some time examining them. The iron wasn't new, its surface rusting, although beneath the rust the metal was still strong. She didn't like the implications. These iron rings had the appearance of fetters, and she could tell they had been placed here for no clean purpose.

She straightened and moved to the center of the circle, where the only other clean surface of stone lay. The central flat stone, or altar stone, set slightly off true center as they often were, was also scraped clean of its covering vegetation, although this had been done much more recently. As the first heavy drops of rain began to fall through the canopy far above, Sullyan realized someone had visited this stone circle within the past few days. Probably no longer than a week ago, judging by the metal scrape marks on the altar stone.

Tension gripped her. This was the first clear indication that this site, her goal and the focus of her fears and suspicions for so long, would play a part in whatever plan the Baron had devised. She refused to believe it could be anyone else. Yet there were no clues within the circle to tell her what those plans might be.

Scouting farther, she found a concealed track leading almost directly northwest away from the site, toward where the mansion must be. Someone had pulled dead tree boughs across the entrance to the path, which was just wide enough to permit the passage of a small cart, and the surrounding vegetation had concealed its presence. By examining it minutely, she could just make out faint footprints in the disturbed soil.

The rain was falling faster by the minute and the sky darkening. She decided to attempt contact with Taran, to see whether he or Ardoch had had any success that day, and seated herself upon the altar stone in preparation. Before she could hone her metasenses, a faint quiver or tension in the air caused her to stiffen. A long low rumble of thunder, perceptibly closer now, vibrated through her finely-tuned senses. Thinking this was what had impinged upon her consciousness, she nearly missed the faint sound when it came again.

It was a footfall. Someone was coming! She leaped from the stone. Slamming down her shield, she retreated to the edge of the circle, away from the concealed path. She swiftly checked the area for signs of her presence. She had left none.

Blending into the undergrowth, she took her long knife in her hand and backed away from the circle. She moved far enough that if anyone chanced to look through the trees, they wouldn't see her. This unfortunately also meant she wouldn't be able to see whoever was coming, but she hoped she'd be near enough to hear any voices. Crouching within the thick ferns, she waited.

✤ ✤ ✤ ✤ ✤

Ardoch once again presented himself at the First Minister's door.

With an ambiguous and stern expression, Levant ushered him into his office, brusquely offering wine. Seated once more in the red upholstered chair, Ardoch accepted the wine, watching Levant's face. His eyes shifted uncomfortably like a man unsure of his ground. Ardoch frowned. Levant's discomfiture could just as easily mean he had found discrepancies in the exchequer as he had not. Either way, he appeared to be facing an awkward decision.

Levant didn't keep Ardoch waiting.

"I have to tell you, Swordmaster, that my perusal of the exchequer accounts today has found no monies unaccounted for."

Ardoch's heart sank. So much for *that* theory. "So you found nothing amiss in the treasury accounts at all?"

The stern line of the First Minister's mouth tightened beneath his peppered beard. "I didn't say that."

Ardoch sharpened his gaze. "But—"

"I said I found no monies unaccounted for. What I *did* find was that a large sum of gold—a huge sum, in fact—left the treasury reserve at the time you specified."

Ardoch's eyes widened. "Then how was it accounted for?"

Levant's face took on a pitying expression. "If it was the Baron who took it, he has made a grave error. If Elias had found this out, he would have been hard-pressed to explain it convincingly."

Seeing Ardoch's eager look, Levant elaborated.

"You know, of course, that the Queen's father, King Lerric, was involved with the rebels who killed Elias's father."

Ardoch nodded. He had been personally involved in the civil war defending Elias.

"What you may not know is that the year before Elias and Sofira wed, he and Lerric spent many long hours in negotiation of their alliance. Lerric denounced his fellow rebels as soon as they'd been defeated, but his loyalty was still in doubt. Elias stipulated there be a period of one year between the betrothal and the wedding, time to allow Lerric to prove his loyalty. If he wanted his daughter to become High Queen, Lerric was forced to agree. But Lerric proved a hard bargainer, and he demanded far more gold for Sofira's dowry than Elias was willing to pay. Elias eventually agreed to pay a certain sum to Lerric on the condition it was used to fund improvements to Lerric's province, which had been sadly neglected during the civil war.

"It was a considerable sum, and the payment was made just before the marriage. Unbeknown to the Queen or her father, Elias sent—shall we say 'delegates'?—into Bordenn to see whether his gold was spent in the way he had specified. It was no surprise when he found it was going straight into Lerric's coffers. Without informing the Queen, Elias instructed me, as Keeper of the Treasury at that time, to inform him should Lerric ever request more in the way of funds. I duly passed this on to the treasury clerks. And although Sofira took over the treasury—or perhaps because of it—Elias never rescinded the order."

Levant paused and sighed. "What I found earlier today was a letter dated at the beginning of the period you mentioned and signed with Lerric's seal, asking for a large sum of gold to help with the rebuilding of an area of southern coastline, citing villages that had been damaged by a storm which brought down a whole line of cliffs. This sum was paid out of the treasury reserves under the sole signature of the Queen."

Ardoch frowned. "But she was the legitimate Keeper of the Treasury then. If Lerric wrote directly to her, did she not have authority to use treasury gold without informing the clerks?"

Levant shook his head. "Up to a certain point. Anything over a specified amount should be checked and approved by the Chief Treasury Clerk as well as the Keeper. The Queen was told this when she took over the running of the exchequer. In the face of

Elias's mandate, the chief clerk would never have allowed her to withdraw that amount without informing the King. I can only assume that the treasury clerks were never shown that letter, nor told about the withdrawal. If the King ever noticed the decimation of the reserve, I have no doubt Sofira, if it was actually her doing, would have pleaded her father's cause and apologized profusely for the error.

"However, if we were to check more closely, I suspect we would find the letter is a clever forgery. Even if it's not—and I'd not bet against Lerric writing that letter at the request of his daughter—I doubt there have been any cliff-falls on Bordenn's southern coastline. Unfortunately, I can't sanction sending anyone to check under the current circumstances."

"But why didn't the clerks notice the depletion of the treasury coffers?"

Levant shrugged. "I expect they would have if the gold had been paid out of the main vaults. Whoever devised the plan cleverly used the reserve depositories, and the clerks would have had no reason to check those. They're only opened when there is an especially large drain on Albia's resources, such as a war, or when the accounts are audited. And wouldn't you just like to bet the Baron offered to help Sofira with the audits rather than 'trouble' the clerks?"

The Torlander regarded Levant soberly. "Well, that could be checked. I take it you realize what this means regarding the Queen, my Lord? Yon Baron couldn't have circumvented the clerks or gained access to the reserves without Sofira's knowledge, regardless of the authenticity of her father's letter. Where is it, by the way?"

Levant's mouth was a grim line. "I left it where it was. If it comes to it, I'll show it to Elias. Until then, given the current situation, I think it best if we kept this matter to ourselves. There's still no proof of guilt on the Queen's part, and I'm inclined to give her the benefit of the doubt. The Baron could easily have obtained her signed authorization without her being aware. Let Elias regain his son, and then he can look into any matters regarding Sofira. It's not our place."

Ardoch accepted Levant's verdict with good grace, acknowledging his sensible caution. At least one other person of integrity now had cause for suspicion, and that was enough for him. He turned to the other matter.

"My Lord, given that you now accept there may have been subterfuge directed against Elias within his very castle, there is another question you may be able to help me with."

Levant's discomfort showed on his face and his blue eyes darkened, yet he waved the Torlander on.

"Do you happen to recall aught about dungeons beneath the castle?"

Levant looked taken aback and replied slowly. "I believe there are some, but to my knowledge they haven't been used in countless years. King Kandaran certainly never used them, and I doubt Elias even knows of their existence."

"Do you recall how to get down to them? Where the entrance is?"

"I don't, but there are ancient maps of the castle, drawings done by some of the stonemasons who built the place. They might show it."

"Can we get a look at these drawings?"

Ardoch could hardly contain himself. Despite the gravity of the situation, he was gripped by his task. He heard a long rumble of thunder as Levant rose to his feet, and realized how dark it was outside.

The First Minister led the way out of his office. "That's going to be some storm."

They walked the corridor toward the Archives and Library, Ardoch glancing out of the occluded windows at the strengthening rain. He was going to get very wet on his way back home, but his efforts would make the drenching worthwhile.

It took them a full half hour of patient searching, but they finally unearthed an ancient and musty parchment showing the castle's lower levels. The plant-based ink had faded and the parchment was poor quality and cracked, but it showed the way to the dungeon levels. Memorizing the twists and turns, they replaced the old vellum very carefully and let themselves out of the Archives.

Once they were back in the hallway, Levant raised his brows. "What now?"

Ardoch knew he had piqued Levant's interest. "Will you come with me to see them?" He was unsurprised when the First Minister agreed.

"We'll need lamps. Those passageways will be damp and slippery. No one's been down there for years."

Ardoch had his own opinions on that score, but they collected lanterns from a storeroom and made their way to the rear of the castle. The entrance to the dungeons in this wing—there was a similar access in the east wing, striking Ardoch as convenient for Reen—was against the rear wall of the castle. There were only storerooms this deep within the massive structure. They were unnoticed as they made their way toward these unfrequented areas.

After two or three twists and turns of the passage, they reached the rear wall of the castle. The hallway they followed turned at right angles here and led to a solid oak door. This had a huge iron lock, and the key to it hung on a hook on the wall. Ardoch took it down and fitted it to the dusty lock. It turned with an effort; if the dungeons had indeed been used, Reen had not entered from here.

They passed through the door and closed it behind them. Ardoch relocked it from the inside and pocketed the key. Levant gave him a look.

"What did you do that for?"

"Insurance."

Ardoch also drew his sword, causing Levant to glance at him sharply. Yet the First Minister said no more and followed Ardoch's lead down the slippery stairs that led to the musty bowels of the castle.

They passed the black, open maw of the stairway that led up to the east wing, and soon the lantern light threw grotesque shadows upon what they could both see was a new door blocking their way. It was stout wood bound with iron and had yet another strong lock, also very new. The key, once again, hung beside the door.

Ardoch cast a meaningful glance over his shoulder and Levant grimaced.

The key turned noiselessly. Ardoch pushed the door open and advanced slowly, his sword held before him. The stench that assailed his nostrils made him gag, and Levant cursed behind him. They followed a line of recent footprints in the heavy dust, prints that were smeared and dragged in places as though someone had carried a heavy burden.

The footprints led to another door. It stood ajar, and beyond it was the source of the stench. Ardoch suddenly didn't want to see what was behind that door. They could hear no sound but their own labored breathing and the occasional far-off drip of water. Even the tolling thunder was inaudible this far down.

Stepping reluctantly to the door, Ardoch pushed it wide with his foot. He thrust the lantern into the noisome air of the cell and sheathed his sword in order to place his free hand over his nose and mouth. The smell made him want to vomit. It was the stink of human ordure, old blood, and infection.

Levant joined him in the doorway and together they looked at the filthy straw, taking in the dark, nameless stains on the stone floor, the effluence of a helpless body, and also the raw echo of unendurable agony.

It was more than they could stand.

Retreating in haste, they left the cell as they found it, careful to walk in the already disturbed dust and to relock the doors. When they finally gained the clean air of the west wing entrance, they were both pale with nausea and grim with anger.

"He surely didn't keep Prince Eadan down there!" Levant's voice was harsh with revulsion and shock.

"Nay, my Lord, not the wee Prince, I think." Ardoch struggled to control his own fury. He couldn't imagine anyone surviving for long down there. "But I fear it's where he kept the Andaryan Prince."

"If he did, the demon didn't live. The *smell* of it, Ardoch! Rot and pain. If a body was kept in that cell until it fell apart with decay it couldn't have smelled worse."

"Aye, man, you're right. I very much fear the Andaryan is dead. Reen must have removed the body. The scuff marks on the floor say as much."

"But there's still no concrete proof it was the Baron," said Levant, "and what I found in the treasury today wouldn't be enough to impeach him, let alone the Queen. Even if we found she did pay out that gold in full knowledge of her actions, it could just be the misguided generosity of a devoted daughter. So, where do we go from here?"

Ardoch didn't miss Levant's subconscious affirmation of his support and allegiance. He smiled grimly at the First Minister.

"You've done enough for now, my Lord, and you have our thanks for your assistance. There's still a bonny wee Prince to find, and I shall be going to the Baron's estate tomorrow for a good look around."

Levant studied his face. "Be careful, Ardoch. If the Baron's as deeply mired in this as you say, he's a very dangerous man. And don't forget, he has his own bodyguard. Many of the Baron's men have been moved into the castle, ostensibly to protect the Queen and the Princess. He still retains a guard, though, led by that commander of his. Izack is a shifty and conscienceless barbarian. It wouldn't take much provocation for him to attack you."

Ardoch waved a hand as he left. "I can handle mercenaries such as yon Izack, my Lord. Don't you worry about me."

Chapter Eighteen

A rdoch made his way home through the tumult of rain and thunder, watching the flash of lightning as it flailed the hills to the east. The storm was steadily heading closer. With flurries of rain-driven wind whipping his sodden cloak about his legs, he hurried toward the shelter of his house.

Taran and Jinny were waiting, and the house was cheerful with lamplight against the murk and violence of the storm. Ardoch wasted no time changing out of his soaked clothes, while Jinny busied herself in the cooking room. There was plenty of stew left over from the night before, and she astounded Taran by producing a creditable meal.

She saw his amazed expression as she brought him his plate, and sniffed disdainfully.

"What, did you think I couldn't cook? How, pray, is a lady supposed to discipline her kitchen staff if she doesn't know the difference between braising and boiling? Give me credit for *some* sense."

Thoroughly put in his place, Taran apologized over Ardoch's rough laughter. The swordmaster had been disappointed not to find Sullyan awaiting him too, but Taran said, "She's not back yet. She did say she might be out all night, depending on what she found. She'll contact me if she can. If not, we'll just have to carry on without her."

Ardoch was also concerned about the friend who had taken

Jinny in, and he asked her if she wouldn't be missed. Jinny replied easily, telling him she'd sent a message saying she'd decided to dine with friends and would be back later. She was as eager as Taran to hear the swordmaster's news, and after a reserved glance at the Adept, the Torlander told them what he'd discovered while they ate.

When the Torlander was done, Taran laid down his eating knife. "So, what's our next move? What do we do with this information?"

"It's obvious, isn't it, laddie? We have to find the wee Prince. And the Baron's estate is the likeliest place to look. With most of his personal bodyguard now stationed at the castle, we'll never have a better time than the morrow. Yon Baron will be at the Minster all day, and the Queen with him. That'll keep him out of the way, at least."

Taran nodded. "Where on the estate shall we begin?"

Ardoch considered a moment before replying. "I can't think of a better place than where Jinny heard the bairn crying. If her uncle never permits children in his mansion, it's a pretty safe bet it was Eadan she heard. I think she may be right. Why would the Baron risk moving him? If he trusted his household servants not to talk when he first took Eadan there, why wouldn't he trust them to keep the Prince?"

Taran looked unconvinced, but found no fault with Ardoch's reasoning. They had to have a starting point, after all. He turned to Jinny.

"What are the usual arrangements for the Baron's servants on a holy day, Jinny?"

She had been watching and listening with rounded eyes and an unreadable expression. "They have most of the day off to attend the chapel in the village. But my uncle always expects a special meal in the evening, so the cooks and the serving maids return midafternoon to start the preparations. And his manservant, Seth, will probably be about somewhere. He'll attend my uncle until he retires for the night."

Taran caught Ardoch's eye. "So we should have the greater part of the day in which to search the mansion. I think we can discount the Baron's own suites and the main part of the house. If he has secreted Eadan somewhere—and the nursemaid, too, I suppose—it's more likely they'd be in the servants' quarters."

Ardoch nodded. "They'll likely be guarded, though. He's hardly going to leave the little Prince and his nanny alone in the house all day, even on a holy day."

Taran grimaced. "You're right. We'll have to be careful. Jinny, we'll need you to tell us the layout of the house and the servants' wing, and exactly where you first heard that baby cry. Can you do that for us?"

Ardoch noticed Jinny's withering stare. "And just how do you expect to get into the house unseen?" she demanded. "How are you going to approach it without being challenged? Any of the estate workers or groundsmen would stop you, you know. And it may be a holy day, but not everyone attends chapel as rigorously as they should. If the two of you are seen sneaking around the house, the alarm will be raised at once."

Taran glanced at Ardoch, his expression rueful. "She's right. Is there any cover near the house that we could use to conceal ourselves?"

She shook her head. "The front is laid to formal lawns and a gravel drive. To the rear is the kitchen garden, the rose garden, and the stables, but they're all separated from the house by an open gravel courtyard. No, gentlemen, you'll be seen however you approach the house. There's only one workable answer, I'm afraid."

Taran shrugged. "We could pose as tradesmen."

Jinny gave him another pitying look, accompanied by a long-suffering sigh. "On a holy day, Taran? Use your wits."

Taran colored as Ardoch let out a snort of laughter which he hastily turned into a cough. Jinny stared at him coldly until he subsided.

The Torlander grinned at her. "What do you suggest, my Lady? It sounds like you have a plan."

"Of course I do. It's plain the two of you will never get into the house unnoticed on your own. The only way you'll do it without being challenged is if you have a legitimate reason for being there. I still have some gowns to collect that the seamstresses hadn't finished, so *I* will be your reason."

Taran opened his mouth to protest, but she overrode him.

"We'll take a carriage. One of you can drive and the other will ride on the footplate. I'll say I've come for more of my things, and that I've brought you along to help carry them. Once we're inside, I can take you straight to where I heard the baby crying, and if there's a guard, perhaps I can distract him or something. The rest will be up to you. And if we do find the Prince, we can use the carriage to conceal him as we drive away."

She sat watching them, hands folded demurely in her lap, a pleased expression on her face. For an instant, Ardoch was reminded of a younger Sullyan, who had often used such tactics as a cadet. Was this some wily female ploy to let the men exhaust the possibilities and then casually toss the solution into the conversation like a pebble into a pool? If so, it was effective, and neither he nor Taran could find fault with Jinny's simple plan. Although Taran clearly disliked the idea of taking her into what could easily become a very dangerous situation, and made a feeble attempt to put her off.

"But what about your friend? Won't she miss you at the Minster tomorrow?"

She didn't even deign to glance at him. "That's easy. I'll tell her I've arranged to go with some other friends. That will enable me to leave her house early so I can come and meet you. The Minster's huge and it'll be crowded. She'll never know I wasn't there."

Defeated, Taran sighed. Ardoch didn't bother making his own effort; he'd clearly be wasting his breath. Taran turned to him, trying to regain some sort of control.

"Suppose we're successful. What do we do once we have the Prince?"

The swordmaster sobered at once. "We'll bring him back here first. Hopefully, we can talk all this over with Sullyan tomorrow. I imagine she'll want to return him to Elias as soon as possible and put a stop to this senseless war.

"Now, if we're agreed so far, I think we ought to get the lassie here back home for the night before she's missed. It's getting late and the storm's still rising. It's not a night to be abroad."

They hailed a carriage to return Jinella to her lodgings. The same coachman was hired to call for Jinny at a certain time the next morning, to bring her back to Ardoch's house. The swordmaster watched as Taran kissed Jinny's hand before she left, and smiled at the look she gave in return. Taran's face was flushed as he waved at the retreating carriage.

✢ ✢ ✢ ✢ ✢

Sullyan waited among the ferns, listening intently. She heard the sounds of what could be a cart being drawn into the circle. She could tell when the concealing boughs were cast aside, and she heard the creak of wheels and the dull thud of a hoof striking stone. There were at least two people with the cart, speaking in low tones, and she couldn't make out what they said. The rain had increased in intensity and a gusty wind had come up. The treetops were rustling and swaying, and their constant susurration drowned out the voices. They were male, but that was all she could glean.

She heard dragging sounds, as if something heavy were being removed from the cart, and also faint metallic noises. She briefly entertained the idea of moving closer. In the tumult of the storm it would be very hard to tell when the circle was once again deserted. Yet she feared to give herself away, especially when she was this close to finding the truth of her suspicions.

She had been crouched within the dripping ferns for a good ten minutes when she detected a surge in the ponderous leakage of Earth force. She had sensed no Artesan's controlling hand on the element of Earth deep within the stones, but that slight heaving of the flow was unmistakable. Something of power had called to the Earth force, and her pulse quickened as she considered what it might mean.

Finally she heard the cart leaving, even above the increasing power of the storm. She was wet through now, but it barely registered. She was impatient to see what had been left in the circle, and whether her guess was correct. Straightening with caution, she edged her way forward.

Just outside the fallen stones of the guard ring, she halted and looked about. The cart was gone, but she could just make out the ruts where it had been. The dead tree boughs that had been used to hide the narrow track were lying where they had been tossed aside, suggesting that whoever had been here meant soon to return.

She had to be quick. She would verify her guess and then return to Ardoch's house. With luck, the storm would keep the brigands of the Forest within their shelters and she could make much better time on the return journey.

Darkness was descending fast, heavy cloud cover hastening the evening. Her eyes were adjusted to the gloom by now, and silently she moved into the circle, toward the altar stone. As she neared it, she could already see her guess was correct. Dumped on the altar stone, gleaming gray in the feeble light, was about fifteen pounds of raw reverse-polarity spellsilver.

It was quiescent, requiring an Artesan's touch to activate it. She was drawn to it, wanted to put out a hand to touch it, yet knew she must not. This unprepossessing accumulation of raw metallic element had probably already been attuned to the renegade Artesan's psyche, and she risked alerting him to her presence if she touched it. Its presence confirmed her worst suspicions. She was still ignorant of the use to which it would ultimately be put, but here was the crux and culmination of the Baron's plans.

And this was where she must be when he put those plans into motion.

Satisfied, elated, yet deeply fearful of the future, she turned to go. The Baron's men would undoubtedly return with the rest of the spellsilver soon. A flash of lightning, still far off to the east, cast a dim flicker over the ancient site. The megaliths, as they often did, reacted to the raw element of Fire by absorbing some of it and casting back an eldritch phosphorescence. A low, labored hiss of agony caught at Sullyan's senses.

She was not alone.

The phantom glow revealed a man's body lying on the ground, his head and shoulders resting against the western cardinal stone. She started toward him, but a heart-wrenching pang stopped her. She knew him.

Prince Aeyron, Heir to Andaryon, lay before her as if crucified, his outstretched arms chained to the iron rings sunk into the stone. They were drawn painfully tight. She could see the iron fetters that bound his wrists to the rings, and also the gleam of spellsilver where a cord wound tightly against his skin. He was unconscious, but that faint exhalation of agony told her that he lived. Just.

Galvanized by this unlooked-for hope, she sprang toward him.

"Highness, *Highness*! Oh, Aeyron!" She flung her senses at him only to reel back as if from a physical blow as the spellsilver that wrapped him like a caul repelled her power. Her gaze limped painfully over his wracked form, taking in the many abrasions and contusions upon his face and naked torso, the rank and fetid smell his body exuded, and, most horribly, the rampant, oozing infection in his right hand.

She could see that the wound had never been tended or even staunched. The blood had simply caked where it had run, and bone shone whitely through the blackened flesh. The stricture of the spellcord had impeded the flow of blood, but the filthy conditions in which he had been kept had allowed infection to spread with impunity. The original knife wound in his upper right arm was also infected, but not as badly as the hand.

Hot tears of rage, sympathy, and love coursed down her face, falling onto his battered chest as she bent over him, desperate to help. "Highness? Aeyron? Do you hear me?"

His eyes opened, but he didn't respond, and she realized he wasn't looking at her. He was staring over her shoulder, and his pale yellow eyes were full of horror. She didn't have time to turn her head before something solid crashed against her skull. She fell over Aeyron's body, drowning in darkness and pain.

✤ ✤ ✤ ✤ ✤

Tad had been helping Goran in the kitchens. It wasn't his place now as a cadet, but his knowledge of Goran's working routines, and his ability to organize the younger lads to cope with the influx of men, proved invaluable to the irascible cook. Besides, it gave Tad an excuse to mingle with the men, hear their gossip, and possibly learn things of interest.

One group he served during the evening meal had only just

been told they would be going out under the command of Parren, their least favorite officer, and they had relieved themselves of some frustration. Tad had already assured them of Parren's general lack of popularity, so they hadn't bothered to guard their tongues. Tad had learned exactly when and where they were going, and as soon as he could get away he ran to the College to tell Ozella.

"It's perfect," he crowed, his voice echoing off the spellsilver-shielded walls of the healer suite. He and Ozella had taken to meeting here to avoid being overheard by Artesans and non-Artesans alike. "He'll be gone for hours. We'll have ample time to search his rooms as thoroughly as we want. If he's hiding anything of importance, we'll find it."

Ozella shrugged. "And then what do we do?"

Tad knew that Parren hadn't made any more demands or threats since the last time, and that Ozella was thankful, but thoughts of his sisters languishing in some dark and musty prison, or being leered over by lustful and violent men, were clearly uppermost in his mind. Tad sympathized, but still had expected more enthusiasm than this.

"Once we have proof of Parren's treachery, it'll no longer be just your word against his. We'll go to Bull or Colonel Vassa and tell them what we know. Once they see the proof, they'll hold Parren and question him. They'll find out where your sisters are and release them. We'll have helped catch a traitor—maybe two, if we find out who has been buying the information. Don't you see, Ozella? Your troubles will be over!"

Ozella didn't look convinced. "Which of us will do the searching? One of us ought to keep watch."

"You watch, I'll search." Tad relished the thought of some sleuthing. "But I doubt we'll need to watch very carefully. No one else would go into Parren's rooms. He's not senior enough to have a valet. Once he's out on patrol, he won't be there to see us. What could go wrong?"

He watched Ozella, hoping the older lad wouldn't back out. Tad was genuinely trying to help him, and it might even work. If it didn't, if they found nothing, Ozella would lose nothing. He had to take the chance, surely. Anything was better than sitting on his hands waiting for Parren's next threat.

Chapter Nineteen

As soon as the extra men arrived to take control of the newly-annexed town, Elias set about organizing his next conquest. General Blaine's arguments for restraint had fallen on deaf ears. Elias was even more determined now to carry out his plan.

Valustin's scouts had reported on the terrain surrounding the next town to the northwest, and also the fact that it was even less defensible than the first. This town was also a center for the distribution of foodstuffs, and the control of two such important food-producing areas should send an unequivocal message to the Hierarch. Elias meant to show how serious was his intent.

Anjer's forces hadn't moved the previous day. The Lord General seemed content to sit and watch. In Elias's estimation, this was a serious mistake. *He* would have attempted to surround the town and contain the invaders. Of course, that would also have effectively trapped the townsfolk, and maybe goaded their attackers into using them as bargaining tools.

Blaine thought perhaps Anjer was hoping Elias would see sense and withdraw. He sighed. Alas for them all, withdrawal was the last thing on Elias's beleaguered mind.

The King wanted to advance on his new target without constantly looking over his shoulder. He wanted to take the town with minimal fighting, to present the Andaryan general with yet another coup. With this in mind, he had Blaine order Valustin to evacuate the town under cover of darkness. The newly-arrived men were instructed to take over the defensive positions established by the Captain, and to range themselves around the walls in order to be visible to Anjer's scouts. Elias hoped the demon general would believe the Albians hadn't moved.

Robin and Blaine had handled the transfer extremely carefully so that Anjer would be unaware they had used the substrate to bring in extra men. Their subterfuge might not hold Anjer for long, but it should give their forces time to march unmolested on the new town. Once they had it under control, Anjer's numbers wouldn't be sufficient to form effective cordons around both towns as well as oppose Elias should he choose to march closer to the Citadel.

These plans went some way toward lessening Elias's fury. He had been enraged beyond measure by the treachery of the demons in attacking his rear while posing under a flag of truce. Every suspicion his unbalanced mind had conceived was proving true, and he was now more firmly convinced than ever his precious son and Heir was here.

Mathias Blaine had given up any attempts to calm his sovereign or convince him otherwise. He had only barely been able to dissuade Elias from torching the town they now held in retribution for the demons' actions.

Thankfully, common sense had prevailed when Blaine pointed out how necessary the town was to their forces, and how vulnerable they'd be without cover if Elias destroyed it. The demon forces would be unleashed against them for sure if they did that. Elias finally agreed, but was determined to do it once they had Anjer on the run.

Blaine breathed a sigh of relief. So far there had been very little bloodshed, and he had Anjer's restraint to thank for that. The Lord General's men had made no move toward the town. They hadn't shown themselves all day. Blaine knew they were still within the trees. Valustin's scouts and lookouts had seen the sun glinting off their weapons. Yet Anjer had withheld his hand, and it was Blaine's opinion the huge Andaryan hoped to catch them in the open. Provided the invading humans left his people largely unhurt, Anjer wasn't going to carry war into their midst.

Blaine kept his thoughts to himself, but he was mightily relieved that *someone* was displaying a cool head.

Clouds began to roll in during the afternoon, closing down the sky. Rain looked likely. Blaine welcomed the cloud cover. A starless, moonless night would make it less likely Anjer would notice their evacuation. It would also render their own march more difficult, but if the rain lasted till dawn, fewer people would be abroad in the next town. The Albians might be able to take it with as little opposition as the first.

Early evening saw them ready, captains aware of their places in the march and the order in which they would evacuate the town. The newly-arrived troops had all taken their stations and Blaine only awaited full dark.

The rain began falling at dusk; a light, drenching rain from low scudding clouds. A favorable cold wind blew from the northeast—less likelihood of sounds being carried to Anjer. Maybe the Andaryans would take cover against the rain and wouldn't expect movement from the humans.

Blaine gave the order to move out and the evacuation proceeded smoothly. The Albians left the town to the south, using the walls as cover between them and Anjer's scouts, angling around it to the northwest before striking out cross-country toward their next goal. Elias rode in their midst, his long scarlet cloak a black mass in the rain and darkness, a grimly satisfied expression on the iron planes of his face.

They marched through the night, slowly and cautiously, and

about an hour before dawn the scouts reported they had seen the lights of the next town. Valustin received Blaine's nod and went to reconnoiter.

When he returned, Elias's forces were in position and ready to strike. The scouts left behind to cover their rear reported no movement from Anjer, and no sign of the other force that had betrayed them the day before. Elias smiled grimly at the news.

"He'll hear of our deception soon enough. Now, let's show these slit-eyed bastards how a fighting force should be commanded."

He gave the order to take the town.

✣ ✣ ✣ ✣ ✣

In the darkness of his command tent, Anjer listened to the rain. His soul was heavy; he had no stomach for this war. The sheer futility of it struck to his very heart. He was a soldier by birth as well as training. His grandfather, father, and both of his uncles had fought in the Hierarch's service, and he had never considered doing anything else with his life. He was passionate about the defense of his homeland and would spend his men dearly in whatever way was necessary to protect his people.

This situation, however, was something else.

He knew both Barrin and Ephan felt he should now throw everything against Elias and force him to retreat, to harry him until he left their lands in peace. Yet Anjer was well aware of Elias's despair, as well as his irrational state of mind. Hadn't he witnessed it in his own ruler? And if Pharikian's distress had unhinged him so far as to declare war on Albia, Anjer knew he would have supported the Hierarch even as General Blaine was supporting Elias. Right or wrong, their duty permitted them no other decision.

Yet the scale of bloodshed, of wasted life, which would ensue from an all-out attack on the Albian King was too expensive for

Anjer to contemplate. His conscience wouldn't permit him to issue that kind of order, and he was confident the Hierarch would have approved. Anjer also had Marik on his side—the Regent's thoughts and views as valid as if Pharikian himself had spoken.

Anjer would sit tight and shadow the humans. He would only attack if they posed a direct threat to the Citadel, or if they attempted to sack the towns they occupied. He would not take the responsibility of precipitating death upon his people unless the humans began the killing. Provided the townspeople heeded the warnings Anjer had sent them, stayed calm, and offered no resistance, Elias had no reason to butcher them.

This was Anjer's fervent hope.

So he was angered, if not greatly surprised, when he heard that a large force of humans had been seen attacking another of the Citadel's market towns to the northwest.

He sighed extravagantly. They had slipped away from him, taken him unaware, and now he would be forced to split his strength. This was something he had feared. He had resisted thinning his command by surrounding the original town in case Elias planned to attack his lines, forcing a way through to the Citadel. He elected instead to stay within the woods, concealing his true numbers from Elias and keeping him guessing.

Anjer was expecting reinforcements from some of Vellet's nearer neighbors, but they wouldn't arrive in any great numbers until the following day. He had hoped Elias might sit tight until then. Now Anjer had lost yet more ground, and his fear for his people grew. He sent orders for a march on the new town whilst leaving some companies behind to occupy the human troops left to hold the first.

As he prepared to mount and lead his men out, Commander Barrin came galloping through the darkness toward him, his charger drenched in rain and sweat. Barrin's countenance was black with fury.

Sudden fear for his ruler surged through Anjer's heart. "What is it, man?"

But Barrin's news concerned another lord entirely. Despite his anger, there was deep satisfaction in his tone.

"My Lord, the men we sent after the turncoats who attacked Elias yesterday managed to apprehend two of them. They killed more—it seems they fought hard—but the rest got away, and I took the liberty of instructing a company to pursue them as covertly as possible.

"Under questioning, the two prisoners confirmed it was Lord Corbyn who ordered the attack on Elias. He's been recruiting men from Sonten's old lands and has gathered support from among both Sonten's and Rykan's former retainers. Although most of them didn't bemoan the loss of their lords, enough were sufficiently fearful of reprisals from Duke Marik to throw their lot in with Corbyn. He now has a force large enough to be a nuisance to either us or Elias, depending on his ultimate design."

"*Damn* him!" Anjer's black eyes flashed. "I *knew* we should have dealt with him before. He's been showing us his true colors for months. I'll have Tikhal's head on a pole for not reporting his insurrection sooner."

Barrin sat his sweating horse and regarded his enraged superior officer. "What shall I do with the prisoners, my Lord?"

Anjer raised his brows. "They're still alive? Keep them that way. They may yet have more to tell us. Corbyn's obviously been this Albian traitor's contact all along, and has been sending his men to raid their lands. If we ever get a satisfactory outcome to this sorry debacle, we might need those two prisoners as proof of Corbyn's activities. Tend their injuries, but don't allow them freedom to harm themselves. Let me know if your men find out if—and preferably where—Corbyn intends to attack next. We must hope to heaven that Brynne Sullyan can achieve what she's set out to do before this degenerates any further. Only she can find the other half to this puzzle now."

Barrin wheeled his tired horse toward the Citadel while Anjer led his men on to Elias's new position. He was running different strategies through his mind. His favored plan so far—to attempt another parley with the King—he now discounted. He couldn't afford to have Corbyn ruin another chance at reconciliation.

Clenching his fists, he comforted himself with thoughts of dire retribution against Corbyn as he rode out into the rain.

✣ ✣ ✣ ✣ ✣

There was darkness and there was pain. There was a rising tide of nausea and there were jagged flashes across her eyes which could have been lightning but probably were not. There was the taste of ashes in her mouth and a fierce ache in her heart. There was a grinding and insistent pain in her shoulders. But most of all there was the terrible, debilitating, all-pervading void of numbness that was the absence of her powers due to physical contact with spellsilver.

It was a sensation she was acquainted with and it drained her spirit like a ghoul.

An involuntary moan escaped her lips. She couldn't tell whether her eyes were open or closed; darkness slashed by sudden brilliance could just as easily have been the storm as the effects of concussion. It was still raining, that much she could feel, but there was a buzzing thunder in her brain like a stampeding of horses, and it interfered with her thinking. She couldn't hear anything but that incessant drumming and it intensified the nausea in her belly.

She tried to move, but a sharp wave of agony shot from her shoulders down her spine, causing her to whimper. She couldn't move. Her arms were outstretched to their limits, held in place with what felt like metal bands. Her hands were numb and her forearms burned with pain. She tried to force her hands to clench, but the muscles were too starved of blood to obey. Her slight movement alerted her to the feel of stone at her back, and this realization cleared some of the ruby darkness from her mind.

Aeyron. The stone circle. Chains.

Another groan escaped her, this one born of self-castigation and despair. She should have been more careful. Her fear and love for Aeyron had caught her out, and now she was as helpless as he and no use to anyone. Her other companions had only the vaguest idea where she was and would be unlikely even to miss her until later the following day, thanks to her warning to Taran. Her only hope was that he would attempt contact with her in the morning and would recognize the spellsilver-tainted void in the substrate where her psyche ought to be.

Very carefully, as even the smallest movement of her head threatened to swamp her in dizzying nausea, she tried to look to the side to see if Aeyron was still alive. She managed to swivel her eyes without feeling as if her head were falling off, but she still had to breathe deeply to stabilize her equilibrium. When she could concentrate again, she found she could now tell the difference between the flashes of lightning and the coruscations behind her eyes. She supposed the blow which had felled her had also cracked her skull. If so, she was lucky to be alive.

That thought very nearly brought an ironic snort. She doubted Aeyron would consider himself lucky right now, and knew that unless a miracle happened, she might well come to rue that the blow hadn't been fatal. Whatever the Baron was planning, he obviously intended she and Aeyron should have an intimate experience of it.

The next flash of lightning showed her the supine form of the Andaryan Prince beside her. His eyes were closed and she couldn't tell if he lived. Moisture ran down his pallid face like tears, and dark rings around his eyes gave him the appearance of a corpse.

"Highness?" she whispered. "Aeyron?"

No response. If he was dead, he was probably better off. If he was alive, she could do nothing to help him.

She turned her focus to fully assess her situation, more out of habit than with any real hope of rescue. Her hands had been thrust through the rings of iron on the megalith next to the cardinal stone, and were secured there by metal chains like Aeyron's. Someone had removed her leather jacket and pushed up the sleeves of her shirt so the spellcord could be bound tightly about her wrists. This had caused the numbness in her hands. She could flex her fingers slightly if she concentrated, but this only brought more pain and the strange, tingling sensation of reawakening nerves. Her shirt had not been otherwise tampered with, nor her sodden combat trousers. That was one relief.

Sick, helpless, and cursing herself for her stupidity, she allowed oblivion to take her down once more.

✣ ✣ ✣ ✣ ✣

Taran woke to the drumming rain and the humid atmosphere of the dark room. He was momentarily confused and lay still, trying to remember where he was. The storm was still active outside, although he thought its intensity had waned.

The memory of the storm restored him, as did Ardoch's light snoring. Taran rose, stretching a stiff back. Blankets on the floor of Ardoch's room were not the softest bed he'd ever had, but not the worst either. He moved to the door, locating it by the flashes of lightning. It was ajar as he'd left it, and he slipped through, going across to the other bedroom door. He didn't think Sullyan would have returned and gone to her rest without waking him, but he pushed it open anyway.

The room was empty.

Trying to ignore his disappointment, he moved to the window and parted the curtain. He judged it to be about an hour before dawn. Jinny would be here soon. He and Ardoch must be ready.

Taran went downstairs to brew fellan. He stood in the small cooking room and stirred the embers of the fire. Not for the first time, he tried to reach out to the fire with his mind, call it to life with his power. He reached within himself as he had been taught and identified the portion of his pattern that was most closely attuned to Fire.

He could see it clearly enough and had performed this exercise countless times under the guidance of Bull, Robin, Sullyan, and even General Blaine once. Yet the necessary strength still eluded him. Nevertheless, he strove with his failure for some time before giving up. He tried not to allow his inadequacies to cow his spirit. After all, it was a familiar failure. He wished he could share Sullyan's certainty he would eventually be able to influence Fire.

Still wrapped in the intricacies of his psyche, he remembered his boyish incredulity and awe whenever he watched his father playing with Fire. Amanus had repeatedly told his young and impressionable son that the influence—and eventual mastery—of Fire was a pinnacle of achievement far greater than the mastery of Water. It was deeply to be desired.

Taran recalled Amanus speaking as if the control of Fire was the furthest most people ever got in their quest for mastery of the elements, and wondered what his reaction would be if he could know his son was personally involved with two of the most powerful Artesans the earth had ever known.

Of course, his father *had* known Sullyan, albeit briefly. Taran couldn't help speculating, with great regret, what his life and level of competence would be by now had General Blaine not refused his father's arrogant demands for help all those years ago. Or if

Sullyan had been able to keep her promise and found the time to seek him out. That had been before Robin's arrival, so maybe....

All this idle speculation was doing him no good. Sullyan was right; he'd drive himself mad if he kept letting his passions rule his body like this. He glanced down at himself and reflected wryly it was just as well she wasn't here to see the state of him. He could do with another ducking in that cold pool!

As he damped the fiery portion of his psyche and turned away from the hearth, he never even noticed the tiny flames licking the wood.

The smell of brewing fellan must have awoken Ardoch, for he soon joined Taran in the cooking room. The two of them broke their fast with bread, honey, and hot fellan. The swordmaster stared moodily at the dripping skies as they slowly lightened toward dawn. The day was unlikely to improve. There was still thunder to be heard and lightning sparked across the skies, drawn down by the high cliffs to the north of the city.

"Is this unusual?" Taran asked, referring to the intensity and length of the electrical storm.

Ardoch shrugged. "Not entirely. It doesn't happen often, but sometimes storms get trapped by the cliffs to the north and the Downs to the south and circulate for hours. But this one's more violent than most." He eyed Taran. "I take it you've heard naught from Sullyan?"

Taran shook his head, buried concerns rising at Ardoch's question. "Do you think I should risk contacting her again? She did say she might be out all night, and I don't want to alert the renegade Artesan if he's listening."

"Best leave it till our bonny lass arrives. If you've not heard by then, I think you ought to try before we leave. If only to let her know where we'll be." Ardoch grinned knowingly. "Just trust her, laddie. She can take care of herself."

Taran flushed. He'd not been aware his feelings showed so plainly on his face. "I do," he murmured.

Ardoch's smile only widened.

Jinny arrived soon after, full of nervous excitement about their proposed venture. This made Taran even more dubious about allowing her to come with them, but she had already informed the coachman she and her friends would be hiring his carriage for the entire day. As he usually made extra gold on a holy day by ferrying passengers to and from the Minster, he wasn't best pleased, and Taran was forced to part with some coin to compensate the man for his loss. He hoped they weren't drawing too much attention to themselves doing this, but Jinny assured him it wasn't so unusual. People of her class often needed discreet transport, and the coachman wouldn't read anything out of the ordinary into her request.

Now that Jinny was here, they had no reason to delay. Taran had still heard nothing from Sullyan, so he composed himself to contact her. Ardoch and Jinny looked on curiously. Ardoch had seen Artesans at work before, due to his long association with Sullyan and others of her kind at the Manor, but Jinny had not. She watched, her wide eyes filled with awe.

Taran quested through the substrate, Sullyan's complex and familiar pattern fixed firmly in his mind. He threw out his strength in the general direction of her imprint the day before, yet sensed nothing. Puzzled, he widened his field of search, knowing roughly where she had intended to go. Still nothing. Growing ever more concerned, he drew his senses back over the ground slowly, trawling for anything he might have missed. When it finally dawned on him what had happened, he gave a frightened hiss, snapping his concentration.

Jinny and Ardoch crowded round in concern and the Torlander took Taran shoulders in calloused hands. "What? What is it, lad?"

The Adept stared at him. "Spellsilver! Something's happened to Sullyan. Her psyche's been covered by spellsilver."

"What's that?" Jinny's distress showed in her voice and puzzled gaze. Briefly, and rather impatiently, Taran explained. Jinny's eyes grew round and her hand crept to her mouth. "She's been captured, then?"

Taran and Ardoch glanced at each other, Taran's heart limping. "It looks that way. What do we do now?"

Ardoch sank into a chair, thinking furiously. "Could you tell where she is?"

Taran shook his head. "Only very roughly. She's on the estate somewhere, I'm sure of it."

"Then maybe we ought to stick to our plan. Your man can't get out of his attendance at the Minster, so he'll be out of the way. We already know Prince Eaden, if he's there, will be guarded, so that won't have changed. If they've taken the demon Prince to the estate, too—or his body, more like—there's a good chance Sullyan's there as well. If we can rescue Prince Eadan, we may be able to force their hand and make them reveal where Sullyan is. Perhaps we can rescue them both."

"Or perhaps they'll kill her, or use her to force us to surrender!"

Ardoch threw his hands wide. "Then what would you have us do? Sit on our asses and do nothing? That won't help her. Think, man. They can't know about us. She's not told them or they'd be here by now. This can still work."

Taran was distraught. He really didn't know what to do, but Ardoch was right. He couldn't just wait at the house. That would achieve nothing.

"All right, we'll stick to the plan. But I'm not leaving there without finding her, Prince or no Prince."

Ardoch snorted. "You think I would?"

Jinny added her approval of the plan and Taran shrugged his acceptance.

They made their preparations. On an impulse, Taran went up to the sleeping rooms and took Sullyan's sword from her bed. The cross straps of her weapon belt had to be lengthened, but he finally had it comfortable on his back. He had a feeling she might be glad of her father's sword before this episode was over. He just prayed he'd find her in a fit state to use it.

Chapter Twenty

A sharp pain against her throat brought Sullyan back to consciousness. The slight movement of her head away from the pain brought renewed waves of sickness roiling within her. Opening her eyes with difficulty, she saw why. Her own long knife was being held to her throat and its wickedly sharp point had already drawn blood.

The cruelly grinning face poised before hers opened its mouth to call to someone she couldn't see.

"Patrin, go tell his Lordship his new 'guest' is awake."

"Yes, Commander."

She heard retreating footsteps, but her attention was held firmly by the man crouching before her, and by the knife still pressed against her windpipe, forcing her to keep her breaths shallow.

The cruel grin widened. "Well, well, so you're the famous Colonel Sullyan. I can't say I'm impressed. You were very stupid to let yourself be taken so easily. If we'd set this up as a trap for you it could hardly have worked better."

I know, she thought, but held herself silent.

The stocky man exuded brutality like a miasma. She had seen his like before, but whereas Rykan had tempered his nature with at least an attempt at aristocratic grace, this man was totally indifferent to what others thought of him. His eyes, dark blue and soulless, betrayed no hint of compassion or restraint.

Right now, they carried another expression she had seen before. As the realization of it struck sick terror into the very depths of her soul, she fought desperately to stay calm.

Still smiling that cruel smile, he slid the tip of her knife down her throat to rest in the hollow, just above the gem she wore about her neck. Holding her gaze, he gently pressed the knife, deliberately nicking her skin. She felt the trickle of blood as it ran down between her breasts, but managed to suppress the gasp of pain.

That displeased him. He pressed harder, and the sharp blade slid farther in, grating on her collarbone. He twisted it slightly so it scraped along the bone. She was unable to bite back the small cry the pain called forth as her blood ran freely.

This acknowledgement of his control over her appeased him somewhat, but the cruel smile never lifted from his face.

A faint stirring close beside her registered vaguely in Sullyan's ears.

"Izack, you bastard, leave her alone!"

Aeyron's voice was husky as he struggled with his pain. His temerity in speaking and the disgust in his tone provoked an instant reaction from the commander. Leaning across Sullyan's body, he struck Aeyron a powerful blow to the face, snapping the Andaryan's head back against the stone to which he was chained.

His groan of agony brought tears of rage to Sullyan's eyes. That Aeyron should attempt to aid her, travailed as he was!

"Stop!" she cried as forcefully as she could. "Have you not done him enough harm? Oh, you are so mighty, to attack a bound and helpless man."

"*Man*?" sneered Izack, turning back to her. "He's not a man. Look at him. He's nothing but a beaten cur."

She spat at his feet. "Beaten he may be, but wretched as he is, he is more of a man than you could ever be."

That earned her the same treatment he'd meted out to Aeyron, and she slipped into blackness as her own head slammed against stone. It was fleeting, though, and she came back to herself, tasting blood on her lips and fighting more coruscations of jagged light behind her eyes.

"Keep silent," the leering face before her snarled. He was straddling her body now, hands braced on the stone behind her, leaning so close she could smell the reek of lust and violence emanating from him. "I've had just about enough of your kind. Well, soon there won't be any of you left and the world will be a better place. Once the Baron comes, you'll see. Until then, I'll show you how much of a man I am."

He gripped the fabric of her shirt with one hand and tore the fastenings apart. She wore her light chemise beneath, and he gripped that too in his strong hand to rend it from her. Her eyes went wide with horror and she could hear Aeyron's frantic, wheezing protests.

She couldn't believe this was going to happen again. She couldn't bear it a second time; it might just send her over the edge into madness. As with Rykan, she was helpless except for defiance, so she glared her hatred of the man before her and flung her disgust into his face as she spat, hard as she could.

He only grinned and tightened his grip on her chemise. His other hand fumbled with the fastening of his bulging breeches as he savored her horror. He leaned forward over her body, slightly raised on his knees.

Up until that precise moment of threatened violence, Sullyan's pregnancy had meant little more to her than a word. For the past seventeen months, it had been a word that could never have any personal meaning for her, other than something that might happen to one of her friends. Rienne's revelation had been accepted but not yet assimilated. Events had forced Sullyan to put the astonishing fact aside, seal it away as something to be brought out and studied later. But the threat of physical violence had always sparked a reaction in Sullyan, and Izack's specific threat of rape awoke fury deep within her, intensified by an instinctive maternal imperative to protect. It flashed into being without her volition. It flooded her soul and took her over completely. Izack was going to regret unleashing this particular beast, for he had overlooked one vital fact—her legs were not restrained in any way.

Without giving herself time to consider the consequences, she channeled all her gut-wrenching horror into a desperate lunge, terror lending her strength as she drove both knees sharply upward between his legs with all the force she could muster.

There was a meaty crunch.

A strangled, agonized scream burst from Izack's mouth and his face turned mottled purple. His eyes bulged and he fell away to one side, writhing in agony, clutching himself, retching and gagging for breath.

"I think ... that may have been ... a mistake."

Aeyron's voice barely reached her ears, ringing as they were with concussion. She closed her eyes against the sight of the contorted form on the ground, his frothing mouth and his gargling breaths.

"I know," she whispered. "I could not help myself. I fear we will both pay for it."

It had been an uncontrollable gut reaction, an unreasoning defense against a violation she knew she couldn't survive a second time. All she could hope was that she had done him serious and permanent damage. At the very least, his pain and bruising would render him incapable of rape, whatever else he may choose to do in vengeance.

"Still ... I am glad you did it."

She opened her eyes and managed to turn her head to face

Aeyron. The hour was yet early and she could barely see his features in the dawn gloom, but she could see well enough to register his split lip and the fresh bruises and abrasions on his face.

Her own mouth was sore and her teeth ached, yet she managed a smile for him.

"I wish I had been able to strike one blow against him," said the Prince, his voice raw. She knew how that felt, too. "In all the days I suffered his torture, I never once found the strength to do him harm, as you have done."

The desolation in his tone struck to her soul. More than anything, his sense of failure told her the depth of his loathing for what he saw as weakness in himself. She had to assuage that self-abnegation if they were to keep going long enough for someone to find them.

"Oh, but you have, Highness," she murmured, her gaze upon Izack's contorted form. "You survived his torture and you have refused to be reduced by his brutality. That in itself is a victory over his kind, believe me."

Aeyron stared at her. "Lady, you surpass me. Now I see why my father loves and values you so highly. Your spirit is indomitable." He coughed dryly. "If these are to be our last hours, then I am proud and privileged to spend them with you."

She had no reply to this heartfelt declaration other than the love in her eyes, but she was spared the effort of speaking by Izack lurching to his feet. He was gasping for breath, his face still mottled. One hand clutched his groin, sweat beaded his skin. His eyes were wild, insane with fury, and he stared death at his captives.

He had lost Sullyan's knife in his agonized writhing and forgotten it in his rage. She could see he wanted to use his hands. He needed to feel their agony with his fingers, experience their death throes through his nerves.

He advanced on Aeyron menacingly, his breath rasping hoarsely in his throat.

Sullyan watched in desperate terror as Izack balled his fist and dealt the helpless Prince another tremendous blow. Aeyron's body slumped.

The Commander spared the Prince not a glance as he turned on Sullyan. She saw the red mist of revenge in his eyes and prepared herself as best she could for his retribution. Her stubborn spirit would fight against giving him the satisfaction of hearing her scream until she lost all control over her body. By then, she would be too far gone to care. So it had been with Rykan. The only weapon she'd had left in her helpless state was to deprive him of the fullness of his victory.

Izack loomed over her, allowing the moment to build, watching her sick apprehension with a rabid grin on his face. His fist curled, smears of Aeyron's blood staining the knuckles. Clutching his manhood with one protective hand, he cocked his fist to begin his revenge.

The blow never fell. A strident voice behind him snapped, "Izack! Control yourself."

Sullyan saw the furious disappointment in his eyes. For one instant, she thought he would pretend he hadn't heard.

The voice cracked again. "Commander. Do as I say."

His face suffused with rage, Izack dropped his fist and turned, allowing Sullyan to see the swarthy form of the Baron standing in the center of the circle. He was dapper in his holy day clothes, his arms folded over his chest, a frown of distaste on his features.

She wondered at it until she suddenly realized he found this gratuitous violence repugnant. She would have sneered if she'd had the strength. His hypocrisy disgusted her. The insight gave her a glimmer of understanding, allowed her to see how he could stand to profit from dealing with those he considered less than human without compromising the tenets of his faith. She was repelled by such blatant casuistry.

"My Lord," Izack protested, "the witch damn near gelded me. I have the right—"

The Baron cut callously across Izack's protestations, ignoring the man's obvious pain and outrage. "You were careless, Commander. I warned you not to underestimate her. Just because she fell into our hands so easily doesn't mean she's defenseless. You deserve your pain. Perhaps it will teach you better discretion. How you could even consider coupling with such as she, I have no idea. You're such a barbarian, Izack. Now go and help Patrin with the last of the silver. We have no time to waste. I must be at the castle soon."

Izack shot Sullyan a look of menacing promise as he hobbled over to do as Reen bid. She stared defiantly back, putting as much of her disdain into her eyes as she could. The Baron approached his captives, holding his dark blue velvet overrobe fastidiously clear of the damp moss. He was smiling almost pleasantly as he ignored the rain and the intermittent thunder.

He stopped, prudently out of reach of Sullyan's feet, and regarded her.

"So, my dear, we meet again. I must say, I didn't expect the pleasure of your company at this late stage."

Over his shoulder he called, "Didn't I tell you we couldn't trust what that fool at the Manor said when he told us she was no longer a threat?"

He grinned with delight at Sullyan's horrified understanding. "Don't tell me you didn't know, my dear? Oh yes, we've had a spy in your camp for some time now. Two, in fact, although I only had to pay one of them. Convenient that, wasn't it, Izack?"

The disgruntled Commander gave no reply. Sullyan could hear him berating the unfortunate Patrin, taking out his frustration and anger on his subordinate. The Baron smiled again, clearly enjoying Sullyan's reaction.

"Yes, we were very fortunate. It seems you're not as popular as you thought you were, my dear. It wasn't hard to find someone willing to pass information to us."

"Parren." Sullyan was fishing, yet she knew she must be right. Who else could it be?

He didn't reply, but she read her answer in his eyes before he could guard himself. She experienced a twinge of satisfaction. Helpless, was she? Well, she could still play the Baron at his own game, although what good it would do her, she didn't know. At least she'd wiped that smug smile from his face.

He snarled at her. "Oh, you think you're so clever. But you weren't clever enough to realize it was also one of your own betraying you, were you?"

Hearing the Baron confirm his use of an Artesan—and his tone suggested willing compliance—struck her like a physical blow.

She glared at him. "What are you holding over him? You are a base hypocrite, my Lord Baron, to use and profit from those you profess to despise."

He cut the air with his hand. "Profess to? I *do* despise your kind. You're abominations on the face of the earth. And let me assure you, I will do more than profit from my enforced association with such unholy creatures. Very soon now, within the day, perhaps, there will be none of you left—none! And even if some of you do escape, you will be rendered powerless. Helpless against those of us who seek to cleanse our world of such unnatural beings."

"You rave, my Lord. Just how do you propose to accomplish that?" She sneered at him, desperate to keep him talking, to buy time, to discover what his plans were. Maybe there was a flaw in his thinking. Maybe there was something she could use.

"You'll see," he drawled. "In fact, you will be a very intimate part of it."

He crouched down before her, still wary of her unbound feet, although, in truth, she was more interested in learning his intentions than doing him harm just now.

"Tell me, my dear, since you are so skilled in your craft. Just how powerful is this particular circle?"

She stared into his fanatical eyes and refused to answer him. The question was devoid of meaning and only served to display his ignorance. She saw no reason to impart information he did not already possess.

He frowned in displeasure. Izack stepped forward, still massaging his bruised manhood. "I'll make her answer you, my Lord."

Reen shot him a look. "I doubt that, Izack. I doubt it very much."

"My Lord—"

"Izack, you're forgetting the fact that this woman fought and killed Lord Rykan. How well did *you* fare against his sword? Oh, I don't doubt you could make her answer me. But how far could we trust what she said? No, I don't think you have the power to force her to do anything, even helpless as she is."

Izack scowled, but Sullyan ignored him. Despite her predicament, she was interested by Reen's reference to Rykan. She had long wondered how the prejudiced Baron had come to be in association with a despised outlander.

Correctly interpreting her expression, the Baron told her, compounding Izack's humiliation.

"I nearly lost my Commander here to a raiding party of Rykan's men. Izack came across them, fought them, and killed one of Rykan's lieutenants. This angered the demon lord. He easily

disarmed Izack and then held him to ransom. I had to do some
fierce bargaining to get him released. I was angry with Izack
myself, but his carelessness worked in my favor, for that was when
I conceived the beginnings of this plan. I soon realized, during the
course of our negotiations, what a scheming and ambitious man
Rykan was. He was laughably easy to approach on those terms. I
gave him to know that I could help him achieve what he desired,
and that all he had to do in return was give me access to a
spellsilver mine. The potential rewards were enough to outweigh
his suspicions over what I intended to do with it.

"We cemented our mutual trust"—the Baron's tone was heavy
with irony—"by collaborating over the making of the Staff.
Doubtless, Rykan intended to renege on the deal once he had the
throne under his control. Like you, he underestimated me. But
enough of history. Tell me, Colonel, what would happen if we used
the forces of Earth, which I'm told are very strong here, to detonate
thirty pounds of reverse-polarity spellsilver?"

The abrupt change of subject took Sullyan by surprise. She
gaped at him. *Detonate...?* "You intend to use Earth force and
spellsilver to create an explosion?" She read the confirmation in
his eyes. "But that amount of spellsilver, and the forces required to
detonate it, would destroy the whole of Port Loxton! In fact, this
entire region from the cliffs in the north to the Downs in the south
would be devastated. Is that what you want? How will that work
the downfall of Artesans? No one would believe we were
responsible."

"Of course not, my dear." In patronizing tones, he dismissed
her protest. "My plans are much more far-reaching than that. I
have no intention of destroying my own estate—even this circle—
let alone Port Loxton."

"Then ... what?"

"Oh, my dear Colonel Sullyan. Where is your famed

intelligence and foresight? They seem to have deserted you completely. No, it is no petty physical explosion that will fulfill my ends. I intend to wreak *my* destruction on the metaphysical plane. I intend to detonate the spellsilver within a—what do you call it?—a substrate tunnel. I intend to strike at the very source of your powers."

He turned a predatory and self-satisfied smirk on her as he declaimed, "I intend to destroy the Veils."

Sullyan was aghast. *Destroy the...?*

She simply couldn't believe her ears. How on earth had he conceived that idea? It was unthinkable to destroy the Veils. They were a fundamental part of the physical nature of the earth, of all the realms. If their destruction were attempted, all five realms would collapse. They simply could not survive without the framework of the substrate within which they existed. Surely he comprehended that?

The Baron stood. He had her discarded knife in his hand and thrust it through a loop on his belt.

"Yes, my dear. Now you understand. No more trafficking with demons, or any other unnatural creatures. No more access to arcane and occult powers. No more Artesans."

"No more world!" she burst out, fighting the effects of her concussion, straining forward against her bonds in a desperate effort to make him understand. Her head was ringing with pain and fear. "Baron, this is madness. If you attempt this, you will destroy the realms. You will destroy the entire world. You cannot do it. You *must not!*"

He continued to smile infuriatingly, his arms folded across his chest.

"Yes, I thought you might try that one. My dear girl, I didn't suffer the overweening arrogance and sickening brutality of that creature Rykan without learning something from him. Where do you think I learned about spellsilver? Who do you think conceived the concept of the Staff? Only he was too impatient for the satiation of his own desires to use the thing as we agreed. Had he not been so careless with it, had he not wasted time dallying with *you*, he would have taken the throne of Andaryon and I would have had access to all the spellsilver I desired. My plans would have come to fruition long ago."

Sullyan's low, compelling voice cut across the Baron's tirade. "Do you know what he did to me, my Lord? Do you know what I suffered at the 'dalliance' of Lord Rykan?"

The Baron shrugged. "We agreed he would kill you. He was going to use the Staff to steal your powers, and then he was going to kill you."

"Yes! But because it was stolen, because he did not have the Staff to compel me, he used other methods. He *raped* me."

She saw him wince and flung the words at him like missiles.

"Yes, he raped me. Not once, but *four separate times*. Trying to break me, to snap my spirit, to force me to surrender my powers. But he failed, did he not? And I will tell you why. He failed *because* he raped me. I refuse to surrender to men such as Rykan, such as Izack. Men such as *you*, my Lord."

"How dare you!" he spat, almost forgetting himself enough to come within range of her feet. "I am nothing like that animal Rykan. How dare you compare us? I am a faithful son of the Matria Church."

"You are a hypocrite and a man of your own desires," she spat back. "You use the holy teachings for your own ends. You twist the texts to suit your own interpretations. Do you think I do not know what the sacred books say? Do you think Artesans are against the Church and its teachings? You are wrong, Baron. Very wrong. We share the same faith as you. We have heard the priests speak on the subject of our powers. We know very well there is nothing in the holy texts that speaks against us. We are no more unnatural than someone who has a gift for music, or swordsmanship, or woodworking. We simply use the natural talents we were born with to the best of our ability. We would offend more against God if we did not.

"*You* are the unnatural one here, my Lord, if you believe the Veils are a source of evil."

The Baron was scarlet with indignant rage. He even forgot himself so far as to raise his fist as if he would strike her. She stared defiantly up at him, daring him to reveal the suppressed violence within him, to shatter the veneer of his gentility and expose the vicious barbarian at the core of his soul.

With a visible effort, aware of Patrin and Izack watching from the edges of the circle, the Baron mastered himself and stepped back.

"Oh yes," he snarled, "very clever. It has ever been the way of evil to use our own arguments against us. But I am impervious to your wiles. You can't trap me with your knowledge of my faith. I recognize your twisted words for what they are—an attempt to cozen me into questioning my beliefs. Well, it won't work. All your protestations have achieved is to convince me that what I do is right. You reveal your fear of me, your tacit acknowledgement that without the source of your powers, you are nothing. You can neither harm nor dismay me."

She nearly sagged then. Her strength for this struggle was fast deserting her. He was too strong in his convictions, too set upon his path to listen to reason. He would never give credence to any of her arguments, valid though they were. She had only served to empower his resolve.

There was one last appeal she could try.

"Then I hope you have not mistreated the King's son, my Lord. You will forfeit all chances of Elias's favor if Eadan comes to harm."

The cruel smile that stole over Reen's swarthy face struck a chill through her spine.

"Elias? Now why should I concern myself with his favor?" Reen chuckled at the look in her eyes. "Never fear, my dear, Elias will not return. Once the Veils are destroyed, he will be trapped. And even had all gone awry—had you somehow managed to thwart my plans—your champion would never live to hear your accusations. My … associates in Andaryon have their orders to kill Elias, if he has not already died in this very convenient war."

His smile broadened at Sullyan's shock.

"What, you never thought I'd take a chance on his coming back, did you? Ah, no. Once I was sure he would cross the Veils to fight, I knew he would stay there."

He laughed. She closed her eyes. He had won. There was no loophole in his thinking, no flaw in his plan. If she couldn't convince him that destroying the Veils would destroy the whole world, there was nothing she could do except be glad his bigoted thinking would die along with everything else.

She had done all she could. Her only hope now lay with Ardoch and Taran. Surely the Adept had tried to contact her and realized what the muffling of her pattern meant? Unless the Baron had found them too, of course.

As if he'd read her mind, the Baron glanced up at the weeping sky. "Izack, it's time I was on my way to meet the Queen. I have a very important address to deliver to the good people of Port Loxton."

He turned a nasty smile on his despairing captive.

"They will hear what the future power behind the throne has to say," he gloated, taking pleasure in the pallor of her face. "How the Queen will exalt me for what I have done. She relies on me totally, you know. She will need me to guide her through the next few years while the little Prince grows and is molded in the tenets of the Church. Together we will revile and seek out any abominations not destroyed by my plans today. The existence of your kind is at an end. When I depart from here, the circle will be activated and the power will build toward an overload. It will take time, I know. Once I am done at the Minster, once I have sown the seeds of my future, I will return to see the culmination of my dreams. I will oversee the opening of the tunnel and the destruction of the Veils. Enjoy your last hours, *Colonel*." He emphasized her title with scorn, turning from her to snap at Izack. "Well? Where is he?"

"In the cart, my Lord." The Commander glared hungrily at Sullyan.

She ignored him and looked beyond Reen. Even in her extremity, she felt a need to know the identity of the Artesan who was being duped, or coerced, into wreaking the destruction of the earth.

"Who...?" she managed.

The Baron turned back, triumph in his eyes. "Oh, you think you know so much! But you never even guessed, did you? Well, I'm not going to tell you now. If you can't work it out, too bad. It will give you something to think on as you feel the power building toward the termination of your life."

He took a step or two closer, unable to help himself, almost hugging himself in his glee. "But I will give you a clue."

"My Lord," warned Izack.

Sullyan experienced brief satisfaction. It seemed she had taught Izack a little respect, at least. The Baron ignored him. Leaning toward her, he hissed, "You know him."

Although that parting shot shocked her to the core, the fact that he was leaving and she had failed to dissuade him from his destructive folly was paramount. Summoning her fast-evaporating strength, she ignored the flashes behind her eyes, strained against her bonds, and tried one final time.

"Baron. My Lord, I beg you. Not for me, not for Artesans, but for all the peoples of the earth. Hear me. *Do not do this*!"

But he was gone. They'd all gone. She heard the sound of a forceful blow striking a body, followed by a small cry of pain. She heard the sounds of the cart departing, felt the familiar surge through her bones as the circle was activated and the magnetic attraction of the spellsilver began to draw the mighty forces of Earth forth from the megaliths.

The Baron's last words rang in her aching brain. She *knew* him? She knew the captive Artesan who was being coerced into destroying the world?

That last blow and cry convinced her that her fellow Master was not acting of his own volition, as she had long suspected. But she *knew* him? How was that possible? Aside from herself and Pharikian, she knew no one else with the power to do what had been done. That meant it had to be someone with hitherto hidden or unsuspected powers. Yet they would still possess a psyche pattern, and she would have been able to detect it. Wouldn't she?

The rain was still falling, thunder growled irritably not far away. She was drenched down to her skin. Now she was alone with her failure, she began to shiver. Defeated by the puzzle, frustrated by the Baron's intransigence, frightened, despairing, and sick to her soul, the concussion clanging in her head finally overwhelmed her. Intense sorrow settled deep within her heart.

Her eyes closed and her head fell forward as slow, hot tears slid down her face.

Chapter Twenty-One

The hallways of the Manor were largely deserted as Tad and Ozella crept toward Parren's rooms. The militiamen not on patrol with Parren were drilling under Vassa or Baily, and although the midday meal was nearly ready, no one was likely to go up to the officers' private quarters until much later. Bull had been Tad's only worry, but he'd checked on the big man earlier and knew he was helping Falkerk train some of the clumsier men. They shouldn't be disturbed.

They reached the corridor where Parren's rooms were situated, and Tad noticed Ozella hanging back.

"What's the matter with you?" he hissed. "You can't back out now. We're nearly there."

Nervous, Ozella looked at him. "What if we don't find anything?"

Tad shrugged impatiently. "Then we look elsewhere. Or we come back and look again. There has to be something, Ozella. We just have to find it. Now, *come on!*"

They moved forward, watching the corridor, ears alert for sounds. When they reached Parren's door they stopped, listening intently. Tad's hand reached for the door latch, but Ozella stiffened, grabbing his shoulder.

The younger lad nearly yelped aloud. "What did you do that for?"

Ozella ducked his head. "I thought I heard something."

Tad rolled his eyes. "It was the beating of your yellow heart," he retorted, but he grinned as he said it.

He lifted the latch and pushed the door. It swung open soundlessly. With a last glance around, the two lads slipped inside.

"Should we leave it ajar so I can keep watch?" whispered Ozella.

Tad shook his head and closed the door. "If someone does walk past, an unlatched door's more likely to be noticed. Stop worrying, no one's going to come. Now, help me look. And be careful. Put everything back as you find it."

They moved into the room. Parren's quarters were like most of the other junior officers'. His sleeping area was in the same room as his settle and chairs, the small bed being against the far wall. There was only one window, which overlooked the rear of the kitchens. Although the day was gloomy, there was plenty of light for the lads to see by. Tad made for the bed and the two chests by it that presumably held Parren's clothes.

"I'll look in here. You start over there."

Ozella looked where Tad indicated. The sitting area held a comfortable settle, two wing chairs, a low table, and a set of shelves against the wall below the window. There were no adornments in the sparse room, no pictures on the walls, and not many hiding places for what they sought. Ozella began by removing cushions from the settle and checking the fabric of the furniture for loose sections where something could be hidden. His hands were shaking.

Tad, on the other hand, was enjoying himself. He checked the bed, looking under the pillow and inside the blue casing, checking beneath the sheets and mattress, careful to remake the bed as it had been. As Ozella had learned, a cadet's early training at the Manor covered uniformity and tidiness, and everyone made their beds the same way.

Tad turned his attention to the chests. The first one held spare sheets and blankets, and also Parren's dress uniform. Tad went through the pockets carefully, being sure to return the folded bedclothes and the uniform to their pristine state. He laid them on the bed. Then he went over the wood of the chest, looking for hidden compartments, and turned it over with a grunt to inspect the bottom. Nothing.

Ozella finished checking the settle and chairs and began to search behind and below the small table and the shelves, in case anything had been secreted there. Also drawing a blank, he began lifting the rugs, wrinkling his nose at the dust. Superficially, the room was neat and clean, but Parren obviously didn't pay the same attention to his floor coverings. Ozella suppressed a sneeze.

Then he froze. "What was that?"

They both stood still, straining their ears. Tad tiptoed to the window and peered down to the kitchens, one story below. "Militiamen gathering for the midday meal," he murmured. He cocked his head at Ozella.

"I thought I heard footsteps," whispered Ozella.

Tad moved to the door and pressed his ear to it. Ozella stood in fear, his heart hammering, sweat beading his brow.

Tad straightened. "I can't hear anything." He shrugged. "You're jumping at shadows. Get on with it. Take a look in the cooking room. He may have hidden something among the plates. But be quiet."

Ozella moved to obey, his hands still shaking. He went through Parren's scant crockery with no success. It looked as if Parren never used his cooking room. Ozella wasn't surprised. He knew most of the men preferred the commons, and although Parren wasn't popular, Tad had told him Parren still inflicted his presence on the other captains and junior officers. Frustrated, Ozella came out of the cooking room and hung around Tad, impatient to get out before they were caught.

Tad had started on the other chest. This one contained Parren's casual, off duty attire. Tad lifted out shirts and trousers, going through each garment, unfolding and refolding. He was nearing the bottom of the chest, and Ozella was sure they were wasting their time.

Tad refused to be hurried or spooked by Ozella's hovering. Carefully lifting the last item of clothing, he uncovered two objects lying in the bottom of the chest. One was a small leather pouch containing more gold than Parren could earn in a year. Tad gave a low whistle, his eyes gleaming.

The other object was more of a surprise.

It was a book. Bound books were rare and expensive, and Ozella knew there weren't many at the Manor who could afford them. Judging by Tad's expression, the younger lad had never even handled one before. Replacing the pouch of gold coins, he reverently picked up the book.

It was small and not very thick. It was bound in brown leather tooled with a simple block design around the edges. There was a title stamped into the spine in gold leaf.

Tad opened it to the middle and his eyes widened in surprise. It was a book of sacred texts.

"What's this doing here?" he murmured. "Parren's not known for his religious beliefs. It's obviously precious to him, hidden away like this."

Then Tad turned to the very first page. A name had been inked there in a schooled hand. The beautiful script read *Cyrus Parren.*

"Oh," breathed Tad, "the captain's father. He must have been a cleric. Well, well, I wonder what he'd say if he knew his son was a traitor and a blackmailer?"

Ozella was beginning to feel nauseous. "Please get on with it, Tad. I have a bad feeling about this."

Tad turned the pages of the sacred book. It wasn't much used. Parren's father had clearly kept it in pristine condition, and Ozella didn't imagine Parren read it very often. As Tad passed the center of the book, something other than the illuminated pages peeked out. Another sheet had been slipped between the vellum. Hardly daring to breathe, Tad eased it out.

Another low whistle escaped his lips. "Take a look at this!"

Ozella looked over Tad's shoulder, his heart thumping harder. "We've got him," he breathed. "I don't believe it. Do you see what it says?"

Tad looked grim. "I do. Here, take it. I'll put this lot back."

Ozella took the damning parchment as if it might burn him. He vaguely registered Tad replacing the book, covering it over once more with Parren's clothes, paying attention to how they had been before he'd disturbed them. The pouch of coins he left alone. On their own they were no use as evidence. As Tad worked, something else caught Ozella's attention and he gasped aloud.

"Quick, Tad! I really can hear someone coming this time."

Tad looked up in alarm. Footsteps and far-off voices could be heard.

"Hurry!" urged Ozella. They couldn't get caught now, not when they had the means of Parren's downfall in their hands.

Sparing one last glance to ensure all was as it should be, the two lads made for the door. Ozella was sweating. He'd pushed the parchment under his shirt, and its rough edges prickled his skin. His breath came hoarsely.

"Hush!" commanded Tad. "I'm listening."

Ozella put his hand over his mouth. Tad eased up the latch of the door and peered out. Voices approached down the corridor. With a cold shiver down his spine, Ozella realized one of the voices was Parren's.

Damn him, he was returning early!

"Quick," he whined, "let's go."

He pushed the younger lad out into the corridor and closed the door behind him. The door latched with a definite *snick* and he heard Tad curse. But it couldn't be helped. Perhaps the voices had covered the sound and the speakers hadn't heard.

His hand between Tad's shoulder blades, they dashed in the opposite direction from the voices and around a bend in the corridor.

✣ ✣ ✣ ✣ ✣

A disastrous tour of duty had brought Parren back early. The militia scouts he had posted to guard the rear of his disorderly group of peasants had failed to spot the Relkorian slaving party before they attacked. Parren detested Relkorians, and these had proved better organized and armed than most. He lost fully half his command before they rallied and beat the slavers off, and Parren himself sustained a small but irritating thigh wound. His only satisfaction lay in imagining those lost peasants laboring in some filthy Relkorian mine for the rest of their lives. He ordered his group back to the Manor, refusing them a hot meal in punishment for their failure.

Once his wound was cleaned and dressed, he made for his rooms, needing a change of clothing. He scowled furiously as he went, totally disillusioned with life. This nannying of useless peasants was a complete waste of his skills, and his underlying annoyance at the Baron's silence and the absence of more gold was growing in him daily. He'd thought the Baron valued him, that he recognized the worth of Parren's service, and that Parren would finally be accorded the advancement he so richly deserved. It seemed he was wrong. The Baron had simply been using him, just like everyone else.

In this frame of mind, Parren was in no mood to be cross-questioned by Bull over the behavior and punishment of his company.

The big man must have heard of Parren's problems from the duty sergeant. He accosted Parren halfway to his rooms, but Parren refused to speak with him. Bull berated him for his obstructiveness and Parren replied with an offensive and physically impossible suggestion as to what Bull could do with his questions.

Parren approached the turn in the hallway that would bring him to his door. As he rounded the final corner, Bull blustering angrily about reports and such, Parren halted abruptly. Surprised, Bull did likewise. When he opened his mouth to speak, Parren shushed him.

"Did you hear something?"

Parren's tone was completely different, almost anxious. Glancing sharply at him, Bull shook his head. His heart clenching, Parren strode to his door, halting with his hand on the latch. Giving Bull a look that was as apologetic as he could manage, he said, "I understand you're only doing your job, but I'm tired and I've been wounded. Give me a couple of hours to rest and then I'll come and give you my report. Will that do?"

He could see he'd confused Bull, who didn't seem to know how to respond. "All right. Just see that you do," the big man said gruffly. He watched Parren over his shoulder as he walked away.

Parren was trying to control the tremble of his hands. He prayed Bull hadn't noticed. He was convinced he'd heard the latch to his door, and maybe the sound of feet running away. He'd been afraid of something like this ever since the Baron gave him the two gold rings and told him what to do with them. Parren was certain Ozella wouldn't have the courage to fight back on his own, but what if he told someone else…?

Once Bull was out of sight, Parren unlatched his door and stepped inside. He stood with his back to the closed door, listening intently. Nothing. He let his gaze rove about the room, examining every piece of furniture, every rug and cushion. Had he left that blue rug at that specific angle that morning? Had his foot moved it as he left the room? He wasn't sure, but a creeping sensation he didn't like ran the length of his spine.

He crossed to his clothes chest and lifted the lid. His folded shirts lay exactly as he had left them. He studied them, his racing pulse beginning to slow. Nothing was disturbed. He was about to lower the lid when a tiny prickle at the back of his neck insisted he check, just to be sure.

He nearly ignored it, cursing himself for unwonted nervousness. There was no need. Ozella wouldn't dare. He was too frightened of Parren, too sure his tormentor held his sisters' lives in his hands.

Still....

Parren lifted out his clothes, seeing the pouch of gold lying where he had left it. Reassured, he reached in and removed the holy book. It was the only personal item of his father's Parren had. The cleric had died four years ago, and although Parren would never admit it, he missed him. Cyrus Parren had been disappointed his son showed no desire to follow him into holy orders, but had been proud of his military achievements. Parren never wondered what his father would have thought of what he was doing now.

He turned the illuminated pages, growing increasingly concerned. He was sure he'd left the parchment near the center of the book, but it was missing. He flipped frantically through the delicate pages, careless of the book's fragility. His heart was hammering again and his skin turned cold and clammy. It wasn't there.

Slamming the book onto the bed with the kind of curse that should have withered its holy pages, Parren stood appalled. His face felt drained of blood, the livid scar down his right cheek throbbing.

It could only be Ozella. His trembling increased, this time with anger. He would teach Ozella the price of his new-found courage. He'd get the letter back before Ozella could run to anyone else with it. He had to. That parchment was a message from the Baron detailing their arrangement, even mentioning their "powerful benefactress at court." Parren had kept it since the Baron first approached him, despite Reen's explicit instructions to destroy it, in case Reen should play him false. Parren never trusted anyone.

He'd almost forgotten it, but his recent manipulations of Ozella's emotions had reminded him that desperate people take desperate risks. He'd moved it from its original hiding place and put it between the pages of his father's holy book. And now it was gone.

Fighting to control his mounting rage, he went to change before deciding what to do.

Chapter Twenty-Two

By the time Anjer's forces came within sight of the town of Sharrett, it had already fallen to the human King. Although furious, the Lord General breathed a sigh of relief. It looked as though his instructions to the elders had been followed. He could see no signs of burning, hear no cries of wounded. It was galling, but he was prepared to accept the humiliation of losing yet more territory if it avoided bloodshed.

He was well aware time was running out. Elias clearly had some kind of plan and would not be long content merely annexing sections of the countryside. It was likely he would soon threaten their safety, and if his son wasn't produced—as he couldn't be—Anjer's people would really suffer.

He thought it likely Elias would try for one more town. Then the hard bargaining would begin.

Some of the Hierarch's reserves were due to arrive today. Anjer had a plan. He wanted to confront Elias on open ground if at all possible. Fighting through the streets of an occupied town would incur the deaths of far too many innocent people. With the arrival of the reserves, Anjer could afford to detail a sizeable force to protect the approaches to the Citadel, leaving him free to deal with Elias.

While his men set up a hasty field camp, he called through the substrate for Barrin.

Barrin's companies of Velletian Guard were acting both as

rearguard for Anjer's forces and also the vanguard of Ephan's Citadel defenses. Once the reserves had gathered in sufficient numbers, Barrin would be free to either withdraw his men behind the walls of Caer Vellet in the event of a siege, or support Anjer in strikes on Elias's men.

"Barrin," greeted Anjer as the Journeyman Commander ducked under the wet leather sheeting of the field tent. Barrin saluted his superior. "Elias has occupied Sharrett. I expect him to try for Medinia next. It's only a couple of miles away, and if he succeeds he'll control three of the most important food-producing areas west of the Citadel. But I don't think he has enough men to take and hold a fourth town without stretching himself too thin. If Medinia is his next target I'm guessing he'll make for it as soon as he can, hoping to catch us unawares again. He'll think we'll expect him to sit tight for a day, as he did at Andeno, and then sneak out under cover of darkness. He might even be intending a double-bluff, but I think Elias is too cunning for that. I doubt he'll try the same trick twice.

"Have the reserves from Gwayeth arrived yet?"

"They're on their way, my Lord. They'll be in position by midafternoon."

"Good. You can leave the defense of the Citadel Plains to them. Send word to their commander informing him the area is now his responsibility. You and I are going to split our forces. We'll leave enough men here for Elias to see, and we'll even make a feint or two on the town, just to keep him occupied and convince him we want to pen him here. It's what he'll expect. He must know how angry we are that we fell for that first ruse. But if he's as keen to get his hands on Medinia as I think he is, he'll already be organizing the march.

"What I intend to do is come around behind him once he leaves Sharrett, to prevent him retreating into the town. I want you to put enough men across his path to block his access to Medinia. Send this letter to Medinia's elders. It tells them to discount my earlier orders, shut the town gates and prepare to resist. For this to work, we can't allow Elias to entrench under cover. When that's done, take your command and deploy them to block Elias's path.

"I intend to force a confrontation, so let Elias think the way is open to him for as long as you can. Wait until he's fully committed before barring his way. Choose your ground well, and be prepared to halt him when I drive him into you. And be sure to keep your eyes open and your scouts deployed for any sign of that louse Corbyn. I don't want him interfering again.

"There's no time to lose, Barrin. Be on your way."

Barrin leaped to obey.

✤ ✤ ✤ ✤ ✤

Elias was itching to get out of this town. He was urgent to begin the march on their third target, which Valustin's scouts had already investigated to the northeast. It was slightly smaller in terms of area than the two they'd already annexed, but was more defendable as it had substantial walls and stout gates. Elias knew that if the townspeople decided to resist, his forces would have much more trouble taking it than the other two.

Yet he must complete this part of the plan before commencing the next phase. Once the third town was under his control, he intended to send an unequivocal message to the Hierarch that he would brook no further delay. First, though, he must consolidate his position.

It was nearly noon and the weather was lifting. Soon the skies would clear, and any cover the rain might afford would be lost. Also, if they left their departure any later, they'd have to attack in the dark. While this was not an insurmountable problem, Elias would rather be inside the town walls keeping Anjer at bay than caught against them in the dark. Anjer's men knew the terrain more intimately than the Albians did, so Elias urged Blaine toward the start of another march.

The men were not exhausted by their efforts so far. They'd not yet been called upon to give their all, and the marches had been relatively easy. This next one would be more difficult, as there were pockets of woodland between the two towns and the terrain was less than favorable. The farmlands and open pastures gave way to fruit trees and orchards to the northeast, and there were hills to be negotiated. They'd have to skirt these in order to reach the town.

Blaine had already made arrangements for the holding of this second town once the main body of men had left, and Valustin had briefed the captains. The scouts had reported no change in Anjer's position. As before, he seemed content to observe while holding his station.

Elias smiled grimly when he heard the report. He intended to give Anjer something to observe very soon.

Giving the order to march and hoping to catch the Andaryan General unawares yet again, the King watched as his companies began leaving the town.

✣ ✣ ✣ ✣ ✣

Taran took the reins as Jinny seated herself behind him in the small covered carriage. He was muffled in his woolen cloak, as much to hide Sullyan's blade as to protect himself from the rain. At the rear, Ardoch took up station on the footplate. He had also wrapped himself in his heavy cloak and pulled the hood up over his face.

The streets teemed with water. It ran freely off the roofs, streamed down the plaster and brick walls, and cascaded down the roads, creating a muddy waterway. The hooves of the dispirited carriage horse splashed to the fetlocks in the bubbling brown froth as Taran clicked his tongue and moved them away from Ardoch's house.

Once north of the castle, they saw no more carriages. People from this area going to attend the religious service would have already left. Nevertheless, Taran breathed a sigh of relief as they left the final houses behind and approached the heavy wooden gates in the city wall which let out onto the road to the Baron's estate.

The gates were open and unguarded. Guiding the small carriage carefully through, Taran urged the horse to a spanking trot. The Baron's mansion was several miles away.

The rain continued falling heavily and the skies were leaden. Occasional flashes of lightning impinged on Taran's senses and the thunder growled and grumbled, vibrating through his bones. He traveled with his thoughts constantly on Sullyan's whereabouts, desperately hoping she was safe.

He wasn't at all sure they were doing the right thing in trying to find Eadan without her, but they didn't know when, or if, they'd get another opportunity. What he did know was that if the Baron had taken Sullyan, her life was in grave danger. The choice was a stark one: look for her or try for Eadan.

If they could wrest the Prince from the Baron's clutches, maybe he'd have no reason to hold Sullyan. Taran didn't really believe this, but it was his only hope. Once they had the little Prince—*if* they found him—he intended wasting no time searching for Sullyan.

Jinny and Ardoch stayed silent. They saw no one. The weather and the holy day kept the estate workers either behind their doors or in the chapel. Jinny had assured the two men it wouldn't really matter if they were seen. In fact, she would make a point of being recognized if they were stopped. She, at least, had a valid reason to be there.

By midmorning, they sighted the mansion house. It was a large, rectangular building from the front, three stories high, and made of the local sandstone. The white-mullioned windows looked out onto the formal gardens to the front of the house and the grand sweep of the gravel drive. Taran felt acutely vulnerable under the blank stare of those windows as he handled the carriage around the drive.

"Continue round to the side of the house, coachman," Jinny called imperiously from within the carriage.

"Yes, my Lady," he responded, only just remembering the part he was playing. He took the carriage around the house, the horse's hooves crunching noisily on the gravel. The sound grated his raw nerves.

To the back of the mansion, more buildings could be seen. A long wing, two stories high, ran perpendicular to the main house and out toward the kitchen gardens. There were many barns and storehouses farther out, but no workers in evidence.

Taran drew the soaked horse to a halt and leaped down from his perch to open the door for Jinny. He handed her out as Ardoch jumped off the footplate and came to stand beside them.

The swordmaster indicated the two-story building. "Is that the servants' quarters?" His voice was muffled by the hood of his cloak.

Jinny nodded. "We're not going in from here, though. It's not something I'd normally do. If we've been observed arriving, as we probably have, I'd better do what I usually do and go in through the house. We might encounter my uncle's manservant, and he'd be curious if I used the servants' entrance."

They followed Jinny's advice and walked deferentially behind her as she approached the rear door to the main house. Taran was distracted and kept looking about him. It was almost as if he could hear or smell something strange.

"What is it, lad?" muttered Ardoch, causing Taran to startle.

"I don't know … Probably just my nerves."

"Keep your wits about you," said the Torlander. "We can't afford to be wool-gathering."

Dragging his lax attention back under control, Taran followed Jinny into the Baron's luxurious private residence. Entering through a set of double doors, they found themselves in a sumptuous drawing room. The carpeting was soft and expensive, and Taran felt momentary guilt for the splashes of rain they left on its soft pile. Jinny took no heed of it, nor the muddy footprints left by their shoes. Taran supposed the servants would have it all pristine again before the Baron returned.

"What now?" he murmured.

"We're supposedly here for the rest of my things," said Jinny. Her tone was confident, but Taran could tell the atmosphere of urgency was beginning to affect her. "So we'll make straight for the servants' wing, as that's where I left my gowns. The room where I heard the child crying is on the second floor, about halfway down. It's where the under-maids have their rooms, along with the laundry maids and seamstresses."

Taran and Ardoch nodded.

Taking a deep breath, Jinny said, "Right, then. It's this way."

She led them through the house toward the entrance to the servants' wing. They heard a door closing somewhere, causing the men to startle, but Jinny took no notice. Her air of confidence was just what they needed, and Taran began to relax as they neared the stairs that would take them up a floor.

Here, Jinny hesitated. "What do we do if there's a guard on the room?"

"There will be, lass," said Ardoch. "If the wee bairn and his nanny are here, they'll not be alone. Will we be able to get a look before we approach the door?"

Jinny nodded. "The passage makes a turn two rooms up from the one I heard the child in. If we're quiet and there's no one around, we can look around the corner. But there's no other cover. If we want to get inside the room, we'll be seen by anyone in the passage."

Ardoch smiled. "You let us worry about that."

Before they could open the door to the stairs, footsteps sounded behind them. Taran and Ardoch froze, but thankfully, Jinny had her wits about her.

"Don't just stand there, man," she snapped at Taran. "Am I supposed to open the door myself?"

Taran gaped at her, but before he could respond, a young man wearing the Baron's livery appeared from one of the other passages. He saw them. Momentarily startled, the manservant relaxed when he recognized Jinny, who had made sure she was visible in front of the two men. Ardoch, who hadn't lowered his hood, kept his head turned away.

The valet wore an astonished expression. "My Lady? His Lordship didn't tell me you were calling today."

Jinny replied acidly. "His Lordship doesn't know, Seth. I've come to collect the rest of my things. I'm doing it while he's absent as I don't wish to speak with him at present. I trust that meets with your approval?"

Seth retreated from the condescension in her tone. He bowed obsequiously. "Your business is your own, of course, my Lady. Can I be of assistance?"

"That won't be necessary, Seth. As you can see, I've brought my own servants to carry for me. I have some gowns to fetch from the seamstresses, and then I will be returning to the city. That will be all. You may go about your duties."

Seth bowed again and withdrew. Jinny took a deep, steadying

breath.

"Well done, lassie," murmured Ardoch. "That's the spirit."

She gave him a quick smile and gestured for Taran to open the door for her. She swept through and they found themselves in a dim, narrow lobby, with a stairway leading upward and a passageway beneath leading to the lower floor.

Jinny started up the stairs, followed by the two men. She ascended in an unhurried manner, holding the skirts of her deep green gown daintily above her ankles. It was gloomy on the stairs, there being no windows. The only illumination came from the floor above them.

Soon they gained the upper level and saw a long hallway stretching before them, punctuated by doors at regular intervals. The rooms were all on the right-hand side; the left was the outer wall of the building. Through the windows they could see the rain still falling.

Jinny turned to the men, whispering, "Halfway down this hallway there's a turn to the right. We take that turn and the room we want is the third door on the left."

The men nodded and followed her silently toward the turning. They heard nothing; no sound from any of the rooms, no sound from the passageway. The floor was carpeted, and although it was cheap and worn, it muffled their footsteps. They gained the corner undetected.

Ardoch laid a hand on Jinny's and Taran's arms to halt them. A finger to his lips, he motioned them to stay where they were. He cautiously edged nearer the corner of the passage and pressed himself to the wall. He leaned slowly forward, just enough to see around, mindful that he'd be silhouetted against the light if anyone happened to look.

One swift glance was enough. Taran could tell by his face that the news wasn't good. Drawing them farther away from the corner,

Ardoch whispered grimly, "There's a guard on the third door down and it's yon barbarian commander, Izack."

Ardoch's comment didn't mean much to Taran, but Jinny's face paled.

"I hate that man," she whispered. "He's a vicious brute."

Ardoch nodded. "We have to get past him somehow."

They stood in silence, both men thinking hard. The last thing they wanted was to rush Izack and risk alerting the household. Jinny clenched and unclenched her fingers while she waited and watched their faces until she could stand it no longer.

"I'll do it!" she hissed, and marched straight past them out into the passage. Ardoch made a frantic grab for her arm but missed. The furious Torlander gave Taran an agonized look, but all they could do now was wait and see what opportunities Jinny's impulsiveness could buy them.

Taran could hear Ardoch muttering curses under his breath.

✢ ✢ ✢ ✢ ✢

Heart thumping, Jinny marched down the corridor, her long skirts swishing about her ankles. She tried to look purposeful and innocent. She had every right to be here—she did, after all, have clothes to collect—but Izack's aura of barely-contained violence always unnerved her.

The stocky Commander had realized the effect he had on her very early on and had taken great delight in reinforcing it at every opportunity by casting her sly and suggestive glances whenever he could catch her eye. Her plain revulsion amused him. She had managed to keep up a superficially polite manner whenever she was forced to acknowledge him, but now her inner strength would be sorely tested.

Izack reacted instantly to the sound of her approach. He leaped to his feet from the chair he'd been sitting in, his hand falling to the hilt of his sword. Jinny saw him partially relax when he recognized her, but even so, he never took his eyes from her.

She walked toward him as if she meant to ignore him, but, as she expected, he wouldn't allow it.

"My Lady Jinella." He moved to intercept her. "What are you doing here?"

His tone was only barely polite, and she allowed her nervousness to transmute into anger.

"What business is it of yours, Commander?" She put ice into her tone and tried to stare him down. As usual, he refused to be impressed, and gave her the coldly evaluating gaze that was calculated to irritate and unnerve her.

"None whatsoever, my Lady, except the Baron didn't warn me you'd be coming here today."

"And why would he? You are only a servant."

That shot home. She saw his eyes narrow. She might have angered him, but at least now she had his attention. If only she could get him to turn away from the entrance to the corridor, perhaps Ardoch or Taran could creep up on him and disarm him or something.

She tried to edge past him so he would be forced to turn his back toward them, but couldn't do it without touching him, which she was loath to do.

"What are you doing in the servants' wing anyway, Commander?" If she kept him talking, maybe he'd forget himself and relax his vigil. But he was too careful for her.

"Well, as a *servant*, I have every right to be here." There was a challenge in his eyes. "But my duties are the concern of the Baron, and if you'll forgive me"—his tone was anything but polite—"his concerns are no longer yours. I ask you again. Why are you here?"

Jinny gave a long-suffering sigh. "If you must know, I'm here to collect the rest of my things. I left some of my best gowns to be cleaned and altered, and I do not intend to leave the city without them. I knew my uncle would be absent from home this morning, and as I didn't care to meet with him again, I chose this opportunity to collect them. Now, are you satisfied?"

Izack relaxed further. Her indignant air, touch of embarrassment, and condescension were all just right, and they disarmed his suspicions as she had hoped. She knew he had never given her any credit for intelligence, seeing her as a superficial socialite with a head full of parties, gowns, and jewelry. This fainthearted attempt to retrieve her precious gowns without confronting her uncle was exactly what Izack would have expected of her.

Jinny still needed him to turn the other way. She was under no illusions. If he even suspected the presence of the other men and realized what they were about, she would likely end up a hostage or even dead. She had to be very careful.

Regarding him frankly and dropping her cold haughtiness, she said, "Commander Izack, are you quite well? I have to say, you're looking a little pale."

A curious expression of anger came over his features. His eyes glinted dangerously and he shifted his feet as if he were uncomfortable.

"I thank you for your concern, my Lady, but I am quite well."

Jinny warmed to her theme. It was a shot in the dark, but it seemed to have yielded fruit, and she thought she could capitalize on his reaction.

She moved closer, as if to examine him in more detail. "I don't think you are, Commander. Is my uncle not treating you well? He keeps you too busy, I fear. All the other servants have the day off, he is at the Minster addressing the city and thoroughly enjoying himself, and here you are, stuck outside this room with no company and not even any sustenance. Is there anything I can get for you? Ale or wine, perhaps?"

The thought had crossed her mind that maybe she could get him drunk, although the possibilities of what he might do in an inebriated state frightened her. But then, she was not alone.

Her offer clearly surprised him and she could see he was tempted.

"You would like some wine, Commander, I can see that. Let me fetch you some. Or should I call one of the serving maids...?"

She deliberately put her hand to the latch of the door he was guarding. He sprang to stop her, taking hold of her wrist. Alarmed, she stared up into his hard eyes.

"Commander, you're hurting me."

He let go of her wrist after pushing her hand from the door. He seemed to be trying to control himself. He stood before her, watching the fear in her eyes. It seemed to please him that she feared his strength.

A sharp sound from the room behind caught Jinny's attention, and she blinked in surprise as the door opened. Another man stood there, blocking her view of the room beyond. He glanced in concern at Izack.

"Is everything all right, Commander?"

Izack wheeled abruptly. "Get back inside, Patrin. I'm in control here. Nothing for you to worry about. Close that door."

"Yes, Commander."

The man jumped to obey and closed the door. Jinny had used her wits yet again and took advantage of Izack's distraction to move past him. He was now obliged to turn his back on the corner of the passage in order to watch her. She mustn't lose his attention now. She took a deep breath, trying to fight down the revulsion of what she had decided to do.

Ignoring the interruption, she kept her eyes on Izack. "You're very strong, Commander," she murmured, rubbing her wrist and glancing coyly up at him through thick, blonde lashes. He stared at her and swallowed.

"I didn't mean to hurt you, my Lady." His voice was rough. It was as near an apology as she was likely to get.

She smiled, trying not to go too fast. She wasn't used to flirting, not with servants, and certainly not with brutal and dangerous men. He would see through her if she went too far.

"You didn't, not really." She brought her bruised wrist up deliberately to the level of her breasts, and massaged it with her other hand. Her gown was not low-cut enough to reveal much of her bosom—it was a holy day, after all—but her gesture had the desired effect. His eyes strayed. She prayed her companions would see their chance soon. She couldn't keep this up for long.

Chapter Twenty-Three

Trying to appear demure, Jinny lowered her gaze, letting it roam down Izack's body. Her heart was racing and her blood pounded in her ears. The increased depth of her breathing was making her chest rise and fall. Izack's gaze was riveted; she definitely had his interest now.

She licked her lips, trying to make the gesture seem innocent. Izack knew she was no courtesan. A girlish impression was what she was aiming for.

To a man of Izack's appetites, it wouldn't matter what she was. She hoped his knowledge of the Baron's current opinion of her would tempt him to forget she was Reen's niece and a lady. He would be aware she was playing with him, but she had already explained her presence adequately. Despite her underlying fear, her manner had been completely natural for one of her class. That she should now attempt to play the coquette—clumsy though it was— ought to whet his appetite.

She knew it was working when he moved toward her, not yet ready to strike but enjoying the game.

He leered at her. "I must have hurt you a little, my Lady. Let me make amends. Show me your arm. Perhaps I can make it feel more comfortable."

She smiled again, wishing she could see past his bulk, hoping desperately that either Ardoch or Taran were behind him by now. She extended her arm and allowed him to take her wrist in his hand.

"You are very gallant, Commander," she said, the words tasting like bile in her mouth. "I had no idea you were such a gentleman."

He bent over her arm, as if examining it. His soulless eyes met hers. She shivered.

"Perhaps if you knew me better, my Lady, you would realize I can be quite the gentleman when I choose."

He stooped to place a kiss on the back of her hand, and she fought not to pull away. She tried a small laugh, hoping for girlish delight, but all she heard was a shrill note of nervous fear. He seemed unaware—or maybe he didn't care—and the touch of his lips traveled up her arm, past the bruises, while his eyes explored her face, her neck, and the swell of her bosom.

She struggled not to glance over his shoulder. If she gave her friends away she would ruin the entire ploy and still end up his victim.

"Why, Commander," she simpered, "I do believe you're feeling better."

He stared into her eyes like a snake mesmerizing a rabbit. "Oh, I am, my Lady, I am. Would you like me to show you how to make me feel even better still?"

"Oh," she said weakly, unable to tear her eyes away from his despite the sickness mounting in her throat, "how would I do that?"

She gasped as he gripped her by the shoulders. He stepped in close and fastened his mouth onto hers. She fought for breath. She hadn't expected the move and he was so strong! She couldn't even whimper. She screwed her eyes shut against the stink of his breath and the crushing force of his kiss, and nearly fell to the ground when he suddenly went limp and sagged against her.

She stepped hastily aside. Taran caught the Commander's slack body before it crashed to the ground. Ardoch slid his roundpommeled knife soundlessly back into its sheath after checking it was clean.

Shuddering with revulsion, Jinny stared at the unconscious form in Taran's arms. She wiped urgently at her mouth, trying not to gag at the memory of Izack's brutal kiss. "What took you so long?" she hissed.

"Softly, my Lady," cautioned Ardoch. "Don't forget there's another one in there."

He helped Taran lift Izack, and together they manhandled the limp form into the next room, which was a storeroom. Jinny found some cord to bind and gag the helpless Izack.

"Aren't you going to … kill him?" she asked.

Taran and Ardoch shared a look. "Do you want us to?" the Torlander asked tonelessly.

Jinny stared at him. "I don't know … What if he wakes up and gives the alarm?"

Ardoch grinned. "He'll not wake for hours, and I'll truss him like a chicken. He'll not be able to blink an eye, let alone give any alarm. I balk at murder, lassie, so I'll not be killing him, if it's all the same to you. Now, if he'd gone much further with you, it might have been a different story, but I think we managed to stop him in time."

"You're laughing at me!" she accused, her voice trembling.

Taran stepped close and took her into his arms. "We're only relieved you're safe, Jinny. You took a huge risk, baiting him like that. But it was a very clever and a very brave thing to do. We're proud of you."

"Really?" She tried to still her trembling while looking up into his warm, hazel eyes. She read his sincerity and blushed. He flushed also and quickly released her.

Ardoch shifted impatiently. "Enough of that, ye lovebirds. We still have at least one more to deal with. Any suggestions?"

Jinny didn't hesitate. The success of her ploy and Taran's approval had strengthened her spirit. "Stand beside the door," she said. "I'll call him out and tell him Izack's ill or something. It's the truth, after all. He'll have to come out to look, and then you can do what you did to the Commander."

Ardoch looked at Taran, who shrugged. "I don't have any better ideas."

"Go on, then, lassie," said Ardoch. "But stay in the passage. Don't you go into that room, no matter what he says."

Jinny nodded and they went back into the passageway, closing the storeroom door behind them. Jinny moved to the other door and listened for a moment. She heard nothing. Ardoch drew his long knife, and Taran did the same. They positioned themselves on either side of the door.

Seeing their nods, Jinny swallowed. She tapped at the door.

After a few seconds, during which Jinny feared she would have to knock again, she heard movement. A man's voice called, "What is it?"

"Patrin?" Jinny called weakly, trying to sound scared and succeeding. "The Commander isn't well. I think he needs help."

Patrin sounded wary. "What's wrong with him?"

"I don't know. We were just talking and then he went red in the face. I managed to get him into the room next door, but then he collapsed. I think he's unconscious. Oh, help me, Patrin, please! I don't know what to do."

The lock turned and Patrin opened the door. Jinny put on a very credible act, wringing her hands, her brow creased. "Hurry, please! Look, he's in here...."

She stepped back, drawing Patrin with her. He never saw Ardoch's sharp blade, but he did feel it as it pricked high under his throat, warning him not to cry out. The Torlander's strong arm pinned him around the chest so he couldn't move. Taran stepped swiftly forward and disarmed him, taking the sword and knife from his belt. They hustled the sullen man into the storeroom, and Taran fetched more cloth and cord to bind and gag him securely.

There had been no sound or outcry from the room Patrin had vacated. Once they were sure that both the Baron's men were immobilized and silenced, Taran and Ardoch instructed Jinny very firmly to stay behind them while they investigated.

The two men drew their swords and advanced cautiously into the room, Jinny hovering at their backs. It turned out to be a suite, the first room being given over to the seamstress trade. There was a large table for the laying out and cutting of fabric, and there were various chairs for the seamstresses to sit at their work. It was currently empty, but two other doors led off this large room and the men picked one each. Moving soundlessly, they approached their chosen door.

Nodding to each other, they pushed the doors open together, springing through them, alert to any movement.

The one Ardoch had chosen was a cooking room. It contained no hiding places and was deserted. But when Jinny looked in, the small trestle bed in the corner, out of place in a cooking room, caused her eyes to narrow, as did the neat pile of high quality child's clothing laying upon it. Her pulse quickening, she allowed Ardoch to guide her over to Taran's room.

This one was the largest of all, and was full of wooden storage racks. They jostled for space on the floor and were also fixed along all four walls. Each one was piled high with bolts of cloth of every hue, texture, and length. It was impossible to see much through them, and the three companions stood in the doorway, listening.

Yes, there was sound in here. Someone was hiding, someone too frightened to conceal the hiss of their breath. And then Jinny heard what she was sure was the whimper of a young child, hastily muffled. She glanced at Taran and Ardoch, her eyes alight.

Taran stepped forward. "It's all right," he called softly, "no one's going to hurt you. You can come out now."

There was no response, but the breaths came quicker. Taran tried again, using a persuasive tone.

"Come on," he wheedled, "the other two men have gone. You'll be quite safe, I give you my word. We don't want to hurt you. We just want to make sure you're all right, that the baby's safe. We're going to take you somewhere more comfortable. Don't you want to leave?"

Jinny held her breath. Very slowly, a plump young woman stood up from where she'd been hiding behind the huge rolls of cloth. She'd been crying and appeared to be terrified.

"It wasn't my fault, sirs!" she whined pitifully. "I didn't do it."

Jinny frowned, but Taran spoke softly. "Of course you didn't." He moved slowly forward. The girl shrank back, her hand at her mouth, and he stopped. "Is the Prince there with you? Is he all right?"

She nodded. "He said not to tell." Tears slid from her eyes. Then she broke down and words came tumbling out.

"I've been so frightened I didn't know what to do! He said her Majesty would be furious with me if I told, and that I'd be thrown in prison if anyone found me. But it wasn't my fault, I swear it wasn't. We were only walking in the park, like we always do. Then the demons came and grabbed me, and I couldn't get away. I screamed and screamed, but the guards were too far away. I tried to fight them, I tried to save the Prince, but they were too strong. They took us somewhere—I don't know where. I thought I was going to die, and the little Prince with me. But then *he* came and got us and the demons ran away. He said their Majesties were furious with me and blamed me for the little Prince's disappearance. He said it wasn't safe for the baby to stay in the castle because the demons were there. He said I was to hide here with him and when the demons had all been killed, we'd go back. He said perhaps if I stayed very quiet and looked after the little Prince well and kept him safely hidden, I'd be forgiven. Are the demons dead now, sirs? Have you killed them?"

Taran and Ardoch exchanged pitying glances. Jinny could see the poor girl was terrified, and no wonder if Reen had told her the King and Queen blamed her for Eadan's abduction.

Ardoch tried to calm her. "You're Bessie, aren't you? The Prince's senior nanny?"

The girl started, staring at him. "Master Ardoch? Oh, Master Ardoch, are the Queen and the Princess safe? I've been so frightened for them, thinking of the castle overrun with demons. And the King—is he safe too? Is he really angry with me? It wasn't my fault, sir, I swear it wasn't."

Jinny knew they didn't have time to unravel the girl's ravings. Reen had obviously concocted a story to terrify her into submission. Their priority now was the baby.

Ardoch approached the girl and took her shoulders in a fatherly manner.

"Come now, Bessie lass, we have to go. It's not safe here anymore. This is Taran. He and the Lady Jinella have come to take you and the wee Prince to a much nicer place where you can be comfortable as well as safe. Will you fetch him for us?"

Bessie nodded tearfully and turned to where she had been hiding. She bent and picked up a long woven basket with handles, and Jinny saw the baby Prince asleep within, snuggled inside a royal purple blanket. He must have been heavy, for Bessie had trouble lifting him.

"Here, let me," offered Taran. At Ardoch's nod, Bessie allowed him to take the basket from her. The Prince didn't stir.

They led Bessie out and Jinella took charge. She directed Ardoch to the laundry maids' room where the rest of Jinny's gowns ought to be. They needed to complete their assumed task if they were to leave without arousing suspicion.

Once Ardoch had collected her gowns, Jinny turned to the tearful girl. "Bessie, my dear, you have to stop crying now. We're going to take you with us, but we have to leave through the house, and you can't. There's a carriage outside. If you look through the window, you'll see it. We'll go back the way we came and get into the carriage. You wait at the back servants' door with the Prince, and we'll pick you up as we pass. All right? All you need to do is be quiet and keep the baby quiet too. Can you do that?"

Bessie stared at her, clearly thinking they meant to abandon her. This was too much after her ordeal of the past few days and she didn't reply to Jinny's instructions.

Jinny's temper snapped. "Bessie! Pull yourself together. The Prince needs you, do you hear me? Do as I say or you'll be dismissed. Do you understand?"

She heard Taran gasp at her harsh tone, but her snap of temper seemed to work. Fresh tears came to the girl's eyes, but she said, "Yes, Mistress," and bobbed a little curtsey. She took the baby from Taran before fleeing for the stairs to the rear of the building.

Taran turned reproachful eyes on Jinny. "Weren't you a little hard on her? The poor girl's terrified."

"Well so am I!" Jinny flashed her eyes at him. "Do you *want* to throw all this away just to save a servant's tears? We've rescued the *Prince*, Taran. My uncle will be furious. Who knows what he might do if we're caught?"

Taran let it go. He knew she had a much better idea than he of how to deal with servants. Whatever he might think of her methods, he couldn't deny they had worked.

✳ ✳ ✳ ✳ ✳

Taran followed Jinny and Ardoch back the way they had come,

the swordmaster carrying Izack and Patrin's weapons concealed under Jinny's gowns. They gained the luxurious drawing room without incident, and Taran noticed that the muddy stains they had left on the carpet were gone. Stepping out into the incessant rain, they made for the carriage. Someone had given the carriage horse some hay and had also thrown a blanket over its back. Ardoch handed Jinny into the carriage and passed her his burdens under the concealment of her gowns. He turned to Taran, expecting him to take up his position on the driving box.

But as they'd emerged into the early afternoon, the rain still beating on their heads, a strange and unpleasant sensation came over Taran. He'd felt something like it before they entered the house, only now it was much stronger. It vibrated through his body and he almost felt ill, as if his bones were being slowly shaken apart.

Ardoch noticed his distraction. "What is it, laddie? Are you ailing?"

In answer, Taran held out his hand. Ardoch took it reflexively. He dropped it with a startled yelp as a static shock shot up his arm.

"What the Void was that?" he hissed, shaking stung fingers.

Taran didn't have time to explain. "Drive the carriage back, Ghyl. I'm going to look for Sullyan. Someone's activated that circle she was searching for, and they've done it for no idle reason. Take Jinny, Bessie, and the baby back to your house and leave them there. They'll be safe as long as you're not seen. Then go to Levant or Denny. Tell them what's happened. Bring them here if you can, or get them to arrest and hold the Baron. I have to find Sullyan. She's in terrible danger if she's being held in that circle in spellsilver."

Ardoch nodded, concern etched into his face. "How will I know where to find you?"

Taran grimaced at the sky. "If the power continues to build

like this, even you'll feel it soon. And if it overloads, the whole earth will know. It was somewhere to the east of here, that's all I can tell you. If I can rescue her, we'll make for the Forest. Look for us there."

Before the Torlander could answer, Taran drew his sword. With Sullyan's weapon still at his back, he ran off across the rose garden, following the compelling and dangerous signature of Earth that was pulling so insistently at his senses. He barely heard Jinny's urgent call to Ardoch, or the sound of the carriage moving round to the servants' wing. And he only vaguely registered the shadowy figure at an upper story mansion window.

✤ ✤ ✤ ✤ ✤

The pressure and power continued to build. The puissant forces of Earth had been called forth from the ancient menhirs by the unknown Artesan, and they ran sunwise around the megaliths until the circle was sealed. The presence of the power awakened the reverse-polarity spellsilver, and with its natural repellent properties twisted and altered to attract and enhance, it drew those mighty forces irresistibly toward it. Collecting, gathering, storing, the raw element sucked in every shred of power. If left unchecked, it would eventually be unable to contain any more.

When that happened, a substrate tunnel would be opened directly within the circle, and the unbelievably potent forces would be allowed to shatter within it. The Baron believed this cataclysmic event would bring down the very structure of the Veils, thereby sundering the Five Realms from one another for all time.

He was right.

Unfortunately, with a certainty born of long mastery over the elements and her own vast powers, Sullyan knew that those same titanic forces would also destroy the world.

Once the Baron and his Commander had departed, leaving her

with the inert Andaryan Prince, Sullyan descended into sick despair. Bound painfully by her wrists to the prehistoric monolith behind her, bared to the fury of the storm, she bowed her head to Fate and tasted the bitter dregs of impotent failure. With Aeyron unconscious beside her, she let go the last of her hope and prepared to accept the end.

Of Taran and Ardoch she thought little. The odds against them finding her were great. Even if Taran had tried to contact her and realized what the muffling of her psyche meant, even if he'd sensed the activation of the circle, still he'd have to reach her. For all she knew, the Baron now had guards set around the estate—surely at least around the circle—and her two companions would be foolish in the extreme if they tried to break through. Besides, she had already failed Pharikian. And she knew from Bull that Elias had commenced his assault on the Hierarch, so she had also failed her King.

She felt a tiny twinge in her stomach and gasped. Her vision blurred. What a time for her child to make its presence known! This first kick, her first real experience of the new life inside her, was now just another reminder of what she would lose. Another failure to lay at her door: her failure as a mother. Tears of loss streamed down her face, burning their way into her soul. This final failure was her just reward, and she allowed black despair to envelop her.

Yet around midmorning, with purple skies still bleeding rain and the electric storm still lashing the cliffs to the north, one tiny measure of hope returned.

With a stir and a deep groan, Aeyron opened his eyes.

Sullyan could hardly credit his stubbornness. She almost regretted his return to consciousness, except that it gave her the comfort of companionship. That was selfish, she knew. He deserved peace and a surcease from pain. Now he would have neither.

She turned her head and smiled as warmly as she could into his yellow eyes, so like his father's. She spoke softly.

"Highness? Aeyron, do you hear me?"

His answer was a groan as he tried to move, forgetting his bonds. She could read the ache and strain of his shoulders in the lines on his face, and see the cording of cramped muscles. Her own body, she knew, betrayed the same pain.

His pale eyes flicked to hers. "Brynne? Has the circle been activated, or am I suffering from concussion?"

His voice was barely audible over the storm; she was amazed he could speak at all. Yet he was an Andaryan Prince and a Master Artesan. His reserves ran deep.

"Yes, Highness, to both questions. It has begun. The Baron will achieve his objective in a few hours' time. I regret I was unable to convince him of his folly. The entire world will now pay the price for his prejudice."

"You did your best." Aeyron's lips moved in a smile and she felt her heart bleed. He had been through so much. She read the concern in his eyes and guessed his next question even as she wondered how to answer.

"Do you ... have you seen ... can you tell me how my father is? I have been so worried for him. Does he know...?"

She sighed. She couldn't keep the tale from Aeyron without betraying her love for his father. Yet she balked at telling him the whole truth.

She told him of her visit to the Citadel, of Marik's help and support of his father and sister, and gave him a near-truth account of events after the Baron's ransom note arrived. She couldn't keep the sorrow from her tone, but neither could she bear to give Aeyron further hurt by relating his father's incapacitating distress. Hearing what she had been forced to do to preserve Pharikian's life would do nothing to bolster Aeyron's courage.

Instead, she allowed the Prince to think Marik had taken the Regency under Pharikian's orders, to give the Andaryan ruler time to comfort his pregnant daughter. And although the deception grieved her, the tale gave Aeyron some measure of relief.

"I'm glad you were able to comfort my father," he rasped, the pain of his cracked ribs making breathing difficult. "He loves you very much, you know."

"As I love him, Highness." She closed her eyes. "He is the nearest I shall ever have to a father."

The vibration of Earth force passing through the ancient stone behind her thrummed through her bones, interfering with her thought processes and raising nausea within her. Sullyan was helpless to block it out. Coupled with the effects of her concussion, it threatened to overwhelm her. She knew Aeyron must feel the same, and his body was much weaker than hers.

"Brynne?" He'd called her back from the brink of fainting. She turned her head, trying to focus on his words, to stay alert—or at least conscious—for his sake.

"Highness?"

"Will you do me the courtesy of dropping the 'Highness'? There's no need of such formality between us. You have been as a daughter to my father, and that makes us siblings. I have come to know and love you even as he does, and I know what you feel for my sister and me. You are Ty Marik's closest friend, and he is my brother also. I am proud to acknowledge you as family, so please use my name."

He was unable to see the tears that slid down her cheek. They mingled with and were lost in the rain that streamed down both their faces. But she hoped the love and gratitude shining in her eyes was unmistakable, and they shared more in one look than words could have said.

Chapter Twenty-Four

Silence fell between them. Aeyron's physical condition was dire and Sullyan fared no better, although privation hadn't weakened her muscles as much as despair. Aeyron broke the silence again, seeming to need what solace he could find in discourse.

"Do we have any chance at all of coming out of this alive?" His voice was husky, his eyes fixed upon hers.

Too far gone now in bitter despair, she didn't even consider her reply. Her back against the stone, her head resting on its hard surface, she turned her face to the suppurating sky.

"Not much. I did not come to the city alone, but I left my companions yesterday morning. I do not know whether they have tried to contact me. I told them I might be away until the dawn of this day, and until Izack hit me, I was shielded. I did not want to risk communications via the substrate."

"Why?"

To while away the time, and to keep them both from black despondency, she told him of the events which had led to the conclusions she had drawn, and also what she now knew as fact from the mouth of the Baron. The Prince listened carefully and was especially interested in her discovery of the strangely familiar psyche pattern over the place where he had been taken.

"Did you ever encounter it again?" He had closed his eyes.

The effort of keeping them open against the rain was too great.

"I did." She told him of the raid she had repulsed and the backlash that opposing the strange psyche had dealt her.

"And you have absolutely no idea who it belonged to?"

She frowned. "No, although the Baron's parting shot as he left was that his captive Artesan was known to me. Yet how can that be? To be an Artesan, he has to have an active psyche, and I have never met anyone with that particular signature. I would have remembered if I had. And neither your father nor I could think of anyone with the power to create the Staff. Was the Baron toying with me? Was he trying to confuse me? I cannot see what he would gain by doing so; I am no threat to him now. But Izack's reaction when he thought his lord was about to reveal something important was genuine, of that I am sure. I cannot puzzle it, Aeyron. I do not have the strength."

"How similar to yours was this pattern?"

"Identical." When he glanced at her in surprise, she amended her response. "At least, that is what I first thought. When I encountered it again and was able to study it in more detail, I saw it was not identical, of course. But it was near enough to repulse me when I sought to counter it."

Aeyron's face bore a puzzled frown and he spoke slowly. "To be that similar, the Artesan to whom it belongs would surely have to be related to you." She gave a start and he continued. "My father's pattern is incredibly complex, deeper and broader by far than mine." Aeyron was a Master Artesan, but Pharikian was Senior Master, two full levels above his son. The complexity of his psyche reflected that. "But essentially the patterns are the same. Were we of the same rank, you would be hard-pressed to find the differences. They would be incredibly subtle."

He opened his eyes to look at Sullyan, her head still resting against the stone behind her. She raised her face to the rain as he said, "Your father's pattern would have been the same in relation to yours."

She nodded slightly, even that tiny movement setting off the nausea of her concussion.

"Agreed, but my father is dead. And my parents had no other children."

"Hmm. But the offspring of a sibling of your father or mother would be almost as close a relation as a brother or sister."

His simple statement affected her like a kick in the stomach.

A cousin?

She gaped at him. This was a question she had never even asked herself. Knowing so little of her parents—nothing at all, in fact, until two years ago—she had never dwelt on her ancestry. And once she'd had the tale of their lives and deaths from Pharikian, she drew a line under her family, believing herself alone. Pharikian had never mentioned anything about her parents' relatives. He hadn't even known what region of Albia they came from. The question of wider family members had simply never arisen.

She was stunned into silence.

Why had she never seen the connection? The image of her father's psyche pattern was etched onto the hilt of his sword, the sword she had been given by Pharikian before going out to defeat Lord Rykan. And though it was only a flat representation of the incredibly complex whirls, spirals, helixes, and gyrations comprising an Artesan's personal signature, she could still see the parallels between his pattern and hers.

Why had she never realized the significance of the similarities between this stranger's psyche and her own? Had she not discussed this very point with Elias before they left the city for the Manor? How could she have been so obtuse? If her face had possessed the blood, it would have flushed with shame.

Aeyron had been watching her. "So the Baron was right. You do know this renegade Artesan."

She blinked. Even if he was related to her, it still didn't change the fundamental fact that she had never met the person possessing that pattern.

"It must be coincidence," she said. "The Baron was toying with me. How could he know? He cannot see psyche patterns. No. The fact remains that I would know if anyone possessing that particular pattern had come near me. Even a Supreme Master could not hide or disguise it."

Her stomach gave another nauseating heave. What thought or memory had those words triggered?

Aeyron noticed her distraction. "What is it, Brynne?"

Her tone was distant, her eyes unfocused. "We were talking about the last Supreme Master. Gaslek brought me some parchments. They were a record of the life and powers of Liyan Tamilane, the last known Supreme Master. But that was not all."

She struggled with her memory. The answer was so close, but her brain wasn't functioning well. The clamor of concussion was loud in her ears, and the steady increase in the power levels of the circle was gnawing at her bones, grating on her nerves, screaming at her to control it or run.

"Gaslek had other papers," she continued doggedly, working laboriously through her memories. "There was one report from a father about his six-year-old son. The boy was a sport, a lay-Artesan."

"Yes," murmured Aeyron. "I have heard they exist."

Then she had it. Something the father had said struck a chord within her at the time, but she'd never chased it down. She wondered now what difference it might have made if she had.

Her eyes filled with tears. Her head fell forward. It was yet another failure to lay at her door. Not only had she failed to understand the nature of the Artesan concerned, an understanding which might have enabled her to protect him, but her failure also meant that their present straits—those affecting the entire world, not just her and Aeyron—were undeniably her responsibility.

It was too much. How could she bear it?

She was so distraught she didn't at first hear Aeyron's fearful and insistent calling of her name.

"Brynne. Brynne! What is it? You know who it is now, don't you? *Brynne*."

She turned appalled eyes on him, her voice flat with failure. "I do know him. I have spoken with him, I have touched him. I was so close to him, yet I never realized. I even probed him and still I could not see. I met a blank wall, a void where there should have been some hint of a signature. Even those who are ungifted have a rudimentary pattern, yet there was nothing. The father of the other sport reported exactly the same thing. Why did I not realize? Why did I not push harder? I knew something was wrong, but at the time my thoughts were elsewhere."

She haltingly described the events surrounding the horse race at the castle, and the "accident" that had befallen Elias.

"He was there, our captive Artesan. As was our treacherous Baron. He must have orchestrated the whole thing. *Now* I know why he was so keen to accuse me, why he sought to keep me away. He was terrified I would detect the presence of his captive and uncover his nasty little plot. But I had already encountered his prisoner, close enough to detect him a hundred times over had I realized. I had already failed, even then, and never knew it."

"Who is he?"

She sighed heavily, closing her eyes once more. "A boy who is doomed, I fear. Even were we able to win free of this, he would be unlikely to survive. He is a sport, but he is also crippled of body and deformed of mind. He has the mentality of a four-year-old child, and he would be as easy to manipulate in the hands of one as unscrupulous as the Baron as if he were a four-year-old indeed. His name is Huw, and I fear you are right. The poor boy must be my cousin."

They fell silent again, listening to the sound of the rain, the intermittent thunder, and the ever-increasing hum of Earth force within the circle. The twisted mass of spellsilver upon the altar stone was glowing faintly as it absorbed more and more power, an indication it would soon reach its limits. The raw energy thrumming within the ore was burning away the dross, allowing pure silver to shine through. In the gloom of the advancing afternoon it shone with eldritch light, reflecting off the mica within the granite, throwing the blue of the menhirs into shadow.

Aeyron gathered the strength to speak again. "You weren't the only one who failed to see. You mustn't take the blame on yourself. How could you have known he would be a sport? The confusion of his brain would have hidden his powers from you. A sport is notoriously difficult to detect, even when you know where to look."

"It matters little now," she breathed. "His powers are vastly greater than mine, and even if your father and I were to act in concert, I doubt we could stop a determined attack from him. From what I know of his character, he has no idea what he is being forced to do. What does a child understand of cause and effect? To coerce him, the Baron threatens him—I heard the blow he struck to force Huw to activate the circle—but Huw has no knowledge of the resources he possesses, no idea how easily he could defend himself. A simple raised voice can terrify him. He would do anything to save himself from violence."

She gave a strangled half-laugh, half-sob. "All this time I have tormented myself by imagining the hold the Baron must be exerting in order to force his captive to commit his acts so far. Yet in reality, all he has to do is threaten the lad with a slap. It would be ludicrous if it were not so tragic."

The beginnings of hysteria were plain in her voice. The inexorable increase in the power levels was setting her teeth on edge with its subliminal vibrations, slowly driving both captives crazy with its unreachable potency.

"What did your King Elias think of your theories?" Aeyron asked.

She stared vacantly into the horror of her memories. "He was maddened by the abduction of his son. He refused to listen to me. He has carried war to your father."

Aeyron gaped at this new revelation and she cursed herself. How much more could one soul take without breaking?

"How could he do that?" Aeyron's tone was incredulous. "He must have been mad indeed. What does he hope to gain by waging war on my father? How will that assuage his grief over his son?"

"He believes your father took his son in revenge for your abduction." Sullyan's voice was flat and cold. "He received a message to that effect, signed with your father's seal."

"But they are trade partners! Surely Elias knows my father would never stoop to something like that?"

"So he was told, but by then he was beyond hearing. And I no longer held any sway with him."

"So who leads the Albian forces against my father?"

"The King has gone himself, folly though it is. With him are General Blaine and ... Robin."

"Robin?"

Aeyron stared at her in horror. She could tell he intuitively knew there was yet more pain to be told. "Tell me, Brynne. Tell me everything. It may help to purge your spirit."

His gentle care of her while in such a damaged and needy state himself finally undid her tenuous self-control. Only Bulldog had ever seen her break down so completely. Not even Robin, though she loved him with a fierce and binding love no breach between them could ever diminish, had ever seen her descend to such depths of grief.

For some time she was completely unable to speak. Aeyron, horrified by what he had unleashed within her and desperate to ease her, could only murmur her name over and over, trying to give her some measure of comfort.

The storm within her eventually subsided. She was able to breathe again, able to raise her head and offer a small smile of assurance to the wracked man beside her.

"I am whole, Aeyron. Hurt, but whole. It will never mend now. It is too late—too late for so many things—but I wish now I had told him. My friends were right. He had the right to know."

"The right to know what?"

The storm of weeping had cleansed some of her self-denial, her bitter self-blame. Her lips even formed a wan smile as she said, "That I am pregnant. That I carry Robin's child."

✠ ✠ ✠ ✠ ✠

Finally, Aeyron understood, and in his understanding he could not imagine the anguish her condition was causing her. To know that against all the odds she had conceived the child of the man she loved above life itself, and that both her life and the life of her unborn were imperiled, must have been tearing her apart. And Robin didn't even know.

"When did you find out?" he asked.

"Only a few days ago, though I am more than six months along."

His eyes widened and his gaze traveled her slim form in disbelief. "Oh, Brynne," he breathed, eyes filling with tears. "So you finally healed enough to conceive. Deshan always said you would."

Sullyan looked surprised. "Did he? He never said so to me."

Aeyron responded with a smile. "How could he? What if he was wrong after all? He'd never give you false hope, and he'd never risk his reputation. You know what he's like."

False hope. His words seemed to hang in the air. After all her struggles over the past two years, all the abuse, the fear, the pain, the betrayal; all the love, companionship, friendship, and lives lost. All false hope in the end. And now there was no hope left at all.

Aeyron sensed what she was feeling. He was glad she had been able to tell him, but it made him profoundly sad. He remembered her wedding day, which had also seen the marriage of his sister Idrimar to Ty Marik, and Cal to Rienne. With a sudden cold shock, he realized that if the Baron's plans came to fruition, his sister would never hold her babies, either. He swallowed hard past the lump in his throat, his chest tight and painful from far more than mere cracked ribs.

"Why didn't you tell Robin? Had he already left with the King? I know it would be no easy thing to tell to a man who was leaving for war, but it might have made him more careful, more determined to return. If it was me, I think I would want to know."

He didn't look at her as he spoke, but stared out across the circle. The very air within the space encompassed by the megaliths was now beginning to shimmer like heat haze with the intensity of the building forces. The spatters of falling rain fizzed faintly as they passed through it. The spellsilver was glowing so brightly it hurt the eyes, and some of it was already beginning to slump. The end was very close now.

She slowly raised an ashen face, eyes huge and dark with pain, the whites red-veined with all the bitter rue her soul had to bear.

"I never told him," she rasped, "because we are estranged. He no longer trusts me, and I no longer merit his trust. I forfeited that the day I turned my powers against him in anger. I can no longer even trust myself. We are sundered, Aeyron. My soul is rent in two, and now we will never have the chance to repair the damage. He is forever lost to me, and me and his child to him."

Aeyron had no words to express his pain. He wanted to offer solace, to speak words of comfort, but words seemed inadequate. The raw abrasion of her spirit was plain to see. She had told him all, held nothing back, and the purging had brought her no relief. Still he felt unable to stay silent. If all he could offer her was the companionship of his voice and the dubious anodyne of listening to her, that is what he would do. Perhaps if she talked it through, her hurt could work past the tight knot of despair and she would be able to find the still point of peace. At the very least, it might distract them from having to watch and calculate the very last hour of their lives.

Drawing as deep a breath as he could against the fierce ache in his heart and chest, he forced himself to ask, "How did it happen?"

She turned hopeless eyes upon him, but he wouldn't give way. He was not about to abandon her now to sink alone and friendless into black depression. He could tell that she discerned his intent and was not angry.

Haltingly, her voice raw, she told him what had occurred between her, Robin, and Taran. Then she told him the story of her early life and the experiences that had molded her into the person she was. How she had learned, mainly alone, to master her powers in a life devoid of family love; how she had traveled with and learned of the other races of the realms; of the friends she had made and lost, and of the pivotal moment of her life when she had saved Mathias Blaine from certain slaughter and thus been brought to live at the Manor.

When she was done with her tale and fell silent, Aeyron spoke. He related his life as the son of the Hierarch, told her tales of the intrigues at court, of the growing menace that had been posed by the cunning and ambitious Lord Rykan, and of his sister's long and melancholy search for someone worthy of her love. He even made her laugh—more than once—and was astounded anew by her capacity for life, her stubborn extravagance of spirit, and the depths of her loving and generous heart.

"My father greatly wished for me to find a wife," he said, remembering long wrangles with Pharikian over the subject, "but it's not as easy as it sounds. Oh, there are many who would gladly wed me were I to ask them. I am not so ugly, after all."

Sullyan's eyes lightened as she smiled.

"But I never wanted just a pretty ornament for a life mate. I wanted a woman like my mother. A beauty she was, but she was also able to help my father in his many tasks and duties. That is what I want, but in a society such as ours, where tradition dictates women should not be encouraged to use their brains, the desire for such a life is rare."

"Then you should lead a revolution."

He managed a grin. "Wouldn't that stir the nobles! But it would take too long. I wish I could wed one of your race. You humans are lucky. The trait of the Artesan runs true in your blood. Two gifted parents can be sure their child will inherit the talent. In our race, the trait runs only through the male line, and even then it is not certain. The gift may miss a generation, or even two. Marik cannot rely on either of his twins developing Artesan powers, even should they both be male. At least that's one thing you can depend on. You already know your child will be an Artesan."

The violent jolt that wracked her body was visible even to the Prince. Her face had been pale throughout; now it was gray. Even her lips were bloodless. But her eyes! Her eyes burned with the same intense fire that shot forth from the opal at her throat. The heat of their regard struck Aeyron like branding irons. The rigid shock of her body as she stared blindly at him caused panic to well in his breast.

"What did you say?" she rasped.

He stared at her, fearing she had finally lost her mind.

"*What did you say?*"

"I said that your child will be an Artesan."

The look she turned on him then nailed his heart to the wall of his chest. What had come over her that she should look so strange?

She let loose a string of vicious invective that burned the air between them. He had heard from others of her famed capacity for cursing in times of stress, but had never witnessed it for himself. Some of the words she used he didn't even understand, but their import was clear. She was berating herself unmercifully for gross stupidity.

"Brynne, for the Void's sake…!"

She fell silent at last, almost gasping for breath. But she was smiling now, though its edges were grim.

"Oh, Aeyron, I am such a fool. I sit here helpless watching the world turn toward ruin while all the time the answer stares me in the face. There is yet hope. Just pray I have not left it too late."

His utter bafflement would have been funny under other circumstances. She hastened to explain.

"The spellsilver on my wrists prevents me from reaching outward with my powers, but it does not prevent me from reaching *within*. And it does not touch my child. If I can link with my baby in the womb, perhaps I can channel some of my power through the child's mind to halt the march of Earth force. My baby is closest to Earth at this moment. Earth and Water surround it.

"I can do it, Aeyron. I am sure I can."

He gaped at her. The very idea appalled him. A six-month-old fetus? An unborn? The most precious thing she would ever carry within her? What of the risks? What if—?

"Aeyron." Her hoarse voice cut through his thoughts. "If I do not try, we are all doomed. This child will never be born. Idrimar's twins will never be born. You will never live to father your own children. If I damage my baby by this—if I damage myself—at least the world will be safe. I have to do this. I *have* to."

It was almost as if she was asking his permission. He couldn't accept that burden, that much responsibility. But it was true what she said. If they did nothing, then the whole world would suffer. The Veils would collapse, the realms would die, and all those within them would be snuffed out as if they had never existed. Measured against that cataclysmic tragedy, the risking of two human lives seemed unimportant.

"What can I do?" he asked.

She smiled and his heart tore. "Nothing. Watch and be at peace. You have done enough. It was your words that opened the way to this chance. If I fail now, there will be no blame to you."

Chapter Twenty-Five

Sullyan closed her eyes and leaned her head once more against the stone behind her. The vibration through the rock was potent. It raised nausea once again, but she ignored it. She let slip her awareness of Aeyron, of the rain and thunder, of her wet clothes and the soaked ground, of her pain. She sank down within herself, through the layers of her consciousness, toward a tiny, faraway, vibrant mote of life that murmured contentedly to itself, swaddled within the warmth and security of her body.

She could scarcely believe this was the first time she had attempted such contact. When Rienne had requested that Sullyan confirm her pregnancy, she had guided and shown her friend how to do this for herself. She had even touched lightly upon the forming mind of Rienne's child, just enough to verify her sex.

But this was different. So different.

Since acknowledging Rienne's startling revelation, Sullyan thought she had accepted that the impossible had indeed happened; that she had finally conceived where she had never thought to fulfill the potential of her life. Yet the events surrounding and after this acceptance had prevented her from fully assimilating the fact. It had not been real, not *personal*. Although she knew herself to be pregnant, it had taken no meaning among the ruin of her life.

But now—ah, now!

As she slowly approached the developing life within her, the full import of its presence crashed against her soul. A new life, made by her and Robin. A child—a son!

She marveled at the incomplete yet beautiful embryo psyche revolving slowly within its protective cocoon. Sleepy, murmurous, it responded to her delicate touch as intimately as her own powers did. The trust and love she sensed there stunned and amazed her. It was a part of her, so fundamentally joined with her, and yet was a separate entity.

She could hardly believe it. She had never even guessed it could feel like this.

The warm, irresistible rush of love that flowed through her overwhelmed her senses. The response and recognition of her own child was nearly too much for her. How could she bear to endanger him? How could she even think such a thing? So helpless, so dependent on her, so trusting.

And yet she must. They had no future if she didn't. And she owed him a future if it was even barely within her power to procure it for him.

Whispering reassurance, begging forgiveness for what she was about to do, she slipped within the tiny mind.

There was no resistance, only trust and love. Her heart cried out against the violation, yet her son was not hurt, not frightened. He was where he belonged and so was she. Why should he fear her? They were part of each other. Soothed by his calm acceptance, she reached for her power.

Through her son's unfettered psyche, it now lay accessible. Ignoring the areas linked to Water, Fire, and Air, she drew the signature of Earth around them both. Reaching into this nimbus of elemental forces, she wove it into protection, an unbreachable barrier which she placed around her son, so that if she failed at the last, if the Veils were ripped asunder and the world destroyed, he would never know. He would cease to exist in peaceful ignorance as her own heart ceased to beat.

She owed him that, at least.

Once the barrier was fully in place, a grim strength infused her. Her determination, her instinct to protect, and her rage at the Baron's destructive prejudices all combined to fill her soul. Her baby would remain unaware of this terrible passion; she would never let it touch him. She fed it like a fire within her, and when it was stoked and avid for use, she reached out through the passage open to her son and attempted to take hold of the power of the circle.

The pressures within the circle were almost unbearable. She could feel her skin reacting, sense her eyes bulging under the weight of Earth as it slowly crushed down upon her. The spellsilver was incandescent and melting; soon it would flash into vapor. There was no time. Already it was too late.

Perspiration slid down Sullyan's face, joining the incessant rain. The straining of her body against the bonds that held her was subconscious, but it echoed the struggle of her mind. She could touch the awesome powers of Earth and influence them, but the quantity of spellsilver the Baron had amassed was just too much and the power already accumulated too strong.

She had feared this. She could not channel the full measure of her power through her son's psyche without bursting his unformed mind.

She cried and cursed within her soul. Too late! Why had she not thought of this sooner? She could have handled the power before it grew too strong, but against the levels now stored within the spellsilver and the continuing, relentless march of those puissant forces, she was helpless. The only way now to avert the awful consequences of the Baron's plans would be to destroy the spellsilver.

Crying aloud in her frustration and despair, she opened her

eyes.

Aeyron's head fell forward. "You tried. Don't blame yourself. You tried."

A jagged flash of lightning streaked across the leaden skies, striking with a vast crack upon the hills to the north. It threw into harsh relief the imposing bulk of the menhirs and struck sparks from the straining spellsilver.

The spellsilver.

The *reverse-polarity* spellsilver!

She suddenly knew what she had to do. With the help of the storm, there was a way to change the ore's polarity so it would repel once more rather than attract.

She scanned the skies. Would there be time?

"Aeyron!" she hissed, her urgency startling him. "One last attempt! One final hope and then I am truly done. I may kill us both with what I intend, and so I ask your forgiveness. If I fail again, then I am sorry. Close your eyes, my friend. This is our last chance. If this goes amiss and we lose our lives, maybe we will meet again in some other place. I do not know.

"Pray for me, Aeyron. Pray for us all."

Aeyron didn't understand, yet she sensed his trust. He obeyed her and closed his eyes, his voice raw as he said, "I'd forgive you anything, Brynne Sullyan. I love you."

Not registering his words, she sank once again toward the contented mind of her son, still wrapped securely within his cocoon of Earth. This time, Sullyan reached for the element of Air. It was a fractious force, capricious and slippery, but the mighty storm clouds above them were already trapped by the Downs to the south and the cliffs to the north. She only needed to identify the cusp of the storm and nudge it a little closer. This task was well within her grasp, and soon the dark purple clouds at the center of the violence began to gyre and roil above the ancient circle.

Timing was critical. Too soon and she would advertise all too clearly that she was in control. Too late and it would be too late for them all.

The overload in the spellsilver was reaching crisis point. Soon the touch which would open the substrate would come, and then she must be ready to strike.

Fixing her eyes on the boil of clouds overhead, her powerful senses were fixed on the passion of Fire in her soul. She held her breath and waited.

It wasn't long in coming. The spellsilver reached its capacity. It had already lost its shape and form and was held together only by the tremendous strength of the Earth force flowing through the megaliths. Sullyan could feel the imprint of Huw as he took control of the power. She entertained the idea of calling out to him, but then abandoned it. He was frightened and being coerced. She couldn't take the chance she might frighten him more. He didn't know her pattern, after all.

Resolutely pushing aside her concern for him, she concentrated on the colossal strength of the energy she controlled.

Huw's touch on the forces of Earth was incredibly powerful. It was like seeing her own vast resources multiplied fourfold. He had twice the strength of a Supreme Master, and she raged against the perverse quirk of fate or birth that had crippled his body and mind. She could have done much to help him, using her power to guide his—maybe even to the straightening of the paths of his mind. Certainly she could have healed the bones of his body.

She had to stay focused. He was opening the substrate; she felt the Veils parting at his touch. And then the circle, with its unstable and immeasurably puissant forces, slipped between the realms.

Just before it was enveloped completely, she unleashed her power.

✣ ✣ ✣ ✣ ✣

The two boys allowed their steaming mounts to slow. Their flight from Parren's rooms, and then from the stable yard, had been instinctive. They had no reason to believe they were being followed, but adrenaline had flooded their bodies when they'd heard footsteps approaching Parren's rooms, and only the wild gallop through the trees dispersed it.

Besides, the deserted woods offered them the privacy they needed to review what they had found.

They glanced at each other, sharing the trembling excitement of their discovery. Reining the sweating horses to a halt, they dismounted. Unconsciously, Tad had headed for the stream where Ozella had told him about Parren's blackmail. Hitching their mounts to a tree, they made for the boulders by the pool.

The woods were wet, but the rain had finally eased. The sky was lightening to the east, and it looked like the clouds would eventually clear. The stream's flow had increased with the additional rainwater and the little fall cascaded over the rocks, splashing noisily into the pool.

They seated themselves on wet boulders. Ozella brought the crumpled parchment out from under his shirt, smoothing it over his knee. As Tad looked over his shoulder, he read it through. They'd only had time for the most cursory of glances before, just enough to verify its damning contents. Now they scanned it carefully, assimilating and understanding its import.

Tad's eyes were alive with triumph. "We've done it, Ozella! We've nailed him. He can't argue his way out of this one. It's too plain, too explicit. There's enough here to damn him forever. I doubt they'll even let him live once this becomes known."

Ozella's emotions were more complex. He was clearly excited by the parchment, but also troubled. He looked up at Tad.

"But will Colonel Vassa take this seriously enough to imprison Parren immediately, or will he wait and do nothing until the King returns? Isn't it the King's right to deal with treachery among his forces?"

Tad took a breath to reply, but Ozella wasn't done. His voice rose in panic.

"I can't take the chance, Tad. What if Parren gets a message to whoever's holding my sisters? What if he's already discovered the parchment's gone? What if Rozlin and Surine are already dead?"

Tad tried to hide his exasperation. He understood Ozella's indecision, but things were very clear-cut to him.

"Ozella, listen to me. No one's going to ignore or sit on evidence like this. If we show this to Bull or Vassa, Parren will be in the cells in chains before he can blink. Think about it. They've been trying for months to find out who's behind the attacks on Artesans. And don't forget, the King's life has even been endangered—twice. Not to mention that this parchment means Parren is at least partially responsible for him carrying war—in person!—to Andaryon. Do you think they'd let anyone even remotely involved in that walk free? Parren's the link, the one person who can lead them to the enemy."

Ozella stared, still unconvinced.

"And do you see what it says here?" added Tad. "'*Our powerful benefactress at court.*' Don't you see who that refers to?" He lowered his voice. "It's the *Queen*. She and the Baron are in it together. Colonel Sullyan was right after all. So what does that say about the disappearance of the Prince?"

There was still no response from the older youth, and Tad's exasperation overflowed.

"Oh, come *on*, Ozella, use your wits! Where's your courage? If you didn't intend to use this, why go to the bother of stealing it?"

Ozella wrung his hands, indecision and panic plain on his face. "Colonel Vassa will be out on patrol. Shouldn't we wait for him to return?"

Tad scowled. "Bull's in charge when Vassa's not here. He'll command the duty-sergeant to arrest Parren."

"But what if Parren's already issued orders to kill Rozlin and Surine?"

"Then it's already too late. Parren will be accused of murder as well as treason."

Ozella flushed. "Well, what if he's discovered the theft of the parchment and has fled the Manor? What if even now he's running to his new master in the city?"

Tad grew angry. "Then a company will be sent to apprehend him, and both Parren and his treacherous paymaster will end up behind bars. Come *on*, Ozella!"

Ozella had run out of delaying arguments. He looked deflated and gave a resigned shrug.

"Are we agreed, then?" Tad moved away from Ozella and glanced back up toward the track. All was still. "We'll go to Bull now—and Vassa if we can find him—and tell them everything. We'll show them the parchment and let them make the decisions, yes? Ozella?"

The older lad was silent—surely he couldn't still be undecided? Tad turned around to encourage him some more, and froze in shock.

A foot of bloody steel stuck out the front of Ozella's chest. The youth's mouth hung open in a silent scream. Slowly, his body slumped to the ground.

Parren withdrew his sword and stooped to wipe it on Ozella's jacket. Then he flicked the parchment out of the youth's lifeless fingers. He raised his eyes to Tad and smiled.

Tad's whole body went rigid, his mind telling him both to fight and to flee. He could do neither. His chest was tight with grief.

"You bastard," he panted. "Oh, you bloody bastard!"

Tad silently cursed himself for not taking more care. Parren was too experienced an officer to be duped by two cadets, and now Tad's inexperience had brought Ozella to his death. His heart hammering, he weighed his options. It didn't take him long; he didn't have many.

Using grief and anger as substitutes for courage, he said, "You won't get away with what you've done, Parren. Don't make it worse for yourself."

Eyes that reflected the thrill of killing bored into Tad's. Parren's lips quirked lazily as he replied, "And how is that, runt? Who's going to inform on me?" He glanced at the body on the ground, cushioned by dark red moss. "Ozella won't, that's for sure. That only leaves you, and you won't leave this place alive either."

Tad swallowed and played his trump card. "I don't have to. I'm an Artesan. I can call Bull through the substrate. I may not be able to stop you killing me, but I'll tell him everything first. You'll still be finished."

Parren was silent. Tad was beginning to think his ploy had worked when Parren's cold, cruel smile returned.

"Oh, very good. You nearly convinced me. But you're not that clever, are you? You're about as skilled with your feeble mind as you are with that length of steel at your side. You're only an Apprentice, kitchen boy. You can't even control your own bowels, let alone the dubious power of your mind. You shouldn't be out of swaddling bands. I've nothing to fear from you."

Tad's heart lurched. He was going to die. It had been a long shot, but worth a chance. He hadn't expected Parren to know what Apprentices were or were not capable of, but he should have known better. Parren had lived among Artesans for years. The fact that he despised them didn't mean he was ignorant. Weren't they all taught you should get to know your enemy?

Tad couldn't call Bull, it was true. He didn't yet possess the strength. And he couldn't hope that Bull would call for him, either. The big man had been far too busy recently to bother with Apprentices.

Tad was on his own with only one option left.

Cold panic gripped his heart and a strange tingling like static thrummed along his nerves. Moving deliberately, Tad drew his sword. He saw the glint of dangerous amusement kindle in Parren's flat eyes.

He advanced on Parren, not taking his eyes from the Captain as he had been taught. Parren raised his own sword. Scornful as he was of Tad's fledgling skills, he wasn't about to leave himself unprotected.

"So," Parren drawled, "the useless kitchen runt thinks he can take on an experienced Captain. Well, I admire your spunk. Shame it's about to be splattered all over these rocks."

Tad's heart was pounding so hard the pressure hurt his ears. The vibration he could subconsciously sense was growing stronger. Forgetting all his lessons, he sprang wildly at Parren, slashing and cutting with all his might.

The Captain countered Tad's swings easily, the sneer never leaving his face. He kept Tad at a distance, his ripostes pushing Tad back, forcing him to struggle for balance on the uneven ground.

Tad was surprised at his own courage. Having decided to fight, he refused to back down. His blood was up, furious that Parren had sniffed them out just when they had the upper hand, shocked at what Parren had so casually done to Ozella. He wanted revenge. He wanted to wipe that smug smile from Parren's cruel mouth. The electric sensation in the air that crawled across his nerves like trails of fire impelled him to action.

Parren easily held him off. He played with Tad, flicking the tip of his sword now and then to nick an arm or a leg. Each time Tad gasped, he grinned.

"Don't you have the sense to see when you're overmatched, runt? Well, that's your lookout. It's not my fault. I can always blame your deaths on raiders. Oh, what a good story that will be. I'll say I came across a party of Relkorian slavers attempting to carry off two unwary lads. I fought them, naturally, even though I was wounded and outnumbered. It's a pity both boys were killed in the fight, but at least I tried."

The nasty smile that stretched his lips turned Tad's blood to water.

"It's a shame you'll never get to see your idol again. How do you think he'll feel when he hears of your senseless death? Mind you, the war's not over yet. Tricky things, wars. Tamsen might just take a sword in the back, just like poor Ozella there. And even if he comes home safe, he won't live long. I've already accomplished Sullyan's downfall. Tamsen will be easy meat."

This was too much for Tad. Shrieking his rage and grief, he flew at Parren. This time, he didn't completely lose his head. He remembered his lessons and tried to channel his rage into strength instead of mindless slashing. He was now more dangerous than he had ever been.

Yet he was still no match for Parren. The Captain was older, taller, stronger, vastly more skilled, and merciless. No pity or concern marred his responses. He might have been fencing with a dummy for all the humanity he showed.

He pursued Tad relentlessly toward the stream, across the boulder-strewn terrain, forcing him ever backward. Tad could do nothing except counter his blows as best he could, struggle to keep his footing, block and defend. The cold glitter of Parren's dead eyes revealed nothing; no hate, no fury, no compassion. He was a killing machine and Tad his next victim.

Then Tad's back was to the stream. He could go no farther and remain upright. Valiantly, though his untrained muscles were afire and he burned from numerous wounds, he strove to hold his own. Parren was toying with him. The sneer never left his thin lips. Tad read his death in those cold eyes and his courage failed him.

"You know, runt," said Parren as he rained blows down on Tad's blade, "you were right all along. I don't have any men with which to hold Ozella's sisters. In fact, they're not being held at all. They were released some days ago, completely unharmed. What a shame your friend will never know."

Tad's eyes filled with tears. He saw the final stroke, registered the intent in those pale gray eyes, and did the only thing he could. As he felt the cold steel bite into his flesh, he gathered all his strength and shrieked out through the substrate, forcing his underdeveloped psyche to carry his last silent, despairing scream to the one person he desired to reach above all others. He never really felt the incredible detonation that surged all around him as the cry left his mind:

ROBIN! HELP ME!

Chapter Twenty-Six

Taran had never wished harder for a horse. He was all too visible and noticeable, running afoot in obvious urgency through the foul weather lashing the Baron's lands. His cloak was wrapped tightly around him, the hood drawn up to cover his head and face, but he would still be remembered, dashing across the landscape in the pouring rain on a day when most sensible folk were warm and dry indoors.

There was no help for it. The incessant vibration through the earth and the air and its effect on his metasenses urged him to speed with alarming irresistibility.

Rain drummed from the skies, turning the lanes to rivers and the fields to a sodden quagmire. Visibility was poor. The warmth of the land and the chill of the rain caused steam to rise and mingle with the downpour, producing a clinging kind of mist. The light was leached from the day by the purple clouds above, the air split by regular bursts of forked energy.

Taran ignored the storm. It was concentrated more to the north of the city now, attracted by the cliffs overlooking Loxton Bay. With any luck, it would break and fray on those cliffs and lose its vigor.

The power he could feel through the substrate was constantly growing, akin to the forces of the storm. It was a tsunami of Earth force that would rend the whole world if released uncontrolled. His flesh, his very spirit, quailed before the promise of its violence.

His direction was determined by the pull of those forces. Squinting into the pummeling rain, he could see few markers to guide his way and was compelled to open his senses to the dangerous energies in order to track them to their source.

He wondered how on earth he would stand it when he was closer. The tightest shield he could form would quaver before such potency.

He was taking too long. His sodden cloak hampered his movements; the rain beating into his eyes stung like hail. The increasing power screamed at him to hasten, and yet he could not. The fields were too mired for him to force a way through. He had to stick to the flooded lanes and had no idea whether he was really going in the right direction.

Breath rasped through his burning throat and his heart hammered against his ribs. He was unpleasantly reminded of his flight from the huntsmen of the Andaryan noble he had killed—Sonten's nephew, Jaskin—and the huge, vicious tangwyr that had been flown at him. There was no waiting portway to save him this time, and he ran toward the danger, not from it.

He was forced to slow to recover his breath, although his nerves screamed at the delay. He panted as much from urgency as lack of oxygen. His sight was blurry from his exertions—or was it the rain? Forcing his burning muscles to obey, he pressed himself back into a run. He had a fierce stitch in his side and his head was pounding from the hum of raw power.

He saw no one, which was a blessing. He had passed unseen beyond the immediate boundaries of the mansion house and had deliberately avoided the village. There were outlying houses and barns, and he saw candles and lamplight in more than one window, but no one was abroad. It was not so surprising. Only a dire emergency would force people to brave such foul weather, especially on a holy day.

Taran ran on. He crossed stiles and leaped fences and took turnings which seemed to pull him in the right direction. He passed orchards and pasturelands, saw fleece-draggled sheep attempting to shelter in the scant lee of hedges. Cattle stood dejectedly, rain pelting their hides. No herders or farmers accosted him, no carters or shepherds delayed him. Only his own protesting muscles forced him to slow.

He finally had to lean against a five-bar gate, gasping for breath. His nose was assailed by the smell of sodden sheep. His eyes searched the gloom of the fading afternoon. His head came up sharply, his senses slapped to wakefulness by a tiny alteration in the timbre of the Earth force.

He opened his mind, but not so far as to reave himself of all protection. Was the build of Earth force lessening?

Desperately, he sought confirmation of Sullyan's psyche. What he sensed caused a frown to gather on his brow. This was like nothing he had ever felt before. It was akin to her pattern, yet different. Almost as if it were superimposed upon something else. It was unresponsive, and the Adept received a sharp and painful reminder of what spellsilver felt like.

He had experienced it only once and had no desire ever to go through that again. How she would ever bear it, he had no idea. Yet she had borne many things he was sure would have finished him, and he knew the depths of her courage could never be plumbed.

The power snapped back with renewed vigor and Taran was forced to throw up a shield. He gasped as the Earth forces crashed against his mind with manic strength. He'd only just been quick enough to save himself from serious harm.

Thoroughly alarmed by the failure of that strange psyche to control the spiraling Earth force, Taran thrust away from the rain-slick wood of the gate. Leaving the mournful sheep to their dejection, he ran on.

Now his gaze was drawn to the sky. Was the storm coming closer? Hadn't its center of violence been concentrated over the cliffs? A vagrant breath of wind from behind him caught his cloak, flapping it about his legs despite the thick, sodden weight of its wool. He turned his head as he ran, glancing up over his shoulder.

He was brought up short by what he saw. The heavy clouds were approaching, turning ponderously like some titanic, inverted whirlpool. He had never seen the like and stared transfixed, half in horror, half in amazement. The dark purple clouds seemed to boil and roll ominously, and they were coming steadily closer.

He was watching the exact spot when a colossal bolt of lightning struck the ground, the after flash imprinted on the backs of his eyes. He blinked, forced to clap his hands over his ears at the air-splitting crack of thunder that followed.

The cusp came overhead, but it was still moving. Its sinister violence smote his senses, making him want to cringe to the ground. The very strength of Fire and Air within it staggered his brain. It was a cataclysmic storm, and it was building even as the Earth forces below it were building.

Taran knew with intuitive clarity that the storm and the circle were linked. If he followed that whirl of dreadful cloud, it would lead him to the site of the circle and, hopefully, Sullyan. Could he feel her influence on the storm? No, but he could feel something. A tiny hope infiltrated his heart and he grasped at it. Trying to ignore the huge blasts of lightning striking perilously close, he dashed after the cusp of the strange storm.

It halted, seeming to gather itself. The speed of its gyre intensified. The clouds were bulging, rain-heavy and pregnant with violence. Taran felt a prodigious Fire building within the storm—held back, honed, readied—and its potency crawled across his nerves. He watched as the center of the cusp began to descend, forming a narrow purple funnel as it reached for the ground.

It was holding station above some woodland. To Taran's eyes the trees were impenetrable. Helpless, unable to hinder the might of the storm or affect the march of Earth power, he could only watch and wait.

Nausea swamped him. The vibration through his body and the static coursing along his bare nerves frayed his consciousness. He hugged his arms tightly across his chest as if to hold his spirit within. He approached as near to the woods as he dared. Any closer and he might imperil his life. He had no idea what was happening.

Panting, he leaned against a tree, prepared to observe the culmination of this strange occurrence as it played out before him. He could sense the overloading of the spellsilver. He was appalled at the amount of Earth power it had amassed. *Thirty pounds of spellsilver,* he thought. How could it contain so much? Then, abruptly, he felt it fail.

In that instant, and with deep and utter horror, he sensed the opening of the Veils.

He wanted to scream—*No! NO! We'll all be destroyed!*—but he had no voice, no vehicle for the shock in his soul. His eyes stretched wide as the titanic forces of Earth were sucked into the substrate, for he knew that if they exploded, the resulting detonation would shatter the world to its very roots.

Then a vast, apocalyptic bolt of lightning struck.

✣ ✣ ✣ ✣ ✣

General Blaine surrounded the King with his forces, placing the Manor men on one side of him and Valustin's on the other. Blaine himself rode around the mass of marching men, encouraging, watching, exhorting. He had an uncomfortable feeling about this march, although it was probably just the culmination of all the misgivings he'd had about the campaign from the start.

If Blaine had been able to influence the King at all, he'd have recommended initiating diplomatic approaches instead if this damaging rush to invade. Talks with the Hierarch and his ministers would surely have proved to Elias that although the demon ruler had no idea of the little Prince's whereabouts, he'd have been perfectly willing to cooperate with finding those who did.

After all, there was no question some of his subjects were responsible for Eadan's abduction, as well as the recent raiding into Albia. It was also not in doubt that demons had perpetrated at least one attempt on Elias's life. That alone would have guaranteed Pharikian's compliance. And the Hierarch was also in the unenviable position of having firsthand experience of how Elias was feeling, having lost his own son and Heir.

Blaine reflected ruefully that Sullyan's special relationship with the Andaryans would have proved invaluable. Had he been in his right mind, Elias would have utilized it to the full.

The General was still trying to come to terms with the King's shocking denouncement of Sullyan. The fact that Elias had gone so far told the General just how unstable his monarch was. He knew how fascinated Elias was by Artesans—Sullyan in particular—and how proud he was to have such powerful people loyal to his service. He had trusted them all implicitly, but the damage done to his mind by Eadan's abduction had warped his view of that trust. Sullyan's refusal to obey his direct command must have seemed like the ultimate betrayal.

He had tried to contact her twice since she'd left, but she was always tightly shielded. He had no doubt she had gone to seek both the King's son and the Hierarch's Heir. He had questioned Robin as to her whereabouts but had received evasive answers. And that worried him.

He had, of course, heard the rumors that had spread around the Manor. He credited them with no more truth than her other friends had, but he'd seen how troubled Robin had become, and now feared the two of them had not settled their differences before Sullyan left. He had also noticed Taran's absence. Busy though he was, not much escaped his attention. As the Adept had never been under Blaine's command, he was free to come and go as he pleased. Blaine had assumed Taran was lying low to let the rumors die down. Now he found himself wondering whether the tall Adept had gone with Sullyan. Taking another Artesan to stand for you was one of the first lessons drummed into all Apprentices.

The General dragged his thoughts back to the task at hand and rode another circuit of the marching men. Whatever the reason for Taran's disappearance, one thing was certain. This campaign had sharpened their minds and the rumors were long forgotten.

They had evacuated the second town in good order on Elias's command and even now were leaving the farmlands behind. In the advancing afternoon, the terrain was becoming more difficult as they neared the region of hills and woods reported by Valustin's scouts. They had to negotiate this region before seeing the orchards and vineyards of their next objective, and the General was uncomfortably aware of its suitability for ambush.

He gazed around at the orderly, massed ranks of trained men, surrounded by the mounted companies, and gave Valustin the signal to send out yet another band of scouts. The Manor men were providing the forward scouts while those from Port Loxton ranged away to the rear. So far, they'd brought no reports of pursuit from Anjer.

Elias had been euphoric at the news, believing his ploy had worked. Blaine found it hard to credit they'd duped Anjer yet again by their swift taking and then abandoning of the last town. It just didn't correspond with what he'd heard of the Andaryan general.

Surely such an experienced warleader wasn't going to let the Albians annex portions of his territory without lifting a finger to stop them? From Sullyan's reports, he knew she respected Anjer highly and considered him a formidable strategist. She would have had a good idea of what he was up to right now.

The Manor men galloped off to the north to scout around the hills and investigate the woodlands. They would inform the General of the safest route for their forces to travel. The weather was improving steadily as the afternoon wore on, but the cloud cover was still heavy enough to exclude all sight of the sun. The quality of the light meant they were unlikely to see the next town before dark. The unfavorable terrain had slowed them considerably.

A shout from behind caused the General to turn sharply in his saddle. Every captain barked orders to alert their men to possible action. Peering back over the massed ranks, Blaine could make out a small band of riders heading their way at a ground-eating gallop—Valustin's scouts, by the look of it.

They identified themselves as they came and were let through to the General and the King. Captain Benett, the leader of Valustin's scouts, came forward and saluted his King, but his eyes were on the General.

"We've spotted Anjer's forces, General. His whole command is on the move and following fast. They didn't come direct from their last position. That's why we've not seen them till now. They've swung around behind us to the west and are coming up on our left flank. We didn't expect them from that quarter, so they've gained some distance on us. They've blocked the way back to the last town, so we can only go forward—unless, of course, we're going to hold them here."

"Hold them here?" The King's tone was irascible. "Of course we're not going to hold them here. What purpose would that serve?

And let them block the way back if they choose, I have no intention of retreating. No, we're going to press on and we're going to take this next town before they reach us. Coming up fast, are they? Well, we'll just have to move faster than they are. General, give the order for a forced march."

Blaine had long since learned that raised voices or protestations only hardened the King's stubborn resolve, so he spoke quietly. "Your Majesty, we ought to consider this development. If Anjer's trying to push us, he must have a reason. He can't want us to gain the next town. There must be something up ahead that is advantageous to him, either in the terrain or, more likely, a second body of men. He might even have sent reinforcements to fortify this next town. If so, it would be madness to throw ourselves against it. Captain Benett's idea is a sound one. We'd be better advised to consider our position and find a place for defense. If we order a forced march we may leave ourselves vulnerable or even run blindly into a trap."

Robin spoke up in support. "At least wait for the advance scouts to return and report, your Majesty."

Elias was in no mood to wait. His face was red with anger and his eyes glittered coldly as he stared Blaine down.

"And maybe scaring us into milling about here like witless sheep while his slit-eyed demons round us up like dogs is exactly what he wants!" he snapped. "Have you lost your courage, Mathias? Will you back down at the first threat of battle? We expected opposition, didn't we? My orders remain unchanged. I will not be deflected from my purpose like this. We will gain the cover of the town by full dark, and from there we will carry war to the demons and give them a taste of our anger. I will not be intimidated into a rout nor forced to change my plans just because there are a few barbarians behind me. Order a forced march, General, or I will do it myself."

In the face of the King's direct order, Blaine had no choice. Both Robin and Valustin registered the reluctance with which he passed on the King's wishes, but they were all helpless to do anything other than obey. He knew both senior officers agreed with him, and Robin in particular would know that Anjer and his men were not barbarians but intelligent and wily opponents who were, moreover, on their own land and fighting for their own people. The Albians were isolated and vulnerable, and Blaine knew how risky it was just having Elias here when he possessed no powers to return himself to Albia should this campaign go awry.

That responsibility lay very firmly on the General's own shoulders. He and Robin had made an agreement—without Elias's knowledge—that if things went badly, whichever one of them was capable would force Elias through the Veils and ensure his return to Albia. They might risk instant dismissal or worse, but at least the King would be safe. It was as much as they could do.

The men picked up the pace, the King refusing to remain hidden among them. He rode at their head, fully visible and highly vulnerable to crossbow bolts or longbows. Blaine had Valustin send men far out on either flank to watch for any such attempts, and he scanned the hills and woodlands nervously.

Benett had been sent back with his band to keep watch on Anjer's forces. He was to send a runner to the General at frequent intervals to report. But the scouts that had been sent ahead had not been seen for some time, and Blaine was reluctant to send another group until they knew what had delayed the first.

They marched on into the waning afternoon, the heavy clouds shutting out early what light there was. The increasingly frequent grassy hills and broadleaf woods were fading into the twilight, causing them all to strain their eyes. Benett's messengers reported no slackening of Anjer's pace; indeed, he had increased it to match theirs and, if anything, was gaining on them. Elias's determination to reach the next town and entrench began to take on the feel of a rout.

Knowing they weren't going to make it in time, Blaine tried twice more to convince Elias to halt and prepare to defend while they still had the option of choosing their own ground. He feared running into the opposition and being forced into unfavorable terrain where the enemy would hold every advantage. He was sure this was Anjer's plan. Blaine's every instinct screamed at him to pick his ground, deploy his men and prepare to fight.

Elias, however, wouldn't be reasoned with. They would gain the town, he insisted, and defend from there. Blaine's response was that should they be too late, the Albians would have hostile forces before and behind them. If they couldn't breach the town walls before Anjer reached them, they would be caught like a nut between rocks. The townspeople could shoot at them from behind their defenses while Anjer picked them off from outside.

But Elias didn't believe Anjer was that close. He also didn't believe the townsfolk would resist. Hadn't the other two towns proved how lily-livered these demon peasants were? He'd fire their walls if they dared defy him.

Frustrated, Blaine pointed out that this would disadvantage their own forces, and that sight of Anjer's men would put heart into the townspeople and encourage them to resist. Elias's only response was to growl that they'd better get a move on, then, and secure the town before the demon hordes appeared.

Around dusk, Benett himself came charging up through the ranks to the King. His report was grim. Anjer had fanned out his lines and was advancing fast. There was now no chance of the Albians reaching the town walls before Anjer forced an engagement.

Blaine glanced at Robin. The forward scouts had still not reported, and both men feared the worst. They must have been captured or slain.

Blaine had had enough. The King's intransigence had given him a throbbing headache and he rubbed irritably at his temples, trying to massage it away. The time had come to assert his authority, whatever Elias might say.

They were not in the best of positions. There was a wood to the east and some steep hills to the north. The town was probably just over the next rise, but the General wasn't going to commit his men to rising ground without knowing what was at the top. Without consulting Elias, he gave the order to halt and prepare to defend.

Elias was furious and roared a counter order. Robin and Valustin stood fast with Blaine. They were on the verge of an all-out argument, the men standing by awkwardly, when a frantic shout cut the air. A lone rider came pelting out of the hills to the north, crying words they couldn't hear. It was one of the forward scouts, and he galloped straight for the General, panting out his message of doom.

"A second force, your Majesty! They took us—all of us—and we couldn't get free to report. They're camped at the top of these hills. You'll never get past them. They let me go deliberately so I could warn you. We're caught, your Majesty. We're trapped."

It was exactly what Blaine had feared. Nevertheless, they still had options. Anjer had spread out his men, and that meant he would have weak spots. The force ahead of them was not as large as that behind, judging by the scout's report, but they held the high ground. It would be folly to attempt them with Anjer so close on their tail. The woods to the east were their only hope.

Blaine ordered the men into the cover of the woods. The trees would fragment Anjer's ranks if he attacked, and also help conceal the Albians. They would hamper the Albians too, of course, but at least they would offer some measure of protection.

Elias made no comment, but his expression was murderous, and the General threw Robin a meaningful glance which the young Major understood. They couldn't permit Elias to throw his life away just because the balance of his mind was disturbed.

The men entrenched, efficiently and swiftly. Elias was forced into their center, furious but no longer attempting to countermand his general. The light was fading fast; there was unlikely to be much in the way of fighting during the night. It was Blaine's private view that Anjer, who had shown no sign of wanting to attack them so far, would use both the forces at his disposal to intimidate Elias into surrendering by surrounding them and negating their threat. Why else had the force to the north allowed the scout to escape?

The General's only real fear was that Elias would play his trump card and use the towns he was holding hostage against Anjer. The King had stationed runners along their line of march to communicate with the men left holding those two towns, and they had orders to fire the houses if Elias sent the signal. Blaine knew this action would result in nothing but unnecessary bloodshed, and would undoubtedly goad Anjer into attacking them. The best this strategy could produce would be an angry stalemate.

Grim-faced and frustrated, still plagued by the thrumming headache, the General could only order his camp and wait to see what dawn brought.

* * * * *

Once Robin had done his habitual rounds of the camp, he returned to Elias and Blaine. The young Major was experiencing a grinding headache which his metaforce seemed unable to relieve. It had made him snappy for the past two hours. As he approached the circle of tents that served as the King's and the officers' quarters, he felt a tremendous blow, as if his head had been cloven in two.

Giving an involuntary shriek of pain, he dropped to his knees. Blaine was beside him in an instant, reaching out with his own psyche, supporting and defending. Robin's first thought was to suspect some underhanded attack by Anjer or one of the other Andaryan Artesans, but he soon realized it was nothing of the kind. The echo he'd caught fleetingly before his shields snapped down had been of a desperate but ill-formed cry for help.

His first intense fear—*Sullyan!*—proved groundless. He knew her signature well, and this was nothing like it. This was faint, raw, and immature.

Blaine, helping the trembling Major to his feet, demanded gruffly, "Who the Void was that?"

Robin shook his head, unable to answer. The contact was so unexpected, so swift, so full of terror and desperation that he couldn't think.

"Give me a minute," he gasped, pressing his hands to his aching temples.

Once he was calm again and the curious who had gathered round him had been sent back to their duties, he was left with Blaine and Elias. He sat down on a fallen log beside the small fire that had been laid for the King, still holding his head in his hands.

Blaine watched in concern. "Well, Major?"

Robin sorted gingerly through the layers of his mind. The touch had been so fleeting and so inexperienced he had to search hard to find the pattern that had sent it. When he finally did, he couldn't believe it. "Tad!"

Blaine's brows creased. "You mean the cadet who used to work in the kitchens?"

Robin nodded.

"Why would he call you?"

Robin held his gaze. "I don't know, sir. I didn't even think he *could* call me. He's just an Apprentice; he shouldn't have the strength. But I could tell, even from that brief contact, that he was terrified. It's the only thing that could have lent him enough power. He was desperate. But I can't reach him now. I can't even sense his psyche."

Blaine frowned. "Was he in Albia?" When Robin nodded, Blaine snapped, "Then contact Hal Bullen and check all is well at the Manor. *Quickly*!"

Chapter Twenty-Seven

Despite his reluctance to bespeak Bull and feel his erstwhile friend's censure, Robin obeyed the General immediately. He felt for Bull's strong, familiar pattern and contact was swiftly established. Bull confirmed that all was well at the Manor, although he had been concerned by a sudden surge through the substrate that he didn't understand. He had no explanation for why Tad should call to Robin.

The Major passed on Bull's report to Blaine, and the General gave his permission for Bull to investigate.

See if you can find him, will you, Bull? asked Robin, worry coloring his tone. *Something must be badly wrong. The poor kid sounded in terror of his life. Do your best. That boy means a lot to me.*

More than your wife, by the looks of things, was Bull's underhanded parting shot. He cut the link before Robin could reply.

Tears came to Robin's eyes and he felt his heart contract. He had thrust his love and fear for Sullyan deep down within himself after the anguish of her betrayal. Now he felt ripped in two, confused and hurt, and he didn't know how to bear it. He was frightened for Tad. He had a deep and genuine affection for the boy who, after all, had saved his life once. If Tad should be badly wounded or worse, he would have no more room in his soul for the pain.

✤ ✤ ✤ ✤ ✤

Bull had been at the level of Adept-elite for some years now. Once he had gained enough strength to learn the technique for influencing Fire, he had reached a plateau, unable to overcome his very natural aversion to something that could cause him serious harm. Eventually accepting he'd never have the power to serve Sullyan as she deserved, he had channeled his energies into finding someone who would. Someone stronger, more determined, more worthy of her. And finally, he had found Robin.

When he had realized this extraordinarily handsome young man who was also a talented soldier possessed the capacity to match Sullyan's force, he just couldn't believe his luck. Robin was only two years older than she was; just the right age for a potential mate. The eventual results of bringing them together were more than even Bull could have hoped for.

He was content where he was. He was serving the woman he loved, watching her grow in power and into the heart and soul of the young man who had become her life mate. A young man who had professed himself to be more blessed than he ever thought he could be.

So why the Void had the silly sod allowed some ill-conceived and patently erroneous rumor to ruin all that? After four years together, hadn't he learned better than that?

The big man realized he was allowing his anger and frustration to distract him from his task. *Gods*, he thought sourly, *let's not hold the wake before the bloody funeral.* Emptying his mind of thoughts of Robin, he delved through the substrate for Tad's immature psyche.

His initial failure irritated him, but didn't trouble him unduly. He was aware he was not always as methodical as he might be. Perhaps the nagging headache he'd had for a couple of hours now had affected his concentration, although it had been steadily fading since that strange surge through the substrate.

Closing his eyes and clearing his mind once more, he tried again. This time he thought he caught a faint glimmer, but it vanished as soon as he tried to catch hold of it. Puzzled and a little concerned, he decided to try for Ozella.

He met with even less success there. Thoroughly alarmed, he left his rooms and ran for the commons. The communal room was crowded with men, both militia and cadets. Bull threw open the door and roared Tad's name over the throng. When he received no response except the amused and curious looks of the inmates, he strode into the kitchens to ask if Goran had seen the lad.

The cook was busy and in no mood to be helpful, but Bull gathered Goran hadn't seen Tad. He wished he had; he could have done with his help. He bitterly regretted the day Tad had been accepted for military training.

Abandoning the sour cook to his grumbling, Bull ran for the College. If Tad and Ozella were practicing in the healer suite, the spellsilver in the walls would muffle their patterns completely.

Wondering why he hadn't thought of this before, and convinced the boys were trying out some forbidden experiment where no one could sense them, Bull prepared to blister the air when he finally found them. He wouldn't be surprised if Tad had induced Ozella into playing some prank or other. If so, he'd tan their hides, not least for daring to distract Robin in the field.

That thought brought Bull up short. If the boys were indeed in the nullified room, neither of them could have called out to Robin. Striding through the dark corridors of the deserted College, roaring their names with no response, he thrust open the healer suite door. As he had begun to fear, it was empty.

At a loss now and thoroughly frightened, Bull took a moment to consider. He could check the barracks and any number of other places in the Manor, but there was nowhere Tad could hide where Bull couldn't sense him. That left only two options. Either the boys had been captured and were unconscious or in spellsilver, or—and this one really scared him—they were dead.

Biting his lip, he decided to verify one more hunch before he roused the place.

Bull headed for the stables and accosted one of the stable lads. The lad told him two horses had been taken out earlier in the day, and one of them was Ozella's. Bull immediately instructed the lad to get horses ready and sent another lad scurrying for Rienne to alert her to a possible serious injury, or worse. He then pelted back to the commons, his heart laboring fearfully.

Once there, he identified two of the more competent militia leaders and ordered them to pick and send out search parties from those peasants who were good enough riders. They were to scour the Manor grounds. It was fortunate that most of the men knew Tad and Ozella by sight if not personally. The former kitchen boy was popular with many of the peasants, and Ozella's olive skin was unusual in those parts, so no time was lost issuing descriptions.

Bull picked half a dozen men to go with him and worked out a search pattern with the other leaders. Gratified by the instant and good-natured response to the emergency, Bull hurried out with his men, some of them still finishing mouthfuls of food. He led them back to the stables and soon they were mounted and moving out into the gloom of the early evening, torches at the ready, followed closely by the other two search parties.

Bull chose the southeastern section of the Manor grounds. Here there were broad tracks through the trees where Ozella could have raced his desert-bred stallion, plus enough in the way of fallen logs and other obstacles to provide jumps for such a race. Fervently hoping the lads had simply fallen from their mounts during some wild, competitive ride, but knowing deep down the situation was far more serious, Bull set his party to search.

After half an hour of searching, Bull's party was increased by two when Rienne and Chief Healer Hanan joined him. Hanan had heard the stable lad's news when he came to fetch Rienne, and had sent healers out to join all the parties in case immediate medical care was required.

It was full dark by the time the healers joined the search. Their torches shed a flickering light and threw out more shadows among the trees than they dispelled, but Bull was loath to give up. They continued in a line, each keeping their neighbor just in sight. Eventually, Bull heard what he had both hoped for and dreaded.

One of the other search parties set up a great holler, bringing all the men galloping dangerously fast in the dark. When Bull arrived he saw it was not the boys that had been found, but their mounts. Both horses were hitched to the trees where they had been left.

Bull eyed them with concern. "No sign of ambush or attack," he mused, searching the ground as best he could in the guttering torchlight. The men's feet had disturbed what signs there might have been, but to Bull's experienced eye it looked like the boys had ridden out here together, left their mounts tethered, and walked off into the woods.

"Right, men," he called, "fan out and search the woods. There's a stream to the left through the trees and it gets boggy, so my party will go that way. The rest of you spread out around us and keep your eyes open. Remember, there might be raiders around."

Bull drew his sword and led his party toward the small stream that ran through the woods. It fed a series of small watering pools in the breeding herd pastures and always ran swift and clear. He knew roughly how far into the trees it was and cautioned his men to be careful when they were close. He positioned himself and the women in the center of the line, with his men ranging both up and downstream of him.

It was from upstream that the call came.

They ran in haste to where the cry came from. The two men who had made the gruesome discovery stood within a little clearing, one next to Ozella's body, the other by the stream.

Bull went first to Ozella, followed by Hanan, who bent to examine him. Rienne, with a small cry of grief, waded into the shallow stream. Bull could tell even by the guttering torchlight that there was no life left in Ozella. The wound in the youth's breast had severed the arteries of his heart; he had been dead before he'd fallen. Fury on his face, his eyes blurring, Bull turned to Rienne.

She was crouched in the stream over Tad's body, her fingers to the vein in his neck. Her eyes were unfocused as she strove to utilize her empathic senses to ascertain whether any signs of life could possibly still linger within.

"Bull," she called, "can you reach into him? I think there might be a flicker there, but I can't be sure. Oh, if only I were a proper Artesan!"

Bull joined her in the stream, ignoring the pull of the cold water around his feet. Sheltered by the trees for much of its length and coming from the waterfall and pool, this stream never lost its chill, even in the hottest of summers.

Gathering his wits and his powers, Bull reached out to Tad's psyche. He strove with all his strength to find what Rienne had glimpsed. Yes, it was there! Faint and quailing, but still there. The slightest hint of his soul clung doggedly to the final thread of his life. Bull grunted with the effort of bolstering that feeble spark.

"He's fading fast," he said, his words clipped with the effort of split concentration. "If I can pour all my strength into him, I might be able to hold on to him until we reach the infirmary. Will you be able to do anything for him there?"

Rienne swiftly explored the wound in Tad's side. She called for more light and the men brought their torches closer.

"His main problems are shock and loss of blood," she said. "I don't think any of the major organs are damaged, although he may have lost a kidney. I'll be able to tell better when he's more stable." She glanced up at the men around her. "Two of you lift him—very carefully!—and keep him as flat and still as possible."

Packing some cloth around the gaping wound, she nodded to the men. With Bull keeping a hand on the boy's clammy brow to facilitate the link and using all his concentration to shore up Tad's limping heart, they bore him from the stream.

He vaguely heard Hanan say, "Bring the other lad as well." Two men leaped to obey her. With two more bringing the boys' horses, they made their somber way back to the Manor.

Someone had sent word ahead of them to ready the infirmary. Tad's mother, one of the junior healers, met them on the way, wringing her hands, her face white. It was only two hours off midnight, but all the healers had turned out to see if they could be of assistance.

For Ozella, they could do nothing. For Tad, they would have to work a miracle.

All the men at the Manor had heard of the search by the time they arrived. Colonel Vassa wasn't there; he was due back very shortly with the last patrol of the day, and the next wasn't due out until just before dawn. So it was that the party bearing the two boys was met on the approaches to the infirmary by Captain Parren. Bull barely noticed the sallow young man as he fell into step beside a pale-faced Rienne.

"What's happened here?" he asked, his voice full of rough concern. "Been dueling, have they?"

Rienne looked sharply into his scarred face. "Why do you say that?"

He shrugged, studying the boys' gray faces. "Oh, I heard them arguing in the stables a few hours ago. The kitchen lad was insulting the foreign boy's horse and the other was defending the beast. It got quite heated, so I'm not surprised they came to blows. Shame they killed each other over it, though."

Bull frowned. That didn't sound like Tad. The boys may not have been instant friends but Tad would never come to blows over any argument, however serious. He knew dueling was strictly forbidden.

Rienne clearly agreed because she snapped, "Well, it would be, but they haven't."

"They're not dead?" Parren's tone was sharp. There was a rapid change as he said, "Well, that's a relief! But are you sure? They look dead to me, and I've seen many a fatal sword wound."

Bull wished Rienne would push Parren aside and get on with it. Thankfully, she did.

"Yes, Captain, I imagine you have. And yes, one of them is dead. But if we are allowed to proceed without further interruptions, I may be able to save the other. If you don't mind?"

As she hurried them past Parren, Bull caught a glimpse of pale eyes fixed on the boys' bodies. A shiver ran the length of his spine that had nothing to do with his wet feet.

✤ ✤ ✤ ✤ ✤

They laid Ozella in the mortuary, and two of the healers set about cleaning him up and making him presentable. General Blaine would have the sad duty of writing to his father with the grim news.

Tad was taken into a small, private chamber and laid gently on the bed. His mother stood by his side, sobbing and wringing her hands. Rienne guided Bull to a seat beside the bed and pushed him down. The big man's hand was still on the boy's brow and his eyes were totally unfocused, his ears unhearing. She didn't even attempt to speak to him; he was intent upon his task and would be drained enough without her distracting him. In fact, he would probably need attention himself once they were done, whatever the outcome.

Ignoring Tad's distraught mother, Rienne and Hanan stripped Tad of his stained and sodden clothing, revealing the awful extent of his wound. Hanan pursed her lips at the sight, her face hard.

"Ozella wasn't a very experienced swordsman, was he?" she murmured.

"No, I don't think so," replied Rienne, sponging the wound with an antiseptic solution. She did this out of habit, though the stream had cleansed the wound very thoroughly. She thought that the frigid water might even have helped staunch some of the bleeding. Otherwise Tad would surely have bled out by now. "Neither of the boys was very competent. Ozella was lazy and didn't work very hard at his lessons. Tad was more diligent, but still very new to his sword."

Hanan leaned toward Rienne and lowered her voice still further. "Then there's more to this than two lads fighting over an argument. Look at all these little cuts. They're almost artfully placed. And no inexperienced hand delivered this large wound. It's clean and precisely positioned. Only the temperature of the water and Tad's stubborn spirit have saved him thus far. If I'm any judge, I'd say that thrust was meant to be a killing stroke."

Rienne believed her. Hanan was an experienced healer of many years' service, all of it spent among fighting men. She had seen every conceivable type of wound and would be able to recognize the skill, or lack of it, behind the hand that dealt it.

Rienne frowned. "So who did this? Who could possibly want to kill them? What harm have they ever done anyone?"

Hanan brushed the question aside. "Let's just concentrate on not losing him. If we can help him hold on to life, he'll tell us himself."

✣ ✣ ✣ ✣ ✣

When Taran finally opened his eyes, he was completely unable to see. Afterimages of stark white light coruscated across his vision, and rubbing his eyes only turned the light to yellow motes.

He realized he was lying on the ground in the mud and that rain was still pouring over him. Despite the burning in his brain, he could tell the rain was easing. How long had he lain here insensate?

Struggling to a sitting position, fighting down incipient panic and sudden nausea, he strove for calm. He was an Artesan. He had control over some of his bodily functions. He could heal himself. Concentrating on the area behind his eyes, he brought his power into focus. He closed his eyelids and tried to ignore the sparkling, flashing lights. He soothed his outraged nerves and cooled the damaged area. He quietened his breathing, forcing himself to inhale and exhale deeply a couple of times. Then, gingerly, he opened his eyes.

He could see again though the wet air now had a ruddy tinge to it, like a sunset. The clouds still massed heavy above him, although he could tell that the cusp of the storm had frayed and broken apart. That last, prodigious blast of lightning must have destroyed its heart.

He climbed to his feet, shedding water, and looked around. There was no one about, and he wasn't surprised. That tremendous explosion must have rocked the earth for miles around. What with that and the terrible weather, who would dare venture out of doors?

Then a strange sensation on his skin caught his attention. Despite being wet through, he was warm.

Warm? How could that be? Hadn't he been chilled to the bone by the rain and the sweat of his earlier exertions? Hadn't he just been lying in a pool of muddy rainwater? How could he possibly be warm?

And yet, he was.

Perplexed, he shook his head. The world still existed. At least the titanic forces gathered by the circle hadn't been released to wreak their wanton destruction.

Gathering his wits and ignoring the strange warmth, he turned toward the seemingly impenetrable woodlands to search for a way in. The rain was definitely easing and the very air was warm. Not with the sultriness of a storm; just pleasantly warm. He could also hear a faint humming, not unlike the vibration of the building Earth force before the lightning struck. He puzzled over it as he scanned the brambly edge of the woods for a pathway, but came up with no answers.

He did, however, find the track. Cunningly hidden behind a barrier of branches, faint cartwheel-ruts had been filled and made visible by the rain. Pulling at the boughs, Taran entered the wood.

It was an ancient wood, he could see that. Firs, birches, elder, and oak all twisted together to form a dark, dense mass. The narrow cart track cut an arched pathway through the tangle. As he traveled it, his cloak thrown back from his sword hilt and his hand resting lightly on the pommel, he saw that the ruddy light was increasing, matched by the humming in his ears.

Treading cautiously, listening intently, Taran reached the end of the track. He gasped.

The huge, powerful outer megaliths, those still standing and those which had fallen, were scoured clean, their blue surfaces glinting in the rain. The inner ring of granite stones was just as clean, just as imposing. Taran could see no farther, nor approach any closer, and he stood aghast and totally lost.

For not only was the circle ancient beyond his ken, puissant and impressive in its majesty—it was also incandescently afire.

Taran had never seen anything like it. *How can such stones burn?* As an Artesan who had mastery over Earth, he knew the various properties of rock and stone. And while no Artesan would ever boast they knew everything, still he was aware that granite and bluestone did not burn.

Yet these did. Here was the source of the ruddy light, the humming in his ears, and the warmth in the air. When he recovered from the worst of his shock and looked more closely, he could see the fire wasn't actually consuming the stones, nor affecting them in any way except to cause them to glow and emanate the heat he had felt even outside the wood. Neither did the fire affect the trees. He could also see that the flames were running sunwise about the circle, forming a roaring, opaque barrier that sight couldn't breach.

It wasn't actually the stones burning, but Earth force.

This, he understood. Fire fed on Earth force. This was what allowed it to live in its natural state, from where it could be called by one skilled in the knowledge, or skilled with flint and steel. That vast current of lightning must have reversed the failing silver's polarity and flung the Earth forces back on themselves. Unfortunately, it had also ignited the power, which was being consumed and summoned in a continuous loop. It was not the silver that kept those forces flowing, but Fire itself.

Understanding how the circle burned, however, wouldn't help Taran. How was he to pass the barrier? If Sullyan was inside the circle, how could he reach her?

He tried to sense her psyche, but the muffling of spellsilver was still there. He had hoped it might have been destroyed with the other silver when the lightning struck, but apparently not.

He called her name, softly at first, wary in case whoever had set this in motion was still about, and then louder and louder. No response. She could even be dying for all he knew. He couldn't tell the state of her psyche through the spellsilver. He couldn't even tell if she was nearby. She could be miles away.

This circle was his only clue. He had to breach the flaming barrier and find out if she was within it before he could leave to look elsewhere.

It was Fire, though, and he didn't possess the skill or strength to influence Fire. He did have mastery over Earth, but the Fire was feeding on the forces of Earth, calling it forth as it consumed the sluggish energy, and it would have to be dampened before the circle could be returned to quiescence. Taran shook his head. He couldn't do it.

Still, he had to try. There was no one else. Advancing until he was as close as he could get without being burned, he delved within himself for his own unique pattern, isolating the element of Fire. As he had been shown so many times before, he attuned himself to it, letting it flow through his psyche, ignoring the knowledge of burning, of pain.

That was the tricky part. Fire could kill with a touch, unlike Earth or Water, and overcoming that innate and instinctive fear was the key to mastering Fire. Gritting his teeth and shoring his courage, Taran stretched forth his hand.

He snatched it back with a cry. Cursing, he sucked the tips of his fingers, trying not to lose his concentration. It was the same familiar problem. Like Bull, he simply couldn't get past his fear. Try as he might, he knew the Fire would burn him and he couldn't unlearn that knowledge.

He was going to fail again, he knew it. Berating himself for a craven fool, he tried again. Murmuring a calming and bolstering mantra, he extended his hand once more, with the same stinging result.

His cry and the obscenity that accompanied it were born more of frustration than pain. The Fire had only scorched him, but the painful shame brought tears to his eyes. He sank to the steaming ground, staring in desperation at the burning circle.

The light was fast disappearing. Soon it would be full dark. Would whoever had called these forces return to see what had happened? The Baron was no Artesan, but would his skilled captive, whoever he was, tell him his plan had failed? Taran didn't know, but he had to breach this barrier soon or give up. And he couldn't give up.

He beat his scorched fist on the ground and cried aloud, "For the Void's sake, Sullyan, *where are you*?"

He stiffened in shock. Had he heard a reply? A tiny groan of pain? He was sure he had. He called her name again, rising to his feet, his ears intent for the faintest sound.

This time it was unmistakable. There was definitely someone alive within the circle. Whether it was Sullyan or not, he couldn't tell. His frustration became urgency. No one could survive this burning force for long, and if she was wearing spellsilver, she'd be helpless to protect herself.

He didn't even think this time. He gave himself no preparation, no time to consider. He grasped his Fire-attuned psyche and wrapped it around his body, forming a glowing cloak almost like the Firefield he had once seen Robin cast. Surrounded by fiery power, he dashed between the blazing stones.

Chapter Twenty-Eight

He emerged unscathed into the calm of the circle. He stood amazed. He could see the flames from where he stood, but they didn't touch him. Not even a thread of his clothing was scorched. At any other time he might have shouted with delight at his achievement, but now all his attention was riveted on the two prone figures on the other side of the circle. He ran toward them.

He immediately saw one of them was Sullyan. Her tawny hair, drenched and bedraggled though it was, marked her clearly. The other was a man, but Taran couldn't see his face.

He ran to Sullyan's side, kneeling in the wet grass. He put a hand gently under her chin and raised her head. Her eyes fluttered open at his touch. He grimaced at the sight of her split and bloody mouth, the bruising around her face, the bloodied fabric of her chemise, and the cruel way her arms were bound to the stones.

Softly, he called her name.

Her eyes, darkened with fear and pain, sought his. "Taran?" she whispered, trying for a smile.

His breath caught and his chest tightened with love. "I'm here, Brynne."

"Aeyron," she said weakly, trying to turn her head. "Does he live? Did I kill him?"

Kill...?

Taran didn't stop to ponder her meaning. He turned to the beaten and half-starved figure beside Sullyan and put two fingers to the great vein in Aeyron's neck.

"He's still alive."

Sullyan sighed deeply. The news seemed to strengthen her and her eyes cleared somewhat.

"Can you cut the spellcord?" she asked hoarsely.

Taran cursed himself. He should have done that first, knowing how it must be paining her. Drawing his knife, he moved to her left wrist, noting the swelling of her hand and the abrasions caused by the burning of the silver. This wasn't the first time she'd borne such wounds.

He carefully slid the knife beneath the spellcord, trying to avoid the raw flesh below. She gave a small gasp of pain as he slit the cord. He unwound the bloodstained length of it and she attempted to flex her numb and swollen fingers. He moved to the other wrist and performed the same task.

The abruptness with which his impression of her psyche leaped to clarity was almost shocking. He could feel her reaching down for her own vast powers, using her metaforce to bolster and shore up her failing physical strength.

"Quickly, Taran," she urged, her voice stronger now, "do the same for Aeyron. He is in a very bad way and we need to support him."

Careful not to touch the metal entwined within the rope, Taran removed the spellcord from Aeyron's wrists. His blade just nicked the blackened, puffy skin of the right wrist and infection oozed out, the stench causing Taran to gag. He felt Sullyan reaching out to Aeyron's spirit, pouring strength into him to counter the virulent poisons in his infected arm. The tall Andaryan groaned.

"How do we get you out of this?" Taran asked.

She turned semi-focused eyes on him, most of her attention

caught up with Aeyron.

"If you can help steady the Prince, I can deal with these chains."

He did as she asked. He had to touch Aeyron in order to learn his pattern. He'd met the Heir to Andaryon before, but they'd never meshed psyches. Once he was familiar with the Prince's personal imprint, Taran took over from Sullyan, dismayed by the extent of the other man's injuries. Sullyan withdrew reluctantly. She would not risk losing Aeyron now, not after all he'd been through.

The chains holding the captives were made of ordinary iron. Iron was an element of Earth, easily affected by one who had long held mastery over that fundamental force. Taran watched as the links of the chain that clasped Sullyan's wrists rusted with accelerated aging. Brown flakes fell away from the metal until it was so thin and weak that even in her depleted state she was able to snap it with a gentle tug.

She took a moment to bring her arms down from their cruciform position, clasping her wrists between her knees. Her attention focused inward as she slowly increased blood flow and soothed outraged muscles and strained nerves. It wasn't long before she performed the same feat for Aeyron.

Soon, they were both free. Taran helped Sullyan lay Aeyron flat on the grass, his naked torso cleansed of blood by the fast-diminishing rain. Only then did Taran notice the blood caking the back of Sullyan's head, trailing in long streaks through her wet hair. He could also see the wound that had caused the bleeding.

"That's a nasty head wound," he said. "Will you be all right?"

"How bad is it?"

He didn't like what he saw when he studied it. "Pretty bad. Your skull might be cracked. Do you have concussion?"

"Of course, but there's no time to worry about it now. We

have to get Aeyron to safety before the Baron returns." She turned a serious gaze on the Adept, who stared back at her, wondering what was coming. "We were right about his involvement. And I now know who the renegade Artesan is, the one Reen has been controlling and forcing to do his will."

Taran raised his brows, guessing the news wasn't good.

"Do you remember the deformed boy we met at the castle? The one who was so concerned about Darius the day of the horse race?"

"Huw?" Taran was surprised. "You can't mean that poor boy's an Artesan? How can that be? We stood right next to him. You *touched* him. How could you not have sensed him?"

Her eyes closed as she crouched beside Aeyron in the gathering gloom. "He is a sport, a lay-Artesan, and outside the normal rules. He also has twice the power of a Supreme Master. But that is not all he is, although it should be enough. I am quite convinced he must also be my cousin."

Questions crowded Taran's lips, but he knew they'd have to wait. He accepted Sullyan's words and turned his attention to their present predicament.

"Will he know what's happened here?" he asked, indicating the circle.

"Almost certainly. And what he knows the Baron will know, too. Did you come here alone? Did you have to deal with any guards on the way?"

Taran shook his head. "There was no one about. And I came alone. I left Ardoch at the Baron's mansion. We found Prince Eadan there. He was being kept under guard in the servants' wing. Ardoch's taken him and his nursemaid, along with the Baron's niece, back to his house. I told him I was going to look for you, and he agreed to go to Denny or Levant and tell them about Eadan. Hopefully they'll raise the garrison against the Baron."

Sullyan looked dubious. "It was a good thought, but I doubt the Queen will allow the garrison to move against the Baron. Unless Levant has the courage and the conviction to overrule her, Reen will be safe under her protection. I am relieved you found Prince Eadan, but was it wise to involve the Baron's niece?"

Taran heard overtones of suspicion in Sullyan's voice, brought on by Jinella's part in the rumors that had so blighted her life. The Adept couldn't really blame her.

"It was Jinella who enabled us to rescue Eadan. Without her, I doubt we could have succeeded."

The slender woman smiled. "I see you have much to tell me. I am proud of you for what you have done, Taran, proud and grateful. Do you realize what you have achieved here today?"

He frowned, flustered by her praise and not fully comprehending her meaning. "What?"

She grinned despite her sore mouth. "You influenced Fire, my friend. That means you are an Adept-elite."

The shock of seeing her and Aeyron chained to the stones had pushed all thoughts of that achievement aside, but it came flooding back as he recognized the truth of her words. He had finally attained his life's goal—to reach the level of expertise his father had held before he died. A slow smile crept over his strained visage.

"We will have to deal with that later, though." Sullyan's tone held genuine regret. "We need to get Aeyron to safety. I have no doubt the Baron and his men will soon be heading this way, if they are not already. When he knows his plan has failed yet again, he will be even more determined not to lose his two captives."

She took the torn ends of her linen shirt and tied them together over her stained chemise. Taran hadn't noticed the ripped shirt before in all the excitement, but the nature of the damage and her bloodstained undergarment brought a frown to his face.

"Sullyan, you weren't ... hurt?" he asked delicately.

She saw the direction of his gaze and smiled grimly. "Not this time. The Baron's mercenary commander, Izack, thought to have a little sport with me while he considered me helpless. I taught him never to underestimate me, even in spellsilver and chains."

"We ran across him in the servants' wing. Ardoch gave him a lesson, too."

Sullyan made an appreciative noise, but just then Aeyron regained consciousness. She knelt beside him on the wet grass.

"Brynne?" he whispered hoarsely.

"Hush, Aeyron," she soothed, placing a hand on his shoulder. "You are safe now. Taran is here to help us and we will take you to safety. But you have to help us a little. We cannot carry you, you will have to walk.

"Come, Taran," she requested, and together they helped Aeyron to stand. "Be careful," she cautioned, "he has some cracked ribs."

Aeyron put an arm painfully across each of their shoulders and they helped him walk. He was weak and trembling in every muscle, but he managed.

"What about the Fire?" asked Taran.

The circle was still raging with flame, the Earth forces still surging.

Sullyan gave a nod. "I need to touch the southern cardinal."

They moved in that direction, Aeyron staggering between them. Once they reached the southern cardinal, the stone that was linked to Fire, the slender woman put out her free hand and laid it upon the rough, wet surface of the megalith. Her need for physical contact told Taran how much of her power was being used to support the tortured Prince. Her face was pale, tired, and strained. Her golden eyes, black now with hugely dilated pupils, turned to the Adept.

"When I damp down the Fire, you will be able to dispel the Earth force. Are you ready?"

Taran attuned his psyche to Earth and nodded. He could feel the tremendous flow of power shooting through every nerve and fiber of his body, strangely imbued and altered by the presence of Fire. The sensation slowly faded as Sullyan took hold of the Fire and forced it to return to its quiescent state beyond the substrate. The incessant humming of the Earth forces lessened to nothing as Taran reversed the flow and dampened the power.

Then all was still. He could feel the aftereffects of those tremendous energies, but for now, all was quiet. The night was absolute without the flames to mitigate the darkness, and they took a moment to adjust their sight, Aeyron still sagging between them.

"We must go, Taran," urged Sullyan. "We have just advertised beyond any doubt that someone with power has been here. If Huw's senses are turned this way—and I have no doubt the Baron still has him under duress—Reen will soon know of it. He cannot afford to let us escape. If he has also discovered Prince Eadan is gone, all his plans are in ruin and his life is in jeopardy. He will be a desperate man. Let us go."

Holding Aeyron between them, they left the circle. Sullyan shied from the cart track, knowing the Baron and his men were bound to use that path. Difficult though the going was, they had to move through the trees. She took them in the direction she had come from, the most direct route back toward the Forest. As they went, Taran told her he had directed Ardoch to look for them there. Sullyan wasn't hopeful.

"I doubt we will make Loxton Forest undiscovered." Her voice was breathy from the effort of supporting Aeyron both physically and metaphysically. Taran, being much taller, tried to take the majority of Aeyron's weight, but in his current state the Prince was barely able to place one foot before the other. His right arm, which Sullyan had taken across her own shoulders, was black and raw with infection, and it still seeped horribly from the small cut on his wrist.

Taran had no idea how they would deal with that problem. With infection in his system, Aeyron was unable to travel the Veils. The Adept had a nasty suspicion the Prince would lose his arm.

✠ ✠ ✠ ✠ ✠

They struggled on into the dark, wet woods, senses alert for sounds, but their own awkward progress made more noise than they could cover. Although Sullyan was blanketing her own and Aeyron's psyches, she knew the Baron would force Huw to seek them. He must know Aeyron couldn't travel far. Izack's ministrations had seen to that.

Sullyan felt malice rise hot in her breast at the memory of Izack's brutality. She had struck one blow against him. If it was at all in her power, she intended to do more whenever the opportunity presented itself. He would pay the ultimate price for his cruel and perverse pleasures. She promised herself that.

Taran looked up and halted, causing Sullyan to glance sharply at him. More than half her attention was centered on Aeyron. She had less than her usual alertness and was relying heavily upon Taran's senses to ward them. She held her silence while he verified what he'd heard.

His face was grim and set. "Someone's coming."

She glanced around. "I will not be taken unawares and encumbered," she told him in a low voice. She spied a large oak tree nearby and nodded at it. "Help me get Aeyron over there."

They maneuvered the stumbling Prince toward the tree and lowered him gently to the ground. He groaned as they released his arms, his painful chest and torn shoulder muscles protesting. He murmured, "Brynne? Where are you going?"

She crouched beside him and laid a tender hand upon his brow. "Be still, my Prince, we will not leave you. Neither will I let them take you again. You have my sworn word on that."

She stared meaningfully up at Taran in the darkness. He nodded briefly. She didn't intend to be taken again, either.

Carefully, fearful of slicing off his ear with the unaccustomed motion, Taran reached behind his own shoulder and drew her sword from his back. He presented it to her hilt-first. Acknowledging his formal gesture with a slight bow of her head, she accepted her father's sword from his hand.

How she had missed its comforting weight! Her father's sword fitted her like a third arm. With it, she would defend Aeyron to the death, and she promised herself that even should she be overcome, Aeyron would suffer no more. Now she was free of the spellsilver, she could at least be certain of that.

They could hear someone plowing through the underbrush, and it was plain there was more than one. Standing on either side of the prone Prince, they faced the direction of the sounds. Sullyan couldn't tell exactly how many there were, but she thought it was not many. She just prayed one of them would be Izack.

She got her wish.

They weren't being careful, the two of them. They were intent on capture, not stealth, clearly expecting two injured and feeble captives, not two dangerous and armed opponents. Izack and Patrin came blundering up to the Artesans' concealed position almost unaware. But they were also trained fighters and hadn't quite forgotten all they'd learned. And Sullyan knew Izack still burned to repay her for his humiliating and very personal bruising.

The two men stopped when they saw Sullyan and Taran standing by the oak tree. They looked puzzled. She smiled grimly. They probably thought Taran was Aeyron, on his feet and wielding a sword. Advancing slowly once more, they revised their initial impression when Aeyron's slumped figure came into their view.

Izack stopped once more and smiled a slow, cruel smile. He addressed himself to Taran.

"I suppose I have you to thank for the lump behind my ear?"

Taran shrugged. "Actually, no. I'm afraid I can't claim that pleasure."

It was a good reply, and Sullyan gave a smile of her own. It unsettled Izack because it implied a third able person, and the stocky Commander glanced swiftly around the small clearing.

A faint movement by Sullyan's feet caught her attention and she glanced down at Aeyron. Terror rose in his eyes at the sight of Izack, and perspiration started on his brow.

"Beware of him, Brynne," he croaked. "He's very dangerous."

His care for her in his pitiful state cut straight to Sullyan's soul. Her own strength came surging to the fore, her primal urge to protect transferring now to him. Her face was set and grim as she gazed down at him.

"Have no fear, my Prince, for I too am dangerous. And for this man, I am very dangerous indeed."

Izack heard her and his lips curled in a scornful sneer. She could understand his reaction. She didn't look dangerous right now. She was soaked and bedraggled, bloody and beaten, small and insignificant. The sword in her left hand must look almost too heavy for her to lift. He would have heard something of her reputation, but clearly could not equate the stories to this young, slender female before him.

She could guess his thoughts. His black heart would be aching to repay her for the blow to his manhood and pride. His stocky frame was packed with honed muscle. He was taller, heavier, and with a longer reach. How could he fail to best her, even if she did know how to use her sword?

As she mused on Izack's thoughts, she also guessed his plan. Izack would engage her—deal with her swiftly and have his revenge—while Patrin engaged Taran. Izack wouldn't care who Taran was. He was helping the captives escape, that was all the Commander needed to know.

She knew she was right when Izack's eyes locked on hers and he advanced with purpose.

She was forced to withdraw some of her strength from Aeyron. Her wrists were still sore, her hands tingling with the pain of long-restricted blood flow. Her shoulders ached fiercely. But the chance to repay Izack for his brutal abuse of the Prince could not be ignored.

She allowed the red mist of fury to rise up and warm her unresponsive muscles. They would remember their work soon enough, and she would pay the price later. She advanced to meet Izack's threat.

Out of the corner of her eye she saw a startled Patrin watching his Commander. He would be wondering at Izack's choice. Why would he choose to fight the woman when there was an obviously trained swordsman nearby, blade in hand? But Patrin was a follower, not a leader, and he wouldn't dare question Izack. He moved to confront Taran, who was ready for him.

Sullyan and Taran moved forward and apart, so as not to be hampered by Aeyron's prone form. Just as they did, Izack leaped to attack. A rush over such uneven ground was a mistake. Sullyan never moved until the last moment, her eyes locked on his sword arm, reading his intent plainly even through the gloom. Her blade rang sharply and painfully on his as she countered his stroke and spun him away from her.

Then she was behind him, slashing his bicep as the tip of her weapon caught him on the turn. His roar of pain and fury filled the woods. He whirled to face her, only just blocking her next stroke, which had come from an unexpected angle. He had no time to form a riposte of his own and was forced to let her blade shiver off his. Unbalanced, he leaped away.

The tangle of bramble underfoot hampered them all. Patrin and Taran had moved farther away and were using the trees to try to block each other's thrusts. Patrin, she briefly noticed, was a competent fighter with no great finesse. Taran was used to training with Robin and Bull and many of the other talented swordsmen at the Manor. He knew far more about swordplay than Patrin. She could see he was more than holding his own against the younger man.

Izack's initial failure seemed to have taught him a measure of grudging respect. The fire in his eyes hadn't diminished, but he was experienced enough to realize Sullyan knew what she was doing. It was his left bicep she had scored; his sword arm was unaffected. She continued to press him hard, always away from Aeyron.

They were moving toward the edge of the woods. Between the trees she could see the marginally lighter sky over the fields. She tried to keep her face toward this tenuous light, to silhouette her opponent. Izack realized what she was doing and fought hard to reverse their positions.

Sullyan had already changed hands twice during the fight, her strained and aching muscles protesting violently. But the heat of her fury kept her supple, and the revealing of this unusual talent kept Izack from double-guessing her moves. If she felt herself flagging, she only had to remember Aeyron's tortured form and fear-filled eyes, and new strength flooded into her.

✣ ✣ ✣ ✣ ✣

Patrin and Taran came together time and again in a flurry of blows. Their blades rang and shivered through the woods as they fought each other off. Taran was unencumbered by abused muscles and knew he was capable of taking Patrin. Yet he was fearful for Sullyan and had to concentrate hard not to let his attention wander to where she struggled against Izack.

Patrin came at Taran again, pushing him off balance. The Adept stumbled over a tree root and nearly went down. Patrin was on him in a flash, but Taran raised his blade and held off Patrin's killing stroke. Regaining his footing, he came back at the younger man. As he righted himself, he snatched his knife from his belt with his free hand, keeping it concealed from Patrin.

The next time the other man tried to close with him, Taran allowed it. He fell back, as if wrong-footed, drawing Patrin closer. As the younger man saw his chance and drove in, Taran turned his blade deftly aside, Patrin's momentum driving his exposed chest full onto Taran's knife.

The man went down with a gurgle, a froth of blood escaping his lips. Taran sighed with regret, then realized the woods around him were silent.

He went ice cold. He could hear no sounds of fighting. Fear brought a metallic taste to his mouth. Sheathing his bloody knife and hastening back to where they had left the Prince, he could see no sign of Sullyan or her adversary. He helped the trembling Aeyron to rise, taking the Andaryan's left arm over his shoulder and supporting him with his other arm about the Prince's narrow waist. Together they stumbled as best they could toward where the Adept had last seen Sullyan.

✠ ✠ ✠ ✠ ✠

Sullyan and Izack reached the edge of the woods. Sullyan had beaten the Commander farther and farther back, raining blows on his upper body, catching his flesh on more than one occasion. She bore wounds too, and although none were serious, they sapped her already depleted strength as she expended metaforce to stem the bleeding. She had to end this soon.

One thing in her favor was Izack's fury. His inability to best her was making him clumsy. Instead of cooling his temper and thinking rationally, he let his embarrassment overtake him. Snarling his rage and disgust, intending to use his bulk to intimidate her, he raced at her.

Seeing her opportunity, and appreciating the irony of having cause to be grateful to Rykan, Sullyan sidestepped Izack's rush and let her shoulder clip his. Her footing was secure; his was not. He sprawled at her feet, and her blade found his neck in a flash.

He lay panting, face up, staring in disbelief at the length of steady steel in her hand and the iron resolve in her eyes.

Sullyan glanced up, seeing Taran and Aeyron slowly approaching. She nodded to the Adept, who smiled in relief as he lowered the Prince to the ground. She stood breathing deeply, her blade unwavering, her eyes locked with her foe's.

"So, Izack, you have stared death in the face at least once before. You know what it looks like. Then, you were saved from Rykan's killing thrust by the intervention of your master. But the Baron is not here to save you now. He is not here to stop me avenging your crimes by taking your life."

"You're wrong, Colonel Sullyan."

Her head snapped up as a voice rang out, shockingly close, shattering the silence of the woods. "I wouldn't do that if I were you."

Chapter Twenty-Nine

Sullyan's blade never wavered from Izack's throat. The steam of her breath shone faintly in the light of the newly risen moon. The heavy storm clouds had unraveled and were drifting away, and the cold glimpse of stars could be seen.

Izack lay motionless on the sodden ground, slowly recovering his breath. Sullyan's eyes were not on her captive, nor indeed were they on the Baron. They were focused instead on the knife in the Baron's hand—her own knife—pricking dangerously close to the big artery in the neck of his terrified prisoner.

Reen's other hand was wrapped tight in the spellcord noose circling Huw's throat, causing the boy to struggle and wheeze for air. Physically, she knew, Huw was much stronger than the Baron, but the bleeding of his powers by the spellsilver and the catatonic effects of his own terror held him limp and helpless. His mismatched eyes were wild with fear and confusion, his face was white and sweating, and he darted frightened glances around him, shying away from Izack on the ground and the implied violence of Sullyan's steel.

He drooled and whimpered in his distress.

"Release him, Colonel," came Reen's smug voice. "If you don't, I'll kill the boy. I have no use for him now."

Sullyan didn't move. She was caught between her disgust for Izack and her natural pity and care for Huw. If he really was her cousin, as he surely must be, he held information about her family.

Izack's life meant nothing compared to that knowledge, but if she released him now, he would kill Aeyron, Taran, and then herself. She couldn't allow that.

"A trade, my Lord Baron. Release Huw unharmed and I will release Izack."

The Baron grinned. "Oh, my dear Colonel, you're mistaking me for someone who cares. I'm afraid I don't have your sentimentality. Izack means little to me. He's a servant, a tool. If you kill him, I can always buy another. But this boy"—he jerked on the noose around Huw's neck, making the crook-backed youth sob for breath—"he means something to you, doesn't he? He's one of your kind and you value him. So I regret you've nothing to trade. If you don't do as I say, I'll spill the imbecile's life. Now, release Izack."

Sullyan recognized the sincerity of Reen's threat. She'd gambled the Baron would still have a use for Huw. His plans to destroy the Veils might have been thwarted, but surely he wouldn't throw away his most valuable tool against Artesans? Yet he had no mercy and less compassion. She couldn't take the chance he'd kill the boy in front of her for vengeance. She had no choice.

Izack's expression had turned murderous at his master's cavalier betrayal, but he didn't move. Sullyan's blade still menaced his neck. Any rash movement could have seen him slit his own throat. Sullyan sighed, unwilling yet to give up.

"Admit you have lost, my Lord. The spellsilver is destroyed, the Veils still stand, and all the realms with them. I have Prince Aeyron safe, and Prince Eadan has been taken from you. What will the Queen say when she hears you have been holding her son captive? What will the King say? You are finished, Baron. Accept your defeat. There is no place for you here anymore. Leave Huw unharmed and give yourself up to justice. I will let you live and even plead your cause. I give you my word. The King might be merciful if you confess. He might be persuaded to let you retire to some cleric's retreat where you can live out your life serving your faith, misguided though you are. I urge you to consider my words. The alternative is death."

Reen spat, his eyes glinting in fury. "I don't think so, girl! I am protected by the Queen. She detests your kind as I do—detests your demon friends. She knows how you have cozened and bespelled Elias and wormed your way into his favor. You will find no kindness in the Queen. And my allies in Andaryon will already have dealt with Elias, so I have no cause to fear him."

Sullyan's heart lurched, but the Baron wasn't done.

"You may think you have defeated me, but it is *you* who have lost—*your* life that is forfeit. You are already branded a traitor, are you not? Even if Elias does live to return here, you no longer have the favor of the King. But I will be praised as a liberator of the land when I bring you and your sorcerous friends to justice.

"You may think you have won here today, but you cannot threaten me. I am following the Queen's orders. I am safe within her protection."

Sullyan risked a swift glance at Taran, who nodded to show he understood. He was hanging on the Baron's every word; his testimony could be crucial later.

"Are you telling me the Queen understood and supported what you tried to do?" she snapped.

The Baron couldn't help crowing. "You never knew, did you?"

He pressed her knife ever more firmly against Huw's neck. The poor boy squirmed in his grasp and the Baron twisted the cord cruelly tight around his thick neck, cutting off his airway. Huw's face turned purple and his tongue stuck out. Saliva hung from his slack lips in thin ribbons and trailed over his chest. He didn't have the strength or courage to struggle.

"Did you think the Queen supported Elias's misguided views on Artesans? Of course not! She is a true daughter of the Church. When she rules in Elias's stead, when I proclaim her Regent after the King's death, she will look to *me* to guide her, not you. You think I've failed, do you? This is only a setback. With this imbecile boy here, whom I control utterly, I could also control all of *you.* Do you think I don't know he's stronger by far than any of you? I learned at least that much from my dealings with Rykan. Huw could burn your brains out if I ordered it. He could have you on your knees, begging for my mercy, with no more than a thought. But don't think my knowledge of his power would prevent me from killing him. I would rather destroy him now than leave him alive. Don't forget, I still have my allies in the demon realm.

"If I instruct her to, the Queen will order every Artesan in the land to be delivered to her for execution. So if you don't release Izack *right now,* not only will I order the boy to destroy you, but I will make sure you survive just long enough to see me cut out his living heart before your eyes. Now, *do as I say!*"

Reen's single-minded oration had caused him to miss the sound of approaching horses. Sullyan had heard them, though, and she thought Taran had, too. Izack certainly had, for a light of hope had entered his eyes. Would the riders be the Baron's men, summoned to his aid, or would they be the King's, sent by Ardoch?

Taran was alert. Out of the corner of her eye, she saw him lower Aeyron to the ground and pass the weakened Prince his knife so that Aeyron wouldn't feel totally helpless. It was a token gesture, although one Aeyron would appreciate. He was so weak he probably couldn't wield the blade against a foe, but at least it gave him the option of taking his own life should the Baron emerge victorious. Then Taran stood with his hand on his sword hilt, unwilling to make any move that might precipitate disaster.

The Baron finally registered the sounds of men's voices and the drumming of hooves. He smiled a nasty smile.

"It seems I get to keep both my tools after all, Colonel. Unless I am much mistaken, that's the rest of my guard approaching. You may drop that sword now. Do as I say and I might not kill you just yet. Tell your other friend to throw down his weapon, too. You'll both be taken to—"

He never got to finish his sentence. He was right, it was his men approaching, and they were coming fast. But they were not alone. They were being pursued by a group of Kingsmen from the garrison, Ardoch and Lieutenant-Major Denny at their head.

Reen saw them at the same time as Sullyan, and his mouth dropped open. His men shot through the area and he cried out to them. One of them swerved toward him, heeling his mount hard, hurriedly clearing the stirrup so Reen could climb on board. The Baron screamed at them wildly. "Stay, you fools, stay and fight! I order it."

The rider shook his head. "My Lord, we are outnumbered. Levant has raised the garrison against us. You must come!" He leaned down, tugging urgently at the Baron's arm.

Snarling, Reen swung toward Sullyan, who hadn't moved. The sound of the pursuing Kingsmen grew louder in the night air. "It's not over yet, witch!" he shrieked. With a vicious thrust, he sank her knife up to the hilt in Huw's back. Dropping his hold on the boy and shoving the collapsing body away from him, Reen allowed his man to drag him onto the curveting horse and spur after his fellows. Denny's men were hard on their heels as they disappeared into the night.

Sullyan gave an agonized cry as Huw crumpled to the wet grass. Seeing his chance, Izack raised himself swiftly on one arm and swung his sword. The blade opened a long gash down her left thigh and she let out a gasp of agony as she stumbled. She dug for her power to numb the pain and stem the worst of the bleeding. Izack scrambled to his feet and charged her, and that sight, coupled with Huw's fate, brought a storm of uncontrollable rage welling into Sullyan's breast.

Something within her had snapped with the Baron's senseless cruelty. Huw's fall was yet another failure, another grief, and her soul was already brimming with pain she couldn't bear. She drew on the upwelling of her fury, deliberately allowing the red mist of a berserker rage to take her over. The change in her face, her eyes, and the sheer primeval savagery of her caused Izack to recoil.

An inchoate snarl burst from Sullyan. She spun, attacking Izack double-handed. He fell back, really frightened for probably the first time in his life. Sullyan was unstoppable. No grace or finesse directed her movements now. She used all the elements within her psyche to fuel her fury and guide her steps.

The heavy power of Earth was her strength and endurance. Water became the supple fluidity of movement. Fire was the passion of rage in her blood and the determination in every stroke of her blade. Air swept into her lungs to provide her body with the energy it needed to fight. She was raw power stripped of the beauty of her skill, honed to kill or be killed.

And she had no intention of being killed.

She hunted Izack mercilessly across the grass, her attacks coming too fast for him to counter. He fell back constantly before her, unable to touch her. Finally, gasping, he could take no more. He left himself open and, with no conscious thought, a vicious sweep of her sword opened his belly from chest to groin. With a cry of agony, he sank helpless to the ground, clutching the spilling mass of his guts.

She was vaguely aware of eyes watching her in the scant moonlight. Ardoch and Denny, who had hung back, had dismounted and stood some way off. Taran was bent over the prone form of Huw, urgently removing the spellcord. Sullyan only had eyes for Izack. She stood over him, her father's sword resting on his heaving breast. She leaned on it so he would feel her touch. The defeated Commander, his hands uselessly clutching his opened belly, stared up at her in despair.

She spoke in a low, cold voice, bowing her head over his, her words meant for him alone. "That was for what you would have done to me earlier today, when I was at your mercy, and for what you have doubtless done to other, less fortunate, women. But this, Izack … this is for Aeyron. For his fear and his pain. For the torture and debasement of his proud spirit. This is my gift to him."

Staring Izack in the eyes, dispassionately and mercilessly, she leaned harder on the hilt of her father's sword. The sharp steel slid effortlessly through muscle and bone, severing arteries. He gasped once, and was still.

As life faded from his eyes, she thrust once more on the engraved pommel of the sword. It passed completely through his body and into the ground below. Feeling a tremble begin in her limbs, she left it standing, rearing like a sign of forgiveness that Izack would never have, and took two steps away from his body.

Then she collapsed to the ground.

Ardoch hurried over and knelt beside her, seeing the blood on her body. "Are you all right, lassie?"

She managed to meet his eyes as she hugged herself. Already she was paying the price for the power she had used to fight Izack, and she still had a long night of toil and strain ahead of her. She couldn't afford to give way now. There was too much at stake.

Huw. A sharp pang of grief stung her heart. "Help me up, Ghyl," she panted. He stood and raised her unsteadily to her feet.

"You need to rest, lass," he said, his eyes on the bloody wound in her thigh. She just moved past him, stumbling to where Taran knelt over Huw's contorted form.

The Adept had removed the spellcord and was attempting to reach into Huw to bolster his life force and stem the massive internal bleeding. Huw was resisting. All his life he'd known only revulsion and compulsion, the goad of fear and the threat of violence. He didn't know how to respond to kindness. He didn't even recognize it.

Despite this, Sullyan knew how to reach him. She knew his psyche intimately, as it was nearly identical to her own. Falling to her knees beside the wounded boy, she took his head and shoulders into her lap. She grasped his hand in hers and drove inward with her psyche, seeking the seat of his power.

Their patterns were so similar he didn't see her as a threat. They meshed seamlessly together and she felt the inestimable, unfathomable spread of his power. She was immediately lost. This was so vast, so incomprehensible! The pathways of his tortured mind were a maze. Nothing was familiar, nothing safe. She saw how twisted and deformed he was and wondered how he had ever managed to survive as long as he had.

She didn't know where to start. There were no reference points to guide her. She was lost in a tangle of meaningless neurological pathways that seemed to lead nowhere. There were no connections. She couldn't access his power, couldn't find the seat of his life force.

And if she couldn't find that, he was lost.

The internal bleeding was serious. The knife had missed his spine but had nicked a lung, and also one of the chambers of his heart. Blood leaked out with every beat, and unless she had access to his power, she couldn't stop it. Already his lungs were filling. He was drowning in his own blood.

This was too much. Why was she always too late? She dug frantically down through the layers of his jumbled memories, hunting backward for some clue that would give her access to what she needed. In the process, she read the story of his life.

She saw the Baron's cruel hold on him, how he'd used Izack to terrorize and cow the gentle boy who'd never known the power he held. Huw did what he was told without question, without conscious thought. He didn't understand how he did it. He just thought of it, and it was. How she cried inside when she realized that without his instinctive fear of violence, he could easily have freed himself from the Baron's tyranny. He had no idea what his power could accomplish, and never even saw the results of what he had been forced to do.

The creation of the Staff was one cataclysmic memory of Fire, power, and heat in Huw's muddled mind. There was no connection to the innocent-seeming metal rod such forces had brought into being. He wouldn't have known what to do with the thing had it been given into his hands. Rykan had taken it and used his knowledge of Huw's psyche to imbue the Staff with much of his own inner force. Had Jaskin not stolen the thing to further his uncle's bid for power, Rykan would have reigned supreme.

She saw other pictures, too. Reen forcing Huw to touch certain people—herself and Robin included. Their odd encounter in the King's audience chamber before the horse race had been no chance occurrence. Reen had to make sure Huw learned her pattern. In order to defend against her, or subtly influence her, Huw had to have personal contact with her. He'd also been made to learn the King's pattern, inert and inactive as it was, and Ozella's, before the Beraxian left for the Manor. Much uncharacteristic behavior was explained by Huw's subconscious memories of Reen's control.

Sadly, Sullyan also saw memories of a long time of living friendless and alone, of scavenging for food, avoiding the thrown stones of people's suspicion. Memories of their revulsion. There was also his love of horses, strong as Sullyan's own, and his feeling of kinship with them.

And over all of this, pervading every memory, every emotion, every sense, was the overwhelming loneliness of the outcast.

Hot tears ran down her face, fell onto Huw's cheeks. Her gaze was fixed and swallowed by his mismatched eyes. His pupils were as dilated as hers and she realized with shock that she'd never met anyone else whose eyes reacted to the use of power as hers did. Yet another confirmation of their blood tie.

"Huw," she whispered desperately. "Oh, Huw! Do you know who I am? Can you hear me?"

He stirred in her arms. She still thought of him as a boy, although physically he was much her own age. Maybe a year younger. He frowned slightly, trying to focus his failing eyes.

"Brynne?" he managed, blood frothing at his blue lips.

She smiled through her tears. "Yes, Huw. Let me in. Open your heart and mind to me. I can help you. I can take the pain away. Only show me your life force, let me use your power. I can save you, Huw."

She could tell he didn't understand her. He used his metaforce instinctively. He'd never had to learn to channel power through the elements, or even his psyche.

In desperation, Sullyan tried another tack.

"Your mother, Huw, do you remember your mother? Your father?"

He lay silent, dying. She held him tenderly, no longer probing him. He was lost to her. The potential of his friendship, his companionship, his physical link to her past—all were lost. She thought only to comfort him, to ease his last moments with happy memories.

Her words, however, raised a storm of rage that nearly swept her away. At nine years of age, unable to develop further, his crooked back, strange eyes, and unmanageable ways had caused his parents to cast him out. Only the dimmest of recollections—an auburn-haired man with honey-brown eyes and a tearful blonde woman with soft hands—came into Sullyan's consciousness. Huw thrust all else away, as he had been thrust away. With the last of his strength, he rejected his origins.

Sullyan sat helpless, her face wet with tears. She whispered Huw's name as he slipped away in her arms, surrounding him with all the love she could muster. It was all she could do for him. She couldn't reach him and so was unable to grant him even the ease of opening the Void.

Just as the brightness of his incredibly complex psyche began to fade and slide past her on its final journey, something about the familiarity of their imprints seemed to register with him. Somewhere in the vast recesses of his tortured brain, he recognized her.

She couldn't believe it. Too late *again*. It was too late to reach out and help him. Yet as he died in her arms, as his crooked body relaxed finally into the peace he'd craved for so long, he reached out gentle fingers of power and stroked them like a benison of love across her soul.

Soft words echoed in her grief-stricken mind: *Pretty Brynne*. Then he was gone.

All she could do was weep. Cradling Huw's limp body in her lap, she bowed her head and sat motionless as the tears ran freely. He was her cousin, her family, and she had been unable to help him. If only she had sensed something within him the day they'd met at the castle.

She wondered if the disabled boy had instinctively known who she was or guessed she had some connection to him. He had certainly seemed drawn to her. His time with her hadn't felt forced. How she wished she'd paid him more attention when he'd sought her out. She would never know what difference it might have made.

She remembered the look in his eyes when she used her power to dampen the pain his too-strong grip on her hand had caused her. If not for the King's accident, she might have recalled it sooner. She also recalled the Baron's urgency when he accused her, and how he had ordered Huw away. She realized he had been testing his control over Huw, as it had to have been the Baron who gave the signal for the Earth shift that threw the King's horse to the ground.

He must also have been able to communicate in some fashion with Huw over longer distances, otherwise the attack on Elias during the storm—the attack that cost Fiann his life—couldn't have been so precisely coordinated. Huw must have been able to perceive Reen's thoughts, like the sport she had read of in the archives Gaslek showed her. It all made perfect sense. She never stood a chance. How Reen must have laughed at her.

Taran, Denny, and the swordmaster stood awkwardly nearby, watching her, not wanting to disturb her. A movement in the gloom just past them caught her eye, and she saw that Aeyron, temporarily forgotten in the sorrow of the moment, was trying to rise. Taran turned at the sound and crossed swiftly to him. He took the injured Prince's arm over his shoulder, helping him gain his feet. Aeyron waved him toward Sullyan.

When Taran brought him close enough, he spoke. "Brynne."

She tilted her head up, eyes brimming. He smiled for her, his pale yellow eyes reflecting what moonlight there was.

"You did what you could for him. Please don't blame yourself like this. He was a raw talent, untutored, unaware. He didn't know how to let you in. It wasn't your fault."

His voice was hoarse, but she heard the kindness and care he was trying to convey. She could see the effort he was making for her. And he was right. There were yet more vitally important tasks awaiting her that night, and their outcomes would all rest very firmly on her shoulders.

She sighed deeply. Would she ever have time to grieve?

"He was my cousin, Aeyron, my family, yet I could not save him. And now, another link to my lineage is lost. How will I ever find out where I came from?"

Aeyron frowned. Denny and Ardoch widened their eyes. This talk of cousins was new to them.

Aeyron's voice was low and full of strain. "If he was truly your cousin, then he had parents. And they may have had other children who yet live. This need not be the end."

She stared up at him. This thought hadn't yet occurred to her. Perhaps she could trace Huw's origins, discover where he had come from. It was even possible the Queen, who had permitted Huw to stay at the castle, knew something of his background. Whether she could be persuaded to tell remained to be seen.

Looking down at his peaceful face, Sullyan promised both of them she'd do all she could to find out more about him and whatever other family they might still have.

She placed a tender kiss on Huw's shocking red hair and laid his head down. Ardoch extended a hand to help her up and she stood unsteadily, still looking down at Huw's body.

"I'll see he has a proper ceremony, lass," Ardoch said. She nodded her thanks, unable to speak past the lump in her throat. "So, what now?"

Sullyan glanced over at Denny, who remained some way off, embarrassed and unsure of his reception after the consequences of his scandalmongering at the Manor. Although she made no reference to it, her tone was a touch hard as she asked, "Lieutenant, what orders were you given concerning the Baron?"

Denny moved stiffly as he came forward. "Lord Levant ordered the garrison raised against Baron Reen and instructed us to confine him to his home, along with his men. We outnumber them, so my men should have them secure by now. The dogs have run to their kennel."

"Good. What was the Queen's reaction?"

Ardoch answered. "We don't know yet, lass. Levant was persuaded to act by his discovery of the discrepancy in the treasury accounts, the use of the dungeon, and my testimony of finding the wee Prince at the Baron's mansion. He has the authority to take control of the garrison and issue orders in the King's absence, even against the Queen's wishes if he considers there's sufficient cause. More than that, he cannot do. The best we can hope for is to pen the Baron in his home. But Levant can't stop the Queen from seeing the Baron if she wishes, nor stop the Baron from sending messages."

Sullyan nodded. "Then we had best hope I can reach the King in time to thwart the Baron's assassins." She saw Ardoch's alarm and repeated what Reen had told her. "At least Reen can no longer initiate communications with his Andaryan allies. But neither can we force him to call them off."

She sighed heavily, glancing down one final time at the poor crooked body on the ground. "We must get Aeyron to your house, Ghyl. I must tend to his injuries before I can return him to his father."

She turned to Denny. "Lieutenant, do you have sufficient men to guard the Prince's nursemaid and the Lady Jinella while I am gone? They may need protection from the Baron's supporters, as they hold vital evidence against him. I think it would be best if they stay with Ardoch until this is resolved."

Denny was about to answer when a signal whistle sounded out of the darkness. He whistled back, and three of his men rode out of the gloom toward them.

"We've penned him and his men in the mansion and surrounded the place, sir. Not a mouse could creep out of there without us knowing."

"Good man." Denny waved an arm. "Chaz, Fergus, you two go with the swordmaster. You're to stand guard outside his house until the King returns. I'll arrange for you to be relieved at dawn. Yadrin, I'll ride double with you back to the Baron's mansion.

He turned deferentially to Sullyan, deliberately ignoring the fact she was no longer entitled to her rank. "Colonel. Please take my horse. You can leave him at the stables near the city gates. I'll collect him later. And ... I earnestly wish you every success in warning the King of his danger. I ... oh, never mind."

He gathered the reins of his horse. Sullyan's eyes had softened and she gave him a small but genuine smile of thanks as he brought the stallion over and held the beast's head while she mounted. The wound in her thigh was stiffening despite her flow of metaforce. She had too many other hurts that needed healing power and her resources were already strained.

Ardoch and Taran helped Aeyron up behind her, the Andaryan clinging to her waist with his one good arm.

Taran and Ardoch rode double on the swordmaster's gray, and the four of them, flanked by Chaz and Fergus, left the bodies of Huw and Izack lying on the sodden ground as they made their way back toward the city. Denny hauled himself up behind Yadrin, and they spurred for the Baron's mansion to check on the deployment of his men.

Chapter Thirty

The ride back to Ardoch's house was uneventful. It was nearly midnight and the soaked streets were empty. Lamplight reflected off every wet surface, and the eaves of the houses sparkled with a myriad glittering droplets.

Sullyan had to pour vast amounts of her own strength into Aeyron to enable him to keep his seat behind her. The Prince had lapsed almost into unconsciousness once more and his weakened body lay heavy against her back. She was thankful when they finally reached the street of Ardoch's house and saw the welcoming light shining from the windows. Jinella could be seen anxiously hovering behind the drapes. When she saw who approached, she ran to open the door.

Ardoch and Taran slid from Morlech's back and went to help Sullyan with Aeyron. One of Denny's men took all the horses to the stables as the other took up his guard post outside the door.

Jinny gasped when she saw the wounded man and wrinkled her fine nose in disgust. "Ugh! What on earth's that vile smell?"

"That is the scent of your uncle's malice," snapped Sullyan as she limped behind the three men into the house. Jinny cringed from her acerbic tone, one hand to her mouth, her green eyes tearful. Sullyan ignored her. She was in no mood to spare the sensitivities of Jinny's sheltered spirit.

Taran spoke over his shoulder, his tone reproving. "Jinny

helped us courageously today, Brynne. Without her assistance, Prince Eadan might still be in the Baron's power and you and Aeyron still in chains."

Arrested by the tone of his voice—he had never dared rebuke her before—Sullyan halted. She had allowed her grief over Huw and her fear and love for Aeyron to color her response. Despite the pain lodged deep within her soul, she was shamed. Taran's mild reproof gave her pause and she regarded him speculatively, the merest hint of a smile on her lips. Then she turned to Jinella and met her nervous gaze.

"I ask your forgiveness, my Lady. I am not at my best. Prince Aeyron is in dire need of care and attention, and I fear for him. I apologize for my sharp words."

Jinny smiled tentatively and the awkward moment faded. Taran and the swordmaster guided Aeyron into the small cooking room. There was a long wooden table in the center of the floor and they helped the weak Prince to lie upon it, a folded cloth beneath his head. Jinny was asked to heat as much water as she could, and Sullyan began stripping the Prince's befouled and sodden breeches.

Taran took the knife firmly from her hand. "Let me do that. Take care of yourself first."

Ardoch came to help too, and they soon removed the Prince's clothing. They threw it into the tiny backyard outside the cottage's rear door. Jinny gave a small squeal when she turned and saw the naked male outlander lying before her. She averted her eyes.

When the water was ready, Taran and Ardoch began carefully washing the grime, filth, and blood from Aeyron's flesh, taking especial care over his many wounds. He made no sound. Sullyan had put him to sleep with a thought to spare him any pain or embarrassment, although he was probably far past the latter. Then she asked Jinny to help her wash, and stripped off her own fouled, torn garments.

"Colonel!" exclaimed Jinny, her voice full of shock. Sullyan stared at her, arrested in the act of removing her bloody chemise, the last of her garments. Jinny indicated the men with an emphatic nod of her head, her eyes wide and disapproving.

Sullyan shrugged. "They are far too busy with their work to notice me, my Lady. Besides, they have seen it all before." She completed her disrobing.

She could almost hear Taran thinking, *Not entirely true*, and saw the quick glance he couldn't resist. She followed the direction of his gaze, glancing down ruefully at her belly. She could definitely see a difference and wondered how much longer it would be before everyone knew. This reminder of the future brought a resurgence of grief, but she clamped it tightly down. She must keep a clear head for the work still ahead of her if she was to get Aeyron fit enough to travel the Veils.

With Jinny clicking her tongue over Sullyan's many scars and wounds, the two women thoroughly cleansed Sullyan's body and washed the blood out of her hair. During their work, they talked of the events that had brought them to this hour. For Sullyan's benefit, Ardoch recounted his two interviews with Lord Levant, and also their expedition to the dungeons. He reassured her Levant was suspicious enough to withstand the Queen's anger at the imprisoning of her countryman, at least until the King returned. Sullyan didn't allow herself to speculate on what might happen should Elias be killed.

Then Taran took up the tale and told her of his fortuitous meeting with Jinny in the park, what she had suffered at her uncle's hands, and how she had helped them rescue Prince Eadan. Jinny herself chipped in with her own thoughts as he recounted the actual rescue. Sullyan praised her for her courage in distracting Izack at the crucial moment. She well appreciated how frightened the gently-reared Jinella must have been.

Then it was Sullyan's turn to tell the story of her incarceration in the circle and how she had managed to foil the Baron's plans. She had no wish for Ardoch or Jinella to learn of her pregnancy just yet, so she glossed over the actual mechanics of the breaking of the circle's titanic forces, and as neither Ardoch nor Jinny had any concept of how it could have been done, they accepted her words at face value.

"So," said the Torlander when she fell silent, "is that the end of yon Baron's threat to Artesans?"

Sullyan applied a towel to her wet hair. "Only if he can be discredited and removed from power. He still has at least one ally in Andaryon, and although he cannot communicate with him directly now he has lost Huw, he can, perhaps, still send messages. But I am sure now I know who his ally is, and that is another reason why I must lose no time in returning to Andaryon. I have to warn the King before Corbyn can send his assassins against him. As soon as we are finished here, I must contact Bulldog and find out the state of the war. Then I can contact Marik and warn him of Corbyn's treachery."

They finished their washing and Sullyan donned clean clothes from her pack, loosely binding her still-damp hair. Her stained and ripped clothes she deposited with Aeyron's outside the cottage door. "Burn them, will you, Ghyl?" she requested in distaste.

They wrapped Aeyron's body in a warmed blanket, as much to spare Jinny's blushes as to keep the Prince from chill. Sullyan's work would now begin in earnest, and she was already exhausted by her recent trials.

She turned to Jinny. "Are you squeamish, my Lady?"

Jinny frowned. "Why? And you don't have to keep calling me 'my lady,' Colonel."

Sullyan smiled faintly. "I am no longer a colonel, Jinella. My name is Brynne. I ask you because I must drain the poison from Aeyron's wounds, and I need to know if you can help. Ardoch here will have to hold the Prince still, and I will need all my powers to counter the poison. Taran will have to help me direct the metaforce, so we need someone to hold the basin and renew soiled cloths. It will be highly unpleasant. Can you do it?"

Jinny squared her shoulders. "It can hardly be worse than allowing myself to be pawed by that barbarian, Izack. I'll manage."

Smiling her thanks, Sullyan bent to her work. With Jinny holding a basin under Aeyron's right arm, and the Torlander leaning over the Prince's other arm and chest, Sullyan took Taran's knife and made a deep slit in Aeyron's bicep, the site of the original wound he had taken on the day of his capture.

It was just as well Ardoch had laid his own body over Aeyron's. Despite Taran's soothing flow of metaforce, the outpouring of the vile infection must have pained the Andaryan as much as the bite of the knife, for he gave a thin, high scream and his upper body heaved. Sullyan linked with Taran and together they numbed the pain as much as they could.

As the infection oozed sluggishly into the basin, Sullyan showed Taran how to use his powers to help push the flow of it from Aeyron's blood. She followed through with Fire, sterilizing muscle and skin. It took some time and was highly draining on the two Artesans, but finally it was done. Taran's new confidence in handling Fire even enabled him to take some of the burden from Sullyan, and they were both perspiring freely when it was over.

Leaving Jinny to wash the ragged wound once again with warmed water laced with Ardoch's tarn liquor, Sullyan and Taran rested briefly, wiping their flushed faces with damp cloths. Ardoch had produced a needle and suture thread, and his nimble fingers stitched up the long slit in Aeyron's upper arm as best he could. It was only meant to be temporary. Deshan and his healers would do a much more thorough job once they had the Prince back at the Citadel. Jinny made a neat job of binding the wound when he had finished.

Water was constantly being heated over the hearth, and Sullyan took some precious time to brew fellan. She hadn't eaten for twenty-four hours and had drunk only rainwater. The anodyne of the fellan was much needed. The hot brew helped revive her, and she didn't even comment when Taran added a measure of honey to their cups. They both needed the energy.

In truth, Sullyan was dreading the next task and was in no hurry to begin, despite the urgency. Aeyron's maimed hand was in a very bad way and the infection was rife. The dungeon had been fetid and filthy, and the knife used to hack off his finger none too clean or even sharp, judging by the mess it had left behind. Jinny had only just hung on to the contents of her stomach as the stench of raw infection from Aeyron's arm had hit her nostrils; this promised to be twice as bad. Sullyan didn't know if even she could stand it, and she was long inured to wounds and mangled flesh. She sent soothing thoughts to her unborn son, hoping he wouldn't kick at the wrong moment and embarrass her completely.

Her biggest worry was whether she could clear Aeyron's flesh of poison without being forced to remove his hand. Andaryan aristocracy set much store by physical perfection and prowess, and Sullyan knew that if she took his hand, he might never rule after his father. As it was, he would have to relearn the art of swordplay.

Sighing deeply, she drained her cup and forced herself to begin.

✣ ✣ ✣ ✣ ✣

Others had also labored long into that night. It was two hours after midnight when Bull finally left the infirmary, and he felt ancient down to his very bones. He had put forth all his strength, all his power, both physical and metaphysical, and still Tad only clung to life by a knife edge. The next few hours were critical.

Rienne and Hanan had contrived to replace some of the precious blood Tad had lost by taking some from his distraught mother, but it was not a procedure guaranteed of success. As a technique it was still in its infancy, and there was much to learn about why some people reacted badly to receiving another's blood. Whenever possible, family members were used as donors, as that seemed to yield the highest rate of success.

Tad's mother had been sent to rest once she had done her part, and despite her weakness she went with reluctance. Bull had strengthened Tad's heart, steadied his breathing, and kept him warm while his wound was tended and stitched. Eventually, Rienne, mindful of Bull's own weak heart, had made him stop. They had done all they could. The rest was up to Tad. He had held on this long, and both Rienne and Hanan were amazed at his dogged fight for life.

Now, they could only support him and pray.

They had discussed the boys' fates at some length while they worked, and Bull had agreed with Hanan's thoughts on the nature of Tad's wound. He was also highly suspicious of Parren's comments outside the infirmary. He was so concerned that he sent for a couple of militiamen, telling them not to leave Tad unguarded for one second. Hanan would be sleeping in the same room, to keep an eye on him during the night, and she had other healers nearby if she required help. Rienne would take over in the morning.

Despite their exhaustion, Rienne and Bull were still discussing the incident as they walked back to their rooms.

"What possible reason could Captain Parren have for attacking Tad and Ozella?" asked Rienne. She looked haggard. Her recent exertions and her fear for Tad were draining her.

Bull shrugged. "I don't know, dear heart, but I think it might be a good idea to find out."

As they passed into the comfort of the Manor's lantern-bright hallways, a curtaining drape fluttered in some unfelt breeze. Bull hardly even glanced at the shadow behind it, too intent on a glass of firewater and his waiting bed.

✣ ✣ ✣ ✣ ✣

Taran had to take over from Jinella. The gently-bred young woman simply couldn't stomach what came forth from the blackened flesh of the Prince's hand, although she made a heroic effort. The rest of them just gritted their teeth and hung on grimly.

Jinny was tasked with changing cloths and watching over the heating water. Sullyan needed copious amounts to flush the wound clean. It was fortunate there was a drain in the middle of the cooking room floor, and the excess water leaked away outside. The bowls of rank infection were thrown out of the cottage doorway, to be flushed away into the city sewer. Denny's two men soon learned to stand well clear of the door.

Taran and Sullyan labored long to clean Aeyron's blood and flesh of corruption. Sullyan hadn't made any other cuts in the skin. She merely re-opened the wound where the finger had been. Aeyron cried out in agony when she did, then subsided into unconsciousness. By this time, he had accepted Sullyan so completely into his mind and psyche that she had unrestricted access to his metaforce. She no longer needed his volition.

She was almost hopeful for the hand by the time his flesh was clean. Much of the muscle would need reforming, but Deshan could help Aeyron there. It was impossible to stitch the wound—it was too raw and ragged—so she packed it with cloth soaked in tarn liquor and bound it.

They all breathed a sigh of relief when the last bowl of poison and the last soiled cloth was disposed of, and the aroma of fellan took over from the stench of sickness. Exhausted, Taran and Sullyan collapsed into chairs in the sitting room. Ardoch had dressed Aeyron in Taran's spare breeches and shirt and wrapped him in one of his own spare cloaks. Aeyron didn't move. Sullyan had ensured he would stay deeply asleep until she required him to wake.

The hour was early, only a few hours off dawn. Despite her weakness, Sullyan was desperate to know the state of the war, and so she made no concessions to the hour when she attempted to contact Bull. Taran linked with her to provide some extra strength, but she couldn't rouse the big man.

"What does he think he is doing, sleeping so deeply?" she grumbled. "This is no time for dreaming. Taran, I am going to have to use stronger methods to wake him. Be wary, he might hurt you if he startles."

She was puzzled by the depth of Bull's slumber. Those with military training often slept lightly and were easily roused. Yet once Sullyan had given the big man the metaphysical equivalent of a shout in the ear, which caused him to leap, sweating and cursing, to his feet, she learned the reason why.

Fresh tears welled in Sullyan's eyes as Bull related the incident of the evening before. Ozella hadn't been with them long, and she took his killing hard. She hadn't dedicated as much time to his training as she would have liked. Perhaps if she had, he would have been better able to protect himself.

And Tad? she asked. Her own fear for the youngster was heightened by the grief she knew Robin would feel over his fate.

Both she and Taran felt Bull's mental shrug.

I'll go and see now you've woken me. He was in a very bad way last night and Hanan wouldn't commit herself. I did all I could, but I don't have your skill or strength.

Sullyan, there's something else you should know. Parren was sniffing around when we brought the boys in. His interest seemed suspicious to me. He tried to suggest the boys had been dueling, but no one believes that. I've put a guard on Tad's room, just in case.

Anger swelled in Sullyan. *That was well done, Bull. The Baron let slip that he had a spy in his pay at the Manor. It has to be Parren. I suspect he was given some hold over one or both of the boys. They have been forced to pass secrets to him which he, in return for gold, passed to Reen. I suspect that is why Ozella was so desperate for me to take him on that mission to Andaryon. It would also explain why he was so distracted while we were there. Tell Vassa. Get him to hold Parren for questioning.* She sighed heavily. *I have been very remiss, my friend. I should have taken more notice of Ozella at the time. Now, two more innocent lives have suffered.*

Bull tried to reassure her. She refused to be comforted, instead asking after the state of the war.

The big man told her what had happened to Elias's forces since entering Andaryan territory, and how they were now pinned down in a wooded area by two opposing groups. He told her Blaine had been careful to keep him informed of what was occurring, hopeful it would reach her ears.

She was distressed by this turn of events, especially when she heard of Corbyn's attack on Marik's parley party. Bull also told her about Cal recognizing Corbyn.

She nodded, even though Bull couldn't see her. *This confirms Reen's boast that Corbyn is his ally. He also told me Corbyn has been instructed to kill Elias. Anjer and Barrin will know nothing of this. If they keep Elias pinned where he is, he will be a sitting target for Corbyn's assassins.*

Bull's concern was palpable. *Are you going to bespeak Anjer and warn him? Do you want me to contact Blaine?*

Sullyan's frustration mounted. Blaine would accept her word with no qualms, but her current standing in the King's eyes meant Elias was unlikely to heed any intelligence coming through her. This needed careful planning.

Warn the General that Corbyn might try something, she said. *Thanks to Cal's sharp eyes, he already knows of Corbyn's treachery and should be on his guard. I am certain Anjer and Marik have scouts watching for Corbyn's men, so they should be forewarned if he makes any threatening moves. My worry is that Corbyn will send a small group to infiltrate the woods around Elias's position. It would take a similar small group to track them and negate their threat. Anjer cannot move now to release Elias's forces from the trees. The King will be suspicious of his motives and might see the gesture as a trap. He might even order an attack, and I cannot be responsible for precipitating a pitched battle, not after Anjer has been so careful to avoid one. The only options I have are either to find Corbyn and make him recall his assassins, or reach Elias in person and warn him. I have to do one or the other before I can return his son to him, and the Heir to the Hierarch.*

She broke the link, ignoring Bull's amazed exclamation as he realized the import of her final words.

Taran was staring at her. "How on earth do you propose to do that?"

"We have a little time, my friend. Nothing will happen until daylight. The assassins might use the cover of darkness to infiltrate the wood where Elias is sheltering and to approach his forces from behind, but they will need light for a clear shot at him. They will wait, hoping Anjer will force a response from Elias. Entrenched as he is, the King will be surrounded by his men and no easy target, even in daylight. Once the General hears Bull's report he will increase the guard around the King, if he can do it without arousing Elias's wrath. The assassins will likely only have one chance, and they will want to make it count. If they miss, they will hope Elias blames Anjer or Barrin's men for the attempt, and that he will be killed in the subsequent fighting. You and I must find and attack Corbyn's men, and take their lord captive if possible."

The Adept's eyes stretched wide. "What? Just the two of us?"

That brought a faint smile to her lips. "No, Taran. With your help and a bit of luck, we will have a small force of our own with which to fight. First, we must move Aeyron and Eadan to a more convenient place. The city is not safe and is too crowded. I intend to take them to Jed at the Hazel Tree. I can trust him. He will look after them and keep them safe until we can get them across the Veils. It will mean a fast ride. Are you up to it?"

He spread his hands. He'd come this far; he wasn't about to back out now.

She smiled her gratitude for his faith and friendship, and laid a hand on his shoulder.

"Ardoch," she called, "Taran needs a fast horse. Will there be one at the stables we can borrow?"

The swordmaster came into the room. "Ach, lad, take Morlech and welcome. I can always get a remount at the barracks. Return him when you can. But you're surely not going right now? You both need food and rest."

"Both are a long way off for us yet, Ghyl," Sullyan replied. "I thank you for the loan of Morlech. Would you ask one of Denny's men to saddle both him and Drum and bring them to the door?"

When the swordmaster had gone to do her bidding, Sullyan turned to Jinny. "Where is the Prince, Jinella? We must take him with us if we are to return him to his father."

The blonde woman went up the stairs to fetch the baby from

the room where he was sleeping with his nursemaid. She came back down with a warmly wrapped bundle that squirmed slightly. She passed him to Sullyan, and as he was laid in her arms a curious sensation flooded her breast. She gazed down into Eadan's baby blue eyes and gasped. If she could carry her mission off safely and preserve Elias's life, she might have some interesting and unexpected news for her monarch.

The Prince stared seriously back at her. Soon she would hold her own son in her arms like this and be looking down into his face. Would his father be there to see him?

To cover her rising emotion, Sullyan thrust the baby at Taran. He stared at the tears in her eyes as she moved toward the cooking room, and probably guessed the reason for them, for his own glittered with moisture.

"Jinny," he said solemnly. "We'll never forget what you did today. The King will hear of your loyalty and bravery, I'll make very sure of that. But don't forget what I asked you to do to put things right."

"I won't forget," promised Jinny, making Sullyan wonder what Taran had asked of her. How on earth could Jinny put things right? Jinny's next move surprised her and made her forget her puzzlement. Surprising Taran too, judging by the look on his face, Jinny reached on tiptoe to kiss him full on the lips.

"Please be careful, Taran," she urged. "I'd really like to see you again."

Sullyan entered the cooking room, returning with a stumbling and barely-conscious Aeyron, aided by Ardoch. She had her sword at her back again, the hilt rearing over her shoulder.

"Come, Taran, we have a long ride ahead of us."

Taran followed her into the chill pre-dawn darkness and mounted Morlech. The beast was slimmer and finer of leg than the powerful Drum, and more to Taran's preference. Jinny passed the baby up to him and Taran wrapped Eadan firmly against his body in a blanket-shawl.

Ardoch and Sullyan manhandled Aeyron onto Drum's broad back. Sullyan leaped up behind him, one hand lightly on the reins, the other clasped firmly around the slim Andaryan's waist. She hoped she'd be able to hold on to him. He was barely able to stay upright.

They took their farewells of Jinny and Ardoch, Sullyan noting the sheen of tears in the blonde woman's eyes and the slight flush on Taran's face. She might have smiled if their circumstances were not so urgent. One of Denny's men rode with them to the Forest Gate, and also accompanied them through the Forest itself. The main coaching road through Loxton Forest was wide and easily traveled, even in the scant starlight. Sullyan set a fast pace, Drum and Morlech galloping stride for stride, Denny's man just at the rear. The Guardsman turned and rode back to the city just before the Forest edge.

Chapter Thirty-One

Parren was growing frantic. He'd tried twice during the night to gain access to Tad's room so he could finish what he'd started, but hadn't been able to get near for fear of discovery.

Gods damn the stupid boy! How could he possibly have survived that sword thrust? And how had Bull known to look for him?

Parren was forced to conclude Tad had indeed managed to call Bull, as he had boasted. Yet the little runt hadn't told Bull who had injured him, or the big man would have said something when Parren accosted the party on the way to the infirmary. All was not yet lost, although Parren's glittering future was in severe jeopardy unless he could ensure Tad didn't breathe a word of what had happened. He vowed he would end Tad's breathing forever.

He'd been dismayed to find guards on Tad's room and the Chief Healer herself sleeping by the boy's side. Parren guessed his story of hearing the two boys arguing and their subsequent duel had been discounted. Perhaps he should have used the tale about Relkorian raiders after all. Too late now.

There was no way Parren could gain access to Tad's room without alerting either the guards or the healer. The two men on the door were among the most skilled of the peasant militia. Parren knew they bore him no love, and he couldn't approach them without taking the risk they'd been warned against him.

Guards aside, that still left the healer, and Parren, ruthless though he was, balked at the cold-blooded murder of innocent women. Had it been Rienne, it might have been different, but he at least had respect for Hanan.

Momentarily defeated, he slunk away, searching desperately for a plan.

He went back later and the guards had changed. This gave him pause. Would these new men know the full facts? He thought probably not. He'd followed Bull and Rienne back to their rooms and knew they'd spoken to no one else. These men would have been told to relieve the other two and may not have heard any details. Perhaps he could work with that.

His main problem was his next tour of duty. He was due out at dawn, and that wasn't far off. Vassa had returned quite late with his group and it was unlikely he'd been apprised of what had happened to the boys. He probably wouldn't hear of it until he broke his fast. Yet he would be woken and told immediately if Parren didn't go out on time, and would want to know the reason why. Parren fumed. He couldn't afford to be away from the Manor all morning without having silenced Tad. The boy could rouse at any moment and tell what he knew.

Parren had already destroyed the Baron's letter. He'd been stupid to keep it in the first place, but had been reluctant give up his little piece of insurance. The Baron's recent silence had surely justified Parren's caution. After his thrice-damned failure to ensure Tad was indeed dead when he hit the stream, Parren had no choice. He couldn't afford for that letter ever to be seen again. He burned the parchment in his chambers and washed the ashes into the privy.

So much for that.

He also had to get rid of the two gold rings belonging to Ozella's sisters. They were useless now anyway, and he had intended to sell them. That would be foolhardy in the extreme now, so he took them to the well that served the kitchens and tossed them in. Now only Tad's spiteful tongue could link him to the Baron, and Ozella's death.

Could he risk Tad recovering, against all the odds? If Tad did make it, would the boy even remember what had happened? Maybe Parren could still talk his way out of it. He'd already suggested Tad and Ozella were dueling. Should he stick to that story and accuse Tad of trying to blame someone else for the breaking of military law?

He toyed with the idea, but it was too risky. Besides, someone was already suspicious about that story.

With a creeping sensation that raised gooseflesh on his arms, Parren suddenly remembered Tad was an Artesan. No matter what story Parren concocted, those cursed witches only had to rummage around in Tad's immature brain to discern the truth. He *had* to silence Tad. But how?

He hung around the infirmary until it was nearly light, still unable to gain entrance to Tad's room. He thought of climbing to the roof and scaling the walls to Tad's first floor window, but quickly discarded the idea. He'd have to fetch rope, and anyway, someone might see him. He'd never explain *that* away. Even if he did get in, Hanan was there.

Increasingly desperate, he shadowed the corridors, hoping Hanan would come out. If she did, he could easily distract the guards, slip inside, and smother the boy. Problem solved.

For once, things didn't go Parren's way. Hanan didn't come out, but another healer, a man, went in. And the two guards stayed rigidly at their post. Parren was trembling with rage and desperation. He was so close! Why hadn't he made sure Tad was dead? He wasn't usually so lax, and the thrust he'd used on the boy ought to have been more than enough to seal his fate. Damn the runt's obstinate strength!

Parren stiffened when he heard footsteps and voices approaching. Maybe this was his chance. He slipped into a side room and waited, holding the door open a crack. This would be his final opportunity. After this, he would be forced to go and see to his command. If he had to leave on patrol now, he could only hope Tad wouldn't last much longer and wouldn't regain consciousness before he died.

He didn't want to take that chance.

When he recognized the voices, his eyes narrowed in anger. It was Bull and Rienne, coming to check on Tad. Rage burned in his breast. Let the two of them be left alone in Tad's room, he prayed silently. Let the guards be dismissed and Hanan leave for her other duties. Then three of his enemies would be trapped in the room together, and he would deal with them all. How their demise would be explained away, he didn't consider. He'd think of something.

As Bull and Rienne drew closer, Parren made out their words. He shivered as his heart turned cold. Bull knew! Somehow he had learned Parren was the Baron's contact at the Manor. How the Void had he found *that* out? Parren was finished for sure, unless he could kill them all.

He cowered behind the door, seething with hatred.

"What are you going to do?" Rienne asked Bull.

"Tell Vassa, of course. I don't have the authority to arrest Parren, but Vassa does. He'll take the little viper and lock him away until Blaine and the King return. Then he'll be tried for a traitor and probably hanged. Serve him right. It's about time he paid for all his nasty little comments and sly tricks, not to mention nearly killing Robin in that farce of a duel two years ago. He got out of that lightly, but he won't wriggle out of this one. Once we've checked on Tad, I'll go wake Vassa. Sullyan will tell Blaine and the King when she returns the Heir, I expect, but we can't afford to leave the little weasel at large until they get back. Who knows what other crimes he might commit?

"You know, it breaks my heart to think of those two lads facing that cold-hearted, ruthless murderer. Tad must have been very brave to stand up to him, but I know he'd have been terrified. Whatever else you can say about Parren, he's a highly skilled swordsman. Oh, how I'm going to enjoy watching his neck stretch!"

Bull and Rienne passed Parren's hiding place and entered Tad's sickroom. Emerging slowly from his concealment, Parren slunk away.

Damn Sullyan! DAMN her! Damn them all! His last chance had faded with Bull's words. Up until that point, Bull's and Rienne's fates were sealed; they would have died at Parren's hands. But if that witch Sullyan told Blaine and Elias, it was pointless and he was finished. There was only one course of action left open to him now if he was to salvage anything of his glowing future.

His scarred face twisted with fury, Parren stalked away.

✣ ✣ ✣ ✣ ✣

It was a wild ride in the darkness. Halfway through, they changed mounts, Sullyan's physical condition being unequal to holding the barely-conscious Aeyron secure on Drum's back.

Taran mounted the huge black stud nervously, but Drum remained easy and responsive. Sullyan sprang up onto Morlech and settled the baby into her arms. She hardly touched the gray's sides as she set him off again into the predawn light, Drum thundering beside her.

The sun had barely risen behind a bank of cloud when Jed's homely inn came into sight. They drew rein outside his door and it was opened before either of them could dismount. Despite the early hour, Jed had a keen ear for custom. He greeted them warmly and calmly accepted Sullyan's request.

"Of course I can give them a room. There're only two others in at the moment, and they'll be leaving after breakfast. But who is he, Colonel?" Jed indicated the unresponsive Aeyron with a nod of his head. "He looks to be in a bad way."

"They are both very important people, Jed. It would be best if you kept their presence here a secret. With good fortune, we will return for them in a couple of hours. If we do not, you are to release them to no one except Hal Bullen or General Blaine. Or the King himself."

Jed's eyes widened. Taran helped the groaning, semi-comatose Andaryan down from Drum's back and half-carried him into the inn. Jed pointed to the gurgling baby in Sullyan's arms.

"Is that who I think it is?"

"He is a hungry babe who would appreciate some breakfast."

The innkeeper smiled. "Fear not, Colonel. I'll find him a breakfast fit for a prince."

Sullyan couldn't suppress a grin. "I knew I could rely on you, Jed."

They took Aeyron and the baby up to one of Jed's best suites, which had the added bonus of being apart from the rest of the guest rooms. They laid Aeyron on the generous bed and Sullyan tried for some time to reassure the Prince. He was so distressed by her going that she was forced to put him to sleep.

There were tears in her eyes as she turned to Jed. "He will remain asleep until I return to awaken him. Just keep them safe for me."

They returned to their mounts, which were being fed apples by Jed's two sons. The boys grinned at Sullyan and caught the small coins she tossed them. She held out a handful of gold to Jed, but the innkeeper shot her a look of indignation.

"I am no longer a member of the King's forces," she reminded him.

"Still in the King's service, though, aren't you? I don't think he'll begrudge their board when he hears who it was for."

She gripped his arm in silent gratitude. Then she leaped once more to Drum's high back and heeled him away, Taran following.

She only went a short way into the open countryside before drawing rein once more. Drum had caught her mood of urgency and pranced lightly, chin tucked into his muscled chest, breath snorting from wide, red nostrils. Taran drew Morlech alongside him, a puzzled look on his face.

"Why are we stopping?"

Sullyan glanced at him. "We are going to cross the Veils, but I have neither time nor strength for finesse. Drum will not balk, as he has his own knowledge of the Veils, but I must caution you to keep Morlech's nose on Drum's tail. Do not allow him to turn his head or he will shy. You also might find it easier to fix your sight on Drum."

Taran's frown deepened.

"I intend to open a moving tunnel. The substrate will part a yard in front of Drum's feet and close a yard behind Morlech's. Do not deviate from the path or let Morlech falter. I do not want to lose you. Now, are you ready?"

Taran swallowed, nodded, and took a firm hold of the gray's reins. Sullyan touched Drum with her heels and the huge stud leaped into a canter. She urged him even faster. "Keep up, Taran!" she yelled, and he pushed the gray stallion until he was practically running on Drum's black-feathered heels.

Sullyan parted the Veils and Taran gasped. He hadn't experienced anything like this before. The tunnel was unanchored and unstable, flowing and flexing around them. He moved Morlech so close to Drum's pluming ebony tail that the gray's head was almost buried in it. One wrong move and he'd be lost. She wouldn't have the time to search for him.

Drum barreled his way through, heedless of the swirling mist before his eyes. Horse and rider trusted each other implicitly and there were no mistakes. They all burst out of the moving tunnel into a field of barley glistening with dew.

Reining Drum to a halt, Sullyan scanned their surroundings, looking for signs of fighting. The field they were in was on the edge of a cultivated area bordered by a low range of hills ahead. She could see vineyards to their right and dense woodland to their left.

She listened with all her senses, then nodded in satisfaction. "Elias should be within those woods. Commander Barrin has a small force encamped on top of those hills, protecting the town beyond. The Lord General is to the west of us, between Elias and the two towns he annexed. The King's next objective lies behind Barrin's position just over those hills. Elias is pinned in the trees.

"Corbyn's assassins must be hidden within these woods somewhere, waiting for their chance to strike. Taran, I want you to contact Cal and ask if he would be willing to put his command at our disposal. Put no pressure on him, and make sure he knows he would be acting on his own. I will not ask this of Cal if he is unsure."

Taran nodded and did as he was bid. Sullyan relaxed a little when she saw him smile.

"He's agreed," the Adept reported. "He wants to know what you want him to do."

"First I want him to ensure all his men are in agreement," she said firmly. "Any who are not can join another command. When he is sure of his men, I want him to keep his eyes open for stray groups of Andaryans who appear independent of the main force. Once Anjer makes his move, I want Cal to bring his command to the rear, where we will join him. Then we go hunting."

Taran relayed this to Cal. "He's standing ready," he told Sullyan. "He says Dexter's joining him and he thinks *all* Elias's men would follow your orders given half a chance. Are you going to tell General Blaine and Anjer your plans?"

Sullyan was deeply touched by Cal's words and Dexter's support. Her voice was husky when she replied. "Bull will have given Mathias my warning. I will not speak with him directly. It would put him in an awkward position with the King, and I do not want that. I also cannot risk distracting Anjer. "

She turned Drum and sent him trotting toward the woods. Taran followed. As she went, she gathered her will and accessed her metaforce. In answer, a patter of raindrops fell. Taran lifted his eyes to the sky, where clouds were increasing from the east, their tops rearing into thunderheads. An irritated curse slipped from him.

"What on earth are you doing?" he demanded, gathering his cloak around him. "Didn't you get wet enough yesterday?"

She grinned. "My friend, there have been times when I have been unfairly accused of making entrances. Today I intend to make a very dramatic entrance indeed, one that everyone will see."

Her expression turned grim. "We need to keep our wits about us, now. Stay in touch with Cal and let me know as soon as Anjer makes his move. The hunt for Corbyn begins."

✣ ✣ ✣ ✣ ✣

General Blaine sat his restive horse, heartily wishing he had the nerve to render Elias unconscious and carry him off the field back to Albia. Things had taken an odd turn. Late the previous evening, Elias had suffered some kind of episode. He'd suddenly slumped, as if his bones had been turned to water, and Blaine had had to help him regain his feet. For a while, the blank stare in Elias's eyes made Blaine fear the King had lost his mind completely. But then

Elias's vision cleared and his determination to break out of these woods and confront Anjer returned in strength.

Then, early in the morning, Blaine had received a message from Sullyan, via Bull. It seemed Anjer and Barrin wouldn't be the Albians' only problems that day. Corbyn, the renegade Andaryan lord, had allied himself with Baron Reen and had orders to kill the Albian King.

An assassin creeping through these woods was just what Blaine didn't need. He felt anger and frustration mounting. This whole ridiculous war was a waste, and the General railed against the needless loss of life that would inevitably ensue once Anjer began his push.

The fact that Anjer had held off so far and even now was making moves to herd them, not kill them, meant less than nothing to Elias. He didn't see a cool-headed commander trying to resolve this conflict with minimal loss of life. He only saw hostile forces set to prevent him from retaking what was rightfully his. He seemed more determined than ever to resist them.

Blaine was fast running out of hope. He kept thinking about the upheaval he'd felt through the substrate the previous evening when Robin received Tad's despairing cry. He'd never felt its like before. The implosion of the tunnel at the siege of Hyecombe hadn't produced such a backlash. Even when Sullyan had destroyed the Staff housing Rykan's life force, the Veils hadn't trembled so violently.

He very much feared the disturbance heralded some terrible event, and his heart was heavy with worry for Sullyan. He didn't care to voice his thoughts to Robin, or ask him if he'd had any contact with her. Surely, she'd have asked Bull to tell him everything of import.

Or would she? Maybe he had so crushed her trust in him with his refusal to support her against Elias that he'd forfeited all rights to her loyalty. Didn't the fact she'd spoken with Bull rather than her General prove that? Resigned, he sighed. He would just have to make the best of this and hope Anjer had instructed his men against wholesale slaughter.

✠ ✠ ✠ ✠ ✠

Robin felt as if he were drowning in grief. He had sealed the hurt and anguish over his life mate's betrayal inside a protective shell to stop it overwhelming him. This had allowed him to function and fulfil his duty to Elias. Then had come Bull's tragic news about Tad and Ozella. Fear for Tad had shaken the protective shell, allowing sorrow to leak into his heart. Robin had tried hard to push it away, to reseal the shell, but late the previous evening he had failed catastrophically. Something had brought his shield crashing down, baring his soul to a torrent of grief he could barely comprehend. It had felt as if every failure he had ever suffered had returned to crush his spirit, every wrong he had ever done demanded he pay. For an hour or more he had struggled with a compulsive desire to throw everything away, even his life. The feeling eventually passed, but even now Robin couldn't say how he'd come through it.

Since learning of the boys' fate, Robin had heard no further word from Bull. He could only assume Tad was dead, and the fact that his name had been the last word on the boy's lips when Robin was completely unable to help him filled the Major's soul with pain.

Robin was also dreading the coming conflict. Anjer had shown him nothing but respect when he had stayed at the Citadel with Sullyan during the war with Rykan—now he'd be forced to fight against the man. It was wrong. It went against the grain not to offer Anjer some kind of explanation.

With sudden resolution, he decided that though they were foes this day, there was nothing stopping him bespeaking Anjer. Elias and Blaine need never know—Robin would shield his thoughts so tightly the General wouldn't sense them. Gathering his courage, he searched for the Lord General's psyche in the substrate.

He caught Anjer unawares. The Lord General was busy reviewing his men and preparing to march. His first thought on perceiving Robin's contact was that the Major was attempting to spy on him. Robin put him straight before Anjer could block him out.

I just wanted you to know, my Lord, that if I had any choice in the matter I wouldn't be involved in this war. General Blaine doesn't wish to fight you either. He was awake all night trying to convince the King to treat with you and return to Albia, but his Majesty is too distraught, too consumed with fear and rage over his son's abduction. I fear he is maddened beyond all reason.

I needed to tell you that I am not usually in the habit of fighting those I consider my friends.

Anjer didn't immediately reply. It was almost impossible to lie when speaking mind-to-mind with another Artesan, even for those who were highly skilled. Anjer was a Master, the same rank as Robin, and the young man had made no effort to hide his feelings.

Finally, Anjer spoke. *I appreciate your candor, Major, and I will remember your words. We have no wish for this battle either, but I cannot sit by and watch your King take control of large tracts of the Hierarch's lands. Unless he can be convinced or coerced into a withdrawal, I am afraid our course is set.*

Robin broke the link. He had done what he could. At least his conscience was as clear as it could be given the circumstances.

A horn sounded from the edge of the woods and the men stirred, readying their weapons. It was the signal that Anjer was on the move.

The battle had begun.

Chapter Thirty-Two

Sullyan and Taran split up to search the woods to the east of Elias's position, maintaining a link while they did so. Their plan was to locate Corbyn's men and then withdraw. Sullyan wanted to wait until both Anjer's and Elias's forces had engaged before risking a strike against Corbyn.

To Sullyan's puzzlement and annoyance, neither she nor Taran could detect any sign of their prey. They quartered the woods as thoroughly as they could under the circumstances. A force as large as the one Corbyn had to have at his command wouldn't be able to hide so completely. Even a small group of assassins should have been spotted during their search.

Frustrated, she recalled Taran, sitting deep in thought while she awaited him. Reen had told her Corbyn had been given orders to kill Elias during this conflict, and now that Anjer and Barrin had shown their clear intention to engage he wouldn't have a better opportunity. So where in Perdition was he?

When Taran arrived he linked with Cal, and she soon had an answer.

After the horn call signaling the start of hostilities had sounded, Anjer had driven forward into the woods while Barrin moved his men down the hills to flank the Lord General. Their objective, clearly, was to push Elias back through the woods, away from his annexed towns and, eventually, toward the Citadel Plains. If they got that far before Elias capitulated, she thought, Ephan's

Velletian Guard and probably reserves from Gwayeth would be waiting before the gates of Caer Vellet. Elias would be trapped and forced to submit.

According to Cal, Elias had other ideas. He was quite prepared to fight Anjer if necessary, but during the night he had formulated another plan. He had decided to use Anjer's tactics against him.

Elias had told his forces to fall back before Anjer's advance, but to retreat south. They would attempt to come out behind Anjer's forces and then turn against him. If the plan succeeded, Elias would have his captured towns at his back and a line of retreat should he need one. He would also be able to fire one or both of the towns, thus forcing Anjer and Barrin to halt.

Neither side's plan worked.

As Taran related the information from Cal, Sullyan worked it out. While Anjer and Barrin began their respective charges and Elias yelled the order to retreat, a third body of men, hitherto undetected, had come pelting out of the southeast to collide forcefully with both Barrin's and Elias's flanks.

Corbyn.

He must have hidden his men in the foothills, well away from the woods, and set scouts to watch Barrin's command. He would have seen Elias forced into the woods, and observed Anjer deploying his men. Corbyn had split his command, which was comprised of both human mercenaries and his own countrymen, and sent the Albian contingent against Barrin whilst his own liegemen attacked Elias.

She had to admit, it was both cunning and beautiful. Barrin and Elias were convinced each had attacked the other, and Barrin's natural suspicion of Albians coupled with Elias's flawed reasoning caused them to react predictably.

Each retaliated in force.

Sullyan cursed freely. She had underestimated Corbyn. He

must have had his strategy planned much earlier, doubtless with the Baron's help. She should have guessed he'd have human mercenaries among his command. The Baron's personal guard numbered far too few to have been responsible for all the raids into Andaryon as well as the capture of Prince Aeyron. These mercenaries would have been given access through the Veils days ago, long before Huw was killed.

Still cursing, and frightened for her King, she yelled to Taran to follow her. They pelted through the trees toward the sounds of fighting, swords drawn.

Taran warned Cal they were coming, but Dexter saw them first. Despite the fierce fighting, both captains had heeded Sullyan's instructions and kept to the rear. When Dexter clasped Sullyan's forearm in relieved welcome and roundly pledged his command's loyalty on top of Cal's, Sullyan was overwhelmed. The cheering rang loud in her ears.

There was no time for reunions. The threat to Elias's life could not be ignored. Sullyan showed Cal a mental picture of both Corbyn and his son, confirming he had indeed been the black-haired lord Cal had noticed at the Citadel, as well as being responsible for betraying Marik's parley. She gave orders that both Corbyn and Kethro should be taken alive.

She then sent Cal and his command off to the center, to surround the King and protect him at all costs. Blaine was unlikely to notice their change of position given the confusion Corbyn had caused, but if he did countermand her orders, she told Cal to say he'd had intelligence of an imminent threat to the King. She hoped the urgency of the situation would save him from the General's anger.

Taran gave his Apprentice a clap on the back and a smile of pride as the dark-skinned young Captain saluted Sullyan and led his men back into the fray.

She took Dexter and the rest of her old command with her. They penetrated farther into the woods, aiming to circle round to the southeast to come up behind Corbyn. She knew the traitor was likely to stay at the rear of the melee, and with any luck his son would be with him.

Kethro's capture was as vital as his father's, for Kethro was an Artesan. He would hold important knowledge of the Baron's scheming, and had to have been involved in the plot. Whether voluntarily or under coercion Sullyan had yet to determine, but she would ensure neither he nor Corbyn could escape through the Veils.

She guessed Corbyn would want to keep his son out of the fighting. Anjer would have joined the fracas by now. He had to support Barrin at all costs, and she hated to think what needless loss of life there would be this day.

Grimly determined, she and her men stalked their prey, the noise of battle covering the sound of their movements. The sooner she could take control of Corbyn and Kethro, the sooner she could end this futile war.

There were pockets of fighting among the trees and she couldn't avoid them all. Some of the Albian forces saw her. Despite the confusion, news of her presence would inevitably spread through the ranks. It couldn't be helped. Cal's men probably wouldn't hold their tongues, and she hadn't bothered to order them to silence. There was no point. Besides, more rumors could only work in her favor now, although she didn't like to think what the news might do to Robin's concentration.

She had no time to dwell on it because Taran caught sight of a familiar face crowned with unruly black hair. He gave a great shout. She pushed to his side and glimpsed Lord Corbyn riding hard in the middle of a tight band of his own men, his son by his side. Kethro looked terrified. They fled through the trees to the left of Sullyan's position.

She yelled, urging the men after him, though they needed little encouragement. Corbyn, realizing he was being pursued, roared at his guard and rode harder. Sullyan guessed he had already sent in his assassins, probably having opened up a route for them through Elias's men. She sent a hasty message to Cal to be doubly vigilant, but couldn't wait for his answer.

With her men around her, she pursued Corbyn. Their wild flight through the trees made it difficult for his men to protect him closely, and Sullyan watched for her chance. She had her eye on Kethro, whose fear was blinding him to his surroundings. He was pushing his sweating horse too hard. At least his panic prevented him from using his Artesan talents.

Calling to Dexter and the nearest of his men, she swung Drum's head to where she thought a gap might occur in Corbyn's guard.

She was right. At least one of her hunches had paid off this day. She had badly miscalculated earlier and it galled her. She made no concessions to the fact she was wounded, exhausted, and still suffering the effects of concussion. This maneuver would put it right.

Kethro and the twenty or so men near him were gradually becoming separated from Corbyn's group. Sullyan drove in hard and fast to cut Kethro off from his father. Dexter's men closed in behind her, herding the fleeing men. She ordered Taran and the rest of her command to go after Corbyn, and soon they were far out of sight.

It was like rounding up sheep. It put Sullyan in mind of her childhood, gathering the flocks of the Downs with one of her earliest mentors: the beastmaster, Trent. Kethro was inexperienced in matters of war and none of the men around him seemed to have the stomach for a fight. Instead of turning on the Albians, or trying to return Kethro to his father, they simply ran on.

Sullyan and Dexter pursued them. They split their forces yet again, Dexter coming up on Kethro's right flank and Sullyan taking the left. As the trees permitted, they gradually surrounded Kethro's group, slowing his flight. Kethro kept casting frightened glances about him, searching for signs of his father. By the time he thought of ordering the men with him to stand and fight, it was too late.

Sullyan and Dexter had allowed some of those around Kethro to slip the net. Even if they could have overcome them all, they'd have to waste precious time and resources subduing them and guarding them. It was Sullyan's opinion that they would probably run off with their tails between their legs and return home, unwilling to face Corbyn's wrath for having lost his son.

When they finally brought Kethro to bay, only ten men remained.

Sullyan and Dexter, their men around them, sat their blowing mounts and faced the frightened young man. He was visibly sweating, and not just from the wild flight. His sword trembled in his hand. He recognized Sullyan with wide-eyed shock as she kneed Drum toward him.

"Wh-what do you want from me?" He tried vainly for arrogance.

She smiled and spoke softly. "Nothing, my Lord Kethro, except your surrender. Come willingly with us and these men with you will be free to go. We need you to accompany us and prepare to answer for your actions and those of your father to King Elias and the Hierarch."

Kethro tried to scowl, but only succeeded in appearing even more frightened. The men around him whispered among themselves. Sullyan's offer of freedom had caught their attention.

She became aware of Kethro attempting to contact someone

through the substrate. Knowing who it must be, she sat watching the boy's efforts, a look of pity on her face. He struggled manfully for a few moments, but his total lack of success caused him to crumple.

"You are doomed to failure, my Lord. Not only could I block your attempts if I so desired, but the person you are trying to reach will never respond again. The Baron killed him."

Kethro's unthinking reaction betrayed him. "He killed Huw?" Realizing his mistake, he backpedaled. "I don't understand. What Baron? Who did he kill?"

She had no appetite for the game and no desire to coddle the boy. "Too late, my Lord. Will you submit quietly, or must we force you?"

He turned as if to order his men to fight. One of them urged his horse past Kethro, deliberately sheathing his sword. He spread empty palms to Sullyan.

"Did you mean what you said, Lady?"

She regarded him frankly, ignoring Kethro's spluttered protests. "I did. You are free to go unmolested, provided you leave these woods and the Hierarch's lands."

"Agreed."

Kethro cursed and made to spur his horse forward, outraged by the casual betrayal, but the man clamped a hand on his warhorse's reins. "I'm sorry, my Lord. Being massacred wasn't part of the deal. Your father's not paying us nearly enough for that."

He disarmed the boy before he could react, and handed the reins of Kethro's horse to one of Dexter's men, along with the sword. The Albians parted ranks, allowing the Andaryans to ride away, leaving a sullen, fuming Kethro helpless in his enemies' hands.

"Dex, tie him to his saddle," Sullyan said as she reached for contact with Taran.

The Adept and the rest of Dexter's command had succeeded in bringing Corbyn to bay some way off. The demon lord was fighting back, hard.

Tell him we have his son. Even if he does not believe you it will undermine his resolve. We will bring Kethro to you. That should ensure his father's capitulation.

Taran's affirmative reply was fleeting because he was concentrating on the fight. Dexter, who had finished securing Corbyn's son, took his horse's reins. His men dashed off after Sullyan toward where Taran and the rest of their fellows grappled with Corbyn's men.

As soon as Corbyn saw his bound and frightened son, he threw down his sword, swearing in the vilest way. The rest of his men surrendered. Sullyan let his retainers run off. They had orders to keep running until sunset if they valued their skin. She cared little about what Anjer would think of her actions. She only had one thought in mind now.

"Dex, take Corbyn and his son through our lines to the King. Hold a knife to Kethro's throat. If any of Corbyn's men succeed in even attempting the King's life, you are to kill Kethro."

She turned to a venomous-eyed Corbyn. "My Lord, if you value the life of your son, you will immediately recall your assassins. You will direct Captain Dexter to their positions and you will order their surrender. You have heard what will happen if you fail. Do not make the mistake of doubting Dexter. He will be ruthless in carrying out his orders. Do you understand me?"

Corbyn snarled more curses, but he was trapped and he knew it. She forced him to speak his acquiescence, which inflamed him further. She cared little.

"Your ultimate fate will be decided by King Elias and Lord General Anjer, my Lord. For myself, I pray we never meet again."

She turned from Corbyn as if he had ceased to exist. She smiled at Dexter, who grinned back.

"Farewell, Dexter. I hope you will be commended for your work today. Present these captives to General Blaine and the King. You do not have to mention my involvement—the glory is yours and welcome."

Dexter's face fell. "But aren't you coming with us?" The men ranged around him murmured their endorsement.

She shook her head. "My friend, your loyalty today has touched me deeply. I will never forget it. I owe you more than you know—all of you." Her gaze swept over the men, many of whom ducked their heads. "Taran and I have other duties yet. Return swiftly to the King. His life may depend on your speed. Come, Taran."

She urged Drum to a canter and Taran followed.

✣ ✣ ✣ ✣ ✣

Taran ran Morlech a little behind Drum. He was still exhilarated by the hunt and capture of Corbyn, and had caught Sullyan's sense of urgency. Fighting alongside her company again had felt good, brief though it was. He spared a thought for Rienne and wondered how she was faring, alone and pregnant back at the Manor. He hoped Bull was keeping a close eye on her.

That thought jerked his attention back to the woman in front of him. Over six months pregnant, deprived of food for nearly two days, no sleep and not much liquid, wounded and suffering from concussion, and yet she was still on her feet—well, Drum's—and fighting for her King. He could scarcely believe she was human.

Strictly speaking, he reminded himself, she was a half-breed. Did her demon blood give her greater than usual stamina? He doubted it. It was her sense of loyalty that drove her; loyalty and love. She was pushing herself too hard, spending herself too extravagantly, and eventually she would pay for it. Soon, she would have to slow down.

But not right now. Now her eyes were huge and black as she communed with Cal to learn the state of play.

She broke the link and glanced at Taran. "Elias is still safe. It seems Anjer has realized Elias wasn't responsible for attacking Barrin's command. Cal thinks he has ordered Barrin to mitigate his response. Most of Corbyn's men have fled the field, and the fighting is not so fierce. But many of the ordinary soldiers on both sides have their blood up and are proving difficult to control. The raids organized by the Baron and Corbyn have done much damage to relations between our two races. We are not out of danger yet. Come. It is time we collected the Princes and put an end to this farce."

As they raced for open ground, Taran felt Sullyan take hold once more of the weather, urging the rain clouds closer. There had only been a few spots of drizzle so far to mar the morning, but now she called to the Water in the heavens and brought it surging forth. The rain fell in earnest, clouds building and bubbling into the morning sky, their purple heads crowned with thunder.

"Ready, Taran?" she called. "Keep hold of Morlech's head."

As before, her huge black stallion raced into a gray-shot shimmer of substrate, the earth disappearing before his feet. Taran followed closely, holding tight to Morlech's mouth and clamping his long legs about the stallion's barrel to stop him shying away. This time it was easier as he knew what to expect. He still felt a sense of relief when they burst out into morning sunshine, drops of moisture glinting and sparkling off Drum's ebony coat, bejeweling his flowing tail.

She had brought them to precisely the same spot from which they'd left. It was midmorning. Jed's two other guests should have already departed. Certainly there were no other horses as they rode up to the door of the inn and hitched their damp mounts to the rail.

They walked into the cool interior, Sullyan calling for Jed. An answering hail from above drew them upstairs, where they found the innkeeper sitting beside Aeyron's bed, the King's son dandled in his lap.

Taran gazed at the blue-eyed toddler, who was sucking on a crust of bread. The baby looked up and gurgled, one chubby fist extended toward them. Sullyan took the babe from Jed, gazing into his eyes. The baby watched her as if fascinated, his little hands straying to the sparkling jewel at her throat. Taran heard her give a deep sigh.

"How have they been, Jed?"

The small man stood, brushing crumbs from his knees. "Fine. Not a peep out of this one"—he indicated the sleeping Aeyron—"but the baby's been keeping me on my toes. I'd forgotten what they're like at this age. I tell you, I'm glad my two are old enough to wipe their own backsides."

Sullyan's face fell. Taran realized they'd completely forgotten to leave Jed any cloths for the baby.

Jed laughed when he saw her expression. "Don't worry, we managed. My boys have quite enjoyed playing with a Prince, and we had lots of spare cloth to change him with. He'll be quite clean and comfortable for a while. They even gave him a bath."

Sullyan thanked him for his care, causing him to flush. She grinned and handed the baby to Taran as she approached the bed. Seating herself beside the silent Aeyron, she laid her hand on his brow.

Before awakening him, Taran sensed her searching carefully for any signs of wound fever. They'd labored hard to clear the poison from his blood, but it was possible some might remain. Although heat emanated from the worst of his wounds, it was the warmth of healing, not corruption. Breathing a sigh of relief,

Sullyan gently awakened him.

His spirit responded reluctantly. He'd been so comfortable, so secure within the protection she'd woven for him, and it was precisely what his body needed to heal. But Aeyron belonged in his own realm, needed tending by his father and sister, and Taran knew that being reunited would heal them all, especially Pharikian. He still lay wrapped in a cocoon of his own psyche, and could not rouse until Sullyan returned to call him back. She intended Aeyron to be by his side when that happened.

With a deep groan, the Prince opened his eyes. Jed was watching from over Sullyan's shoulder, and Taran heard the gasp as he saw Aeyron's slit-pupilled yellow eyes. Familiar as he was with outlanders, Jed still found the eyes of Andaryans strange and disquieting.

Aeyron's wandering gaze fixed on Sullyan's face as she removed her hand from his brow. His good hand immediately fumbled for hers. He seemed terrified she might leave him again. Much of his self-confidence seemed to have been stripped away by the Baron's abuse, along with his dignity and his finger. Taran wondered if he'd ever get it back.

"Easy, Aeyron," murmured Sullyan. "You are not alone. I will not leave you. We have come to take you home. Just one more short ride, one last effort, and then you can rest. We will take you to your father. He and Idri will be pleased to have you home. Can you rise, my friend? We must be on our way."

They got him upright between them, but he was noticeably weaker than before. His body needed rest and healing, not more exertion. Supporting the gaunt Prince around the waist and under his arms, Taran and Sullyan got him down the stairs. Taran offered to take him onto Morlech, but Aeyron refused to relinquish his grip on Sullyan's hand, as if it was the only thing holding him to life. Her gentle coaxing couldn't sway him, and she wasn't prepared to force him. His mind had been battered enough.

With tears in her eyes, she allowed Taran and Jed to place Aeyron on Drum's back. Taran boosted her up behind. Once there, with her holding him firmly about the waist, Aeyron seemed to rally. Instinct born of years in the saddle took over and the strength he seemed to draw from her physical contact allowed him to remain on Drum's back.

Taran took the baby from Jed once he was settled on Morlech.

They took their leave of the innkeeper, Sullyan promising to tell the King of the part he had played in Eadan's rescue. Embarrassed, Jed waved her thanks away. They rode into the open fields once more, sunlight in their eyes. Taran drew his cloak around the baby, remembering what they were riding into. Sullyan glanced at him.

"We need to form a Powersink, Taran. It will be necessary to throw a tight shield around Aeyron, for although there is no sign of infection, he is very weak and badly wounded. He would not survive the transfer by himself. And I also need to control our entrance. I want all eyes turned our way when we arrive. I want there to be no doubt about the Princes' return. It is the only thing that could guarantee the immediate cessation of fighting."

Taran nodded and she continued. "I will merge with Aeyron, and so we will have access to his power as well as our own. Once we are all linked, I want you to use as much of Aeyron's life force as you can to surround his psyche. Leave me to worry about the tunnel and my display. We will travel a little more slowly this time. I need to place our site of emergence carefully and precisely. Are you ready?"

Taran reached out his psyche to overlay her pattern. With a renewed surge of pride, he saw that the portion of his pattern that controlled Fire was much more like hers. He was indeed growing in strength and skill and could now support being raised to the level of Adept-elite. His heart swelled. He had finally achieved his life's goal: he had attained the same rank as his father.

Sensing his thoughts, Sullyan smiled. Then she schooled herself to the task ahead. Once Taran had formed a glowing nimbus of protection about Aeyron's mind and soul, she parted the substrate, fixing her point of egress firmly in her mind.

❖ ❖ ❖ ❖ ❖

Anjer had merged his men with Barrin's and they fought together to oppose the weight of the Albian forces. Elias had been enraged beyond tolerance by what he saw as yet another sly betrayal from the demons, and had ordered his captains to do all they could to push the enemy back. He ignored both Blaine and Robin's assurances that a renegade was to blame. They were all demons. That was all Elias knew or cared.

Robin had seen Cal and Dexter take their commands and leave their positions, but hadn't had the leisure to ream them out for their desertion. He was needed elsewhere and couldn't afford to split his concentration even by calling to Cal through the substrate. Then he'd seen Cal return, although the young Captain hadn't taken his assigned place.

Robin fought his way to Cal's side, angrily demanding to know what the Void he thought he was doing. He frowned when he heard Cal's answer.

"An imminent attempt on the King? Impossible, among all of us. Where on earth did you get that idea? And where's Dex?"

Cal hesitated, as if unsure what to say. "We heard some of the Andaryans calling to each other, moving about in small groups behind us. Dex suggested I move my men up around the King, to shield him. He's taken his lot off after the group we saw at the rear. He'll be back once he's dealt with them."

Robin eyed Cal suspiciously, but the fighting was too near for him to waste any more time.

"All right, Cal, stay where you are. And thanks for the warning. In these trees it would be easy to miss small groups, especially if they keep their faces covered. Damn this rain! Gives them an excuse to use their cloaks and be anonymous. Send Dexter to me if you see him before I do."

Robin left Cal's side and battled toward the General. Barrin's men had pushed the human flank hard and they were being forced southeastward through the wood, farther away from Elias's subject towns. The King had ordered them to withstand at all costs.

Robin finally reached Blaine. How he wished it was not so impossible to fight and use his powers at the same time. He'd risk a sword in the guts if he tried, so he used his voice instead.

Blaine's face hardened when Robin related Cal's news. "Good work, Major. I'll tell Valustin to keep his eyes peeled and to close up around the King."

The rain was increasing, and the tide of fighting had changed. Many of the Albians had heard the rumor of assassins and indignation lent them strength. They rallied, regaining some ground. Anjer and Barrin were forced to retreat almost to the western edge of the woods. Blaine wouldn't let his forces push farther forward. He wanted the cover of the trees, even more so after hearing Robin's news.

There was a sudden shout behind him, making him turn abruptly in his saddle. Robin also heard and got there before him.

Recognizing Dexter, and seeing his two bound prisoners, the Major sent a group of men to the rear to forge a path for the Captain. Dexter brought a fuming, sullen Lord Corbyn toward the General, Kethro to one side, a knife still pressed to his throat.

"We've dealt with the assassins, sir," called Dexter. "His Lordship here was most obliging in pointing out their positions. They were hiding high in the trees with crossbows. We only just got them in time. This traitor here is Lord Corbyn, and this battle is his doing. His men attacked both our side and Commander Barrin, making each of us think the other was responsible. Just like he did on the day of the parley. Lord General Anjer will be very interested when he hears."

Robin managed a smile, but Blaine glared at Dexter's obvious high spirits. "Take them into the center, Captain, and see they are guarded well. Then get back here and resume your duties."

"Yes, sir!" Dexter saluted and left, the grin never leaving his face.

Blaine turned back to the King, beckoning Robin to follow. The Major felt a keen satisfaction knowing Anjer hadn't played them false. Somehow he'd never believed the man would resort to such treacherous tactics.

Elias, however, wasn't interested in Blaine's news. He was convinced he had Anjer and Barrin on the run, and intended to keep it that way. He ordered Blaine to begin a swing southward, still hoping to come up around Anjer's lines and herd him north. Blaine argued, but Elias roared at him. The General shrugged and gave the order.

This move brought the Albians into the open. They had the woods on their right flank now, bare hills in front of them. Anjer's and Barrin's forces covered the open ground. Robin glanced sourly up at the gathering thunderheads, hoping the threatened downpour wouldn't swamp them. It was certainly going to make the footing much more uncertain.

Lightning struck the crest of the hills and thunder blared virtually overhead. Most of the fighting men, Albian and Andaryan, glanced upward in surprise.

The second flash was colossal—and it didn't fade. It cracked the dark sky open, struck the crest of the highest hill and stayed there, pinned against the inky clouds like a giant signpost to the heavens. Its electric crackle could be heard even over the titanic blast of thunder that beat about their heads and battered their ears with physical force. The sheer immensity of it caused them to clap their hands to their ears.

Cal grabbed Robin's arm and pointed. He needn't have bothered. Every single eye was drawn to the hilltop where figures on horseback stood out against the coruscating crackle of lightning. Robin strained his eyes to see who they were. Taran, bearing a small bundle in his arms, and Sullyan, holding a man slumped in the saddle before her, a shimmering halo of golden sparks surrounding her wealth of tawny hair.

Limned in blue fire, screaming a stallion's war challenge to the heavens, Drum reared his magnificent body. His chin tucked into his powerful chest, feathered hooves beating at the wind, mane and tail flaring. Sparks of fire flicked against the dark, roiling clouds.

Against all the odds, Sullyan had returned the Princes.

The End

Glossary

Albian Characters

Ardoch, Master. Elias's legendary swordmaster.

Baily. A Lieutenant-Major at the Manor under Colonel Vassa.

Benett. A Captain of King's Guard at Port Loxton.

Bessie. One of Prince Eaden's nurses.

Brynne Sullyan. A Colonel at the Manor under General Blaine.

Bull, aka Bulldog, aka Hal Bullen. Colonel Sullyan's aide.

Cal Tyler. Taran's friend, and life mate of Rienne Arlen.

Chaz. A Kingsman at Port Loxton.

Cyrus Parren. Captain Parren's cleric father, deceased.

Dexter. A Captain at the Manor under Captain Tamsen.

Eaden, Prince. Son of King Elias and Queen Sofira.

Elias Rovannon. Albia's High King.

Falkerk. The Manor's swordmaster

Fiann. A master bard from the realm of Sinnia, deceased.

Fergus. A Kingsman at Port Loxton

Goran. Master cook at the Manor.

Hal Bullen. See 'Bull.'

Hanan. Chief Healer at the Manor.

Hezra Reen. An Albian Baron at Port Loxton.

Huw. A young disabled lad living at Loxton Castle

Izack. Baron Reen's personal Commander.

Jed. Landlord of the Hazel Tree, an inn on the way to Port Loxton.

Jerrim Vassa. A Colonel at the Manor.

Jessy. Deceased sister of Robin Tamsen.

Jinella, Lady. The niece of Baron Reen.

Jona. An Albian scout.

Kandaran. High King Elias' father, murdered during Albia's civil war.

Kinsey, Lord. Chamberlain to High King Elias.

Lerric. Client-king of Bordenn, father of Queen Sofira.

Lily. Lady Jinella's maid

Mathias Blaine. The Manor's senior officer and General-in-Command to High King Elias.

Milo. Landlord of an inn close to the Manor.

Owyn Denny. A Lieutenant-Major at Port Loxton.

Ozella. A young Lord from Beraxia, sent to study at the Manor.

Parren, Glinn. A Captain at the Manor under Colonel Vassa.

Patrin. One of Baron Reen's men.

Rendan Levant, Lord. First Minister to High King Elias.

Rienne Arlen. A healer and Cal Tyler's life mate.

Robin Tamsen. A Major at the Manor under Colonel Sullyan.

Royen. Assistant swordmaster at Loxton Castle.

Seline, Princess. Daughter of King Elias and Queen Sofira.

Serrell. Paymaster at the Manor.

Seth. Baron Reen's manservant.

Sofira. Queen to High King Elias Rovannon.

Solet. The Manor's stablemaster.

Tad Greylin. Former kitchen boy at the Manor, now a cadet.

Taran Elijah. An Artesan who is desperate to learn his craft.

Trent. A Beastmaster on the Downs, one of Sullyan's first mentors. Deceased.

Valustin. A Captain of King's Guard at Port Loxton.

Wil. A corporal at the Manor.

Yadrin. A Kingsman at Port Loxton.

Andaryan Characters

Aeyron Pharikian. The Hierarch of Andaryon's son and Heir.

Anjer, Lord General. Officer in overall command of the Hierarch's forces.

Barrin. A Commander in the Hierarch's forces.

Brianne. Baby daughter of Anjer and Torien.

Corbyn, Lord. One of Lord Tikhal's northern nobles.

Deshan. The Hierarch's Master Healer, also a Master Artesan.

Ephan. General in the Hierarch's forces, overall commander of the Velletian Guard.

Gaslek. An Andaryan Baron, secretary to the Hierarch.

Idriana. Deceased wife of Timar Pharikian.

Idrimar Pharikian. The Hierarch's daughter.

Jaskin. Sonten's nephew, killed by Taran.

Kethro. Artesan son of Lord Corbyn, a northern noble.

Liyan Tamilane, one-time Hierarch and the last known Supreme Master Artesan.

Nazir, Lord. One of Duke Marik's nobles, made Lord of Durkos after Sonten's demise.

Norkis. Senior page to the Hierarch of Andaryon.

Rand. Artesan son of Lord Tikhal.

Rykan. Deceased Lord of Kymer province, one time aspirant to the Andaryan throne.

Sonten. Deceased general to Duke Rykan. Former Lord of Durkos province.

Tikhal. An Andaryan Lord, also known as the Lord of the North. Pharikian's premier noble.

Timar Pharikian. The Hierarch, Supreme Ruler of Andaryon.

Torien, Lady. The wife of Lord General Anjer.

Torman Vanyr. Deceased commander of the Velletian Guard, the Hierarch's personal Guard.

Ty Marik. Once Count of Cardon province, now Duke of Cardon and Kymer.

Realms of the World

First Realm—Endormir

Endormirians are sometimes known as 'Roamerlings' because of their itinerant habits. They are small and slim, dark skinned, with brown or black eyes showing hardly any whites. The Artesan gift runs only through the males, and gifted males always become clan-leaders. As Endomir suffers from severe winter conditions, its people cross the Veils into the other realms for the winter months, where they are well known as traders.

Second Realm—Sinnia

Sinnians are tall and milk-haired, with pale skin. They live in clans and were once nomadic but now live in settlements. All are born able to control their metaforce up to the rank of Adept and are thus considered 'sports'. Their race often produces highly gifted musicians and storytellers.

Third Realm—Relkor

Relkorians are small, fierce and stocky, notorious for raiding the other realms for slaves to work their mines and quarries. Their Artesans, both male and female, invariably become slave-lords.

Fourth Realm—Albia

Albia is the human realm. The Artesan gift runs through both male and female lines, each gender being equal in potential. The craft is currently out of favour due to raiding by both Relkorian and Andaryan Artesans. Albians widely believe that all Artesans use their powers only for gain and control.

Fifth Realm—Andaryon

A warlike race characterised by eyes with slit pupils. They fight constantly amongst themselves, vying for position within the Hierocracy. The Artesan gift passes only through the male line and females play a minor and downtrodden role. Only the most powerful Artesan can become and hold the rank of Hierarch. Their battles for supremacy are governed by strict, ritualistic laws.

Terms

Arch Patrio. The leader of Albia's Matria Church.

Artesan.

A person born with the ability to control metaforce and Master the four primal elements.

Brine rum.

Strong liquor, drunk by pirates on Andaryon's eastern seaboard.

Cardinal stone.

The stones in a stone circle that sit at each of the four compass points.

Cheosian Red. A fine Andaryan red wine from Cheos province.

Codes of Combat.

Strict laws governing any conflict between Andaryan nobles.

Demons.

Derogatory term used in Albia to describe those of the Andaryan race.

Earth ball.

An explosive sphere of Earth element formed by an Artesan for use as a weapon.

Fellan.

A dark, aromatic and bitter beverage brewed from the seeds of the fellan-plant.

Firefield.

A barrier formed from the primal element of Fire, through which only Artesans can pass. Firefields formed by those of inferior Artesan rank can easily be destroyed by those of a higher rank.

Firewater.

Incredibly strong liquor.

Free traders.

Another term for pirate.

Kingsman.

Term used to describe members of the High King's fighting forces.

Matria Church.

The Minster in Port Loxton, seat of Albia's primary faith, the Faith of the Wheel.

Metaforce (sometimes also called life force).

The force of existence pertaining to all things, both animate and inanimate.

Perdition.

A state of non-being for the soul – a place where souls with no ultimate destination reside.

Primal elements.

Earth, Water, Fire and Air.

Primal Sacrament.

Andaryan name for the Pact, an agreement brokered between Andaryan nobles. Used to settle wars ending in stalemate, it involves the willing suicide of a powerful Artesan.

Portway.

Structure formed by an Artesan from a primal element – usually Earth or Water – which gives its creator access through the Veils.

Powersink.

An Artesan construct allowing two or more Artesans pool their power. Each can draw equally on the forces contained within the Powersink regardless of rank.

Psyche.

An Artesan's unique and personal pattern through which they can manipulate metaforce and channel the primal elements.

Roamerling.

Slightly derogatory term for the nomads of Endormir.

Sally port.

A small door within a larger fortified barrier, allowing only one person to pass through at a time.

Substrate.

The medium in which the primal elements reside, and in which the world and all things have their being.

Tangwyr.

Monstrous Andaryan raptor trained to hunt men.

The Pact. (See Primal Sacrament).

The Staff.

Mysterious and terrible weapon capable of stealing and storing metaforce. Can only be used by Artesans.

The Veils.

Misty barriers separating the five Realms of the World. Only Artesans have the power to move through the Veils.

The Void.

Dark abyss at the end of life into which all souls pass before reaching their final destination.

The Wheel.

Central principle of Albian faith.

Velletian Guard.

Personal guard of the Hierarch of Andaryon.

Witch.

Derogatory term for an Artesan.

Artesan ranks and their attributes

Level one: Apprentice. Person born with the Artesan gift and the ability to influence the first primal element of Earth. Able to hear other Artesans speaking telepathically but unable to initiate such speech.

Level two: Apprentice-elite. Has some skill in influencing their own metaforce. Has attained mastery over the element of Earth. Able to initiate telepathic speech but only with Artesans already known to them. Able to build substrate structures, identify a person by the pattern of their psyche, and counter metaphysical attack to some degree.

Level three: Journeyman. Has mastery over Earth and is able to influence Water. Able to build portways and travel through the Veils. Has some skill in using metaforce for offense. Also able to initiate psyche-overlay and converse telepathically with any other Artesan. Possesses some self-healing potential.

Level four: Adept. Has mastery over both Earth and Water. Able to build more complex substrate structures such as corridors. Able to influence where such structures emerge. Possesses stronger offensive and defensive capabilities. Able to merge psyche fully with other Artesans. Increased healing abilities.

Level five: Adept-elite. Has mastery over Earth and Water and is able to influence Fire. Possesses great healing powers which can even aid the ungifted (with their permission). Able to initiate powersinks and merges of psyche. Able to construct such structures as Firefields.

Level six: Master. Has mastery over Earth, Water and Fire. Able to control the power of an inferior Artesan against their will. Control over personal metaforce now almost total. Possesses incredible healing powers.

Level seven: Master-elite. Has mastery over Earth, Water and Fire and is able to influence Air, the most capricious primal element. Able to absorb a lesser or even equal-ranked Artesan's power and metaforce provided some link or permission (however tenuous) can be found.

Level eight: Senior Master. Has complete mastery over all four primal elements. Is able to absorb another Artesan's power by force, even sometimes without a link. Possesses a high degree of metaphysical (and usually spiritual) strength.

Level nine: Supreme Master. It has never been fully established whether this rank actually exists. Supreme Masters are supposedly able to influence Spirit - largely regarded as the mythical 'fifth element.' Ancient texts refer only to the possibility; no mention has ever been found of a being attaining Supreme Masterhood.

Sport or lay-Artesan. Freaks of nature, sports are thought to be able to control their own metaforce from birth, to whatever level of strength they inherently possess. As they receive no training their working is often undetectable. They are also believed to be able to 'hear' the thoughts of those around them; gifted or ungifted, and directly, not through the substrate.

Cas Peace was born and brought up in the lovely county of Hampshire, in the UK, where she still lives. On leaving school, she trained for two years before qualifying as a teacher of equitation. During this time she also learned to carriage-drive. She spent thirteen years in the British Civil Service before moving to Rome, where she and her husband, Dave, lived for three years.

As well as her love of horses, Cas is mad about dogs; especially Lurchers. She currently owns two rescue Lurchers, Milly and Milo. Cas loves country walks, working in stained glass, growing cacti, and folk singing. She is currently working on writing and recording songs for each of her fantasy books. The song associated with *King's Envoy* is "The Wheel Will Turn"; for *King's Champion* it is "The Ballad of Tallimore"; and for *King's Artesan* it is "Morgan's Song (All That We Are)." For *The Challenge* it is "Meadowsweet", and for The Circle it is "Larksong."

All Cas's book songs can be found at and downloaded (free!) from her website, see below.

Cas' first novel, *King's Envoy*, won a HarperCollins Authonomy Gold Medal in 2008. Her *Artesans of Albia* fantasy series has earned the critical acclaim of US fantasy, sci-fi, and non-fiction author, Janet E. Morris. Cas has also written a nonfiction book, *For the Love of Daisy*, which tells the life story of her mischievous and beautiful Dalmatian. She is also a freelance editor and proofreader. Details and other information can be found on her website: www.caspeace.com.

Other Books by Cas Peace:

Artesans of Albia Fantasy Series:

Trilogy One: *Artesans of Albia*

Book One: *King's Envoy*
Book Two: *King's Champion*
Book Three: *King's Artesan*

Trilogy Two: *Circle of Conspiracy*

Book One: *The Challenge*
Book Two: *The Circle*
Book Three: *Full Circle* (Spring 2015)

Trilogy Three: *Master of Malice*

Book One: *The Scarecrow* (Winter 2015)
Book Two: *The Vagrant* (Spring 2016)
Book Three: *The Gateway* (Winter 2016)

Non-Fiction

For the Love of Daisy